John Connell was born in 1986. He grew up in County Longford, Republic of Ireland, and is an award-winning investigative journalist, playwright and producer. *The Ghost Estate* is his first novel.

The Ghost Estate

John Connell

PICADOR
Pan Macmillan Australia

First published 2015 in Picador by Pan Macmillan Australia Pty Ltd
1 Market Street, Sydney, New South Wales, Australia, 2000

Cataloguing-in-Publication entry is available
from the National Library of Australia
http://catalogue.nla.gov.au

Typeset in Adobe Garamond by Midland Typesetters, Australia
Printed by McPherson's Printing Group
Map by Pat Naoum

For my lovely Faryl

And for Bill Small
with greatest affection

Public: It's all over.
Private: And it's all about to begin. It's all over.
Public: And it's all about to begin.
– *Philadelphia, Here I Come!*, Brian Friel

Ill fares the land, to hastening ills a prey,
Where wealth accumulates, and men decay.
– 'The Deserted Village', Oliver Goldsmith

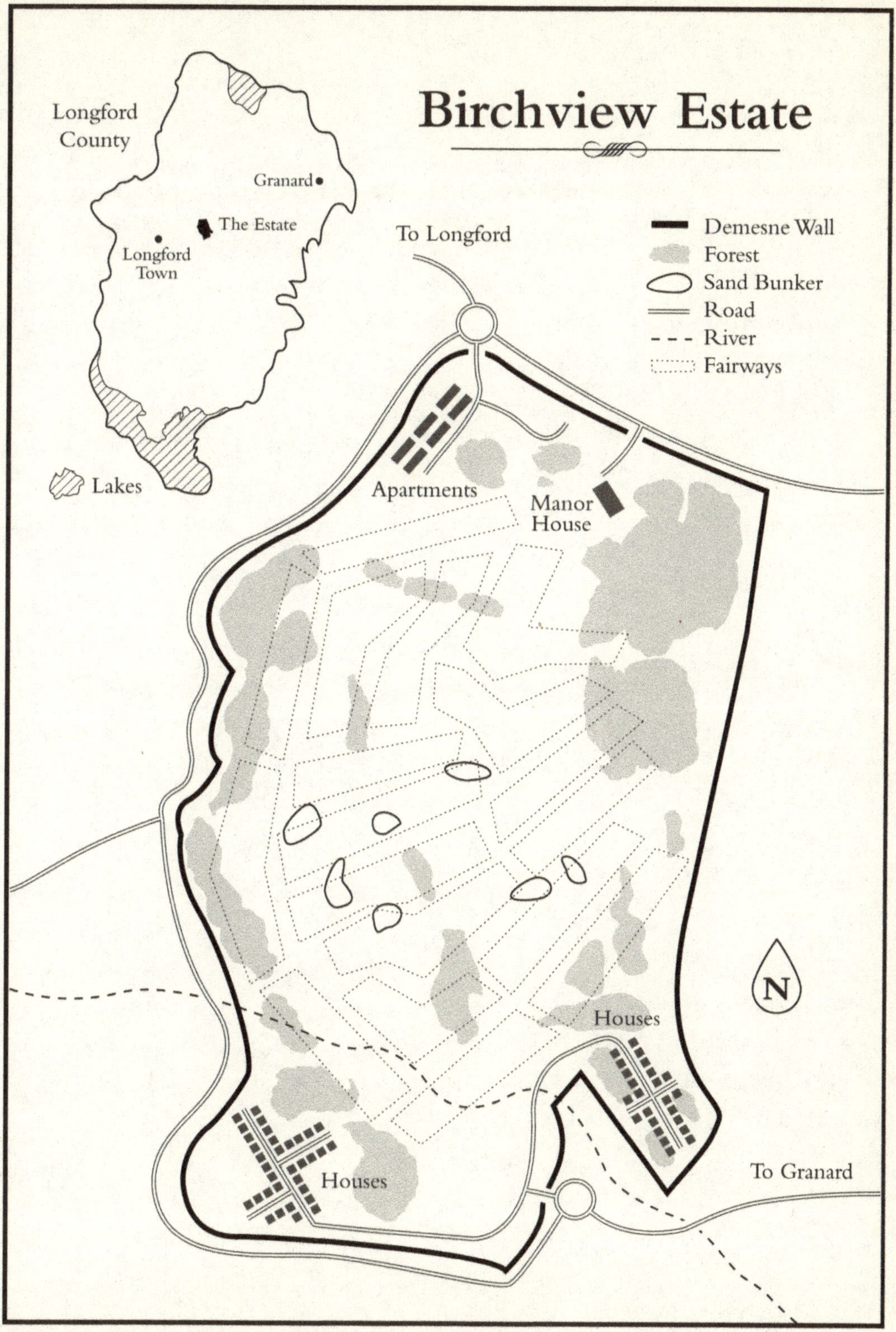
Birchview Estate
Longford County
Granard
The Estate
Longford Town
Lakes
To Longford
Demesne Wall
Forest
Sand Bunker
Road
River
Fairways
Apartments
Manor House
Houses
N
Houses
To Granard

Author's note

1800–1847

The 1800s were a time of great upheaval in Ireland. The entire nation, both north and south, was united in the Kingdom of Great Britain and Ireland under the Act of Union of 1801. The majority of land in the country was controlled (and had been for a great number of years) by Anglo–Irish landlords, many of whom were absentees living in England. Under this system the Catholic Gaelic Irish lived in squalor as tenants at will and serfs. Under the Penal Laws that ruled the nation Catholics could not vote or sit in Parliament.

Following the French Revolution, however, Daniel O'Connell, a lawyer and member of the old Gaelic nobility, led a campaign of reform for repeal of the Union and for the right of Catholics to vote and sit in Parliament. By 1829, O'Connell's followers, sometimes called traverers or repealers, had led the first peaceful mass movement in modern European history, achieving Catholic emancipation. The movement then set its sights upon ending the union of the two nations. In 1845, however, the Great Famine struck Ireland. The landlord class, who had feared an end to their hegemony, were granted a reprieve as millions died and the peaceful movements passed away, to be replaced decades later by modern nationalism and the emergence of the gun in Irish politics once more.

Key dates

1798 Rebellion – Inspired by the French Revolution, an intellectual cohort of Protestant and Catholic leaders known as the United Irishmen lead a rebellion under Theobald Wolfe Tone and Lord Edward Fitzgerald against British rule in Ireland. The revolution ends in disaster.

1801 – The Act of Union is passed, uniting Great Britain and Ireland under a single parliament with control residing in London.

1803 – Robert Emmet leads a disastrous one-day revolution in Dublin, ending in failure.

1811 – Daniel O'Connell establishes the Catholic Board to campaign for Catholic emancipation.

1829 – Catholic emancipation is granted, despite great disruption and disdain from the majority of the Anglo–Irish ruling class.

1845–1849 – The Great Famine (*an Gorta Mór*) starts, and millions die or emigrate. The campaign for the repeal of the Act of Union collapses.

1847 – Daniel O'Connell dies in Genoa.

Modern Ireland

The Republic of Ireland underwent an unprecedented rate of economic growth in the late 1990s and early 2000s. The boom known as the Celtic Tiger fuelled a huge domestic building industry, wherein thousands of houses and apartments were constructed to house Ireland's new and future generations.

Controlled by the Fianna Fáil government under Taoiseach (Prime Minister) Bertie Ahern, the country and banks lent cash recklessly. When the global financial crisis of 2008 struck the world's markets, Ireland's deregulated economy suffered hugely and the inflated economy began to collapse, leaving thousands unemployed and creating a new wave of emigration. Despite bank guarantees, an international troika of lenders had to bail out the once rich nation and a period of protracted and severe recession followed, which will take generations to fully heal.

Prologue

It was the 25th of June. He had returned to the estate. There had been time since he last visited. The big blue foundation stones pierced the soil and slowed his pace. It was still very much a sight. He could hear the Protestant church bell call its hallow chime for one o'clock. The crows overhead were making a racket of some sort as a hawk appeared high above and gracefully swanned the skies. Unhurried.

The cranes like sky rafters had come to a standstill. A tricolour wrapped around itself blew as best it could.

Pioneering *buachalán* and thistles were beginning to reclaim some of the footings. He walked the grounds where they had worked. Some houses were near finished, while others lay like half-built slums. In many the plasterboard sat still stacked on its pallets, the chalk wearing through in tufts. An unfixable twist had come into the board from the damp. It was now worthless.

Another house was partly skimmed, the pink mix of gypsum like salmon flesh smeared on the walls. A drill head lay frozen in a caked bucket. Forgotten or abandoned. It was seized there now.

Stacks of discarded roofing slate, which had come from Chinese mines, littered the grounds in imperfect patterns. The rush owned it now . . .

1
McQuaid

There had been a time when he had been happy to have his wage and his pints at the weekend but now he wanted more. He wanted the big house and the flash car. He wanted to marry her when she came back from college, and later the land with the prize-winning Charolais.

He wanted to be one of them. He wanted to be able to take her to the Brandywell on Sundays for the roast; she could have white wine and he would have his usual beer. The greed had taken him and made him king.

It was in his hands and he could do it all. His future was wire. How many lengths of wire would it take to have that future, he wondered. How many hours on the site? On countless sites, up and down the country. Sweat was the word and the flesh. This was his start and end.

Gerard McQuaid got into his old Hiace van amongst the reek of invoices and crumpled delivery dockets. The smell of work and dirt had worn itself deep into the upholstery. He shifted his body and turned the key in the ignition. The heater blew fusty air in his face and brought on a drowsy feeling.

A radio host on the local station was giving an update on mart prices from Dowra and Granard, and indicated the local deaths were coming up in fifteen minutes.

He passed bungalows and cottages, new houses and for sale signs. Raising his finger in salute to other vans he passed on the road. These early morning fleets of men, each going to different sites, different jobs. There were the Foxes and the roofer Quinn, Greggs in their long white van, and Casey the plumber in his red hatchback. All the men united in their work and hopes, each site a promise of the new. They were all local lads, the sons of farmers and labourers, peasants of yesteryear.

He stopped by the local village, took some coins from the dashboard and bought a packet of cigarettes and a red-top newspaper. He looked through the pages, from back to front, and sighed as he did daily: not much in it except tits and the match results. He threw it on the dashboard, lit a cigarette and continued on his way.

He was on the main road now and the traffic whizzed past him on the way to Dublin offices. There were often crashes at this time of the morning with so many minds fixed not on the road but on reports that were due or meetings to be held. Quick cars and slow thoughts did not mix.

He neared the estate walls, the mighty granite blocks still in place though well over a hundred years old. In parts nature shone through in brilliant greens. The estate had always held a grim fascination in his childhood, those walls of ivy bloom to be passed and never entered.

John Kane the developer had bought it for a song, he had heard men say. The owner, an old lord or something akin to it, had come down from the North, the last of his line. He had only ever lived downstairs in the big manor house, not being able to afford to heat it all. Whether out of poverty or meanness the grounds and land had become a remnant of another time and another glory.

The lord had discussed the matter with the local bank manager, whom McQuaid guessed had let the news slip out, and the place had been sold by private treaty. The lord and his wife had gone back to England, shutting the door on their family's presence in the county forever.

The van moved slowly up the driveway; in the distance he could hear the familiar rumble of track machines. The clearing had already begun. The temporary road was small, with a grass fringe in its centre. He supposed it must have been a tradesman's entrance at one time. He looked and saw along the horizon the giant elms, oak and sycamore planted in another time, in an evocation of another's wishes.

Past the trees further still he could see the silhouette of mechanical diggers pushing topsoil to one side, exposing blue chalky remains. The machines worked with purpose and efficiency. The farmland that had been so hard won from the soil by generations of local men was now being cleared and covered over by their sons. Thin stakes of wood, painted red or white, dotted the property, indicating a road, a house, a stop sign, a golf course. The pegs stretched out into the distance, grandiose in their sheer number.

The main office sat in the middle of it all. A white portacabin with dirty windows. He paused, inhaled deeply and hoped for poise and grace.

'Hello,' he began as he knocked on the door.

Big Jack, the head contractor, a barrel of a man, stepped out to greet him.

'You must be Ger McQuaid, our electrician. Great to meet you in person finally.'

'Same to you,' McQuaid said and they shook hands.

'Ah, but I'd know you out of your father, Lord have mercy on him.'

'You knew him well then?' McQuaid asked with a smile.

'I did. Back in London, we worked on the sites over there. Now *that* was labour, boy. We worked a hopper under an auld cunt by the name of McKeon, a Galway. *Mane* as church water, he was,' Jack added softly.

'Da always said it was tough going, but you kept it up and came back.'

'No choice. It was shovel or shite in those days.'

The pleasantries over, Jack ushered him quickly out of the cold morning air. The cabin had a stark simplicity to it: tea-stained mugs, knife-sharpened pencils, notes from suppliers and tradesmen stacked here and there. The main desk sat in the centre of the room, and to one side there was a small bench with a kettle and bottle of water for tea. A map of the development hung on the wall beside a paper calendar from a machine parts supplier. The calendar was out of date.

'John will be with us in a moment,' said Jack and they both relaxed in their seats.

John Kane had made his money in livestock, an inherited farm, then as a piggery owner; he was a local lad made good. This estate was his biggest project yet.

'Gentlemen, how are we?' Kane enquired as he entered the cabin, his head draped with a sleek mass of fine black hair. He sat down, placed two mobile phones on the desk and switched them both to silent. There was a confidence about him, it seemed to McQuaid, which spoke of wealth and position.

'Jack, could you run us through this?' Kane smiled as the plans were unfurled on the main desk.

They moved through the drawings, turning page after page; one hundred and fifty houses sat line upon line, and within a few blueprint inches, a drawing of an apartment block nestled into a corner. Jack licked his thumb and turned the last page, exposing a sketch of a large square building surrounded by trees.

'What is that?' said McQuaid.

'That's the old manor house. We're turning it into a hotel,' said Jack.

McQuaid looked over the plan. He ran his finger from the houses, across the great lawns, to the manor and the solid black lines of the demesne walls that encompassed the six hundred acres of Birchview Estate.

This was to be his start. He'd served his time with Noodles Begley. He'd worked his way from apprentice to foreman, and when Begley had retired last year, it was he who had taken over the company. The estate was Begley's way of handing on the torch.

Though the work was not difficult it was with nervousness that he viewed those plans. It would be his name on the line and on the safety vests. This would be his moment, his first great push.

He wanted to smile, to clap Big Jack and Kane on the shoulder and thank them for this, and yet he could not act like some yahoo. Any excitement might be perceived as naivety. No, it was better to remain quiet, he thought. The glow of a correctly wired light bulb would be voice enough.

'So the main house is to be gutted?' He tapped his finger on the plan.

'Complete rip job,' Jack confirmed. 'It's a maze in there, neither made nor let alone, there's conduit going arseways all over the place.'

'And the ground works? When will that be done?'

'Two weeks.'

Kane suggested they walk the grounds to get a sense of the scale of the development. Past puddles and freshly turned soil they moved, over and through the yellow hazard tape that surrounded the various plots and sites. Jack held a blueprint out in front of him as they walked, indicating points for drainage, septic tanks and generators. The houses were to be a mix of semis, detached, and a number of cottage-style units.

McQuaid paused on the crest of a small drumlin and looked out over the site. He wondered for a brief moment how Kane had got planning permission for so much. He shrugged his shoulders in confusion that was not his concern, and yet he could not help but wonder where all these families would come from. The county was small and yet there were now more sites than fields. With the flick of a pen, whole farms were becoming villages.

They stopped by a clump of wild whins and Kane explained the golf course would begin there. 'We have a specialist team from England coming to do the job.'

'Are you a golfing man, John?'

'Not at all, but the Dublin crowd love it.'

'Just.'

'Jack speaks highly of you. You're up to the job?'

'Oh, I am,' McQuaid responded and was unsure of Kane's sentiment. 'Worked on lots like this one. It will be a great boost to the area though,' he added. 'Oh, certainly it will, and it's needed. No decent hotel in the county.'

Big Jack smiled at him; he had passed the test it seemed. They continued the walk and in the silence of the grounds he began to figure out the task. He and the boys could do much, and save the headache of extra labour. With Willy, his foreman, by his side, there was a peace of mind that the job would be done.

But what of pricing, he thought as they moved past the large manor house. Quote too little and do himself out of money, too much and it might sour Kane, sour him enough to refuse them the work, no matter what assurances Begley offered.

He would think on this later.

Jack handed him a set of plans and the three men spoke of timeframes, budgets and what was to come.

Kane grasped his shoulder firmly.

'You won't let us down,' he said.

'Not a fear,' interjected Jack, and the three men laughed.

2
McQuaid

She'd be back on Friday. Oh, but how he loved Fridays. They would finish early on the site and he would make his way to the train station, with thoughts of heavy breaths and drinks and laughs.

She'd emerge from the sliding doors all smiles and embrace him on the platform. He would carry her bags and the conversation would begin.

'I missed you,' he would admit and gently clasp her soft hand.

'I missed you too,' she would say and smile shyly.

Now she was here. The first embrace after a week of texts and calls and her lips were creamy soft to the touch.

They walked towards the Railway Bar and stole a drink before going back to her parents' house. The place was old but they didn't mind. It was not atmosphere that propelled them here but absence and longing. He went to the counter and ordered her a vodka and Coke.

She talked happily and gave a light to the gloomy evening. Her blonde hair watched by all those failed creatures of men.

'So I told Dervla we'd have to come up to hers that night. So how does that sound?'

McQuaid watched her, he did not listen for now. He had fallen into her performance.

They had been with each other for years now, though 'with' was a flimsy word. The course of their love seemed to be stolen moments inside cars or that weekend trip to Strandhill where he'd confessed his feelings, drunk as a lord on all that wine. He'd told her of his plans for the future too: of the house and the land and the babies they would have. It had been a dandelion of words.

'And how is class going?' he asked now.

'Yeah good, I'm failing one of my core subjects but I'll make it up at the end of the year,' she said.

'That's good.'

She never asked him about his work, aside from, 'Are you busy?' or 'It's loud there, I can't hear you, what's going on?' He'd come to expect this, and besides, it did not bother him so much. His last thoughts were of work when she was before him. To be with her now was as if Monday would never come again. That they might stay in this cocooned embrace all weekend.

He had fallen into the habit of her, and wasn't this love?

'I suppose you'll be looking for work soon?' he asked.

'Yes, I mean Dublin is just full of opportunity now,' she returned.

She was, he knew, regurgitating what she'd heard in class that week. All the college crowd were the same: full of other people's ideas. And hadn't it been the same when she was finishing secondary school and he had had to listen to her talk about the nervous system and the periodic tables, as if it had been she who'd invented the bloody things.

'So you'll think of looking around here?' he asked.

'I . . .' she began, and looked to the floor. 'I'm considering my options. That's what Brian says I should do anyway. I mean, what is there around Longford?'

'There's lots. Or you could work in Mullingar or Athlone. They're close.'

He did not want to ask and yet the question burned in his mind: who was this Brian? This new name he had not heard before. The tension built within him and he knew, he knew he would ask and the awkwardness would follow.

'Who's Brian?'

'Oh, he's in one of my project groups. He's a mature-age student from Wicklow. Nice guy, he's just doing his masters part-time.'

A television flickered in the background unwatched by all. He could hear the announcer call out that night's lotto numbers: *It could be you.*

'Well, there's lots around here. I just don't want to see you having to do the commute every day,' he said slowly.

She nodded and drank the rest of her vodka in one mouthful.

'Would you like another one?' he asked shyly.

'Yeah why not, it's Friday night. Mammy and Daddy won't mind if I'm a bit late.'

The evening crowd began to trickle into the pub. The clatter of coins and bravado of a week's work done echoed through the building. The young couple finished their drinks, their talk now with a softer quality. They had, they knew, each caused a hurt.

He grabbed her hand and said those words, those words that settled these arguments. 'Always,' he said. 'Always, I'll love you.' He felt his face grow red.

She rubbed his cheek.

There was no winner in these arguments, for to win was really to lose. It was a tightrope for two, this relationship business.

McQuaid dropped her outside her parents' house in the work van. Indeed there had been a time when she was ashamed to be picked up in that same van. She had suggested more than once he get a car, for the weekends. But after he had met her parents, those remarks had stopped. They must, he supposed, have liked him and given their daughter some kind advice.

She leaned over the gearstick and invoices and kissed him tenderly. A soft wet kiss. Her smell, a hint of soap and perfume, filled him. McQuaid stroked her face gently. His palms were clean but the backs of his hands bore a fine tan of dirt from that day's labour. He felt embarrassed, or was it foolish, and broke into a smirk.

As she opened the yard gate to walk inside he lowered the passenger window. 'We'll go for a drink in town at the weekend, Sinead.'

She smiled back at him and gave a nod, her teeth a gleam of creamy white.

*

The weekend brought relief. McQuaid valued this time. There was still work to be done, yes, but it would be his work. His own sweat for himself, be it the workshop or nixers here and there.

It was the repose of men all over the country. Relax on Friday evening, the house full of food from the weekly shop. Saturdays to work in the fields or the yard and then head for the town.

A giddiness filled the bars on those few nights. There was, it seemed, a magical incomprehension by all that they could look this good. A week's dirt baptised in a flurry of hot water, soap and wax. Doors would open and a suite of men with gelled-up hair, cheap aftershave and a thirst for intimacy would burst forth. There was a quiet country sexuality to these nights, but it could not be analysed, for to speak it aloud might also break its spell.

Boy racers toured the town in their hotted-up cars, all exhausts and neon lights. They would do a circuit through the market streets from the army barracks to the cathedral and back again.

The Polish workers seldom drank in the pubs on these nights. They stayed to their own. Groups of them gathered on the street with plastic bags of cheap beer or bottles of vodka. They would sing songs about home that no one else knew or understood. Despite their difference, it was a scene of strange familiarity hidden somewhere in the town's migrant memory.

McQuaid stood by the bar of PV's. One of those modern superpubs built a few years before, it boasted neither charm nor character but the air was thickly warm with gossip and laughter. He sipped his pint and watched the room. Names no longer needed, for a face told your family. The blond hair of the Farrells or the dark skin of the Dohertys. They were traits that had lived on countless faces in different times, borne out again and again. The betrayal of ancestry worn.

He nodded to men he knew or raised his glass in hello. Sinead had not yet arrived and he occupied himself with thoughts of the night that could be. Drinks and passion and an embrace after the chipper in some quiet lane.

'The Connollys could be the boys the year,' a voice sang out behind him.

'Ya have your shite, it's Killoe all the way,' he answered before turning around to see who had spoken.

Willy Brady stood before him, red-faced from drink, his chin a baby glow from a fresh shave.

'Are you trying to rise it, Willy?'

'I might be.' Willy laughed and clapped McQuaid on the shoulder. 'How's the form?'

'Not a loss, just waiting for Sinead,' McQuaid said.

He and Brady had worked for Begley all these years, from apprentice fools to foremen. Willy was in so many ways a friend, and a brother.

They joked and talked of little and lots, the alcohol giving a keenness to every story. The crowd swarmed now and men stood four deep to the bar. In the corner a deaf couple signed to each other, a silent world that echoed with the sounds of dumb laughter.

'How did it go with the estate job?' asked Willy.

'Oh, we got it,' replied McQuaid.

'Good stuff, *buachaill*,' said Willy, and it was odd for he should have been in charge now that Begley was gone, but authority was something he had never sought.

'I priced it fair enough,' McQuaid said.

'I knew you would.'

And McQuaid thought back to the day Noodles had taken them both aside – what was it, a year ago? – and they working on the restoring of that old Protestant church in Ballinalee. They had sat looking out over the parish and the graves.

'Lads, I'm thinking of packing it in,' Begley had announced simply after he finished his black sugarless tea.

'Packing it in?' McQuaid had questioned. 'The business?' he added, scratching his head, with thoughts of his own future and what this might mean.

'The business,' said Begley solemnly.

'But why?' Willy asked. 'We're going gangbusters.'

'You are, lads, I'm not,' Begley said, looking towards the headstones. 'That mix-up with the wiring a few weeks back was the nod.'

'But shor, that was an honest mistake,' said McQuaid, looking at Begley with pride.

'Could have happened to anybody,' agreed Willy.

'It was a fucking botch mistake, lads, and if you hadn't noticed it, Willy, it could have killed someone. It's the eyes, lads. What sort of a ganger has to wear one pair of glasses to drive to work and another to look at wires?'

'Shor, what's a pair of glasses?' said McQuaid.

'It's a sign of old age,' said Begley and a strange emotion entered his voice.

In the distance a flock of starlings moved across the hay-fields; they were beautiful in their form, like a living wave.

'I started this business a long time ago, lads, and well, there's no one to pass it on to now. You two are as close as I have –' and he stopped short.

He stood up and rested his arms on the scaffolding bars. The birds swooped low over the graves, rising and falling.

'You've both been with me a long time, and I'll pass on the business to both of you if you want it,' he said, firmly now. 'You've worked like dogs.' He corrected himself. 'Like men. It's the least I can do. I'll let you chat it over,' he said and climbed back down the scaffolding ladder.

It didn't take Willy long to tell McQuaid he did not want the business. 'It's not for me; you were always the one with the brain,' he said. 'And besides, Noodles thinks of you as a son.'

'Are you sure?' McQuaid said, looking at him.

'I'm sure.'

And they had shook hands, or was it a hug, he no longer remembered. There on top of the church with the country beneath them.

When McQuaid told him the news that evening, Noodles smiled and said he wasn't surprised but that he'd had to be fair to Willy and ask them both.

He ordered the *McQuaid Electrics* safety vests two weeks later and it was an odd sight to see the men he had worked alongside now wear his name.

McQuaid smiled to himself and ordered another drink. He looked at his watch: Sinead was late.

'No sign of her, eh?' asked Willy.

'Putting on makeup or something,' laughed McQuaid. 'Always the way.'

'It's some place, that estate,' said Willy. 'That lord was some boyo to have all that land. Pure greed.'

'Just,' replied McQuaid.

'John Kane fancies himself a bit of a lord I'm sure,' said Willy, his face bright with mischief.

'It's far from golf and hotels he is, the burn artist,' said McQuaid, and they both laughed.

But they would not ridicule the man further, there were too many ears at the pub. It would be foolish talk. They reached for their pints and drank deeply, wiping the foam from their lips, and stood silent a moment, poised in thought. It could be comfortable, this silence, if you allowed it.

At ten, Sinead entered the bar; she was a flurry of apologies and kisses. The sweet smell of vodka on her breath.

He squeezed her hand and was glad she was there. She kissed Willy on the cheek and straightened herself.

'Well, the girls have a table in the corner,' she announced. 'Will we join them?'

'We might as well,' said McQuaid, to which Willy nodded.

The women talked amongst themselves and Sinead turned to him occasionally, stroking his hand. To touch was to speak in a place as loud as this. A collection of handbags and coats littered the seats and booths, and the cackle of women filled the air.

As the night wore on, the bullish energy of young men showed. They would lap the bar in twos and threes looking for women. They were not preying, for in some way they were too innocent to be predators. A look returned was enough to show interest; some would succeed and drinks would be bought, but more were relegated to the sidelines and began a false talk of manhood, importance and work. It was better to be on the outside of these chases; McQuaid did not envy them their solitude.

He savoured the pints and brought his wit to bear. The women now turned to him to direct the conversation. He recounted humorous stories and jokes while Willy interrupted with, 'Jaysus, this is a good one,' or 'Will you tell the one about auld Podge Mulhearn?'

'I fucken won't, aren't there ladies present,' McQuaid returned, laughed and told the story regardless.

By twelve the crowd began to fragment, many leaving for home, while others chanced their hand in the disco downstairs. He did not like the disco; the music was too loud. And there in the darkness you were never sure who you would meet. Traveller girls parading tanned bodies and gold earrings, or townies ready to fight for the sake of a spilled drink. An African waited by the toilet basins with aftershaves, gels and chewing gums. Men would talk to him about rap music he hadn't heard of, or football he hadn't seen. Eventually, McQuaid knew, they would throw him a euro out of some television-learnt guilt.

He walked outside to the cold night air and smoked a cigarette. It was calming, the suck and inhale, or was it a moment of reprieve where he could be himself without having to perform? He was not sure.

They ordered a round of shots but Sinead was now drunk, her naggin bottle deposited behind a potted plant in wasteful secrecy. She offered herself to him, kissing him with those soggy lips that said *I am here and yours but I will not remember.*

Her friends moved to the disco, their skirts riding up exposing tan lines and pale chubby thighs.

'Let's go for a dance,' she said.

'I think we'll grab a chip instead,' he said tenderly, stroking her back.

'No, nah, let's go have a dance, come on, babe, it'll be fun,' she slurred.

'No, I think you're pissed, love. Don't you want to go home?' he asked again.

'I want to dance.'

And so they went downstairs to the cheap R'n'B music that was so alien to this place. Willy had paired up with some local girl and bucked and jumped his way across the floor like some newly released calf.

McQuaid held Sinead in his arms. He kissed her but she had turned almost childlike in her drunkenness, her head heavy against his shoulder. To share in her now, as much as he wanted to, would seem wrong. And it was, he told himself, it was.

He caressed her cheek and whispered in her ear. 'I'll buy you a chip and we'll head home. It's one already, boo.'

'Okay,' she responded sheepishly and offered her hand.

He waved goodbye to Willy, who did not see, and they walked out the door.

The night was well into itself as they finally pushed their way to the chipper counter. The smell of grease and vinegar and piss filled the air. The brown bags unfurled like flowers in their hands and they ate with animal gluttony.

As the taxi approached Sinead rested against his frame, her eyes cement heavy. He would drop her home first and then walk up the lane to his place. He liked these moonlit nights, with the dust around the stars and the midnight chorus of bat song. He would have a cup of tea and go to bed. It was a long way from a bare-arsed, bog-road embrace.

There would be mass in the morning and the comfort of tradition.

3
McQuaid

It was a different site when McQuaid next entered the estate. In the distance he could see that Limerick Mick, the block layer, had begun the houses. They slowly edged their way upward towards a silhouette on the skyline.

He could hear the trundle of the cement mixer, rumbling steadily through the air as the Polish labourers loaded two sand, one cement. Never to be called Lech or Pieter, no; no one bothered to learn their real names. Their shovels moved with purpose and the mortar would emerge in a slick foam of sticky bubbles. The old concrete-caked wheelbarrow would cry out over the emptiness as they worked back and forth, back and forth.

McQuaid watched as Limerick motioned from the scaffolding for a new batch of muck. 'Throw it up here, lad,' he said with a wave of his trowel.

It was a testosterone pace that drove the walls higher as strength and skill combined and set, as did the cement to the block. Each gable bore the fingerprint of the man that had laid it, if only one had the eyes to see.

McQuaid turned towards his own work, to his drawings of driveways and street lamps. Ditches would have to be dug to bear the cables around the estate, across the lawns and fields, the woods and the old outhouses. They would use different gauge wire for different jobs and the lengths stretched on in endless rolls.

He would not enjoy the comfort of being inside the houses yet, not until the temporary road-lights illuminated a way out on rainy evenings and the roofs and tiles appeared.

His fingertips wore a pale mist of blue spray-paint as he walked across bare earth marking out the location for lights and junctions. The spot lamps, far away as they were, would domesticate the grounds, if such a thing were possible after so many years of neglect.

'Waste line is here and the tanks are . . . Where are the fucken tanks?' a new voice called out from afar.

McQuaid looked up to see a middle-aged man in the clearing. A schematics plan in hand, he stood scratching his head. He was about forty, his body lean; a red moustache hung above his lip, and a small scar on his forehead added a strange character to his face.

The man caught McQuaid's eye. 'Well,' he called out, acknowledging the glance.

'Well,' returned McQuaid.

Putting the plans in his pocket, the stranger walked towards him, his palm outstretched. 'How are you?' he asked, and they shook hands. It was not the brute-like grip that so many offered, thinking pain a sign of manhood. 'I don't think we've met yet.'

'No,' said McQuaid.

'I'm Paddy, Paddy Reilly,' the older man said.

'Gerard McQuaid.'

'Ah, the sparky, I know your auld pal Begley well,' said Reilly with a smile.

'It's the plumbing for you so, is it?' asked McQuaid.

'Tis, though for the life of me the shite has to flow an awful distance to get to these tanks,' Reilly said and laughed.

'I heard you there all right,' said McQuaid.

'Oh, sometimes a man has to talk to himself to figure a thing out,' returned Reilly. 'Tell me, young McQuaid, are you working on the manor house as well?' He placed his foot on a length of orange waste pipe on the ground.

'It's on the list, so I suppose we'll have to,' said McQuaid in retort.

'And have you been up to the house yet?'

McQuaid shook his head and clicked his tongue. 'No . . . no, not as yet.' He had avoided the place, that house which was ready to fall in on itself. It was going to be difficult, that he knew, to rip and tear in the hope of finding solidity amongst decay.

'Well, it's like volunteering for sorrow,' Reilly said. 'But it will have to be done.'

They stood stony-faced a moment. McQuaid could hear the distant scrape of stones inside the mixer.

Reilly flicked his arm and looked at his gold watch, all scratched and worn. 'It'll be lunch,' he announced. 'Have you the nosebag with you?'

'I do, yeah,' McQuaid replied.

'Well, we'll have tae,' said Reilly, and the men turned to walk and join the others.

A generator hummed and rattled as an ancient kettle slowly boiled. They waited with their stained mugs and talked of the work. Limerick the block layer produced an iced log roll bought in the filling station that morning, and thick buttery slices were passed about. The ground was a litter of wrappers and containers. No one bothered to clean up, for it would all end up in the skip at some stage, with the broken slabs and the spoiled cement bags.

Reilly's stories of other jobs, other haverals, kept the men in chat for an hour or more. It reminded McQuaid of times past when he would pick up his father from the local pub and find him in the full flight of a story. The character of the long bar. He propped nothing; they propped him.

Reilly was a decent sort it seemed to McQuaid. There was no hidden agenda to the man, no connivances for news or knowledge. He was what it said on the tin.

He'd have to take a look at the manor house, he told himself. After lunch was finished, he walked across the grounds, up the old carriage lane, through the oak plantings and on towards the front lawn. It would humble a being, he thought, to come so far a distance on one man's property. And perhaps that was the idea.

They were all the same, these houses: vassals to another age, to a time when they were important. All gothic and gaudy, a symbol of an older Ireland, a statement of power that said, *We are here to rule.*

And what did it rule now, he thought.

On the windows a limestone rust spread as rainwater slowly found its way to earth through broken gutters and drainpipes. A tree sapling grew out of a gable wall, tall and straight towards the light.

He walked through the front doors and the smell of decay filled his nostrils. In the entrance hall a pair of broken deer antlers hung from the mouldy brickwork, crumpled and damaged from a collapsed ceiling. He walked the rooms, he followed the criss-cross pattern of tiles in the corridors and savoured the house's former glory; it had seen beauty once.

He ran his fingers across the walls and traced the lines of wiring. Cheap and old, they sat exposed on top, clever in their Protestant thriftiness. At least they would be easy to remove.

The rooms were empty now, long since cleared of any value. Patches of wallpaper clung determinedly to the walls, the remnants of countless renovations. Flecks of paint dangled from ancient black cobwebs, and the yellow urine-like ring of dampness graced all the ceilings.

He walked up the stairs and through the bedrooms. There on the exposed floorboards he could see the blueprint stain of furniture that had not been moved in years. Old cupboards were lined with brittle newspapers that spoke of the advance towards Berlin and the Spanish flu wreaking havoc.

McQuaid muttered to himself occasionally at the discovery of something odd in the course of his journey: music rolls for a pianola; postcards from when the last owner had tried to make the house a tourist attraction; a child's misspelt graffiti on a bedroom wall, written a hundred years ago, a hundred years still wrong.

In one room he found a stack of *Farming Gazette* magazines. He knew the places, indeed had seen some of the fields – Granard, Cavan, Leitrim – and yet the names were alien: Harmon and Rutledge, where now Brady and Reilly lived. The said unsaid of separation and a class's fall.

He could hear voices downstairs, and moving back to the landing on the second floor, he peered around the corner of a long room. John Kane stood in the middle of the floor dressed in a crisp suit, assembling posters and stands. Lit by the low ebb of winter sunlight, architects' drawings and aerial photos hung from the walls in beautiful glossy prints. He could hear the clink and rattle of cups as stoves of water boiled for tea and coffee. There was a fixed look upon Kane's face, McQuaid thought, like a bull with new cows, like a man looking for money. He would leave them to their meeting.

He walked back down to the lower floor, towards the kitchen and the main hallway. A huge stained-glass window filled the eastern wall. McQuaid moved closer, and the sun caught the coloured panes, the triangles, the squares, the cut-glass beauty of coats of arms and swans and stags. It illuminated papal purples and royal blues and it shone as brightly as it had always done, he supposed. He watched a moment, transfixed, and imagined the splendour that had been, splendour built on others' backs, but splendour none the less. In his mind he saw those sunlight yellows and the armchairs by the bay windows. He could hear the pianola playing Haydn or Beethoven or whatever it was landlords listened to, the stately lion statues purring silently all the while. It had all been here once.

The walls of the hall were bare. He supposed they must have held many paintings at one time. Portraits of adventurers and statesmen, gentlemen and ladies. Different faces in different times. And now, in their absence, their imagined aloofness seemed all the more real.

The rattle of a text message on his phone broke his reverie and the grey room returned. He found himself not in splendour but in rubble and mildew.

It was certainly a ruin, as Reilly had said. Not nearly worth the effort, but . . . and there was that but. It could be remade and perhaps something of its old charm restored. He walked aimlessly now, looking at his phone.

How are you bebe? xo. Sinead.

I'm gud, just in this old house at the estate havin a look, pretty amazin ☺. And what of his own manor house with Sinead? Would their dream home be beautiful too?

He shuffled in circles typing on the phone and kicked out at the rubbish on the floor. His boot came to something hard, and he kicked again, thinking it a brick, and yet it did not move. He placed the phone in his pocket and bent down, searching through the papers and plastic, and yes, there was something hard.

But it was not some block. His hands moved and uncovered an old painting, pockmarked and worn, black and dirty.

McQuaid lifted the picture. The frame was chipped and broken, the canvas warped and sunburnt; the painting, whatever it had been, was gone. He held it up to the light and turned it this way and that; it must have been a worthless thing to be left here on the floor in a pile of rubbish.

He was about to return it to the floor when he saw what he thought was the hint of fleshy cream paint. He brushed the canvas with his hand, moving over the dusty oils, and a sultan or soot-black figure appeared; the hint of an eye, the crux of a nose. He wiped the twisted surface with his sleeve and a pair of eyes emerged from their dirt-bound hibernation. It was a portrait hidden in the slag. A middle-aged man with flowing hair, parts of his face missing, but the eyes, those eyes, were still vibrant and strong.

It must surely be the only painting left in the house, McQuaid thought, and the hint of a 'Jaysus' rolled from his lips.

It had been forgotten or lost, he reasoned. The old lord must have misplaced it. The only portrait left in all of Birchview Manor and how odd, how odd, he thought, it looked a sorry figure there on its own, like a blackthorn in a meadow. He propped it by the ledge of the stained-glass window, the man looking out again, after how long he did not know, at what might perhaps have once been his.

McQuaid finished his inspection, wrote some hasty notes and left soon after, the image of the figure still vivid in his mind.

4
Kane

John Kane balanced the car keys and mug of tea in his hands as he opened the sleek black door of his new Land Rover. It was a bright if somewhat cold morning. He let the engine warm before he turned the ignition. One, two, three. He sipped from his mug quietly, as the window slowly defrosted.

He was used to this morning routine now. The Land Rover moved smoothly along the country roads. He could hear the scrape of briars and overgrown branches against the vehicle as the lanes narrowed towards the cottage.

How many times had he come up this lane? It was beyond measure now. The house was still the same, had been since Noel lived there. Old Noel, his distant cousin, the bachelor, the man who had left him everything in his will.

But wasn't that what he had wanted, he reminded himself, all those visits, the shopping trips to Longford, the dinner in the Landmark. Had it all been for the hunger, the want of land, those twenty acres and the plot of turf in Kelleher bog? Yes, he admitted, and no. He and Noel *had* shared a friendship, and while it was not a surprise that one day the man had asked to be brought to the solicitors in town, some part of Kane felt that he was entitled to it. It was in a way a gift. Though Noel's niece had never seen it in that light. Not at the funeral, when he had taken the front pew reserved for immediate family, nor at the reading of the will when she had received nothing, despite nursing him in those last few months.

Friendship had a price and that was not his fault.

He rolled to the door and beeped the horn. The vehicle hummed quietly as he waited on the cracked concrete. The house was old. Sheds dotted here and there around the yard were filled with turf and old creamery cans. The turf was never burned any more. The house ran on oil.

The Poles emerged with their shaved heads and their plastic bags full of sandwiches. Odd that they never seemed to have a lunchbox, not one between them, Kane thought to himself.

They had lived here for over two years. He'd done little with the house: put in some bunk beds, a lick of paint and that cheap oil burner instead of the range. The walls were still damp on cold winter mornings. They had probably brought on Noel's bad chest and would, in time, make the Poles sick too. But they were young and hardy.

'Good morning, lads,' Kane said as Jans and the others slowly climbed into the vehicle.

'Morning, boss,' said Jans quietly.

'We're all well, I hope?' asked Kane, looking in the rear-view mirror at the others.

'We well, yes,' they agreed sullenly.

Each morning was the same. A half-hearted chat that petered out. There existed in the car two different worlds with many incomprehensions.

'I drop you at the manor today, okay?' he said.

The group nodded.

'Jans, can you come with me to office? I need you to give me a hand.'

The Polish had arrived with the boom, come like a wind indeed. The country had woken up to find new names and faces that spoke of towns and villages no one had ever heard of. They were good workers and in so many ways were what the Irish had once been, Kane thought. Strong-backed, fond of a drink and, yes, ignorant. They were in search of a better life in another land and yet dreamed only of returning home.

Jans, who spoke the best English, had been a teacher of sorts, but there was more money to be made lifting blocks than teaching children. He, like all the others, had made that Ryanair migration across Europe and somehow, somehow, ended up in Longford.

It still puzzled Kane, Longford was becoming multicultural, and was there not already enough trouble between the two native groups that lived here, not to mention the travellers? How were they ever to come to terms with foreigners when they had yet to come to terms with themselves?

But there was work to be done, and these men, these Poles, were ready to do it. They never complained, they never questioned, they simply shrugged and worked. They had become serfs in a way; a man's success could be measured by how many Poles he had working for him.

Kane drove towards the estate. Big Jack would be waiting for them. It was the same routine each morning. And they would be set to work on some menial task around the sites, something a contractor would refuse to do. They were the workhorses of this boom, and when it ended, whenever that might be, they would be sent away like all old nags.

On Fridays after work he would bring them to town to wire their earnings back to Poland, back to their families. It was perhaps paternalistic but he knew the minds of young men well.

If they had the money, they would spend it, and an arsehole pub in the middle of Ireland was no place to waste a week's wages. He would give them their pay slips and drive them to the Western Union branch and the rest was their own choice.

It was not really a life, Kane often thought, to work and save and never be able to fully communicate your thoughts and fears for the lack of words. It was little wonder the men took to the cheap bottles of vodka.

They were not so different, not so very different at all, Kane thought. A picture of Poland instead of Ireland on the cheap bedroom walls and a set of rosary beads under each man's pillow. Poverty had a way of repeating its motifs.

'Come on, Jans,' he said as Lech and the others packed out of the Land Rover. 'The gutters in the office need a good clean. They're full of fucking weeds.'

'Yes, boss,' Jans said simply, and returned to silence.

Was it better than teaching, Kane thought. It must be. It must be.

5
McQuaid

He loved this time in the life of a house, just before it became a home. He could walk the rooms, each empty and yet full. Full of promise of the character that would be: the children, the fights, the late breakfasts at the weekend. These were other people's dreams, but right at this moment he was part of it all like a voyeur in the night. There could be such emotion to a light switch.

McQuaid turned the van towards the estate. He could see the various contractors gathered in the makeshift parking lot. Men leaned against doors talking and laughing. The air was thick with the breath of cigarettes and exhaust fumes.

'There, like a cackle of hens,' Willy sang, pointing at Reilly, Limerick and the others.

'There, like women, they wouldn't function without the cup of tea and the yarn in the morning,' returned McQuaid.

'That's for sure.'

Peter, the security guard, walked out of his hut and handed McQuaid the sign-in papers.

'Peter, good man, will we be entering the Kingdom today?' quizzed Willy.

'Have you heard the news?' the guard replied in his birdlike voice, missing the joke.

'No, we haven't,' Willy said.

'Oh, but there's a shocking amount happening this morning.' Peter looked set to burst for the want of human contact. He would waste a day's news in those few morning minutes. 'Well, another bombing in Iraq – serves that twisted cunt Bush right,' he said, to which they nodded. 'And of course Rooney is out of next week's match. He'll be missed.'

'Oh he will,' said Willy with a sympathetic smile.

'And there was a lad killed off a motorbike in Tarmon last night. That'll be a big funeral.'

McQuaid marvelled at how Peter seemed to have a conversation with himself. He did not need a reply, for he had his own prepared. And then with the emptying of his news, of himself, he would return to silence, nod, and limp back towards the security hut.

'Go on in, lads,' he shouted and lifted the gate.

'Poor bollox, he's going odd with those all-night shifts,' said Willy.

'He's harmless,' said McQuaid.

Once John, Pat and Declan arrived, McQuaid threw the blueprints over the hood of the van and, using his phase tester like a baton, mapped out that day's work.

The men nodded, arms pressed against the vehicle. They were busy, the first houses ready for fixing. Fuses, wires, junction boxes, joists. It was all ahead of them. All to be done.

They would work in teams. John and Pat were the youngest and he did not like to separate them. In so many ways, they knew life only through the grit and dirt of work. Willy took one group and he another.

'I'll see you at break,' Willy said and produced that calming smile.

'Grand,' McQuaid replied. Willy would not, would never, let him down.

The sun broke the grey sky and filtered through the cement-dusty windows of the house, and McQuaid set to work. The reel spun easily in his hands as he walked the distance to the living room. He would bore the joists and run the wires through. The drill squealed as the metal bit sank into the wood. He worked his way across the room, timber after timber. The aluminium steps sang out as he scraped it along the concrete floor, again and again, as he screwed and tied, screwed and tied. The timber crackled with a bee-loud hum. He held a pencil in his mouth to mark the X; saliva ran down it and drooled to the floor. The drill bit was hot to the touch when he was finished.

All the wires of the house would run to what would be the circuit breaker; in the small cupboard a fat clump of grey and white cables sat waiting for the eventual mains connection.

A house needs two fixings, the first to put all the wires in place and the second to fit sockets, lights and circuits. The second could not happen without the first or without the work that other men would do. The roofer, the plumber, the plasterer, on and on it went, an orchestra of labour.

He wiped the sawdust from his forehead. He was dirty but it was an honest dirt. As he drank from the water bottle, he heard the front door open and the sandy scrape of boots on the concrete.

A voice called out to itself. 'Ah, Jaysus.'

He stopped and listened.

'Arra, fuck's sake,' the voice said again.

McQuaid cleared his throat and made himself known. 'Well,' he said, and the greeting rang through the empty rooms of the house. But there was no answer, only the grumble of curses again.

He walked towards the front door, to the source of the noise. Turning a corner he found Paddy Reilly, crouched on the floor, a smear of grease on his face and a drill in pieces before him.

'How's himself?' he said.

'Ah . . . fucking drill is banjaxed,' said Reilly, holding up a screwdriver in explanation.

'Always the way when you want a tool,' McQuaid replied. 'You're in here today so?'

'Yeah, yeah,' returned Reilly, looking back at the drill, a vexed expression painted across his face.

McQuaid waited a moment, unsure.

'Botch of a young lad a mine was working with it yesterday, pure annoyance to me,' said Reilly, more to himself than anyone else.

McQuaid turned to go back. He had work to do, too much to do.

'Aha, ya cunt . . . I have ya now,' cooed Reilly, clicking the drill back into place, and his dirty face gave a great smile. 'I'm grand now,' he added, standing up, and clapped McQuaid on the shoulder. 'Children. All they're good for is eating and shitein',' he said and laughed, to which McQuaid could not help but smile.

The men worked in separate rooms the rest of the day, a wall between them as they went. Occasionally they would call out to each other, across the house and through the concrete blocks. It was, in a way, a strange confessional.

McQuaid opened the window and lit a cigarette. He could hear the sound of a radio as the tones of some country and western track drifted across the site. He pursed his lips on the cigarette and watched as the smoke floated up towards the rafters.

'That picture – do you know anything about it?' he shouted

to the wall. A moment passed as he waited for the words to seep through the block.

'What's that?' said Reilly. 'A picture? What picture?'

'Aye, yon picture up at the manor house. I saw it the other day.' McQuaid looked to the wall for a response.

'No. No, I don't know of any pictures up there. Shor the whole place is in a ruin,' said Reilly.

'I was there a while ago to look over the job and I came across an old painting,' McQuaid explained.

He listened for a moment and heard the muffled shout of, 'Just so.'

Why had he asked such a stupid question? It had just come out of his mouth, come out without him even thinking how odd it sounded. And yet there was something about that picture, something that bothered him. And before he knew it, he had launched into the rant again. 'Aye, the only one in the whole house. Rotted to bits, it was.'

'Can't say that I saw it. Are you sure it was a painting, not an old calendar or a poster?' returned Reilly distractedly.

'No, it was a painting. A man with longish hair. It was old, I know that.' There was silence again as McQuaid looked to the wall for an answer. A hint as to what the painting might be and if it might hold any story.

'And where is it now?' questioned Reilly from behind the mortar.

'I left it sitting by that big stained-glass window.'

'Ah, shor, wasn't I there yesterday, there's no painting there now. A lot of rubbish, mind, but no paintings. Are you sure it wasn't a print?'

McQuaid stubbed his cigarette on the window board and walked back to the wall, intent. 'I wonder,' he called out, looking up at the block. 'I wonder who is he?'

Reilly cleared his nostrils and coughed. McQuaid could tell that the man had grown weary of this chat. A painting, a ghost painting that only McQuaid had seen. Of what interest was it? No one had time for art in the country, save it was some picture of Our Lord or that Constable *Hay Wain* that seemed to appear in every kitchen.

'Some auld landlord, I suppose,' he said, now in a half-breath as he returned to his wiring. 'Some old lord.' He repeated the words to himself, laughing, as he picked up the reel. 'Lord . . . Henry . . . Lefoyle,' Reilly shouted, pouncing on each word.

McQuaid turned quickly towards the wall again.

'And a right *lord* he was, too,' added Reilly.

'Lefoyle?' McQuaid turned the name over on his tongue.

'Yeah, that's the bollox. You're an odd man to be asking about someone dead so long.'

'But you said you didn't see anything up at the house?'

'Well, maybe I did and I couldn't be arsed talking about him with his track record.'

McQuaid snorted and ran his fingers through his hair. 'Jaysus, you're some man, Paddy. And tell me, who was he when he was at home, this Lefoyle buck?'

'Only a thundering hoor and madman,' said Reilly. And there was a venom to those words that spoke of a long-held hurt.

'But who was he?' McQuaid returned, his mind now full of questions. No answer came and he waited, looking at the concrete, at the blocks, at the rafters, listening for an insight.

'Now, young man, I've to head off, need to get a few things,' said Reilly, emerging from behind a wall, his voice cool.

'Oh . . . grand so.' McQuaid felt foolish to have been caught staring at mortar as if it were the Western Wall.

Reilly left the house, and the silence of the building resumed.

The walls rang with the echoes of unanswered questions, and as much as McQuaid worked that day he could not settle himself on those questions. The figure in the painting had a name. Why not a story to go with it? He took up the drill in his hands again and continued the litany of bit and chase. He would ask Reilly another time, he thought to himself. Another day.

6
McQuaid

Evenings with his mother were coming to an end, they both knew this. McQuaid would be building his house soon, and when it was finished he would move out and she would be on her own. That knowledge, that unspoken reality, brought a silence between them.

She'd manage all right, he thought to himself. And besides, he was only going to be down the road. Indeed you could see the site from the end of the family lane. A man needed his own space, after all. He needed his own castle.

His mother, Frances, was in her late fifties. Her fine face had begun to wear the signs of age; skin untouched since the death of her husband Mick years before.

She and Gerard lived in the family home and kept the rhythm of the house ticking, but their talk these days seemed only to interrupt the clock.

'How is the manor job going?' she asked over the evening meal.

'Fine,' he replied.

'Will you have more spuds?'

McQuaid nodded his head silently as she leaned across the table and spooned out two more. He began to undress them from their jackets; the sound of the knife through the starchy mass, then the cloudy body rolled onto the plate, steaming and hot.

'And school?' he asked. They were used to this dance, this foxtrot of tradition.

'Oh, fine, fine. Those Carrigy twins are just scuts. No homework done again. That's the third day in a row. I don't know what's going on in that house but it's not decent.'

'Right.'

'But . . . I've told you all this before,' she sang in her maternal coo.

'You have,' he said.

Winter evenings would wear on like this; to look out the window and only see one's reflection for the want of daylight. Waking to the darkness in the morning and some days finding the moon still in the sky like a mockery of time. Was it a wonder people went odd in winter, he thought. Oh, for summer and long nights, the smell of hay in the fields, and a pint outside after work.

'I'll boil the kettle,' he announced, standing up abruptly, his chair scraping on the tiled floor.

They slumped in front of the television and watched the evening news. Mugs of tea in hand, shaking their heads at the story of another drug death or car crash.

'Every weekend there's two or three killed on them bloody roads,' she would say, almost prayer-like. But wasn't she right? Hadn't Moran's son been killed a few weeks back? The family had put up a cross at the side of the road where the accident had happened. But no piece of wood could reverse the tragedy.

He read the local paper for a time. *The Leader* carried the stories of the county, in this time of plenty. He picked it up to see who was dead, or what division-four team had lost in the local football. It was all a well-rehearsed routine.

'Can you sort out them gutters for me this weekend, son?' his mother asked.

'The what?' he said, looking up from the newspaper.

'The gutters,' she repeated.

'I will.'

'Well, I asked you the last two weeks to do it. They're full of old moss.'

'I'll do it,' he said.

'But will you?' she said, looking at him now.

'I will, didn't I say I would?'

'Well, I don't want the neighbours to see.'

'The bloody neighbours, as if any of them dole artists would ever lift a finger to clean their own gutters.'

'They have a mouth the same as anyone else in the area and I don't want them saying I'm letting the house fall apart.'

'Right, right,' he said.

He took up the paper again but could no longer settle himself to read. There was an irritation to these menial tasks; as if he was not already busy, as if she did not know it would be done when he had the time.

The weekend was approaching and with it the men's wages. Each Thursday night he would sit at the kitchen table, the brown envelopes laid out in front of him like little love notes, each with a man's name upon it: John, Pat, Declan and Willy.

It was still odd that *he* would pay Willy, but they had come to that arrangement. Willy was foreman and McQuaid boss, and it had thankfully not caused any friction or upset. They were still equals. Still friends.

He knew now finally the pressure of being in charge. Cheques had to be written each week and there was no money yet from Kane. That would come at the end of the first fixing. Bills would be paid then, and materials bought, and he might bring Sinead somewhere for a nice meal, maybe a trip to Carrick or the Purple Onion.

Begley was right to have retired when he could. There was no big money without big sweat. McQuaid set the pay slips to one side and, sighing, closed the accounts book for the evening.

He might play the Xbox later or watch a film. But they held little for him any more, he'd outgrown them in so many respects. He went to his room and lay on the bed. The same posters from youth still littered the walls: the county team, the Manchester United line-up, the photo of his father from that Sunday trip to the zoo. Here he was a grown man and still in his childhood bed, still to be treated as a child by the mother. What could one do but laugh?

At nine, his mother walked through the house and pulled the curtains in all the rooms, even the empty ones. Each night closed, each morning opened; it was the habit of a thousand bedtimes and she would never break it.

'Goodnight, son,' she called from the hallway.

'Goodnight,' he replied.

He settled on a film, an old thriller. It played in the background as he prepared himself for sleep. Under the covers now he thought of Sinead and what they could do together if only she were here. He reached for his phone to text her.

How are you? his text read.

Yeah good bebe, just watching telly ere xoxo, she replied instantly.

How is college?

And the phone shook with her words.

Gud ☺ got a few projects on, but they handy enuf. How is your mam?

Yeah grand the usual. You in bed?

But the phone did not buzz with the instant excitement of her words, and he waited; one, two, three minutes. A flurry of words and then this silence. What was she doing? Was she out of credit or on a phone call? A phone call from this Brian bollox, whoever he was? The shadows of the mobile light played on McQuaid's face as he sat waiting in the darkened room.

You dere? he wrote now, impatiently.

He tried to watch the film but it brought no ease. Would he call her? Maybe he should call her. As he scrolled down the contacts list to select her name, the phone vibrated with forgiveness.

Soz bebe got a phone call. Yeah am in bed now ☺

Was it Brian, he wondered to himself, and then let the question go. It was bedtime, there was no point to this. No point in starting a souring match before sleep.

What ya wearin?

Just me jammies hehe.

And that laugh made the feeling grow in him. She was his. He could ask anything of her. Here, in the darkness, their words brought them together. They could feel close. Dublin and her classes were a reality that could be faced another day, another time.

He moved in the bed and the metal creaked nervously as he gently found himself.

Wish you were here ;)

I wish that too.

Remember Sligo?

He thought of their journey to Strandhill and the beach. He had taken her in the van, the gearstick in the way. Her skin had been so soft as they moved. Beads of sweat had formed and rolled down her back. They had kissed, kissed with the passion of pent-up emotion, and he had sucked, bit her lips. She had looked into his eyes and watched his excitement grow. She had watched him until the sounds of the beach and the sea had returned to the van, to their ears, and they had hugged and laughed. They went for oysters after.

So gud you felt amazing, like doing it dat way, she replied.

Wish I cud do it right now.

I wish that too.

There was a sweat on his fingers now, and he was slow to type. The rush of blood made him tremble.

Tell me more, he wrote, with the anticipation of what was to come.

Wud kiss ur neck and bite your earlobes, then wud push you on the bed and sit on u.

Her words were real and the memory of Sligo and the beach conjured a bull lust in him. The bed creaked faster now and there was no thought of sin, only of her and their times together. Her image in his mind's eye.

Mmm sounds gud, tell me more.

Would lick u and then we'd do stuff.

Can imagine it you feel great, he replied.

So do u my big man, wud love to touch u x.

And his lust grew now, too quickly, before she could reach her pleasure, and the phone, forgotten, fell to the floor. Her image, the van, her hair, her touch on him. Her eyes locked on him and then thoughts of work and the eyes of that painting. No, he told himself, no, he must focus: Sinead and the next time they would be together, and he was mechanical in his insistence on that vision.

His seed spilled and then the remorse came. The loneliness

and the reality that she was not here, she was not here, and it hurt him so, for he longed only to touch her. She was in that fucking city. McQuaid cursed openly, the words rasping from his paper-dry mouth.

There was frustration and shame upon those bedsheets. He still at home in his childhood bed. He paid men's wages and yet here he was in this limbo. Waiting for the weekends to come so he could feel alive.

If they were together there would be no shame. Only the embrace of afterwards and their laughter. And he cursed again. The phone lay on the floor. McQuaid turned to angry dreams and then the forget of sleep. He would text her in the morning.

7
Kane

As John Kane put on his suit that morning, none would have known. None would have known how close it had all been. How it might never have happened, never have been built. What would all the men who had been engaged and set to work think if they knew that?

They were in the air now, coming over Knocknagow then Westmeath and Lough Owel with its little birch and ash island, past Moydow and Ardagh with those Fetherson-built cottages and then Cairn Hill in the distance and the manor, *his* manor. They'd flown even though they could have driven, had driven before, but today was different. It wasn't some sod-turning, back-slapping event. Today they were the investors and he the developer, nothing more.

He'd have to impress them once again and assure them that the houses would sell, that the golf course would be green for next spring, that the hotel with all its little rooms would be a success. He had come this far, sunk his own money into the mix and made the start. He needed these investors; he needed their money.

The girls should have the tea ready, he mused, looking at his watch. There were sandwiches being made up, though they might only be pushed around plates. And a bottle of wine was to be kept in the kitchen, just in case.

They would fly over those few fields he had grown up on. The ground he had walked as a boy and worked as a man. Those fields had seemed so big then in the vastness of the past. But he saw the reality still, like a painter and his canvas, the foundation of ploughed ground, turned again and again, ditches cleaned and shored, fences fixed, lime spread and rushes sprayed. To an outsider it was but a green field, yet to him it was a lifetime of work and hopes.

The helicopter would touch down soon and he would have to be all smiles. Grin and show his teeth.

Kane looked in the mirror. The face that looked back was still his own, but time was beginning to lay some territorial claims. The suit, he conceded, was good; it gave him shape.

He thought now oddly back to that first year at the piggery. Only a small business and yet it had seemed every bit as important then as this day did now. The corrugated-iron roof and the pecking of the birds' feet upon it haunted him still. The swallow nests in the rafters and the metal bars in rows and rows. The sows sat in their cages, their piglets around them, all swelled tits and feet, and each one had a different face, and those eyes like the eyes of a man.

They were fed three times a day. The piping ran through the buildings, wall to floor, carrying the grain and water. It was all liquid; the slosh and then the shit. The sows would look out and see only the concrete wall on the other side, where the patches of plaster crumbled. They would never see a green field in their lifetimes; the notion of it was a smell hidden beneath all that concrete.

The piglets were weaned after four weeks, he remembered now, and taken to those hot rooms. The heat made them grow. And he remembered the old boars in their pens, whose calls were heard across the parish on quiet Sundays.

His small office had sat above it all, with those corrugated-iron walls. There was the desk from home, the green lamp, the grain dockets, the sawdust on the floor stained black in places, and the old Casio calculator that had seen him through so much. None would know how hard he'd worked that first year.

He'd bought the place and turned it from those few unloved slatted sheds into a *business.* There had been those who had gone against him, the naysayers and begrudgers, but the pig squeals from the export truck through the village each week had deafened all doubt.

Returning to the present, Kane fixed his tie in the mirror and sneered his lips upwards, inspecting his teeth. The mirror was old. Liver spots disrupted his view. He moved a fine comb across his scalp, sending a small electric tingle of sensation down his spine; a wafer of powdery dandruff clung to the teeth.

He looked again and thought of that snowfall Christmas Eve. That first Christmas Eve when they were all ready to head home for the holiday. Someone had sawn some sprigs of wild holly for good luck and a cutting sat atop his desk. As the last few minutes of the working day passed away, the door of his office burst open.

'Mr Kane, Mr Kane. Ten of the sows are after goin' down in the slats,' said young Moran in that thick flat accent.

'Going down? How do you mean, Padraig? Are they stuck?'

'No,' said Padraig with a shake of his head, as his lips rounded on the word. 'Der . . . der gone thru the slats into da tank.'

'In the slurry tank?' The image came to him: ten dead sows drowned in their own shit.

Moran nodded, his knuckles white on the door handle. Then he and Kane rushed from the office, while a current of *fuck*s and *glory be*s followed. The sheds had never seemed so big. Moran unravelled more details from his panic as they made their way through the labyrinth of sows, piglets and boars. The concrete had collapsed under the weight of the heavily pregnant pigs. It was in the middle of the big shed and no machine could be brought in to lift them out.

Their footsteps echoed loudly through the corridors, and the swing of the light bulbs up above added a chaos to the journey. Shadow and light swung back and forth across the hallways. And then, to look in on the hole.

There was squealing and shit and concrete dust. Kane could see a small rainbow slick of blood floating on the slurry of brown bubbles and the undigested seeds. Three of the men were in the watery mix holding up the beasts' heads.

He looked and God forgive him he could not tell the men from the pigs. He ran his hand across his forehead and breathed out heavily. He thought not of the safety of the men but of the price of the pigs, and to recall that hurt him still. He knew then, that Christmas Eve, that his piggery would be a success.

They spent Christmas Day in the slurry and the stink but the animals lived. They were freed from the tank that afternoon and as they each came up, it was like the wrapping coming loose from all those presents that had come down from attics the night before. Each man was given a bonus and a bottle of whiskey.

Men and pigs, he thought. Who was it that said that? Was it Yeats? He guessed so, but Yeats had never sunk as far as that night.

Kane shrugged his shoulders forward now, cautiously raised an arm and gave a sniff. They would be coming soon.

He walked the length of the house to the front door; he felt as though he wanted to say, *Wish me luck*, but who would hear? It was only his own voice rattling around in the house and his head.

The Land Rover moved quietly along the country roads; occasionally he could hear the sound of briars scraping against the metal frame or the hiss of the tyres through puddles.

They would meet in one of the lesser drawing rooms. The rolled glass windows looked out on the building site and the men in the distance were tangible and solid. He wanted them to see this view. The site and its progress was a fact. It had moved beyond blueprint dreams. This was a project moving forward with them. There were millions at stake now; the councillors and ministers had made their speeches. The tourist board, the golfers. A hundred million was no small sum. How many pigs would that buy, he laughed to himself.

He got out and walked to the ruined glasshouse of the manor and looked out on the front lawn. Birchview was a long way from finished, but a start had been made, they could all agree to that, and he gave a nod of his head in agreement with his thoughts.

It was then he heard the rhythmic thumping. He watched as a plastic bag climbed in spirals through the air. The contractors on the site watched until the helicopter touched down and its roars subsided.

Quickly he moved towards the chopper. The investors emerged, their heads stooped. The air, still swirling fast, pushed their clothes to the skin, showing outlines of heavy, desk-bound stomachs.

'Austin, how are you?' asked Kane, shouting over the noise of the blades. He took the man's soft-palmed hand in his and shook it firmly. 'And Sean . . .' He turned, helping the second figure and guiding both gracefully out of the way. As if helicopters landing were an everyday occurrence.

They moved indoors and all welcomed the touch of warmth from the mobile gas heaters.

'You had a better view than all of us this morning,' Kane said in a manly tone.

'Yes, it was really something,' replied Austin. And they talked of flying and the weather and enquired of family. One could have thought the familiarity friendliness.

They took tea in the drawing room. The girls quietly brought in the trays, and for a moment no words were said as they politely sipped and nibbled.

'It's lovely China,' said Austin, raising his cup to the light.

'Good *delph* is hard to find,' Kane said smartly.

Sean quickly drained his tea, fixed his trouser crease with a routine observance and leaned forward. 'John, as I mentioned on the phone, we wanted this meeting to have a review.'

Kane nodded. He did not have to speak yet. He would let them say their piece.

'And . . . well, we have a few concerns,' said Austin, shuffling forward in his chair. 'Today confirmed it,' he added, almost as an afterthought.

'I see,' said Kane slowly.

'Well, John, on our flight today,' Sean explained, 'we flew over two hotels. Two substantial builds.'

Kane looked at them both, taking in their full appearance. A gold watch peeked out from beneath Sean's shirtsleeve, bulky with expense. Austin's socks were a perfect priestly black, pulled up tight and close.

'I'm concerned about them, John,' said Austin. 'How close are these places? Are they going to interfere with us? It's issue enough that both Sean and I have mixed feelings about being part of this.'

He would need to answer carefully and shrewdly, Kane thought. 'Well, as you both know, this is going to be the only hotel in this county. The only one of substance,' he began. To which they both nodded in agreement.

'As to how *far* these other places are . . .' He sank on the word, and then savoured the silent pause. 'They're within forty minutes drive, I suppose.'

'Forty minutes,' Austin repeated softly, nodding his head as though prayer-like all the while.

The mood of the two men changed, and they shifted in their seats again, leaning back and then forward. 'This is a real concern, John. We're not talking about small money here,' said Sean.

'Those businesses are just hotels. One has a guesthouse, the other a golf course. Nine holes, not eighteen. But neither has what the manor offers: the trifecta,' said Kane, raising both hands in benediction. 'Residential houses in a commuter belt area, hotel and a full golf course.' He counted each item on a separate finger.

'But what makes you think people will go in for this?' said Austin.

Kane wanted to remind Austin of his own excitement before he had got into that helicopter. How he had called him last night to say he had a few issues but he was more or less happy to be coming on board as a shareholder. But that would not do, that was not the way of meetings. The past was the past.

Kane paused. He knew both men wanted to invest their money. They had seen the development, the plans; there was that telltale grin that had revealed their true feelings in previous meetings. They wanted in. And he needed them. It was, he thought, a matter of confidence now. As with a young hunter, if the rider was weak, the beast wouldn't chase.

He went on, but softer, placing the business talk to one side and adopting that more rural musical air to his voice. 'Let me tell you something that I think will explain,' he said. 'Not three weeks ago, I happened to be at the launch of an estate. Nice little place, about thirty houses, nothing fancy, but decent. I knew the agent, and we were going to talk over a few things. When I arrived there was a queue of, must have been, fifty people. They were all there to buy, and they were buying off the plans. Stroke of a pen – mortgage for twenty years. It was shooting fish in a barrel. They wanted to spend money.' He breathed deep, the first ditch in sight.

'It was getting on in the day, I'd say must have been four o'clock, and the queue was moving slow like. The agent hadn't planned it well, didn't have enough people. I was ready to leave and as I was walking out an old car drove in.

'I knew the car, knew the man. Everyone did. Old Pat – mean as two planks, wouldn't piss on you if you were on fire – Clyne. Now, Pat had been a government artist for a good twenty years, but he was rich, nixers here and there, selling sites from the bit of land he owned. He had money, but he was a miser. An auld Silas.

'So me seeing Pat was unexpected. Like snow in June it was. His grandson was driving him, a nice quiet chap, wouldn't say anything to anyone. But when Pat saw the queue, he let out a roar I won't forget, 'twas like a beast's. He said, "Ya bollox, we're late, we'll never get one now." They were that mad to spend money, to buy a house.'

Kane stopped for a moment to let the words sink in.

'Austin. Sean,' he said, looking to each. 'If men like *that* are buying, this manor is as good as sold already.'

There was silence in the drawing room once again. They had nodded their heads and given the occasional smile at Kane's rustic intonation. He knew, as they did, that the project could not continue without them. He had come so far: the blocks, the grass, the golf, the men. They wanted faith to go with their money. For, as he reminded himself, there was more sentiment in the ink of a cheque than in that of a mass card.

'Gentlemen, you have the figures in front of you, your shares, your percentages. The manor will be a wonderful development. But I'll let you think.' Kane did not get up or leave the room. To leave now might show a lack in his own confidence, and so he clasped his hands and smiled at them. It had been a good performance.

The men looked through the reports absentmindedly.

'The figures do add up,' said Austin slowly, the paper limply folded over in his hands.

'They do,' agreed Sean. 'There is the risk of Longford, but I suppose it's part of the commuter belt now.'

'I think subject to a few solicitor's details, I can sign today,' said Austin.

'Yes,' said Sean. 'The manor will be a lovely development, a lucrative one.'

Kane smiled and thanked them. He assured them that he'd get his solicitor to draw up the necessary papers and that things would all be squared away before he took their cheques. He did not offer them wine, as he thought it might show how relieved he was. It had been a skirmish of words.

'Perhaps I might show you part of the golf course,' he suggested in an effort to move the proceedings along.

The men agreed and the party moved with a happiness now through the old house and on towards the lawns. The green of the former meadow grass had not been green enough for the course. Woodland, fields and lawns would be consumed by its eighteen holes.

Austin and Sean walked slowly down the temporary road, taking care of puddles and muck.

'The contractors have started this last week,' said Kane. 'So you'll see what the innards of the grounds are like.'

They traversed the fields, and Kane felt a smile upon his face. The scale of it all was impressive. He could see Austin and Sean grow in certainty as they felt the air of the place around them. It had an allure of its own, this estate. Old and new.

They stopped by the former farmlands and he stretched out his hands across the expanse of horizon. 'There she is,' said Kane. He picked up a clod and held it dangling in the air like some snared rabbit. 'It's powerful stuff. We'll have competitions here yet.'

'We will,' agreed Austin, who then remarked on the wonderful quality of the bunker sand.

'Brought from a Wexford beach,' replied Kane. 'Only the best.'

It was nearly seventy grand a hole, Kane thought to himself. The local men might never understand, and would perhaps view it as a wanton waste of land, but the wild grass and thistles had had their day here.

8

McQuaid

Winter could be spectacular in its palette of greyness. From Jeyes Fluid silver to hooded crow black, there were pastels of nature and monotony. The days seemed to roll as a week of Mondays, in a movement of repetition.

This time of the job was the hardest, McQuaid thought. To come each day, pick up tools and see little change in the work. They were stuck fast in the middle of their labours and the end was far away.

Returning from the van, he carried the new drill and transformer across the great lawn. The grass was mottled in places, it had seen so much activity and movement in these last few weeks and months. More than it had in years.

The heaviness of the rain was a shock, as suddenly great sloppy drops soaked his jacket and made a *pok* sound as they hit the tools and plastic cases. Stranded in the middle of it all, he looked for shelter, trying as best he could to hold the gear and pull his jacket over his head, but both were now wet.

He heard a shout and a figure he could hardly make out through the rain gestured to him. McQuaid ran towards the voice and found a lean-to, of a few corrugated-iron sheets against a tree. Paddy Reilly stood underneath with the look of a drowned rat, his hair pasty wet upon his forehead, his hands cold and shoved in his pockets.

'That came out of nowhere,' said McQuaid.

Reilly grunted and shuffled his feet, which McQuaid saw were also soaking wet.

He stood for a time in the cold silence, put the tools in a dry corner and zipped up his jacket. A pair of soggy tits floated up at him from a puddle; the page three girl's smile was watering away.

'How are things, Paddy?'

Reilly grumbled a disjointed response amounting to: 'Shite . . . fucken . . . wet.'

Then neither talked; they blew on their hands and rubbed them together. The rain seemed not to want to ease up and the growing dilemma of a cigarette loomed in McQuaid's mind. Only two left, but if he *was* to smoke his, he'd have to offer the other. And so with reluctant generosity he mutely thrust the opened box towards Reilly.

They smoked in silence. McQuaid looked out on the scene, an occasional figure ran by with a newspaper or jacket held over their head. The static of the rain carried a whole conversation and, hard-faced, the two men stood unmoving as the trees.

'Grand fag,' said Reilly, his eyebrows softened.

McQuaid nodded. ''Tis,' he said and snorted his nose and spat upon the ground.

'You're busy?' Reilly asked.

'I am,' McQuaid said. He'd grown sullen at Reilly's silence and now having worked himself into a scowl did not want to talk. It was, he mused, harder to get out of a mood than into one.

They watched as the raindrops rolled down the sheeting, falling like icicles. A pair of woodlice crawled between the stale timber and roofing nails.

Reilly rustled in his pockets and produced a sandwich; the wrapper squeaked as he undid the silver foil. McQuaid watched from the corner of his eye. Saying nothing, Reilly began to eat, the bread and meat clacked loudly from his lips.

McQuaid cursed him in his mind. *Cunt wouldn't share, last fag I give him that's for sure.* As then a half was pushed in front of him. *The sneaky bastard, you'll have to take it.*

He did not move.

'Well, take it,' said Reilly briskly. 'Won't offer again,' and he shook the sandwich as if to illustrate.

It was, McQuaid thought, the nicest sandwich he had eaten in a long time, the ham and cheese seeming a quiet feast in that cold wet lean-to.

'Grand bit,' he said after a time.

'Herself made it,' said Reilly.

'She's a great woman to put up with the likes of you.'

The mood began to lift and the momentary resentments were forgotten. Both men talked freely of work and sport, or the hopes of not much frost this winter.

As the inanities were exhausted, a real conversation loomed, and seeing his opening, McQuaid pounced. 'That Lefoyle man you told me about a while back,' he said and let the sentence sit in the air.

'Aye, him; what do you want to know about him for?' said Reilly.

McQuaid thought a moment; there was no particular reason save curiosity and the picture, which entered his mind by times. It hadn't been seen in the house again; he had looked, had asked. He had thought perhaps he could take a photo of it. But all had shrugged their shoulders in reply. It was missing again. Gone back to the depths of the house.

'Dunno,' he stated simply, in summary of an array of thoughts. 'Just, just interested, I suppose.'

'Interested in an auld Tory?' said Reilly. 'That's no interest to be having. Isn't there enough bad luck around this place without that vampire of a man? Didn't he leave it in rack and ruin.'

'I know, I know,' McQuaid replied, though he was not sure what Reilly meant.

Reilly snorted and relented. 'Well, what do you want to know?'

'Ah, just who he was, like. That's all.'

Reilly snorted again and spat upon the ground. He remained silent and looked again towards the skyline. McQuaid slouched back. Reilly wasn't going to say anything. It had been foolish to ask, a sort of childish ask. He cursed himself and wished he had a cigarette to pass this moment of embarrassment.

'Well, I suppose you'd have to start at the beginning,' said Reilly. And he drew himself up, sucking in his chest as the ghost of an old bard emerged in the man. 'Mind you, it'll take days to tell the story.

'They didn't just own the manor, you know, they owned all the land around here, away up to the Camlin River and as far back as the widow Collins's near the football pitch.'

'Just so,' said McQuaid.

'But the real history of the place goes back further before Lefoyle. It goes back to them walls,' and Reilly gestured at the granite demesne blocks. 'There was a man the name of Newcomen owned all this, killed himself, mind you, and shor that in itself was the start of the bad luck, not to mind that they took the fucking land off us in the first place. It's a hard thing to get rid of, that bad luck.'

McQuaid watched as Reilly began to paint the story. With

a flourish of words the palette was blank no longer, strokes and slashes of verbs and adjectives allowed Newcomen and Lefoyle to appear on the canvas of the mind. It was helpless before them, and the painting of Lefoyle he had found in the manor that day took to a new world, jumped from its own constraints of frame to the boundless world of the past and the imagination.

9
Lefoyle

1811

Newcomen was dead and the manor his. He repeated the words to himself. Repeated them with an almost zealous repetition. At times he repeated them aloud. To think was not enough. He would bring them into the full reality of mouth and tongue. Newcomen was dead and the manor his.

Henry Lefoyle stood before the grounds. He'd noticed the first lichen on the demesne wall; sign of age. It gave him a feeling of pleasure, but also stirred something irksome. He would examine it more closely on his next walk.

The wall was the relic of Newcomen, the wall and the archway, but all else was his doing. There had been the villa, yes, but not finished it could hardly count, the folly of a fallen man. It had been a cruel fate for Newcomen to lose first his money and then his life – even if it was all by his own hand. But it had been that same fate that had brought Lefoyle Birchview Manor.

How long ago had it been? Years now, he thought, and he a younger man. He'd escaped that childhood of poverty in Limerick and worked his way up from clerk to the Munster law circuit, to a more stable situation. And then had come Rose and her dowry, and it was agreed by all parties to say yes to marriage.

Edward Newcomen had operated a successful private bank in Dublin and financed small firms and exports, indeed his interests had extended as far as France, but like so many, he had lost much in the upheaval, and then that Atlantic wave of rebellion had cost him dearly. Newcomen had been Lefoyle's golden calf; a client who needed representation, a man against the law, with too many bills.

Had he been surprised? Yes, he thought, it had been a surprise.

They had spent the better part of two years in the courts battling against the debts Newcomen had incurred. Edward had been so strong throughout the case, he'd given him hope that they might win. He had a defiance and strength. So many nights Newcomen had come to their house to continue research on the trial, and Rose had always provided him with a meal.

'You're too kind, Rose,' Newcomen had remarked one night at dinner. 'Henry, you are a lucky man.'

The compliment had pleased him. 'Edward, we must return to the subject of the finances,' Lefoyle remarked and tapped his finger upon their notes for tomorrow's court proceeding.

'My boy, my accusers will strip me penniless, there shall be nothing left to pay your fees when this comes to an end.'

'Nonsense, Edward, we will win,' said Lefoyle. 'Granted, it won't bring back your fortune, but it will keep these dogs from the door.'

Perhaps it had been his own family's past that had made him so fond of Newcomen. Agincourt had cast them out and now once again the French had caused havoc; they had pulled down their betters and descended to the mob under the guise of good and right.

And are all just things noble? Are all good things just? Right and wrong were indeed easy words to use. Too many jumped in and out of the rhetoric. And poor Newcomen left to bear the fruits of *the revolutionary's* pursuits: bankruptcy.

It had been a cold night months later and he and Rose asleep when the messenger boy had arrived at the door.

Thy glades forlorn confess the tyrant's power. Here, as I take my solitary rounds.
E.N.

He had known immediately that Newcomen was dead. It had brought a grief to him; after all, he had come to know the man and like him. The pressure of the case had been hidden so well, and yet it was with a certain clarity that he saw now why they had dined together so many evenings. Newcomen had been alone, and perhaps those evenings with him and Rose had been a window onto domesticity. He did not enquire as to Newcomen's method.

His case was dismissed from the courts; his debts died with him. The surprise, however, had been his generosity in death. Lefoyle had not received his fee at the close of the case, but instead Birchview Manor in Longford had been willed to him in exchange for services rendered. It was typical of Newcomen. He did not want the debtors to have it, nor anyone to lay claim to what was his, save under his instruction. Perhaps it was Newcomen's fate that had instilled in Lefoyle the fervour of politics.

Birchview was indeed forlorn; its acres, though numerous and tenanted, were in despair. Rose had just given birth to Eliza and it was agreed that the country was the place to raise children. With Rose's dowry, they had begun the restoration of the manor.

Fate and God, it seemed, had intended all these things, for he was approached to join the Tories soon after and with it came the promise of position and power.

Lefoyle stood before the manor now. The house was finished and held Eliza's laughter. He had come to love the place; its sprawling woods of oak and ash, its rivers, the farmland, the lawns, all of which he and the workmen had restored. And the house itself, which had become a home: they had pulled it into modernity, cast out its narrow-minded architecture and allowed the subtlety of light to play amongst its rooms and hallways once more. They had spent months repairing the stained-glass window, but it had shone again. However, there was no motte and bailey any more; it need not be some gothic fortress, the Wild Geese were dead and gone.

Yes, he admitted, it had taken years and most of Rose's dowry, but Birchview had come into bloom. With time he would acquire more land and, in turn, tenants. His position had followed his age and he had a base from which he would not now be shaken. Not by an Agincourt, nor a Terror, nor Papists. Newcomen was dead and the manor his.

10
McQuaid

Friday was a grand day. The week's work done and a man could relax. As the teams gathered the tools into their respective vans there was the collective sigh and thoughts of a pint to see out the working week. They would make for one of the local pubs and their talk would sound as if they had not seen each other in days.

'Done!' exclaimed Willy as they sat into the van.

'Done,' McQuaid replied as he lit up both their cigarettes.

They made their way down the newly forming roads of the estate. At the gate, they waved to Peter, the security guard, who gave them a somewhat envious but energetic nod. The day's light was not yet spent.

'McKeon's, so,' said Willy as the van pulled onto the main road.

'We might as well,' McQuaid replied and smiled.

Driving towards the village, they were greeted with the flashing lights of a new tractor and a figure waving an arm to them to slow down. He recognised Noodles Begley; he saw him only by chance now, their lives on different flows. Two young heifers stood boldly on the long green verge of grass at the roadside.

'The very men,' Begley said with a smile. 'These pair of scuts has broke on me,' he added with a nod to the beasts.

Without invitation the two men climbed out of the van and hushed them towards an open gate. The cows, knowing themselves outmatched, ran back across the road and home to safety.

'Cunts,' said McQuaid.

'Cunts is right, you wouldn't do it on your own,' said Begley, glad of the help.

'Not with the roads so busy now,' agreed Willy.

The men gathered around Begley's new tractor and complimented its shape and power. It was a fine machine, McQuaid thought. Begley had thrown himself into the farm full-time with his new-found liberty.

'You don't know yourself with that new vehicle,' said Willy.

'It's a great help,' said Begley. Leaning against the front wheel, he gingerly unrolled his pipe and tobacco and began to prepare a smoke. 'You're off for the Friday sabbatical, boys?' he said as he lit a match.

McQuaid smiled and nodded his head.

'Do you miss it? The work?' said Willy after a moment's pause.

'No. Aren't I as busy as ever, carting fodder and moving animals? God, it would be a comfort to have a good run of land round the house. The job is going well?' Begley added.

'Oh, tis yeah . . . slow, you know, no money out of it yet,' McQuaid replied. He would not talk so freely of work with others, but Begley commanded his confidence.

'I know, I know, but let me tell you one thing about Kane, he won't go bust, he's rotten with money,' Noodles assured him, leaning forward to emphasise his point.

'I suppose so,' McQuaid said with a half-breath.

Willy stoically nodded his head, looking all the while out towards the fields and cattle.

'It'll be fine,' said Begley, catching McQuaid's gaze. 'Fine.' He changed the subject. 'How is Sinead keeping?'

'Oh, she's all right . . . in Dublin *full*-time now.'

'Is that so,' said Begley. 'And Willy, still flying solo?'

'Had one,' said Willy, pulling some dried plaster from his jumper and throwing it to the wind. 'But she's gone again.'

The men laughed and relaxed. There was a relief in talking to Begley, McQuaid thought. Noodles had been through it all before. It would be slow, he told himself, but it would be worth it.

Begley extinguished the pipe and climbed back into the tractor cabin. '*Garsúns*, I'll go before the light. Call up to the home place some evening. Mary would love to see you.'

McQuaid agreed, and as the tractor roared to life he slapped the mudguard in manly salute. Turning on his indicator, Begley raised his hand in a pontifical wave as he drove away. Nuncio to forty head of cattle.

The pub held the jolly air of workmen. Willy went to the bar and ordered two pints from Paul the barman. McQuaid looked at the different faces, he knew them all. There were the Bradys, the steel-fixing Reillys, the roofer Quinns and the haggard faces of the men who lived the drink each day. A slow life sentence, he thought. At the end of the counter was Trapp, who'd drunk a farm of land and only a shake in the hand to show for it, and next to him Maguire, who'd lost his son in the Camlin River and had never been the same. And away in the snug cradling a whiskey was the Nasty Quigley, who visited his wife in the nursing home each day, only to be asked, 'How is everyone in Camden? Will we have the passage money for summer?'

And each day the response of, 'We're home from England, that was twenty years ago.' It was a slow life sentence.

Taking his place at the counter he wished health to Willy and they both savoured the silence of their first mouthful.

The talk of the pub was the next day's rugby match. The rise of that team had been as the nation's. All those bar-stool Saturdays of hope, and from a place of strength and skill a pride had been earned. The roll call of names seemed to echo the new Ireland. It was everyone's game now and everyone had an opinion.

He had watched as the Bull cried on that day months before when both the anthems played and all realised Mrs Windsor was but an old woman and flags were but coloured cloth.

'I'm telling you, lads, Stringer is a concern, they say he may not start,' said one of Brady's crew from the far end of the counter.

'Ah, ya have your shite, he'll be up, isn't it only Italy,' Willy replied.

'That's the truth,' called another from the depths of the bar.

'Suppose so, but we need the win all the same, that scrum of theirs is getting stronger.'

'Italians, shor all they're good for is praying.'

'And what would you know, never been outside the county, let alone Italy.'

'Neither of you cunts'll make the lineout,' McQuaid snipped, and the bar laughed in unison.

After returning to silence a moment, the various groups set about their own private conversations once again.

McQuaid ordered another round and turned to Willy with a smile. 'Wouldn't know a good game if he saw it.'

But Willy did not smile; his brow furrowed, he took a moment, then came to his words. 'Are things all right, Ger?'

'What do you mean, things are grand,' McQuaid replied, his voice rising slightly higher.

'With the job, with Sinead, I mean,' Willy said softly.

'Ack,' said McQuaid and turned to his fresh pint and took a deep sip. He did not wish to talk.

'Because you can always talk to me,' Willy said. 'I'm always here.'

'Will ya phwist, they're fine,' McQuaid answered, and thought about Willy's silence at the talk of money with Begley. What did he know, what did he know of the pressure?

'It's a big job, that estate, is all I'm saying,' Willy pressed further. 'I'm happy to help.'

McQuaid did not wish to talk of money with Willy, or the lack of it. Or the worry of wages each week.

'He'll pay on time,' said Willy in echo to those unsaid thoughts.

'I'll tell you now what you can do,' McQuaid said. Thoughts of all he could confide were ready to unfurl. 'You can get us another round, mine's gone dry,' he said and backed away from truth.

'Right so,' said Willy with a smile.

They moved outside for a cigarette as their drink settled. It was grand to watch the world pass by, he thought. He noted the time; his mother would have the dinner ready soon. And though he wished for a longer evening in the pub, he would not abandon her and their traditions yet.

'I'll go after this one,' he nodded.

'Right you are, no point in a row. Is Sinead down the weekend?' Willy asked. 'Only I thought we might all go into town to watch the match, I've a fella giving me good odds on it.'

'No . . .' McQuaid replied with a sigh. 'She has an exam and can't get away.' He cast a spit toward the public road.

'I see. It's going well with her, though?'

'Ah, it is, but I don't nearly see her now from one week to another.'

'That's college, she's nearly done too. I suppose you'd be busy with that.'

'Yeah, suppose.'

'It'll be a different story when she's done,' said Willy, looking out into the distance. 'Qualified and all.'

'I'd like to get a move on with the house before that. At least if I had it started Sinead would have something to tie her here.'

'Are you far from it?'

'I have the site, but it's the money.'

Willy nodded his head in sympathy. 'God will provide,' he stated simply.

'Aye, maybe. Provide us with that pint, will ya,' McQuaid joked and walked back inside.

He quickly gulped his last drink and grabbed the van keys. As he made to get up, men called for him to stay, and wasn't he leaving early.

'I'll see ya Monday, lads,' he announced. 'You're grand to get home?' he asked Willy.

'I am.'

McQuaid gave a salute to the evening and walked to the van. He would take the chance and drive home the last few miles, eat his spuds and deny the drink to his mother, though well she knew. The match was a welcome distraction, he reminded himself, and turned the van for the house.

11
Jans

Ty Pizdo, ty dupek, ty kurwa, ty pizdo, ty pizdo!

The words whirled around his brain. Flew as the hawk did now across the walls and ceilings. Echoes in the gypsum. Plaster could contain sand and cement, why not regret?

Matka, ojciec, obcy.

He picked up the empty beer barrel, skitter of cement on its side, and placed it in the middle of the room. He shifted the mortarboard on top. Keep the men fed.

Pies!

And the only sound an occasional grunt as the muck was thrown up and spread thin.

'Jans,' a voice now called from the other room.

He would finish this job first.

'Jans,' the voice came again. 'Jans, ya fucken eejit, are ya there?'

He walked around the corner. Brady the plasterer stood in the middle of the room, wearing a pair of metal stilts. The stilts a new innovation so as to reach ceilings with ease. It had a look of the circus about it.

'Yes, boss,' he answered now, in his laboured English, tongue still unused to its twists.

'Will ya scud that next room for tomorrow?' Brady said. It sounded like a question, but as he thought on the words, he knew that it was Brady's way of ordering. This linguistic delicacy. Questions as orders and answers as questions.

Jans nodded his head. And slowly a softly spoken 'Yees' could be heard.

'And Jans, will ya try and fucken listen in future.'

'Yes, boss, I try,' said Jans, and the men smiled at each other.

Brady nearly lost his balance on the stilts and a roll of curses reeled off a roll. 'Fucken peg leg *baastard* of a yoke.'

Jans made sure there was enough mix and then moved to the next room to scud the two block walls in preparation for the plaster.

Bubbles in the black bucket, where the lime and water mixed. He flicked the brush and wet the stone. The smell reminded him of something, something from youth. Something of youth, the low flat fields for miles and miles? The Tatras in the early morning? Or was it Bledow Desert that summer many years ago when the family were together still?

A shared past. That was solidarity. And now what? A private present?

Siostra, how could she, he thought. How could she have done it? But it wasn't her, it was him, *balwan*. Jans spat the curse into life, the spittle landing on the naked cavity block. The details like a trowel twist in the mind.

They had lived together in the family home. She, both sister *and* mother, managed the sawmill and had his dinner ready each day after school. The table with its two extra, vacant seats, and the placemats no longer used, though always set. Untouched cutlery.

Then she had met him. The *rosyjski*. Tall and handsome, in his white shirts, Caspian-black chest hair.

He and Jans would play football in the garden on Sundays, and once he had taken Jans to see Legia Warszawa in the cup final.

The *rosyjski* joined them for dinner some evenings. Ritual of the placemats still observed. They were careful with their affection in front of the boy, but the walls of old houses are thin.

The wedding came soon after. She had looked beautiful in her white dress, he remembered now. More Russian than Polish heard that day. Though the vodka was all the same. The best man was drunk when he got up to speak. The groom told him to shut up and thrust him back into the chair.

What was the Irish word for that?

He had sat beside Pieter, the sawmill's accountant.

'*Matka*'s little girl, all grown up,' Pieter had said, his eyes watery with joy.

Jans remembered now the *rosyjski*'s family and their ill-fitting suits. They started to come to the house, first to borrow tools and later machinery. But Jans did not mind, he was going to university in a few months and he would not have to worry about this.

Siostra gave him money for his books and accommodation. At first he came home every week, and they met him at the train station. But the pull of the city soon grew strong and his visits became less frequent. He would send a letter instead. *More money, sister.* And the money always came.

He found he was academic and good in debates. His lecturers liked him and the girls did too. He began to tutor some classes soon afterwards. With his new-found freedom he could spend Saturdays in the park with friends talking of poetry and politics. Such college nonsense, and yet . . .

Exogamein, that was the word for it in Greek, he suddenly thought. Satisfaction of remembrance. Still the English would not come.

'*Ty Pizdo*,' Jans spat, and kicked the block.

'What?' Brady roared from the other room.

'No-thing, boss,' he shouted back.

He picked up the trowel and began to throw the dash on the wall. It fell like sticky rain.

He thought now of that Easter break when he had come home and found that his room had become a nursery.

'We thought you wouldn't mind,' she said.

And so he slept that night in the guestroom on the old bed with the flat pillows, filled with self-pity. 'Poor Jans,' a voice now sneered at him from the darkness.

College finished that summer and he returned home, but home was changed. The *rosyjski* busy in the mill, his sister at the accounts. There were fights now over money, and Jans would have to ask her for a few marks to go to the bar in town.

One evening he came home and found the *rosyjski* in his father's chair.

'That's *ojciec* chair,' he said.

The *rosyjski* said nothing and looked at his wife.

'We don't do that any more,' she calmly explained as the children ran around the kitchen. The baby in the high chair gurgled. 'Times have changed,' she said, and she clasped her hands together like a priest.

'This is Father's house, and that's his chair. How dare you!' Jans shouted at his sister, the anger starting to rise from some unknown depths.

'*You* watch what you're saying,' the *rosyjski* calmly threatened.

Jans turned on him, 'You're one to talk.'

'Jans!' his sister pleaded, knowing what was to come.

He raised his hand to silence her. 'You've made yourself quite at home, but then you people were always good at moving in.'

'You ungrateful little rat,' the Russian spat, standing up from the table. 'Didn't I send you money every week for your studies in that city, or was it for chasing girls?'

The blow struck deep. 'It wasn't your money to send, it was ours, our money from the sawmill.' Jans stood beside his sister.

'A sawmill! You call that a mill!' The *rosyjski* laughed, nodding his head like a horse all the while. 'When did you ever work at the mill, Jans? When did you ever pitch in? I haven't seen you at the bow saw, or in the yard.'

Jans did not have an answer. He turned to his sister but she took a step towards her husband.

'Your sister and I have built it up. It's this mill that pays for your running around the city, drinking wine in the park,' he said. 'Oh, yes, we know!'

'I'm going,' Jans said.

The Russian muttered something under his breath; his sister was silent.

'It's obvious I'm not wanted here,' Jans added, and the baby began to cry at the strange new emotion that filled the room.

He regretted his words as soon as he had spoken them, but he could not unsay them – they followed him all the way to the city and eventually the airport.

He knew they expected an apology and peace could return. But he would only return now to take back his father's mill.

The horizon here was different. It was so close together, no big skies and rolling plains, just valleys turned in on themselves, like the people.

The rented cottage with the other men had such damp walls, such a barely hidden poverty to it all. And the talk that the landlord, Kane, had burned houses before for the insurance. A sulphur king, Lech had called him.

He'd heard from a friend weeks before that they'd changed the name of the mill. But what was in a name, only a word.

Jans let out a manly grunt as he finished the last of the dash. The wall would be ready for tomorrow. There would always be another wall and another tomorrow. He could at least take satisfaction in that.

What was that word?

Gobshite.

'A gobshite,' a voice called.

He listened.

'Is he a gobshite, that fella a yours?' the voice called again.

'Who?' said Brady.

'That labourer of yours, is he a gobshite? I was calling him for must have been five minutes yesterday to give us a hand. Never *even* looked up at me,' the new voice said.

'Ah, don't mind him,' said Brady slowly.

'And why's that?'

'Shor, he's Polish, I have him on loan from Kane,' said Brady.

'Ah,' said the man. 'Built for the blocks, them boys.'

'They are that. Poor dumb bastards.'

Brady walked out now for a cigarette with the newcomer. Looking through the dusty window, Jans recognised him as one of the electricians on the estate; they were around the same age, might perhaps have been friends in another life.

What was that word in English, he tried to think. But the word would not come.

12
McQuaid

He parked the van in the usual spot outside Sinead's parents' house. Her mother was all smiles and a big welcome as she stood in the doorway. That same doorway he had kissed Sinead by so many nights, so many nights in fear of being caught by the hallway lights.

'Come in, come in,' her mam said. 'Jimmy is just watching the football.'

The fire crackled slowly in the sitting room. A picture of Sinead sat on the mantelpiece, from the night of her debs' ball, and he had arrived in that cheap suit to be her date. God, he had changed in those few years and so, so had she. Jimmy's old football trophy sat in the high press amongst imitation prints of rural scenes and countless mementos of trips to Spain, to England, to Lourdes.

'Will you have tea?' Jimmy asked, not looking up from the game.

'I won't say no,' McQuaid replied.

'Mary, Mary, will you get the lad a cup of tea.'

The television played to the chorus of supporters' shouts.

Oh, Sundays, those sleepy days. Football and mass, roast dinners and packed bags. It was decided that McQuaid would bring her back up to college, it was better than taking the train. They would talk in the quiet of the van as he zipped along the motorway, and she would place her hand on his knee and smile as they overtook that small Golf, or the lorry loaded with pigs for God knows where.

'Where has that girl got to?' Mary said as she placed the tray of sandwiches in front of McQuaid. 'Sinead, Sinead, will you get a move on,' she called out.

'Women,' Jimmy said.

'Yes,' agreed McQuaid. 'Women.'

He sipped the tea and ate the sandwiches and biscuits that were placed before him. He knew Mary and Jimmy so well now, and yet he still could never fully relax in the house; perhaps it was that way for everyone.

'How is work going?' Jimmy enquired.

'Oh, no big complaints, we're moving along slow and sure,' McQuaid said.

'And everything else? Your mother, she's well?'

'No loss on her,' McQuaid said.

'The mass will be soon,' Jimmy added.

'It will, yeah,' McQuaid answered softly. He wished they might change the subject, and he thought now of telling Jim about his plans for the house. 'I . . .' he began slowly.

'Oh, Jesus, would you look at that for a score!' said Jimmy, cutting over him. 'Sorry, were you saying something, son?'

'No, no, nothing at all,' McQuaid lied. 'Is Sinead nearly ready?' he asked.

'Oh, she's coming. The pair of them had a row earlier, so she's been in her room all day.'

'Oh, right. Nothing serious, I hope?' said McQuaid.

'I have *no* idea what it was about,' Jimmy said and laughed. 'And anything else strange?'

'Well, actually, actually I'm looking at . . . well, I'm thinking about . . .'

Jimmy turned around in his chair to look at McQuaid, fixing his eyes upon the young man. 'Hmm,' he said, and stroked his chin as he always did when he was listening. Jimmy Toher, local councillor, man about the village. Man about the town, he could get a pothole fixed all right. But how would he take to this proposal, McQuaid to build a house and Jimmy's daughter to live in it with him?

'Well, the thing is, I'm half-thinking about starting work –'

'Hello,' said a voice from the doorway, and Sinead swooped in on top of him. She gently kissed his forehead; he could smell her perfume, how sweet it was, sweeter than the last time, sweeter than every time before. And how glad he was that she had come down from Dublin, if only for a short stay.

'Will you let the lad eat his sandwiches, Sinead,' said Mary from the doorway.

'I'm not stopping him, Mammy,' returned Sinead.

'Don't start at that now,' said Jimmy.

'I'm not starting anything,' said Sinead, and she leaned closer to McQuaid.

'Right so, we'll have a few minutes of peace, this match is nearly over,' said Jimmy.

'God forbid we'd miss the match,' said Sinead under her breath. To which McQuaid could not help but laugh.

'What was that?' quizzed Mary.

'Nothing. I was saying God forbid Cork lose.'

McQuaid watched as Mary pursed her lips and looked at her daughter, her face a grave piety; he supposed she felt the oncoming loss. They had been such good friends all these years, more than just a mother and her child, best friends as Sinead had so often put it. But now that college was nearly finished Sinead seemed different, indifferent in fact. And the rows seemed to happen every weekend when she came home, or so she said. And yet Mary still washed her dirty clothes and gave her meat for the week. That was, he thought, the unyielding love of parenthood, for good or bad.

'Oh, would you look at that! Hoho, we have a match on our hands now,' roared Jimmy as the final minutes of the game neared and the sides had drawn level again for the third time. 'There'll be some sport out of Begley if Kerry win. Ha? Am I right?' he added, looking at McQuaid.

'The woman won't be happy,' said McQuaid.

'Too right, she won't, her a bloody Cork woman,' Jimmy said. 'Oh, he'll take to the pub tonight for sure. There'll be sport.'

'True enough,' said McQuaid.

'We better get going,' said Sinead as the game wound down its final minutes.

'Ah, don't go yet,' said Mary.

'No, we'll have to go, don't we, love?' said Sinead, looking imploringly at McQuaid.

'Well . . . the traffic,' he mumbled, offering up his hands.

'What's another five minutes?' said Mary. 'Finish your sandwiches. This boy has barely drank his tea.'

'I'll get my bags,' said Sinead, standing up. And it was as if the atmosphere in the room changed. Jimmy no longer cared about the match, and Mary, Mary had forgotten the resentments of the day. It would be another quiet week with just the pair of them at home, rattling around the empty house.

'I've those steaks in the freezer for you,' she said, making her way to the kitchen. 'And, and your clothes, your clothes. I just have to run the iron on that blouse,' she said in a flutter.

'It's fine, Mammy. I'll get it next time,' said Sinead.

'No, just wait a minute and I'll get it ready for you, it won't take a minute.'

McQuaid made to stand up; he felt awkward amidst the goodbye, as though he was in some way the one who was to blame, the one who was taking their daughter from them.

'Sit down, eat your sandwiches, you won't get a decent feed on that road up to Dublin,' said Jimmy energetically.

Mary clucked around the kitchen, he could hear her opening presses and freezers, packing the last of her daughter's things for the week. He could not help but feel the emotion that welled in both parents now, that same emotion which was so starkly absent in Sinead. She was young, and perhaps took for granted that both of them would always be there, if only to bicker with.

Jimmy turned to him intently now. 'You were going to tell me something, son?'

'Oh, no, nothing really,' said McQuaid, brushing it aside.

'Because you know, you can tell us things. What I mean to say is Mary and I like you, you're a good fit for Sinead, and all we want is her happiness . . . you know,' Jimmy said.

'I know,' said McQuaid.

'So if you had something to tell me, anything about work or a certain plan for the future, I'd be happy to listen,' said Jimmy.

'I know you would,' repeated McQuaid. He was nervous and Jimmy could see this, the sweat on his brow and his cheeks flushed red.

'But we'll talk again,' said Jimmy tenderly.

'We will.'

Jimmy stood up suddenly and walked out of the room. McQuaid sipped the last of his tea. He should have told old Toher, he said to himself, should have just blurted it out. Jesus, what did it matter anyway, it wasn't like he needed his permission, it wasn't the fifties. And yet he was not sure why he could not bring himself to tell them.

He could hear Jimmy talking with Sinead down the hall. 'Just take it now,' he said.

'Daddy, I'm fine.'

'No, that Dublin is expensive,' he said.

'I have enough money,' she replied.

'Look, you can bring it back to me next weekend,' Jimmy said calmly.

'I might not be home next weekend,' she said.

'Well, all the more reason for you to come back.'

'You're funny.'

'I love you, ya know, Sinead,' McQuaid heard Jimmy say.

'I know,' she said quickly, her footsteps coming back up the hall.

'Are you ready to go?' she said from the doorway of the sitting room.

McQuaid loaded the bags into the back of the van. Mary and Jimmy stood waving from the front porch. The dog ran around the yard, confused at all the noise, confused at the leave-taking. There was a sadness to the goodbye that they knew too well, an understanding that each week they grew just that bit further apart.

'Thank God we're gone,' Sinead announced as they drove away.

'What do you mean?' he said.

'Oh, nothing, there was a fight today.'

'So your father said.'

'He was part of it and all too,' she said.

He turned to her slowly, looking at her face. 'Well, what's wrong?' he said softly.

'Nothing,' she said.

'If you're sure,' he said and returned to driving.

She played with the radio reception distractedly and then, flustered, turned it off completely. 'It's just Mammy and Daddy. We had a big row about after I finish college,' she said.

'I thought it might be that,' he said.

'They want me to move back home, back to live with them. I mean, what was the point in all the years of college just to come back to my parents' house?'

'It's because they miss you,' he replied.

'It's because they're lonely and bored and they want to live through my life,' she snapped. 'You understand, don't you?' She looked imploringly at him.

'I understand living at home, but that's not forever.'

'I want to see the world. I've spent so long in books and exam halls. I'm just fed up of it all,' she said. 'I mean, I have dreams and they extend beyond living with Mammy and Daddy in Longford! It makes me not want to come home.'

'At least you have *both* of them, if only to fight with,' said McQuaid. 'It's only love that guides them, and maybe it misguides them a bit, but they only want the best for you.'

'I suppose,' she agreed sullenly.

He had not meant to bring his father, his loss, into the conversation, but he hadn't been able to hold his tongue any longer. At least she had both her parents; for good or bad, she had them. The sooner she realised the fortune of this, the better off she'd be. And yes, he told himself, he too wanted her in Longford, someone to come home to on those dark nights.

'You'll be finished soon, and I'll be starting the house. It will be a new page, a new chapter,' he said.

'The house, the house, you haven't even started that yet,' she snapped.

'Well, I've got the site,' he retorted, rather briskly.

'Right . . . but what about work? I mean I might be in Dublin and you'll be here.'

'Well . . .' He paused and thought and found himself without the necessary words, or the necessary money, to achieve those dreams. 'We'll worry about all that when we come to it,' he said soothingly. 'God will provide,' he added as an afterthought.

'What?'

'Oh, nothing, something Willy said.'

They were silent a while and once again she tried with the radio but no station could be found. Switching it off once more, she sat back in her seat and adjusted her belt.

'I heard you trying to tell Daddy about the house,' she laughed, and he felt that softness return to her sweet voice.

'Oh, you did?'

'I hear everything,' she said and leaned over to kiss his cheek.

'It will all work out,' he said and gripped her hand tightly as the van moved towards the motorway lights and the road to Dublin.

13
McQuaid

It was not their parish and yet they went. Despite the abuse, the dogma, they went. It was a way of being close to their father in his drill-deep bed.

McQuaid cast his mind back now to Sunday mornings all those years ago, loading into the car and the rain-sticky window. His father saying how the Brits had wanted to turn the cathedral into a train station. Oh, what an exciting place it might have been, the smoke, the goodbyes, the running on the platform. The possibility of destination.

That building was, he imagined, what all Rome must look like, the vaults, the columns, the power of faith. But the priest did not come into it for him any more, not now. There were funerals, yes; car crashes kept the numbers up, and the community would never let it be said that a man was buried with a bad turnout. The dead would get their dues.

It had become for him a place to think: bend the head and Sinead, stand up and the rafters in the manor may have to be gutted, kneel and incense of the welding rod on metal.

The father spoke. 'We offer up this mass for the memory of Michael McQuaid.'

And at the words they blessed themselves, and McQuaid was thrown back once again to that last summer with his father. Their silage had not yet been saved, and at the news all the neighbouring men had arrived with all those tractors the ground had never known. One might have enjoyed this mettle of men if the reasons had not been so. The plastic of the stacked bails had blown like sails in the yard, and it had been a great gather, they had all commented.

'The boyo.'

That had been his father's word for it the evening they had found out, nothing ever to be called by its proper name. The bowel cancer had already spread but they were hopeful. He would battle it. The weekend months later when he had been found collapsed on the kitchen floor, everyone had feared the worst. Found there by his wife, McQuaid's mother, and her words to him: 'Stay with me, Mick, the ambulance is coming, stay with me.'

That night in Mullingar hospital, a corridor for a ward and the smell of sterile cleanliness. He had not been brought to see his father; he was still in secondary school and it was agreed it might upset him. But he imagined it and the imagined memory seemed just as real.

The aunts and cousins had come down from Dublin, impatiently tapping car keys on the table as they waited for news. In the hospital they each bought different papers: the *Sun*, the *Star*, the *Independent*; the banner told of different lives thrown together one last time.

McQuaid thought of how his aunt had made him dinner all that week but her spuds were never the same.

And when his father had at last come home, the first he called for was Gerard. An aunt had tried to hush him out of the room, saying his father needed rest, but with a wave of his hand Mick silenced them all, and summoned him to the bedside.

'You've been taking care of things around here, son?'

'I have, Da,' he answered.

'Good man.'

They did not talk of his sickness, or the hospital, or the trauma of that night on the kitchen floor when he had spied his father from the hallway door.

'Do you have a taste on you for anything, Da?'

'No . . . no, I'm okay,' Mick said weakly, and his eyes grew heavy, indicating he might go back to sleep for a while.

The sunlight was trapped behind the closed curtains all that week, he remembered. There was a dull tinge to the room.

McQuaid stood in the church now for the Nicene Creed, blessed himself and returned to sitting.

It was only in the village shop a few days later, he reminded himself, he had learned the full truth.

'Riddled with it, poor fella,' Tom Frank, a neighbour, said to the shopkeeper.

'Is it that bad?'

'He's home all right, but he's home to die,' Tom Frank said and then, seeing McQuaid, stopped short and produced a sad smile.

'Just getting some milk,' McQuaid answered their looks of pity.

'Okay, son, no problem,' the shopkeeper said.

He wished they had treated him normally that day and not given him that forced sympathy. But he knew then that the pubs and shops of the town and parish would have the news. They had passed their sentence, not one of punishment but rather more as a jury who had been deliberating the length of his father's forty-odd years and who had now returned the ballot drawn; he was for off.

He knew then, too, what was to follow: the wake, the visitors, the endless handshakes, the covered mirrors and tea-stained lips. The body in the house. He knew all this and he only a boy, that his father *would* die, that his aunts and cousins would return to Dublin with their different keys and different newspapers, and that when it was all over it would be him and his mother alone in the house.

When his father did pass, he had been calling to go for a walk outside all day. He was too weak to move, so a window was opened; the swifts and swallows thrust and dived outside, but the face lit up was as yellow as the sunlight that had been trapped days behind those curtains.

He remembered the rainy day and the coffin and the neighbours saying, *Happy the corpse the rain falls on*. The ground in the cemetery was trampled, and Brid Collins, the fat bitch, had stood on someone's grave and it had given way under her weight. And when it was all over and the crowds had gone, his mother began to clean, clean death out of the house.

After, the clocks were set to work again and the visitors became fewer in the evenings. He was the man of the house now. The fields were rented out soon after.

McQuaid wiped a wetness from his eye and looked up at the congregation. Most had never heard of his father. His name was but one in the long roll of the dead and he hated himself for having delved so deeply. In part he wished not to volunteer for this sorrow; let the dead mind the dead, he thought and sighed.

At communion his mother went to the altar and he leafed through the parish newsletter. A marriage, a baptism, and a staging of Goldsmith at the Temperance Hall.

'The mass is ended, go in peace,' the priest announced.

Walking outside, McQuaid commented to his mother that they should get a newspaper and a mineral for the dinner.

'And maybe a *romantica*, day that's in it,' she said with a smile.

'Why not,' he said and squeezed her arm lovingly.

'Poor turnout from the others,' he said as they walked to the shop.

'I told the relations to stay up in Dublin. You know he has the twins and she is working nights at Crumlin. They can pay their respects in their own way.'

'Right . . .' he said.

'I thought we might see Sinead with you?' she returned.

'She couldn't come back in time,' he said flatly.

'Oh . . . I see.'

He looked out at the car park and the dispersing congregation. 'Did you light a candle?' he asked.

'I did, yeah, one for your father and one for Tom Frank, he's a burying this week.'

'I forgot that.'

'He was a good 'un,' his mother said.

'He was,' he answered and quickened his pace towards the shop.

14
Lefoyle

1829

Curious how a window becomes a mirror, he thought. That which gives us vision of the world in the day *shows* us vision of ourselves at night. And were not both landscapes?

Lefoyle mused on this as he gathered himself in the downstairs bathroom. He had court today and, later, meetings. These traversers, these hidden republicans, were beginning to be the subject of yet more conversations.

Tonight perhaps he might spend an hour at his astronomy charts, if he had time. Rattling around this old house, the children gone, he might as well. He could look out on the moon, see the calmness of the Sea of Tranquillity, the afterlife of waves. Laid to rest in that black chasm.

Outside the demesne walls lay stars and planets, and earthly problems too. Lefoyle sighed to himself at the thought of the latter. Emancipation had brought change; the papist mob had their vote now and would they touch the wreath of loyalty still? Perhaps. Or perhaps seek to break with Home completely.

He moved through the house to the drawing room and sat by

the fire. It was a wet day and the flame in the hearth seemed all the more inviting. His portrait hung above the mantel; Rose had commissioned it years before, on his appointment to the courts. What was it, only another glazed figure caught in the artist's crosshair, and yet looking at it, at himself, brought thoughts of her to mind. Lefoyle contemplated taking it down, putting it in another room, but in the end, faced with the power of memory, he left it be.

Rose was dead two years. Good wife, faithful companion, mother to his children, but had she been the love of his life? No. He could admit that now, there in the privacy of his mind, great tormentor of men. They had known love but only that born of the habitual. Of other love he knew that answer too. But she did not bear thinking about, and it had been so long ago in his poor youth. She had given him words; those letters, sent back and forth across the sea, rolling with the waves, lost now in the shadow of a dresser or backroom chest.

The world had been as dark then, he a young man and another rebellion in the air. That dog of Elba come to murder them in their beds. It was 1798 and he was twenty-two.

He remembered the reports from Wexford and the Scullabogue massacre, Protestant children burned to death in that barn. Oh, the traitors had set fire to so much. He remembered the spruce and fir trees and the lime over everything beside that river in the beautiful hollow near the village of St Johnstown. And later those same rebels red-eyed, was it from fear? There had been oaks too. Yes, that he knew, the shackles of the hangman were still on those same trees where the bodies of the traitors had been hung. The pit was empty and the graveyards full.

He had met her two days later, so that both images now mixed together. Her skin as pale as the pit and theirs white from it. Jane of the quicklime. The reverend's bookish daughter, sweet young thing. The reverend had come from Yorkshire to minister to a small parish in Wicklow, and had taken Lefoyle in one night after a thunderstorm on some remote country road. He and Jane had spent but two days together, and yet on their leave-taking it had been decided they would write to one another.

The letters had been courteous and polite at first, but as their friendship grew the language had changed. They had met and exchanged promises, promises of love and running away together. And though he was young, his heart had never felt such true emotion.

It was with anger his uncle had learned of their intentions. She had no fortune. He never made it to the boat, nor to see her face again, and the letters, the letters were a memorial to a life, a love, that could have been different.

Morbid thoughts.

'Morbid thoughts,' a voice called.

Lefoyle, waking from the depth of himself, saw the figure of Harmon James before him.

'I said, morbid thoughts, Lefoyle?'

'Harmon . . . how are you? Morbid? Does one count the death of that papist as morbid?'

'And what papist are you talking of?' questioned Harmon.

'The only one of whose death I should like to hear,' replied Lefoyle, a smirk across his face.

'Ha, O'Connell – no, he is well, seen in Dublin not two days ago. Still ebullient in the aftermath of his bill's victory.'

Lefoyle produced an odd croak from the back of his throat. 'Only the good die young, Harmon.'

'I see you are still with us!'

'There is life in me yet, life enough,' said Lefoyle as he got up to shake Harmon's hand.

Floral patterns of dirt speckled Harmon's boots in a sort of rococo filth. He must have ridden the grey here, Lefoyle thought. Harmon's body was lithe despite his age, his hair a mop of wiry grey. Embracing him, Lefoyle invited Harmon to sit, then called the maid to bring tea.

The Harmons were an old family long resident in the country and owned some thousands of acres in the county. Indeed, Harmon had been Lefoyle's first true friend when he had come to Birchview; they had immediately found in each other that longed-for fraternity. There had been a time when he had hoped their families might be joined in more than friendship through a possible marriage of children.

The marriage had never taken place; Harmon's George had died two months before the union, taken by consumption, and in some cruel imitation Eliza took her lover's illness. Both gone the way of the romantics, the dying had buried the dead.

'What news, Harmon?'

'Another election looks set here in Longford, and White has taken the Roscommon seat for O'Connell.'

'Another election here?' Lefoyle asked.

'Yes . . . yes, it seems likely, they are looking to run a candidate against us, against you.' Harmon sighed, running his fingers through his hair.

'This is news to me. I heard no word of this in court or Commons.'

'Called today,' Harmon said simply.

'Am I to get no peace? Isn't it we who are being intimidated? Good men not let leave their houses on election day, for fear of priests' mobs. We must defend our position.'

'All will change,' said Harmon.

'All will change and nothing. Us out and them in. A junta!' said Lefoyle, his voice harsh now.

He settled himself again and was silent a moment.

'Harmon, it seems that there exists the unignorable and growing reality of Britain's Ireland and Irish Ireland. It is thanks to that Popish pretender O'Connell that this has entered the imagination definitively. We are coming to a time, I fear, when we live in two places at once. In a place of resolved contradiction.'

'A sort of category of Irishness, then?' questioned Harmon.

'A category of allegiances,' replied Lefoyle. 'Patriotism is not a flame you light occasionally but something that must burn at all times, Harmon. All will be lost if we do not defend ourselves.'

'It was my thought that emancipation would give us the Catholics' hearts, and in so doing secure the future for us,' said Harmon after a time.

'It has only served to make them bolder still,' snapped Lefoyle. 'There can be no compromise with an enemy that seeks to destroy you. Emancipators and now repealers, they are one and the same.'

'Rebels then,' said Harmon.

'We might well eulogise and quote Edmund Burke, lamenting the Penal Laws and how a conquered people were mistreated. But I know full well their lot; you might well quote me Burke, but I daresay you would cry different when a pike was going through your side or a fire was rampant in your house. And what has emancipation changed for them? The poor are still poor. The virtue of the tyranny of want is that it lives in all systems.'

'Then better ours than theirs?' Harmon surmised.

'Know thyself and be thyself. It would be better if they liberated themselves from their history,' replied Lefoyle.

'*Mutatio est semper*,' said Harmon quietly.

'Not by me.'

A silence filled the room and neither spoke for a time.

'Do you know, Harmon, that I have a passion for astronomy?' said Lefoyle.

'I do.'

'Do you know much of astronomy, Harmon?'

'I do not, I must admit,' said Harmon with a twist of his boot.

'When I look up I am seeing time, I am looking into the past. The light of a star, which takes so long to reach us, is already spent. The past, yes, but I sometimes wonder, could one see the future too in those same stars?'

Harmon nodded his head and made to respond, but at that moment the tea was brought in.

The two sipped their drink and enjoyed some of the cook's porter cake. Their talk turned to softer subjects and the occasional laugh was shared.

'So it's back on with the armour, Harmon,' said Lefoyle at the close of his friend's visit.

'And the opening of the purse strings,' replied Harmon, tapping his breast pocket and sighing.

'It seems that way.'

'I'll inform Stanley and Foster to ready themselves.'

'A good idea,' Lefoyle said.

He bid Harmon farewell, and told him to call again and that the election was a long way off yet, there was a year to prepare and not to worry. God was on their side.

Returning inside he sat back in his chair, tired now, and the word kept spinning in his head like an eastern mantra.

O'Connell, O'Connell, O'Connell.

15
McQuaid

'That first fixing is done on the houses,' he said to Reilly as they sat down to their lunch break.

'Good man. I'm not too far behind you,' Reilly said.

'I'm done a week.' McQuaid laughed confidently and winked at him.

'Aye, but did your cheque come?' Reilly snipped in return, leaning in close.

'Two days ago.'

'Good.'

'Not much left over from it though,' McQuaid said with a sigh. 'Between the bills and wages.'

'Don't fucken talk to me, but you have a bit there for yourself anyway I'd say?' said Reilly.

'I do . . . I do, a bit, but not nearly enough.'

Reilly poured out the last of his soup from the flask and calmly closed the lid. The steam rose to his face and he inhaled the brothy liquid with a smile. 'Well, patience, lad, it'll come right. Is it more work you're needing?'

'Well, I've the woman, Sinead, I told you about her.'

'You did,' said Reilly as he slowly blew over the hot cup.

'And shor I want to make a start on my place, but she's been awkward about it.'

'Say no more, it's work you're after.'

'Well, yeah, it'd be the difference between getting the thing this year or five years from now,' McQuaid confided.

Reilly nodded understandingly. 'Well, we won't sort this today, and a bank holiday on top of it.'

'No,' McQuaid said. 'Not today.'

'I'll have a think,' said Reilly and scratched his bristly chin. 'Isn't that woman of yours coming down for the night?'

'Oh, she loves Halloween. We're going to a bonfire tonight. You're more than welcome to come.'

'Would you fuck off. An auld boy like me standing in a wet field, it's home I'm going after this shite!'

The men looked out over the houses, how they had grown these last weeks, a real shape had come into them, roofs, floors, windows, they were emerging out of the fleshy soil and their forms had come to make a new silhouette on the estate, a horizon of progress in Longford.

A bouquet of litter-stuffed yoghurt containers covered the ground where they sat. Clearing it to one side with his boot, McQuaid made to stand up. 'I'd appreciate that . . . keeping your ear out like,' he said, and bade Reilly goodbye. 'I'll see you tomorrow, I've enough of this spot today.'

Paddy nodded and waved him off. 'Enjoy the day when you have it, there's always more work to be done.'

'Just.'

McQuaid walked back through the site, past the manor and the golf course; the course had grown, and through the muck and turned-up soil he was finally beginning to see the potential of this vast place. The apartment block would be next, but that, as Reilly had said, would be the work of tomorrow.

By six o'clock he could see the fires in the distance. Oh, how they lit up the hills. How many were there? Thirty or more? It had always been this way, even in childhood, when they had danced and sung around the bonfires. The church bells vainly rang out over the townlands in competition with this pagan night.

Halloween was something special, he thought. The day when one could not wait for the night, for the darkness to come. The boys of the parish would have been collecting for weeks, all those pallets and bits of timber, anything that might burn, that might keep the embers glowing.

And he thought of the night when he was a boy and out on some country lane, some bog road, playing with fireworks and that banger had gone off in Sean Kinsella's hand. It had blown his finger clean off, and he had cried and screamed. 'It's gone, it's gone,' he had repeated again and again in shock and disbelief.

What type was it? McQuaid thought harder still. A black cat banger. Well, there was some meow, some screech that night. They had rushed him back to his mother, a plastic bag wrapped around his hand. She had never forgiven them for the accident. Even now, years on, she still did not speak to them, to McQuaid.

But that was also the night he had first met Sinead. She out with her friends knacker-drinking in some field, and they had shared the cheap vodka and told the story of the accident to each new arrival as if it were the first time. It was long ago, McQuaid reminded himself. They were only children. He never, never would have thought that this would be the girl, the woman he would make his life with. She had been small and fair, breasts not yet developed, and her friends had laughed at him as he coughed after taking a big swig of the bottle.

It was years later, on a rampage of drink in town, that he met her again. Willy had pointed her out in the bar. 'Jaysus, she's a right bit of a girl,' he said.

'She's that,' McQuaid agreed.

He gulped down the last of his pint and walked over with confidence, but it was not words that came out when he stood in front of her, only sweat and nervousness. He had been tempted to turn and walk away, run even, he was weak around the knees in her presence.

'Well, are you going to say hello to me or not?' she said with a laugh.

'I am,' he squeaked, his voice high with tension. 'Hello, I mean,' he added.

And she laughed and touched his arm. 'No bangers tonight,' she said.

And he was stunned that she had remembered him all these years. 'No, none tonight. I'm done with demolition,' he laughed awkwardly, and secretly cursed himself for such a line.

She smiled at him. She was in her last year of secondary school then, though she looked a woman.

They had kissed briefly at the end of the night by the chipper wall, and she had given him her number. That had been their beginning.

Now McQuaid looked again towards the flames that dotted the parish. It was a bank holiday and, in a way, their anniversary. She had come especially for it, for him, and those tiffs of late were cast aside. And were they even tiffs? he asked himself.

Ned Crean's still had produced a great batch of *poitín* this year, and McQuaid had dropped a bottle by his mother's back porch that morning as he always did. 'In case of a sick calf,' he had said with a mischievous air.

He must remember to pick it up on the way.

At Sinead's house he beeped the van's horn and she came running out the door.

'It's freezing,' she said as she climbed in, and kissed him softly on the lips.

'Willy says we won't be cold,' he answered, rubbing her hands in his.

'He's going to have a big fire tonight, so,' said Sinead.

'He's had the nephews out scouring the parish for tyres all week, and he'll burn all the rubbish from the yard too.'

'Good, I need some heat,' she said as the van started again and they drove on down the road.

'I'll turn on the heat for you!' he said and winked; they were both in high spirits and he did not want to break that mood. It was so rare now that they had time with each other, he would do all he could to please her. There would be no talk of college tonight, or work, or houses. It was their night.

'Willy is so funny,' Sinead laughed.

The sky was clear, a perfect view of the stars; the plough, the bear, he could not recognise any more. He had tried but he could never see his own constellation in that same sky. The dots did not seem to join up for him.

They walked through the wet grass towards the towering flames. He could see figures dancing and hear the tinny beat of music playing. *Cause you do it to yourself, just you, you and no one else . . .*

Willy greeted them both with a hug and thrust a can of beer in McQuaid's hand. 'Drink up,' he said and handed Sinead a can of cider. 'For the lady,' he said with a mock curtsy.

'Most kind,' she said, and bowed.

There was something beautiful about the fading autumn and early winter nights in Ireland. A crispness in the air, the feel of coming ice. McQuaid could smell timber burning and hear the popping of old paint cans as they exploded in the fire.

By times Willy would run towards the heat of the flame and throw on a dash of petrol, making it jump and roar. The children screamed with joy at each lunge and he was emboldened and repeated the action again and again to hear their giddy laughs.

Soon more figures appeared as the party filled out, and a tinfoil barbecue was produced and sausages were fried.

Sinead stood beside him and they both looked into the flames, transfixed. He felt her clasp his hand, and he squeezed it in response.

Her red hair flowed now in the breeze of the flames and she looked to his eyes like some star. 'Remember when we used to get that excited about Halloween?' she said, pointing at the running children.

'Yes, it was always a great night,' he said.

'It's our night,' she said and kissed him. 'Do you know what the fires are for?' she asked as their lips parted.

'Something about the dead, isn't it?'

'It's to find your true love: you burn the fires and wait until the embers die out.'

'I don't need to wait, shor,' he answered, and then wished he had not uttered such foolish words.

'Neither do I,' she said and kissed him again.

She suddenly broke away and ran towards the bonfire and the children. 'Come on, we'll have a dance,' she laughed, her hair flying higher in the wind.

He watched her a moment, how wild and free she looked; she brought a lightness to him, and how could he hold resentment tonight, not with her like this. He moved after her and they began to dance and howl around the flames. They took the children by the hand and formed little rings and spun and spun.

He pulled her close and their bodies rubbed against one another. He could smell her perfume, and it excited him, bringing him to life. She smiled and kissed him and then ran away again, looking back for him to chase. It was to be a game of cat and mouse tonight. And he did not know who or which he was.

Declan appeared with a shout from behind a watery ditch, his feet soaked, his face covered in muck and sweat, a witch's hat upon his head. 'Well,' he said. 'I'm fucking drenched.'

'Here's the boyo now,' roared Willy as they moved to greet him.

'I was at your place, waiting for you,' Declan said to McQuaid.

'Ah, fuck, I forgot to go home.'

'I had to walk,' Declan said with a slight murmur of anger.

'I'm sorry. Sinead and I came straight here.'

'That doesn't matter a fuck to me.' Declan began to smile. 'I got this in return.' He produced Ned's bottle of *poitín* like a trophy.

'Oh, for the love of Christ, we won't walk straight after that devil's piss,' Willy said.

'She's kept me warm through them fields and gripes,' said Declan, who took a large mouthful and smiled.

He and McQuaid laughed and embraced. 'I'm sorry I forgot you,' McQuaid said.

'No problem. Now take a drop to make it up to me.' Declan foisted the bottle into his hands.

McQuaid hesitated, remembering the story of his father lost in the fields after a drink of the poison one night.

'A wee drop often saved a good animal,' Declan said with a wag of his finger.

'Or killed a man,' chimed Willy.

Suddenly Sinead seized the bottle from their hands. 'It won't hurt me so,' she said and drank a mouthful.

Willy cheered and clapped. 'That's a woman right there,' he said.

She handed it back to McQuaid, and with the pressure of eyes upon him now, he was forced to drink. It was a burning liquid, he could feel it flow down his throat and sit in his stomach. He knew they would all be drunk in a matter of minutes.

'Angel's piss,' said Willy, wiping his mouth.

As the fire grew higher, so did the party. The children went home and the adults now danced more wildly, the music playing in the darkness, out over the empty fields and countryside, over the cattle in their slatted sheds and the elderly women who'd taken their dogs and cats in for the night. A man could feel alive this evening, he thought. And yes, he told himself, he was alive surely.

The music played on and they were now drunk, they were not tired, their bodies and limbs coursed with energy and passion.

He took the sausages in his hands bare and hot and ate them with gluttony, savouring their greasy taste.

'Yahoo! Yup!' Declan roared as Willy poured yet more petrol on the flame and set his boot alight to the shouts of the group.

Pulling McQuaid to one side, Sinead took him to the darkness, to the shadows. 'Take me away,' she said in a breathy voice, the hint of her bust now showing through her loosened top as beads of sweat rolled down her face from all their play.

'Where?'

'The manor house,' she announced. 'I want you to take me in the old house. It's *Oiche Samhain* and I haven't got my fright yet, I want to do it somewhere exciting.'

'Well, it's better than the van,' he laughed nervously.

But she did not laugh, she grabbed his hair with a furiousness and kissed him with her fiery, cider-soaked breath. 'Take me there,' she said, breaking away from his lips.

He did not question her, this was no moment for jokes, she was filled with an animal passion as he now was, and he would take her wherever she wanted to go, wherever it took to be with her, to feel her.

They ran back to the van, not saying goodbye to the group, and kissed as he turned the key and drove towards the estate.

The security gates were locked as he'd expected, and he lifted her up over the wall. She had become a wild woman this night. She had never once come to any of his jobs before, nor, he thought, to any construction site, and yet she did not flinch at the wire, or the walls, or the puddles of muck as they traipsed through an oak forest with only the light from his mobile to guide their way.

When they reached the manor house, she opened the door and led him through the rooms. 'So this is the place,' she said, her voice echoing through the hallways.

'This is it,' he said and kissed her lips. He was trembling now, in cold and excitement, her lips firm then soft, her tongue a wet mass he could not, could never pin down.

'Bring me to the landlord's bedroom.'

'There's nothing there.'

'It doesn't matter, we'll be there,' she said, and took him by the hand. They made their way upstairs, moving slowly through the old house. But there was no thought of darkness now, or ghosts. There was only flesh.

The floorboards creaked as he guided his hand against the wall, looking for the master bedroom. For Lefoyle's room. He opened the door and shone his mobile around the space. It was beyond bare, there was nothing left, of that grandeur, that former life.

Sinead walked to the window and opened the shutters. The bright moonlight shone through the darkness and he could see her face framed by the glow.

By the light of the moon he took in the room, and there in the corner was the picture of Lefoyle. Lost as it had been, it was found again here of all places, in his bedroom. It seemed somehow more complete, the face a brighter hue, as if somehow restored. And the eyes, those eyes had grown stronger.

'Kiss me,' Sinead called, and he made to tell her of the painting.

'That's . . .' But as he pointed at the canvas she pounced into his arms.

There were no other words spoken. They placed their jackets on the floor to make their lovers' nest and she cried out, wild cries as they tossed and turned. It was beyond lovemaking this night, this night it was animal carnality and all its earthy pleasures. And he did not care who saw, not Willy or Reilly or the ghostly eyes of Lefoyle.

Her sighs sang through the walls of the house and spoke of a joy that the building had not known in so long, so long. They spoke of love, young love and its heady embrace, its binding ecstasy. They sang again and again through the night as they found each other's pleasure there amidst the damp and mould.

As they gathered their belongings to go, he was giddy with excitement. 'Jesus, I don't know where that came from,' he said.

'Never you mind,' she said and kissed him more softly now.

'But God, that was wild.'

'Sometimes . . .' She paused.

'Yes,' he returned.

'Sometimes . . . you just, well, have to fuck,' she said and laughed.

'Ha, well I'm glad I was around for that,' he said and kissed her now.

'It's been a while since someone was happy here,' she said, looking around the room as they stood up to leave. Looking now to the haggard canvas, he knew those words were true.

16
McQuaid

Sinead was happy and in her happiness he found his mood had lifted too. Life though poor was on an upward flow. He trawled the receipts and dockets in the van for bills to be paid, some long overdue. He could face them all now. Kane's cheque had come and he could breathe a little easier, if only for a short time.

Halloween had been just what they needed, a reminder of all the good things. Lining up the wage slips for the week, it was with a smile that he signed each cheque. The men had worked hard, they'd earned their pay. He took an envelope and jotted down some figures. He had enough.

Maybe it was time to go and see the engineer and make that long-threatened start on his house. Maybe it was time to start the planning.

A mirth entered his face as he thought of it all. His own house and no one to bother him in it. An end to the childhood bed and those lonely frustrated wanks.

He added the figures further and found that he could begin to say yes to that dream. He might not have a hope of building it yet, but God would provide, as Willy had so aptly put it.

There was time today, he thought, and with that he stood up from the table and went out to the van.

Fergus Kennedy's office was on the outskirts of the town, occupying one of the industrial units that seemed to be springing up everywhere. They were not pretty but they were the future. There beside the Argos, the McDonald's, the vanguard of the new Longford, he'd speak his piece and commit imagination to paper.

He looked at his phone as he parked the van in the lot. Perhaps he would text Sinead and tell her his intentions. He began the message but the words were not right. No, he'd surprise her with all this, he'd get the plans drawn up and arrive with them when the time was right. He could see her face now, excited, and she'd kiss him and maybe they'd take a walk to the site and talk of the possibilities.

The office was a bundle of schematics and plans, notices and slips of paper stuck to the walls. The receptionist told him to take a seat and that Fergus would be with him shortly.

There was no need to worry, and as he looked around the room he could see that same look on so many other faces. They were young nurses and builders and farmers waiting for their dreams to start, waiting to get their foot on the property ladder.

'Ger,' said Fergus as he walked out to meet him. 'I thought you had gone with someone else,' he added as they shook hands firmly.

'No, no, I was just waiting,' McQuaid said and smiled.

'I know well,' Kennedy replied.

'You're busy,' said McQuaid with a nod to the reception area.

'It's like this every day, we can't get them out fast enough.'

'That's good.'

The receptionist offered him a cup of tea and they walked to the back office amidst the architects' desks and scrolls of blue-prints stacked high on cheap metal shelves.

'You're wanting to start,' Kennedy said as they took their seats and waited for their tea.

'It's time I was,' McQuaid said.

With that Kennedy opened a new black folder and began to fill out the basic notes. 'So we'll start with the test holes and see how we are for drainage, and then we'll move on to the plans.'

McQuaid nodded nervously. So many times he'd looked at drawings and yet never his own.

Kennedy moved to the shelf. Paused and scratched his head. 'The way I'm doing it now, I've all the different plans here and we can just pick one and go from there, no need for architects or any of that shite.'

'Suits me.'

Kennedy began to pull down scroll after scroll. 'Bungalow, two storey or dormer?'

'Oh, two storey.'

'Right,' said Kennedy, returning to the shelf and pulling out yet more scrolls. 'How many bedrooms?'

'Five.'

'Ho ho, a big family.'

'Maybe,' McQuaid laughed.

'Five bedroom, two storey,' Kennedy muttered. 'And old style or modern?'

'Ah, old style, I suppose.'

'Irish farmhouse style?'

'Exactly.'

'That's the popular one now, so it is,' Kennedy said. 'Did three this week,' he added, looking back at McQuaid.

'Just so,' said McQuaid.

'Oh, I'm flat out with them, no one wants a small house any more.'

'The day of the cottage is over,' said McQuaid with a nod.

'It is that and good riddance,' said Kennedy.

He took out yet more rolls and moved as some ancient librarian, handling each plan with care. He unfurled one and then, shaking his head, put it back on the shelf. 'Irish country house,' he muttered again and pushed his glasses back tight on the ridge of his nose. 'I have him here somewhere,' he said and laughed.

McQuaid sipped his tea and made to help remove some of the discarded plans.

'No,' said Kennedy immediately. 'I have a system, as fucking chaotic as it looks.'

McQuaid looked out the window and watched the shoppers move in and out of Argos and Homebase. Desks, tables and sofas were being loaded into cars and trucks. The population, it seemed, were furnishing their visions.

'It's a busy spot here,' he said, gesturing out the window.

'Doesn't stop, Ger, doesn't stop,' said Kennedy.

And just as McQuaid's interest began to fade and his thoughts of houses began to feel ridiculous, Kennedy grunted and pulled a faded and worn white plan from the back of the shelf.

'Now, this might do, this might do nicely,' he said. He opened the dog-eared schematic, held it to the light and smiled. 'Ger, this . . . this is what you might call a house.'

He took two bricks for paperweights and spread out the plans on the desk, then beckoned McQuaid closer. 'It's dog-eared, I know,' he said, looking at McQuaid reassuringly.

'You've done a few of these so?'

'No, only one for a chap in Leitrim but it was never finished.'

'Oh.'

'He died, poor bollox, car accident, nice lad too,' confided

Kennedy. 'What you have here is a one of a kind, there isn't another one like her.'

McQuaid looked closely at the plans; the paper illuminated a large two-storey house, bay windows at the front, and a curving stairwell. He could see that the kitchen was large and spacious, and there were not two but three toilets.

'This would make a fine place,' Kennedy announced. 'We can make your own adjustments, of course, your woman might have her own ideas.'

'No, she doesn't . . . No, it's perfect.'

McQuaid closed his eyes, seeing the rooms, the stairs, the windows, the doors, and every door it seemed in that moment was an opening to happiness. The children and the life that would be, the kitchen and a stew – no, a chicken roasting in the oven, and Sinead cooking it with a sprig of wild rosemary from their own garden and salt and raisins in the stuffing as he liked it. All the dreams came rushing forth.

The blueprint was an index of happiness and his future. It was bright and blue. He'd go to the auctions and find himself some old paintings of hunting scenes and place them in the living room, that room where they would spend most nights. And they would make love there. They'd make love in all the rooms, he promised himself that. To christen each room in the place.

It was so much more than lines on paper, it was a plan. And when Sinead saw it, it would stifle all doubt, all spite and talk of worry.

It could all come to life now and life itself could start. What was it, only a bit more work to have this dream, a bit more sweat and it would be his. Those rolls of wire were closer now, coming to a close in fact.

Willy could visit. And Begley and Reilly would be proud,

and his mother. There would be a room for her in that house, perhaps there on the ground floor so she would not have to climb the stairs.

Sinead could take that job in Dublin now, what did it matter, so many people did the commute, and things were good between them again; the bonfire, the manor house had sorted all those issues. So long as he had the house, he would have her there with him and they could come home in the evening and life could begin.

'Are you all right, Ger?' Kennedy asked for the second time, placing his hand upon his shoulder.

'I'm, I'm grand, I was just thinking.'

'She's a beauty, isn't she,' said Kennedy proudly.

'She is.'

'Most people don't appreciate the work we put into these places, but you know, I can tell,' said Kennedy.

'I've seen a few in my time.'

'So that's the one for you?'

'It is.'

'And I can always make the changes, but not after we lodge the planning.'

'No, just as it is, and you're sure no one else has used this plan?'

'I'm certain, that man is six feet under, she's a one-off.' Kennedy smiled.

'Well, she's the one for me,' said McQuaid.

Kennedy nodded and quickly snatched up the blueprint and took it to the receptionist, ordering for copies to be made. And in that brief moment, McQuaid was sad in the absence of the plan.

Returning to his seat, Kennedy took his details and informed him of the test holes and the planning process.

'That won't be a problem,' McQuaid replied, and thought now of Sinead's father. He'd go tomorrow in the morning and tell him he needed this to be sorted out with the council, and Toher would be so happy at the news that there would be no concern of objections. For it would be partly Jimmy's, that dream, his daughter safe and with a good man and a tie to Longford forever more. They might even have a whiskey in the house to celebrate.

'Well, Ger,' said Kennedy, smiling, 'you're an easy man to please. No changes at all?'

'That's the one,' McQuaid said again, binding himself to those lines heart and soul. 'That's the one,' he repeated, quieter still.

'We'll get the holes dug later this week. And the ball will be in motion.' Kennedy handed him a form to sign.

'I don't know what all the fuss is about building a house these days,' said McQuaid excitedly.

'I often wonder that myself, it's a pleasing toil,' said Kennedy. 'Will that be credit or cheque?'

'Credit,' said McQuaid and smiled.

The receptionist entered with the duplicates and handed him a set of plans.

'That's for you and this one is for me,' said Kennedy, and then reached across the table and shook his hand.

McQuaid gently held the paper, not wanting to damage it in any way. 'Thank you,' he said and passed him the credit card.

'We'll fix up the rest when the planning is through,' said Kennedy and they both stood up.

'You won't be going to Argos for the couches so?' Kennedy looked out the office window.

'No, only the best of stuff, I'll go to Mollaghan's,' said McQuaid, caught up still in the fantasy of it all.

'Good man,' said Kennedy.

He walked McQuaid out of the office and they shook hands again. 'I'll give you a bell in a few days,' said Kennedy, and as McQuaid walked out the door, he thought he heard an astonished laugh from Kennedy, that a man could get caught so easily, pick a house so easily. He looked back but Kennedy was already gone. Perhaps it was someone else. It must have been, he told himself, and with a quick step moved to the van.

An hour had done so much. A pleasing toil indeed, he mused as he turned the keys and rattled home again, a prouder soul.

17
McQuaid

Fianna Fáil beat them all, Fine Gael go to jail. That had been the rhyme from childhood, from telephone pole poster to Sunday collection outside the church. McQuaid silently mouthed the political mantra as the van trundled up the briar-heavy lane to Begley's.

It was with the energy of the recently retired that Noodles propelled himself, he thought. Time took new shades in this new life. As he rounded the last corner he could see the tedious cleanliness of the house and yards. The garden had been severely curtailed in its dash for freedom, and widowed bushes stood naked where a small forest had been.

Mary answered the door. 'Hello, dear,' she said with genuine emotion and embraced him. 'He'll be delighted to see you.'

'Hello, Mary, how are you?' McQuaid asked, breaking away from her.

'He's a'din in the room,' she responded with a wave of her hand and made for the kitchen.

Begley sat by the range with a newspaper on his lap. 'Come in, come in, you're welcome,' Pat said and leaned over to shake hands.

McQuaid put himself before the heat of the fire, hands and arse placed against the heat of the metal door. Both men looked at the opposite wall and paused a moment.

'You have the place looking great, you took tea with the garden, too, I see.'

'Had to, there was a rosyedendron getting an awful opinion of himself out there,' Begley said.

McQuaid smiled. The garden had been fine as it was. 'Much on the paper?'

'Much of the same, our man in Leinster House is in bother,' said Begley, holding up an article in illustration.

'That tribunal has been going on a long time, what was it all about?'

'What else . . . money, isn't it always that same culprit?' said Begley.

'I suppose . . . It's over land, I thought.'

'Oh, rezoning of land for houses in Dublin, technical stuff, but *they* were the technical boys to do it.'

'And the big fella is talking at it now?'

'The cutest hoor of them all,' said Begley with a mischievous wink.

'The ten years of government could be enough for anyone. Is he losing the grip a bit?'

'No contact with the small man any more, that party has changed. Cummans of dead lads now and it's probably as much use to them.'

'Or more,' laughed McQuaid.

Begley grew bolder with each jibe. He had been such a staunch supporter all these years, and yet the soldiers of destiny seemed not to want men such as him any more. His only outlet now for talk of politics was the pub, and that was too political a place.

'It'll be wall to wall Shinners in no time, mark my words. Big group of them in Kilnalough now.'

'Is that so? They'll pull the people with them.'

'Walk when everyone else is running, lad,' said Begley.

Mary entered in a steam of trays and tea and sandwiches. She handed Pat his mug and they exchanged a smile. McQuaid knew she treasured these visits. He was, in a way, the longed-for son that had never come. She left the room again to finish her washing, saying she'd be in presently.

'And Blair might well be for off soon too. He was a good friend to us,' McQuaid said as he sipped from his cup.

'Wasn't his grandmother a Donegal woman?' said Begley. 'Conquer the pull of power though,' he added.

'Ha?' McQuaid quizzed.

'That's what he said on stepping down.'

'Oh, he conquered enough all the same,' chided McQuaid. 'It's a credit to them that North though.'

'Peace in our time, Ger, peace in our time. The way things are going now, we may just join back up one day with Belfast and no one would think the differ, the border is only in the mind for a lot.'

'The hardest barrier of all, I suppose,' McQuaid answered softly.

They sat quietly a moment, the range sounding off a steady hum of heat. The chat was out. And yet there was an ease in the silence and he knew he did not need to talk, there would be no forced conversation, and it was comforting in a way. To be taken as you were in that silence. Begley was happy of the company.

McQuaid looked around the sparsely furnished room. Above the range hung a print of the Virgin Mother and Child faded and worn from years of windowed sunlight. On the opposite wall a cross made from used matchsticks, its shape a pattern of black-headed reverence. The table and chairs picked by Mary, bought by Pat, and a television in the corner watched only after six.

'Work's good?' enquired Begley after a time.

'Tippin away. The lads are working well, first fixing done on the houses, it'll be the manor and apartments next.'

'Great to be busy,' said Begley, a hint of ennui in his voice. He would, McQuaid knew, sooner be at work than retired at home. But his eyesight had grown poorer still in the past few months. Age had shown in the body if not yet the mind.

'And the money?' asked Begley in a conspiratorial tone. 'Did it come through from Kane?'

'Oh, yeah, you were right there, no troubles at all.'

'Now didn't I tell you, he's a cunt, but he's *our* cunt,' said Begley with a wag of his finger.

Mary returned with another plate of sandwiches and they ate side by side and it cast him back to all those worksite lunch breaks. Perched on some high nest looking out over the scene, over all those chipboard mansions and their faux notions of grandeur.

'Have you followed this banking crisis in the US?' asked Begley.

'Well sort of, hard to miss I suppose . . . subprime and all that,' McQuaid said.

Begley emitted a snide curling laugh. 'It's more than that, you want to be paying attention to this stuff.'

And he reached to the foot of his chair to the large pile of newspapers. Wetting his thumb he flicked through a week-old copy of the *Independent* with the dexterity of a clerk.

'Now do ya see,' he said as he forcefully folded over the paper, his broad finger tapping the bold headline. *TROUBLE IN THE US*. 'It's all here.'

McQuaid looked over the article and noncommittally nodded his head. It would be easier to agree. 'It is yeah,' he said quietly.

It was fine for Begley to talk of matters far away, he had time to think and read on them. But then again, maybe he should not be so hard on poor Pat. Maybe this new time brought no peace. All the hours of the day and little to fill them with, the garden, the sheds, the farm could only be cleaned and made ready so many times. Soon he could see the television would start to be turned on before six, and the slow rot of docility would set in. To age, he thought, and gave a sad smile.

'Well, tell me what you think of it all, Pat,' he said now with renewed and softened interest.

'Ah, it's bad news, bad news. The world is in perpetual motion but there's a lot of energy going arseways.'

'Well said.'

'There's gypsies living on a roundabout on the M50, and no sign of them to fuck off home. The banks are folding in the UK and the US looks set to follow, and the Chinese, don't get me started on them.'

'What about the Chinese?'

'Aren't they in Africa now!' Begley exclaimed. 'Meanwhile our lot are flying to New York to shop, spend it, spend it, God will send it. Paisley was talking about the blessed harvest on the television the other day, bedad we have little to reap.' He had worked himself into a rage.

'Ah, now Pat, it's not as bad as that. We're as rich, richer than we ever were, and work for any man that wants it.'

'I don't, I can't trust a political leader who says he hasn't been to confession in forty years.'

'Wasn't original sin invented?' joked McQuaid in hopes of calming him.

'By men like him,' spat Begley and threw the paper to the

floor. 'I don't know why people can't see,' he added vainly and grew sullen.

At that Mary re-entered the room, picked up the paper and sat across from them. The dinner was on, she informed them, and wouldn't Ger stay. Her woollen dress rose up, exposing her once shapely ankles.

'I was hoping we'd see you soon,' she said, looking at McQuaid. 'Pat told me he met you on the road with Willy.'

'He did, in the new tractor,' McQuaid said with a smile at Begley.

'And Sinead and your mother, they're well?'

'Not a loss on them. I . . . I got the plans drawn up for the house.'

'You didn't,' said Mary, astonished, and then beamed.

'Good man,' said Pat, then stood up and shook his hand. 'Couldn't be better news.'

'I'll bet Sinead is thrilled,' said Mary.

'Well, I haven't told her yet. I was keeping it a surprise for now.'

'Ah now, isn't that nice, isn't that nice, Pat?'

Pat walked to the drinks cabinet and poured a glass of whiskey. 'Take that now, son,' he said and thrust the drink into his hand. 'Well done,' he said and they toasted health and luck.

His news had brightened Begley's mood and their smiles told him it had brought a lift to their day.

'And you're ready to build?' asked Mary.

'No, not yet, just the plans,' he said.

'Don't be silly, Mary, one thing at a time, isn't that it, Ger?' said Begley and poured himself a glass now. 'That will work itself out, no rush on that at all.'

'Yeah, well, I'd hope soon, if work . . .'

'If work is good,' said Begley.

'Exactly.'

'There'll be wedding bells before long,' said Mary. 'God, I'll have to get a new dress for that.'

'Don't rush the lad, Mary.'

He had not meant to tell so much for he knew now in speaking it that the news would begin to spread. And yet it was the truth, he had hoped for all those things in looking at those plans.

He looked at his watch. It was getting late, but there was still time. The visit had made their day; he'd get Begley to show him around the yard and inspect the cattle, and with a quiet tenderness they'd smoke a fag on the top gate by those young heifers he prized so much.

Mary pressed him to stay for dinner, but he told them he must be getting on.

'Your mother will miss you,' she said. 'I'll have to give her a call. It's been so long since we spoke.'

'She doesn't know, no one knows yet. You're the first.'

'We'll keep it to ourselves for now,' said Mary, to which Begley nodded in agreement.

As McQuaid walked out the door she thanked him for the visit and gave a sympathetic nod towards Pat. 'He thinks the world of you,' she said.

'I know, I know,' McQuaid answered. 'Come on, Pat, show me these prize heifers you've been harping about.'

'I will surely, lad,' said Pat, who quickly got his wellies on and with a youthful stride made for the top field.

18
Lefoyle

1830

At last the longed-for letter had arrived. He inhaled deeply as he broke the wax seal and watched it crumble upon his desk.

To the Right Honourable Henry Lefoyle,

I write to inform you of your appointment to the Privy Council of Ireland.

He tried to read further but stopped short with emotion. And was it not a tear of happiness that rolled down his cheek. There in the midnight court of his study he exhaled in relief. The nights, those long nights of worry had come to an end in a moment of achieved grace. Even though it was not yet the evening, he rang the bell and told the servant girl to bring him a good bottle of wine.

And who to tell? Not Rose, though he knew she was smiling down upon him. He would inform Harmon, and Foster and Stanley. The word would ring out. Perhaps he might make a party and invite old Lady Bond, for proud she would be.

He rang the bell again and the servant girl appeared.

'Anne, tell Murphy there is to be a gathering tonight. I'll supply you with the invitations.'

'Very good, sir,' she said with a curtsy. 'Sir?' she said, delaying a moment.

'Yes, Anne.'

'May I ask the occasion, sir?'

'The long-expected news,' and he held up the envelope in illustration.

'Bless you, sir, it's overdue!'

'It is, Anne,' he admitted.

And with glee she skipped out of the room and downstairs. The house would have it now, and they would be as happy as he, as if they themselves had received the appointment.

By five, Murphy had left with the invitations, the horses washed and gleaming, and a smile upon his own face. The house had sprung to an action of nervous excitement.

Lefoyle cleaned himself up and informed the man to have his evening clothes laid out and made ready. He would take his walk first and deconstruct the future.

The day was still bright and he moved across the great lawn towards the plantings. He stopped a while at his cedars of Lebanon and took a seat among their towering forms. How magnificent nature was. To think of their journey to his home. He had been right to move the groundsman's hut; it had obstructed his view of them from the drawing room and its removal had let in more light for growth. Although, he reminded himself, there were still a number that needed help. He'd get the men to treat them with some ash and soft dung from the stables.

Ah, but it was a glory, he mused as he took his pipe from his coat pocket and savoured that fine Virginian tobacco. He opened the letter again and read the lines afresh.

The appointment would change things. There was the money, yes, but it was the safety he valued more. The repealers would not dare run against him now; the seat would be safe, and Harmon's concerns over the Whites would quickly fade. The Popish O'Connell might try his hand, but there was the full power of law against him now.

And what did these repealers know of governing? All he need do to know what the people of Longford wanted was look inside his own heart.

Taking the pipe in his mouth, he stood up and walked the vast lawn and fields towards the great wall. The cattle grazed happily in the meadow grounds and out across the lawn he spied the young foal. What a fine hunter he would make.

Perhaps Lefoyle might take up the hunt again. He had not ridden since Rose's death, on a point of mourning, but Harmon and Lord Granard would welcome him back with open arms and his days of pace across the ditches and hedges of Clonfin and Ballymahon could begin again. With a hunter like that he would be the envy of them all.

This extra money inspired thoughts of expanding. Perhaps he might do as other men now and push for more livestock and tillage. But then there would be the headache of tenant removals and clearings. He'd not do as Lisadell, a passage paid for and the surrounding neighbourhood in uproar at a thousand people removed and shoved onto a boat to the Americas. But perhaps he might purchase new lands. He'd have no allegiances there, and if there were people to be moved it was not his concern, he owed them no favours. Ah, it was a curious thing to manage the lives of others. Perhaps it was better first to wait and see how the position went. Yes, he confirmed, wait for a time till things settled with these upstarts; there was no point in buying livestock only for them to be stolen out of retribution.

An hour passed as he walked the grounds; he could feel a sweat grow on the back of his neck and he was glad of his health.

On returning to the house he found Birchview in a state of near readiness. The girls had the front step scrubbed and the smell of roasting pheasant and chicken wafted up from the kitchens. Mrs Joyce had the girls rushed off their feet.

'Sir,' Anne said as he walked in the front door. 'Your boots, sir, if you don't mind.'

He saw her disapproving glance at the dirt upon his leathers. With a smile he complied and made his way in stocking feet up the stairs to bathe. The water was warm and cleansing as he poured in more salts and the window frosted with the steam. How Rose would have enjoyed this night. It had been so long since the house had hosted a gathering of any kind.

At seven the doorbell started clanging in earnest. The wheeze of the great door echoed through the house as it opened and closed. The girls gently received overcoats and capes, placing them in the cupboard.

Harmon had ridden the grey and entered with an air of seriousness. 'My dear Henry,' he began as he sipped a welcoming brandy to warm his frame. 'What,' he paused to sip, 'brings us here this evening?'

The pair walked to the study and Lefoyle handed Harmon the letter.

Harmon mouthed the words and a smile erupted on his face. 'My good fellow, I thought it was bad news that you had Murphy send for me in such haste.'

'Not at all. There is an end to our problems, Harmon.' Lefoyle touched his friend's shoulder in affection.

'Maybe just so,' Harmon said and scratched his wiry hair as was his habit.

'What do you mean *maybe*? It is an end in itself.'

'We have the law now, yes,' Harmon said and paused a breath, 'but they still have the people.'

'The people will stay for the sake of security. Think of all we might do for them now.'

'True.' Harmon shook his head. 'Forgive me, Henry, I've brought doubt on a happy day.' He offered his hand.

'You have. But we'll speak no more of it,' Lefoyle said and quickly twisted towards the drinks cabinet.

'When is the ceremony?' asked Harmon. 'I'm presuming there is some official reception of sorts?'

'A week from now, it says so in the letter.'

'Ah, so it does, forgive me. In the excitement I've missed it all, my mind's a muddle.'

'No matter. Some pheasant will fix you up.'

With that the door wheezed again; soon after, Foster and Stanley entered the sitting room.

'It's good news, I'd know by your face, Henry,' Foster sang.

'It's that, it's that.'

'Privy Council,' Harmon mouthed, to which they both raised their eyebrows in happiness.

'Then I was right to bring the brandy,' said Stanley, who was already on his way to merriment. He handed the bottle to the girl and their talk resumed. The fine smell of roasting poultry drifted through the corridors and drawing rooms. The boy had dug the potatoes and carrots fresh from the ridge that morning, they could not have been better prepared.

'Is this the entirety of ourselves?' Stanley asked Harmon.

'I believe Lady Bond will join us.'

'Sweet Maggie, loveliest of the plain,' sang Stanley as he sipped yet more brandy.

'It's been too long since we saw her,' agreed Foster.

They drank and talked for half an hour or more awaiting the arrival of Maggie.

'You might do well to watch those investments, Stanley,' Harmon cautioned him at the talk of Canada.

'Fort York is a far-off place indeed,' agreed Foster.

'What is it, only an investment,' said Stanley.

'Fortunes, gentlemen, fortunes are being made there.'

'But for how long?'

'What do you think, Henry?'

'I know nothing of the place.'

'I have an agent there who assures me I'll see profit before the end of the year,' said Stanley.

'And what if there were upheavals against him? The red man is not one to give up his sod that easily.'

'I had not thought so far as that,' Stanley responded.

'Exports are the only safe bet, come up against the market and let every man use his wits as best he can,' said Lefoyle. 'I'd put my money in something more tangible than a country you've never seen.'

Stanley grew pale and ran to the bathroom.

'I don't know why he insists on drinking the stuff, he has as delicate a mind as he does a constitution,' Harmon joked.

'You know he gets this investment money on the back of higher rates from his tenants.'

'He knows no different,' said Foster, to which they nodded.

With that they heard the scurry of horses and grit of carriage wheels, then the clanging of the doorbell. Anne took Lady Bond's coat and announced her arrival.

'Henry, I've heard your news – you must be a proud man.'

'Pride is for the fool. I am quietly happy, Maggie,' Lefoyle said and kissed her in welcome.

A sherry was produced for her, it being her habit, and they

lounged by the fireplace as Mrs Joyce finished preparing the meal.

Maggie gathered the silken folds of her dress around her as the dinner bell was rung and the party was invited to the dining room. Her family had been the original settlers in the area, a land grant at the time of brave Cromwell. The table was laid out in finery, the cutlery of Denmark, crystal and candlelight. Lefoyle took his place at the head of the table and toasted good friends and happy times.

The boy produced Mrs Joyce's famous broth and after blessings the slurping began.

'A strengthening force, this soup, Henry. I'm surprised you've always kept such a leanness about you.'

'The secret is exercise,' Maggie quipped and a low laugh was taken at Foster's bulky expense.

After eight the pheasant and chicken were produced; a wave of steam rose from the creamy plates as they were placed before the company. Harmon rose to his feet and with the clinking of glasses hushed the room.

'I would like to toast our dear friend Henry – nay, the Right Honourable Henry – on his wonderful appointment. It is a victory for the march of the mind,' and he raised his glass of wine.

'Hear, hear.'

Lefoyle sat quietly and smiled. He looked around at their kindly faces and though the party was small he felt the room was full of pride and admiration.

'In these troublesome times, it is only right and just to see that common sense prevails,' chimed Stanley and they drank again.

They ate now in between grabs of chatter, interrupted by the arrival of side dishes and wine pouring.

'It's funny,' Maggie said, 'that you broach the topic of

common sense, Stanley . . .' to which they smiled in misunderstanding. 'No, Harmon, not Canada – though that might end up a foolish business, my dear,' she said, scolding gently as only the elderly can. 'Yes, I know your affairs,' she added with a smile. 'No, I mean the common sense of human wisdom. I have heard much this week of Wellington's bulwark against change in England. He stands strong and with the confidence of the country to hold out against the cotton lords and their call for electoral change.'

'Franchise, to my mind, is an opportunity,' replied Harmon.

'How so?' she returned.

'If England calls for reform and gets it, why not set Dublin or Kildare on that path as well?'

'We've had reform, dear,' she replied.

'But not the middle class.'

'The middle class: accountants and clerks,' she laughed. 'What use have they for votes?'

'What do you say, Henry?'

'I would prefer this one night a break from our old chat,' Lefoyle said.

'You are right,' Maggie said. 'I have forgotten myself.'

'But,' he went on, 'as the subject has been raised yet again, I am in favour of reform in England. It is not right that Manchester or Birmingham have no voice in parliament. Rotten boroughs do not make for peace. It is the Christian thing to do. A happy workforce makes a better economy, and now that trade between the isles has resumed on the old terms I would not seek to stop it. It is the only way for the greater part to have peace. But as to our own doorstep, my dear Harmon, you are forgetting that we still fight the Boyne, fight the Pretender, daily with our speech. Though we sit in Westminster, this is a different place and a different time.'

'Spoken like a true man of the law and crown,' Maggie cheered and raised yet another toast.

At length the dessert was produced: a beautiful poached pear and custard.

'From the orchard,' Lefoyle informed them as they sank their forks into the glistening fruit. Mrs Joyce had outdone herself, he thought.

'I wish Rose and Eliza might have been with us this night. Rose was always such a wonderful hostess,' said Stanley.

And a small hurt entered the faces of both Harmon and Lefoyle. They did not talk of their children.

A game of cards was organised after dinner and the group enjoyed the sport of it.

Then, taking him to one side, Maggie invited Lefoyle to sit by the fire and touched his hand. 'He is a fool, that Stanley. I am sorry if he stirred up old memories on a happy night,' she said maternally.

'Life must spring from death, Lady Bond, and am I not at the start of a new one.'

'You are, my dear, but still he is a fool and all.'

'I don't know how we can talk of more votes when men like him are already on our side. God help us.'

Maggie laughed and clasped his hand. 'And wouldn't you know, his mother was a Fitzgerald of ninety-eight,' she said.

'The breeding shows.'

'It certainly does.'

The stars had come out by the ending of the night. A perfect evening. The carriages pulled up at the front and he bade his guests farewell and wished them a safe homeward journey.

'It's a new day for Birchview,' Maggie said as she embraced him goodbye.

'It is,' he agreed.

He sent the last of the pheasant to Murphy for all his hard work this night. He would spend an hour at his telescope before bed. Sleep would come easier tonight.

19

McQuaid

'She's more bull than heifer, that's for sure,' said Big Jack as he finished the last of his watery coffee and threw it on the ground.

'A butch, is it?' quizzed McQuaid.

'I wouldn't know that,' Big Jack laughed and clapped him on the shoulder. He'd pulled him aside that morning as the men unloaded the last of the new rolls of wire from the van. The show house had to be finished for the open day, Jack said, and an interior designer from Dublin was coming to help.

'Ah, fuck's sake,' McQuaid complained now. 'You're the boss man, can't you do it?'

'Do you think I'm doing nothing? I've two meetings about this golf course today, a hauler who won't deliver the precast concrete because his lorry isn't *wide* enough, and to top that I've a review with Kane. So if you'd like to take my place you're more than fucking welcome and I'll sit and look at bloody fabrics.'

McQuaid nodded quietly, knowing his place once again.

'And don't *fuck's sake* me, lad, and don't be cursing around her either. She'll be at the houses at two.'

Checking his watch, Jack walked back into the wilderness of the site; as he strode through the long grey grass, he seemed like one of those Boer men of the Transvaal, wild and hairy.

The street lights would have to wait, McQuaid told himself, and he called Declan to inform him he'd be gone a few hours and to continue with the work. Willy would know what to do.

The show house sat on De Valera Drive; each street on the estate now bore the name of some great Irish hero, from Collins Road to Robert Emmet Crescent. A revolution of tarmac on those six hundred acres and not a single shot fired.

The gable wore a patchwork quilt of sandstone up its face. The work was neat. The Farrells had fitted the double-glazed windows two days before and the stickers were still on the glass. With the wrapped door handles, the house had the appearance of an unopened present. A dream not yet realised.

They were not beautiful houses, nor would they be, for what character was there in monotony, he thought as he sat and looked at the frames row upon row. It would make some civil servant very happy, he reflected and smiled. That new breed of credit monsters dancing at the crossroads.

He checked his phone and smoked a cigarette as he waited. The words of some rebel song from the radio drifted over the plain and he hummed along tunelessly, tapping his foot in accompaniment.

'God save Ireland,' said the heroes,
'God save Ireland,' said they all,
Whether on the scaffold high
Or the battlefield we die,
Oh, what matter when for Erin dear we fall.

Around him the earth was thrown this way and that, gutters of sewage, electrics and water. The landscape crew would be coming soon and false slopes would cover it all. Garden centre trees that would never fully mature, the odd flower here and there and maybe some woodchip in this graveyard of hayfields.

Get your foot on the property ladder, that was what it was all about now, a starter home, your real home, and then a holiday property to escape it all.

McQuaid sucked on the last of his cigarette; it was odd how quiet it could be here amidst all the work. He flicked his finger and the red ember swam through the air. He'd have to go check on the lads soon. And where was this woman?

'There like little portraits, little swatches of lives,' a voice said.

He looked up and saw the designer standing transfixed behind him, admiring the view.

'I always think that too, but then the fuckers move in,' he said slowly and laughed a vicious laugh.

She was perfectly out of place. A Bernhard Willhelm dress draped over her milky frame. Her fingers small and delicate.

'You're the designer?'

'Rhian,' she said and offered him her hand. 'Jack told me you'd be here, he's funny, isn't he,' she added.

'He's himself.'

She took a large number of books and fabrics from her cotton bag and sat on the pallet beside him. Her perfume was strange, unlike anything on the site. It was the smell of a woman amidst the dirt.

'I really think we can make some of the smaller rooms come to life with the right lighting,' she began, her eyes wide, and she pushed the corner of a book towards him.

'Yeah,' he said in a half-swallow.

'They're poky but there's something darling about them too.'

He nodded his head in agreement.

They looked through various booklets, fixtures and fabrics, tones of dark and light. There was something so completely odd about her and yet alluring. All this talk of energy and light and karma, and wasn't it all the one wire and voltage.

They agreed on some insets and switches there on the pallet. Taste and economy would have to meet, and in the end he knew it would look like every other house that had been built in the last few years: a poor imitation of gentility. But one had to admire her willingness.

'Well, we should take a tour inside, get more of a sense of the place,' she announced after a time.

Rolls of insulation sat inside the door, dirt and plastic littered the floors. He kicked the rolls out of the way and invited her in. She walked over the threshold slowly, savouring the experience. She placed her hand on the wall tenderly and held it there a moment. 'Yellow,' she said quietly to herself.

They walked to the kitchen, and taking a pen and paper she began to make some notes, again touching the walls as she scribbled. Under the window where the sink would be, she closed her eyes. 'All those kitchen dreams and dinner wash-ups . . . Do you suppose they'll fight much?' she said, turning towards him. 'The couple who buy this house,' she added, opening her big glassy eyes wide.

'I . . . don't know . . . It's a show house,' said McQuaid, rather stunned by the question. 'It's for everyone, isn't it?'

'I always like to think about these things when I'm working on a place. Colours influence the mood, you know. Red can be so carnal and yet . . .'

Her words hung in the air as she clutched some fabrics and again closed her eyes. 'Hmm,' she purred and scribbled some frail notes.

Again and again she repeated this habit as they walked the rooms: she would touch the walls, pause and rub the fabric in her fingers, sometimes smiling, sometimes laughing.

Spot lamps, light switches, dimmers, candelabras and perhaps a chandelier. She talked of sofas and futons, tables and ethically sourced stools. Wood or carpet, linoleum and rugs. They were all patterns of the showcase life. It would all be in place, she informed him, down to the wine glasses in the press.

'Now, we need a mirror in the master bedroom, something to really bring out more space. I find mirrors fascinating, don't you?' she said as they toured the upstairs.

'Well, they're handy,' he agreed, bemused.

'I *mean* you can really see a lot in them,' she said.

'You can see yourself,' he said patiently.

'Dreams and worries, love maybe, too,' she said, loftily not hearing. 'You know, in Australia the Aborigines don't like to have their photo taken. Something about souls.'

'Mirrors and photos are different.'

'Do you look in the mirror much?' she asked.

'Much as anyone else.'

'I spend fifteen minutes every day, it's very important.'

He did not know what to say and so said nothing, instead taking a cigarette from the box. He tapped it loudly with that tip, tap of awkwardness and placed it in his mouth.

At the landing she brushed in front of him, her buttocks rubbing against his leg. She turned and smiled as she passed. She was odd, he thought, *duine le Dia*, but she was close to something, it wasn't all bullshit.

She asked for a cigarette and placed it to her lips and pursed her mouth around it delicately, her lipstick staining the filter a gentle red.

He made note of the fixtures and told her he'd have the power hooked up soon, and that they could try the lamps then.

She gathered her books and fabrics and placed them in her bag. As they made their way to the front door she ran her fingers along the wall one last time, savouring its feel. 'Yellow is the colour for this place.'

He was glad of the fresh air and distance as they walked outside again. 'Well, you have my number, so you can give me a call,' he said awkwardly.

She was about to answer but her eyes were suddenly diverted. 'Isn't that *darling*!' she said, her face aglow.

He turned to see a tractor in the distance, slowly making its way to a farmhouse. A rusty god of a thing, its red bonnet faded beyond. A dog following behind barking wildly at the engine's noise.

'It's like history passing us by,' she said musically.

'Ah, he's probably home from the shop,' said McQuaid as he squinted at the driver and saw an old man in the seat, a weather-worn jacket about his frame. 'The dog's his too,' he added.

'It's lovely,' she said.

'I suppose you don't get that in Dublin. There's still a few of the old crew left tearing around the place, he probably drives the tractor to the pub and all.'

'I never thought I'd see that,' she said. 'It's like one of those old TV programs.'

'In full colour,' he said and laughed and felt foolish for that same laugh. What did she really know? The loneliness of rural life, the company of cattle all some of the bachelors had left. There was nothing darling in it. It was the last vestige of the poor past.

The tractor drove out of sight and she returned her gaze to

him and smiled. 'Thank you,' she said and placed a kiss on both cheeks, a French goodbye. 'I can show myself out.'

He nodded and watched her go, dodging the puddles and muck with ease.

20
McQuaid

He sat at the table, staring out the window, lost in thoughts. He looked at the things that were not there. Work, the future, and on it went, an assortment of ideas and deadlines. Coming back to the room, a skin floating atop his tea, and the rattling of steaming potatoes sounding off like an alarm in the kitchen.

A magazine lay open absently in front of him, one of his mother's glossy sins, a veneer of smiles and fake breasts page after page. A pop star had got married in Kilkenny Castle, the groom in an all-white suit and with bleached-blond hair. He turned the page and saw that a footballer's new baby had been diagnosed with a rare disease and the parents had started a charity to help the sufferers. They never seemed to start those charities until it affected those same celebrities, he thought.

The pages crinkled loudly as he thumbed through them. There were pictures of social events and wine bar openings, businessmen in black suits with colourful ties, drinks in hand. He turned the page and there were politicians at the opening of yet another golf course; he recognised a minister smiling widely and red-faced from behind a stacked plate of smoked salmon. It always seemed to be so sunny at these parties, and everyone happy. And the women. The women wore tight dresses and pearls, and their hands were not small or chubby but slender and shapely. Their hair was big and powerful. He'd never seen women like that in Longford. They all seemed young, and as he looked he saw their faces repeated again and again at different events, different openings. Socialites or *hoors*, he thought and smiled.

All these pleasures, the new rich, the nouveau riche. The Dublin crowd, builders at wine bars, farmers playing golf, God hadn't they all done well. It was a great moment of feeling that the country had now, and the moment would come too when they had all got familiar with the use of money, he supposed. The Cuchulainns and Ferdias of today were busy managing factories, it seemed. The nation was sated.

As he looked at the photos he wondered might he ever attend such events. And how would it go, he wondered.

'More wine, sir?' as the tray hovered towards him.

'Yes, why not, what is it?' he'd enquire.

'It's a New Zealand sauvignon blanc,' the waiter would inform him with professional condescendence.

He would smell the liquid, sip, and pause a moment as its chilled flavours rolled down his throat. And then perhaps he might close his eyes to add to the unfolding drama.

'From the Marlborough region?' he would ask and know full well.

'Precisely, sir,' and the waiter would smile in appreciation of the man's obvious good breeding.

'Savage wine, lad,' McQuaid would say and smile.

And then some classical music might start, and people would recognise the air but not know the composer. It would be

Strauss of course, the Radetzky March from the Golden Hall in Vienna, or Vien to them that knew.

'Drive 'er up there, Strauss,' he'd say. And strangers would nod to him for that good ear of his. Sign of success.

Sinead would be by his side, in one of those tight dresses like the women in the magazine, the hint of her bust showing, and the feline quality she would possess as she graced the room in her stilettos. A Famine no more.

Pushing away the thought, he closed the magazine and laughed at such foolishness. And yet the thoughts of Sinead had excited him so. Perhaps he might go to Dublin and surprise her. The first cheque had indeed come and the plans, the plans sat out in the van, with only Begley and Mary the wiser of their existence. Perhaps he might go and surprise her, not tell anyone and just go, just arrive on her doorstep.

He looked to his watch; there was time still in the day.

He could drive to Dublin and maybe pick up a dress for her. No, he thought further, he'd tell her to put on a good dress and that they were off for a night on the town. They would go for a meal and pleasure would forego expense. They would have champagne.

What was real champagne like, he wondered. He had had a glass at his graduation years ago, fizzy wine it had seemed then, but that was a sign of the times. They could all enjoy a glass now, even Cuchulainn once he finished work at the factory. They would have it and there would be a *pok* of pleasure as the waiter opened a whole bottle just for them.

McQuaid stood up, emptied his tea in the sink and turned off the potatoes. Brushing the steam from his face, he thought now of a hotel room with oysters and good drink, fags on the balcony and maybe a few flowers on the bed. What was money for if not spending?

As he drained the vegetables in the colander he quickly did

some sums. He had enough to cover the excursion. It would, he further encouraged himself, be a way to present the idea of the house; he could show her the plans and explain that soon, in time, they could build a house out of those same plans.

McQuaid smirked at his visions, but then another voice spoke to him. *What about the job? You should make the orders for the apartments.* He would, but not today. But his mind would not quiet now. *What about that new kango you need to buy?* There would be time for that later. *And your own house? You promised yourself you'd call on Flaherty to ask him to do the groundwork and knock in that ditch for a driveway . . .*

He busied himself and began to set the table for the evening meal to try to silence the disquiet. It would all be done in time, he knew that.

These aren't your people anyway, McQuaid. What are you playing at? Gallivanting, drinking champagne, it's working you should be. He couldn't halt the tide of negative thoughts. *Ah, the blood's up, is it? That's what this is.*

'It is all right,' he said aloud, and no longer gave a damn for the dinner.

He packed clothes into an old sports bag: underwear, socks and a change of shoes. He put on a freshly ironed shirt and those new jeans his mother had bought him. The tag still on them.

He looked to the bedside drawer; the box was empty. Why couldn't she go on the pill, he thought. He would have to buy a pack in town. Walk into the local pharmacy and face Karen Reynolds behind the counter, she who he had gone to school with, and her sly smile as he made for the johnnies. No, he would go to the pub and use the vending machine. There would be no smirks there, save perhaps a congrats from a nosy stranger.

He hastily scribbled a note and left it on the kitchen table amidst the unstarted evening meal. *Back tomorrow, on the phone if you need me.*

There was a heaviness to the day and rain looked set. He made sure the house plans were under the passenger seat and drove to the motorway.

The radio host talked about some new government work scheme. Sighing, he turned the dial to some music and settled his mind on the road as a dance song played out over the fields.

He had been to her sharehouse so often, and yet never as a surprise or with such good tidings. Halloween had been weeks ago, and busy as she was, they'd not seen one another since. This would lift both their spirits. It would be a little Christmas in itself.

The van moved quickly up the N4 and soon the walls of Phoenix Park appeared and the lights of Dublin were around him.

The handbrake croaked as he stopped outside the sharehouse. That unloved terrace with its cheap pebble dash and small concrete garden. The weeds in the gutter were the only sign of life in that grey street. It had been a dream home once, he thought, probably reared a family, and then sold when the time was right. Each year now rented to students and left fallow in the summer break.

He walked to the door, making sure his shirt and jeans were not creased; he fixed his hair and knocked. A silhouette appeared behind the glass.

'Hey,' said a girl he didn't recognise. She had wrapped herself up in a faded panda-festooned dressing gown.

'How are you? Is Sinead in?'

She smiled and, hand still upon the half-open door, turned her head. 'Sinead! Fella here for you,' she shouted. She turned back to McQuaid and with a vulgar curtsy told him Sinead would be right with him. She did not extend an invitation to enter.

There was a rattle from the kitchen and Sinead appeared. 'Hello, Ger . . . what are you doing here?' she said.

'I came up to see you,' he replied.

'I didn't get a text, did you text me?' she asked in confusion.

'No, it's a surprise,' he said and felt foolish having to explain himself to not just Sinead but the panda girl too.

Sinead turned to her friend and explained that this was her fella. Satisfied, the girl moved from her guard duty and left.

'Is everything okay?' Sinead asked, placing her hand gently on his arm.

'Everything is fine, just thought it would be nice to come up and take you out.' He leaned in to kiss her, but misjudged his timing and missed her lips, instead brushing against her chin.

'A surprise?' she asked.

'Yeah, exactly.'

'It's, well, I have an exam,' she said with an air of fatality.

McQuaid looked at her; she too was in pyjamas, her hair matted, and on her feet what he could only guess were her father's thick wool socks.

'Well . . . you better come in,' she sighed and gave him a peck on the cheek as he passed over the threshold.

The house was damp and a cold draught seemed to flow through each room. Cheap furniture dotted here and there added to the bleakness of the place. The smell reminded him of other student houses, every house Sinead had been in during her time in Dublin, that scent of badly cooked pasta meals, mildew and stale drink. It was an orange rot of independence.

He tried to talk to her, to take her to one side, but she had already returned to the kitchen. The girls sat around the television, an oil heater in front of them, each wrapped in pyjamas and dressing gowns. The light was off and only the red ember of the grille and blue flickering light of the television lit up their faces.

He meekly waved his hand. 'How are you, girls?'

They responded hello in unison, never taking their eyes from the box.

McQuaid quietly sat by the table as Sinead boiled the kettle for tea. No one talked, their bodies clung round pillows and blankets. He was utterly lost, and after a time he stood up and walked to her. 'I missed you,' he began.

'I missed you, too,' she said absentmindedly as she prepared tea and biscuits for them. 'They're a bit soft, the biscuits,' she explained as she offered him the plate.

He refused the plate and walked closer to her. 'I thought,' he murmured, not wanting the other girls to hear. 'I thought you might like to go upstairs and put on a nice dress and we'll go for a fancy meal in the city.'

She turned, handed him a mug of tea and smiled at him in sympathy. 'But I just told you, I have an exam, I have to study.'

'But, you're only watching telly,' he said, confused.

'Jesus, Ger, I was on a break. You should have texted me, you know.'

'Well, I didn't think,' he said and returned to silence.

He looked at his watch; it was nearly eight. If she got ready they could still get a booking, they could still have a fine night. 'I've it all planned, we can have a nice meal and stay at a hotel. I'll have you back in the morning for your exam.'

She smiled at his intent but then shook her head once again. 'I just can't,' she said. 'It sounds lovely but I have to get this done.'

'Well, how much more have you left to do?'

'A couple of chapters and then I'll be pretty good.'

'Well, how's about you get them done and then we go?'

She hesitated. 'Well, I'm not saying I will go, but if I do, you'll have to wait until I've finished studying, okay?'

He nodded his head and drank his tea to hide his smirk. Despite the pyjamas and the matted hair and the woollen socks, it was still Sinead underneath all that and she did look beautiful. They'd been apart so long this time. The least he could hope for was to have her to himself for a few hours, just a few.

She drained her tea and placed the cup back on the counter. 'Well, I better get back to it if I'm going to be ready,' she said and smiled.

'Good woman,' he replied.

She told him to wait there and that she would be down as soon as her revision was complete. And that yes, she would put on a nice dress.

He smiled as she told him he was a cheeky fucker for arriving unannounced. But he did not mind, for he had bent her resolve. The new jeans must have worked, he thought.

Sinead went up the creaky stairs to her room and he returned to the television. The girls had not moved from their positions, the patterns of *Eastenders* playing across their faces. He took up his seat by the table again and sipped his tea. He asked at one point was it an affair that was going on, but the Galway women told him to whisht and not be talking over Little Mo.

They only came to life at the breaks and talked as adults.

'So you're Ger,' said the panda girl.

'I told you,' said Lucy.

'The spit of Christopher Mahon from home,' chimed the panda girl, whose name he learned was Kevina. 'You look like a fellow we know,' she explained.

'Right so,' said McQuaid.

'Only he's a bollox,' said Lucy and laughed.

'But you seem nice,' said Kevina.

'Are you studying business too, like Sinead?' he enquired.

'Nursing, with the girls,' she said and leaned towards Lucy.

He began another question, but was told to whisht yet again as the soaps were back on. And so the yoyo of attention went, from telly to break, break to telly. He looked to his phone: it had been a half-hour already. The best of the night would be gone.

He could have gone for a pint with Willy and saved himself the trouble, he thought. He must text Willy and tell him he was in Dublin and that he'd be back down in the morning but if he was late to set the boys to work. The show house needed those fixtures and that Rhian girl would be down again to finish the place. He spent time on the text, tapping out the words in full to pass the time. But still only five more minutes had passed. A pint wasn't a bad idea at all, he told himself, but he would wait, she would not be that much longer.

After the soaps had finished, the girls set about making some dinner; hungry as he was, he refused their offer of food, telling them Sinead and he were off out for a bit to eat.

'I wish my fella would bring me for dinner,' Kevina said as she boiled hot water for pasta.

'What fella?' laughed Lucy.

'Well, if I had one, that he'd bring me.'

'What about that guard from Tuesday?'

'He was only after one thing,' Kevina said and smiled.

'Handcuffs, was it?' said Lucy and laughed again.

The girls ate their pasta and complimented him on Sinead, saying how much smarter she was than all of them, and such a hard worker. He smiled at the praise. He made himself another cup of tea and sat on the couch; it had been an hour and a half now, the dinners would soon be over, he thought. But maybe there was still time.

At ten, Sinead came downstairs and found him alone in front of the television. 'Where are the others?'

'Gone to bed, they said they had to get up early for placements in the hospital.'

'Oh, that's right,' she said and scratched her tired face.

'Are you done?'

She nodded.

'Great, well, go get ready and we'll head out,' he said.

'Ah, babe, I'm tired.'

But he cajoled her and reluctantly she returned upstairs. He heard the shower winch to life and smiled. He walked outside to the van and took out his clean shoes and put them on and fixed his hair in the side mirror. It wouldn't be much longer, he told himself, and nervously checked under the seat to ensure that the plans were still there.

At half-ten she entered the kitchen, a simple red dress on her pale frame, her hair sweet and curled, and on her lips a glossy lipstick shining in the dim, poor light of the kitchen.

'You look great,' he said.

'You're not too bad yourself,' she said and yawned.

She gathered her belongings and they walked to the van. The moon looked out across the skyline, it was late, much later than he had hoped to begin this night. He opened the door for her and she smiled at his manners.

'Now we can go wherever you want. I'd bring us to the Passage but they're closed now,' he said.

'Ah, that's my favourite place,' she said and sighed.

She thought for a time but eventually said she didn't mind. And slouched herself against the passenger seat.

'Anywhere, it doesn't matter,' he repeated.

'You choose,' she said and yawned once again.

He thought a moment and started the van. They drove to

the city centre past Drumcondra and Croke Park, up O'Connell Street and over the Liffey. At St Stephen's Green a fox darted across the tram tracks with a burger in its mouth and scuttled into the park, safe another night.

They walked from one restaurant to another but the waiters told them again and again that service was finished. It was too late and they should have called ahead. At each refusal he grew yet more sullen and Sinead more tired.

'Fucken Dublin,' he said as they walked away from what must have been the fifth restaurant.

'We could always just get a burger,' Sinead said.

'No,' he said now in anger. 'It's a whole plan, there'll be no burgers.'

She did not answer and hid herself further in her thick brown coat. 'Well, it's just that it's getting late,' she said. 'And this exam . . .'

'It's only late because you took all fucking night getting ready.'

'I never asked you to come,' she returned.

'It was a fucking surprise,' he said and, realising the volume of his voice, grew quieter. 'I wanted to do something nice for you.'

'We could always do it tomorrow,' she offered in appeasement.

'What good is tomorrow, I have to go to work tomorrow,' he snapped.

'I don't know . . . it was just an idea,' she said.

They walked in silence now to the last good restaurant he knew. Perhaps the waiter might take pity and let them in for last orders. He could slip him a twenty, he thought. That might calm things. But as their feet approached the holding, they were met by the kitchen staff walking out the door and the manager switching off the lights.

'You were looking for a bite to eat,' he said at the sight of two dressed-up figures. 'Everyone is closed, the town closes early midweek,' he explained with sympathy. 'If you give me your number, I'll get you a nice table for tomorrow evening.'

'Fuck tomorrow, it's tonight I want it,' McQuaid said and took Sinead by the arm and back towards the van. 'Fucking city, fucken Dublin, can't even spend my money when I want to in this kip.'

Sinead began to well up and perhaps it was tiredness but the tears rolled down her face all the same. 'Gerard McQuaid . . . I'm tired, I've an exam tomorrow, I *need* to go to bed,' she said and touched his face.

'This is your fault,' he stabbed now.

'It's no one's fault,' she returned.

'But I had a fucking plan, a plan,' he murmured.

'Things don't always go to plan,' she said.

'Not when you're two hours in the fucking room and I have to listen to fat bitches from Galway drone on and on about *Eastenders* and fucking guards.'

Sinead walked ahead alone. Her coat billowed in the empty grey street, her heels clacking in the silence. 'Take me home now,' she called back to him.

They returned to the van and, driving back to the sharehouse, they stopped for a Coke at the local chipper. They ordered a snack box and a burger and sat in their finery amidst the grease.

The manager looked them over carefully as he rang through the order. 'Good night, was it?' he said in a thick Dublin accent.

'No,' McQuaid said as he paid and returned to the plastic seating.

McQuaid took the chicken piece in his hands and began to suck off the grizzly skin. He wiped his fingers on the paper towel and slurped on his Coke. Sinead pushed her chips around the plate and ate sparingly in silence. The remorse hit him now; so much for romance, he thought, and ate with gluttony to spite her. They returned to the house.

She had been different tonight, his anger-filled mind told him. It was Dublin, it was changing her. And as they made their way inside he thought to tell her of the plans, to at least salvage something.

'Sinead,' he said and paused in the driveway.

'What?' she snapped and turned around.

'I had a reason to come up tonight,' he began.

'Was it to fight with me? Because you fucking did that!' she retorted.

'No, I . . .' and he walked back to the van. He took out the paper tubing from underneath the seat. 'I got the plans for our house drawn up,' he said in an attempt to make peace.

'You what?' she said once again.

'I got the plans, here in my hand.'

'I don't fucking believe this, Gerard. I don't give a fuck about the plans, I don't give a fuck about them, it's after twelve, I have an exam in the morning, just come inside and let me get some fucking sleep, you fucking bogger.'

'I'm a what?'

'I didn't mean that,' she said quickly and strained for them to go inside.

'I'm a bogger, is it? A fucking culchie, a caveman? Well, you're from the same place as me, you spoilt bitch, just because your father's a councillor and you live in Dublin now. You're from the same bloody ground.'

'Shut up and come inside,' she shouted and the girls' lights turned on upstairs.

'You can sleep on the couch,' she said and stormed up the stairs, tears rolling from her eyes.

Fucking bitch, he told himself. And threw himself with force on the couch. He was a fool for coming up, a fool. And all the work that needed to be done. He'd have to drive back early in the morning to beat the traffic, what a bloody waste it all was.

As he turned off the light and found a throw to cover himself with, his phone vibrated.

Grand so man. Have a good night. Ur overdue a good tumble ;) Willy.

21
The Auction

Nobby and his son Rubin got into the old blue Jag that morning, the one with the spider web in the back window. That spider had seen the world, Nobby had commented often. He'd caught flies from Mullingar to Westport.

They picked up the signs and stands from the office and neatly placed them in the trailer. They checked the Jag's fuel gauge and tyre pressure and off they went to Longford.

Comerford Auctioneers had operated from the same family premises these last seventy years. Started by Nobby's father, the Major, it had at one time occupied a favourable position in Westport. Indeed, the Comerfords had at one stage owned much of the town, but certain events had changed that. The old house still stood at least, but the state of its foundations did not bear thinking on. Sugar blocks built on water, a builder had once described them.

'He sounds a gruff man,' Rubin remarked as they made their way through the back roads of Mayo.

'Mr Kane?' questioned Nobby.

'Yes, he sounds a bit rough,' said Rubin delicately.

'Gruff or rough, it's work,' Nobby reminded him.

The Comerfords were not the closest auctioneers to Longford but they did bring a certain clientele: the Dubliners, the Kildares and the elusive Northerners with their pounds and miles. It helped of course that much of the family were still up there. It provided them with an edge. Money did not discern between Green and Orange, the Major had famously remarked at the drawing up of the border. And business had been steady since.

Nobby wore his double-breasted tweed suit, the grey not the green. It was a Donegal weave; it had, he felt, always brought him luck, and though his stomach was not as flat as long ago, it still buttoned comfortably. The stitching of the shoulder gave a stronger shape to his old frame. It was his armour on days like this.

He looked to Rubin, who wore a light linen blazer and a colourful scarf looped around his neck. He'd come to be known for the scarf, Nobby thought; it looked good on him.

They stopped in Sligo at a roadside restaurant to break the journey. Rubin ordered a pot of tea for one.

'And can we have two cups?' said Nobby after the sale had rung through, not a hint of shame in his voice.

They had a bowl of soup and ate the whole basket of complimentary bread. The meal had cost less than ten euro.

Returning to the journey they drove through the remainder of the county. Nobby fiddled with the radio dial and picked up a classical music station; there was the soft recognisable hiss of a live audience and he smiled at the sounds of violins being tuned. Rubin nodded in approval at his father as the opening notes of the Vienna Waltz played.

The stone-wall country of Connaught receded as hedges of rush and birch began to appear, growing more numerous with each field, each acre of ground. The animals too changed from plucky sheep to stocky cattle. The midlands in its bleak flatness was unmistakable.

'John has hired some local boys to help us out today,' Nobby said as they took the last turn towards the estate.

'Wonderful.'

The Jag's wheels crunched on the newly laid gravel of Birchview Estate as they slowly drove up to the manor. Kane was waiting for them by the front door, his face glowing with fatigue and excitement.

Rubin stopped the car and let his father's window down.

'Hello, John,' said Nobby in a slow, correct manner.

'Nobby,' said Kane and thrust his hand ignorantly through the open car window. His grip was fierce.

'We'll get ourselves set up. Have the marquee people arrived?' enquired Nobby.

'They have, they're at it now,' said Kane.

'Right so.'

Kane smiled at them and gave Rubin a wave as the car pulled away again.

'Gruff enough,' said Rubin quietly.

'Enough,' replied Nobby.

They could see the white canvas of the marquee slowly raising itself above the wild laurel bushes. The front garden had been mowed and there was a neatness to the ground. The centre pillars of the tent were a strong round wood, like the mast of a ship, and indeed Nobby observed that the canvas looked like sails. Hopefully there would be no round-ups today, only the sound of the gavel and bear away at the punters.

Rubin began to unpack the small trailer, the velvet ropes and pillars, the stands.

'You finish the unloading and I'll place these signs,' Nobby told his son.

With that he walked towards the main gate where one of the young men Kane had hired stood watch. The boy, for that was all he was, played a game of snake on his mobile phone and wore a bored frown upon his face.

Nobby introduced himself, shook his hand and placed the large auction sign by the wall. 'Now you keep an eye on that today, good lad,' he said, to which the boy nodded.

Comerford Auctioneers present
Birchview Manor Estate
First Phase Sale
150 houses from plans
Showing from 12 today

He went to various gates and entrances, instructed the other boys and placed the signs. He told yet another boy – they did all look the same, he thought – to help him tack the posters to the telephone poles in the surrounding roads.

He went back to the car, cleaned the black tar from his hands and then returned to the estate. It was irrefutable that there would be an auction today. The excitement was building.

Back at the main house he found Rubin and Kane bringing out the placards and information sheets.

'A lot of literature, John,' said Nobby.

'Well, just to do the thing right,' replied Kane.

'Of course, of course, no point in doing it wrong.'

By ten the marquee was ready; the velvet ropes weaved a path from the tent to the manor house, where refreshments would be served, and on to the car park.

Nobby paused for breath and watched the interior designer scurrying around making her final adjustments. She had dressed up the ballroom of the manor, soon to be hotel, to suggest the possibility of the grandeur of life at Birchview.

'I really think the show house turned out well, don't you?' she said to him.

'It's a fine job, Rhian,' he said.

'It will be fine when we get the signatures,' said Kane, overhearing. 'Am I right, Nobby?'

'Right indeed, but there's a place for colour too,' Nobby said and smiled at the girl. 'The ballroom is wonderful,' he whispered to her as he returned to work.

By eleven the local bank managers had arrived. All the major banks were there; each man had a separate room set aside for him in the main house. There he could talk to clients and advise on their mortgage options. Nobby had seen it so many times now; the right person could get approval instantaneously.

They paused for tea before proceedings got underway. Walking through the manor house, Nobby laughed at the sight of the kitchen busy again, in a flurry of excitement it had not known in years, decades even. The steam rose to the high-coved ceilings and the cut-glass light fittings. The girls raced off with a tea for Mr Murphy of the Bank of Ireland and a coffee for Mr Cullen from AIB.

John Kane burst into the kitchen, calling for more sandwiches and tea; his investors had arrived and were hungry. 'Didn't I say I wanted ones without salad cream? God, oh God, but you can't move for the salad cream in this place,' he scolded.

The girl froze and began to well up. 'I'm sorry, Mr Kane.'

'It's fine, it's fine,' Kane returned, frustrated.

Nobby helped bring out the sandwiches and walked with Kane. There was a sweat upon the man's brow, which he wiped with one of the cheap white paper serviettes.

'It all looks fine,' Nobby assured him.

'Are you sure? . . . Good,' said Kane.

He introduced Nobby to Sean and Austin, who further complimented the set-up.

'You had a pleasant drive?' Kane asked Sean.

'Oh yes, a lovely day, hardly much traffic.'

'And the show-house tour, who is to be giving that?' asked Austin.

'My son and assistant,' said Nobby and gestured to Rubin.

'He's a great brain on him,' said Kane. 'He'll go down a treat with the older ones.'

'Lovely,' said Sean, clasping his hands together.

Nobby said that it was time they headed over to the tent and that they could bring their tea and sandwiches. Kane, he noticed, had let nothing touch his lips all morning.

The chairs sat row upon row in the marquee, a delicate pattern to fit as many as possible. The bank managers hovered at one of the side tables, briefcases at their feet.

Nobby and Kane ran through the final arrangements. It was like a big performance, Nobby joked, and the audience would all soon arrive. 'So you'll speak first, John, and give us an introduction, welcome our guests and so on, and then I'll begin. Does that sound fine to you?'

'Hundred per cent, Nobby,' said Kane and gave him the thumbs-up.

The first of the crowd began to appear and meekly took their seats. Kane made his way to the podium, took a bottle of water and sipped. By twelve the room was full of fake furs, chancers, young couples, quiet gays and two local county councillors.

Kane tapped the microphone. 'Hello, can you hear me?' A noisy hiss of reverb filled the room. Rubin adjusted the mic and smiled to Kane to continue.

'Hello . . . and welcome . . .' he said, but his confidence was wrong, Nobby noted. He would never capture the room like this. Kane took another sip of water and breathed in. He placed his hand in his pocket, closed his eyes and uttered a short prayer off mic. 'Please don't let the gearbox go down today,' he said quietly, which only Nobby heard.

Kane opened his eyes, coughed and started again. 'I want to welcome you all here today, to the launch of phase one of Birchview Estate,' he said and paused, at which a small applause began.

'You know, there were many people who told me we would never get this far, that this idea was codswallop,' Kane continued and smiled in dramatic fashion at the local TD, James Brennan. At which the room laughed. 'There were others who said I was mad to buy the place to begin with. Mr Murphy.' He gave a nod of his head towards the bank manager, who threw up his hands in mock surrender. 'But here we are.'

Kane breathed deeply; the room was beginning to listen. 'In my time as a young man, when we were all heading off for England and America, I used to pass this place and I often thought wouldn't it be a wonderful thing to live here and not have to leave. Well, it's a funny thing, life. Now I do have it and I'm leaving it to you.'

'For the right price,' shouted Mr Murphy, and the room laughed again.

'Of course, of course, Peter,' Kane agreed and laughed a big belly laugh.

'It is wonderful to see so many young people here today. It shows no one need leave any more, you can make a life here and prosper. It's a great country we have and it's all our own land now once again, with no outsiders . . .' Kane paused short.

Nobby made a slight cough at this last remark. It was better to leave politics at the door, he thought; Green and Orange side by side were happy when money floated it all along.

'They say that the bad times are over and people are coming back to Ireland to live. The Global Irish; well, I say that too is a wonderful thing. To think of all those generations gone, and it is my hope that when they come back they might choose to live here. In this, the new heart of Longford.

'Birchview is not just houses, it is a community. The hotel, the golf course and our villa-style apartments too – all this is coming. So, welcome to the future.'

Kane breathed deeply. '*Go raibh mile mhaith agat*,' he thanked them.

The audience clapped loudly and cheered him on his speech. Kane took a sip of his water and Nobby watched as his hand shook with nerves.

Kane absentmindedly began to walk away from the mic but then, remembering himself, returned. 'And now I'll hand you over to Mr Comerford our auctioneer, who will run you through the process.'

There was a second, half-hearted round of applause as Nobby came to the podium and adjusted it to his height. Gavel in hand, he signalled to Rubin that he was about to begin.

He stood up erect and adopted his professional tone. 'Now, ladies and gentlemen,' he said in a smooth, direct voice, 'no time-wasters, please. Ladies and gentlemen, if I can have your attention!' he said, and the room went quiet. 'The first tours of the show house will start in fifteen minutes, and we'll be running showings all day. The De Valera Drive, Oak View House is a lovely number. Three bedroom, eastern views, garden at the rear, this is what it's all about, folks.'

He took a sip of water and continued. 'Starting price is two hundred and fifty thousand, a steal really, and as John has indicated, the golf course and hotel are coming online in phase two of the development, so really you are buying not just a house but a private world.'

The gavel was now his paintbrush, as he could see the visions appear before the audience's eyes. 'Woodland walks in the demesne forest, the ladies can have their G&T in the hotel on a nice day, and there are plenty of golf bunkers for the men to hide in!'

There was a lot of new money here, he thought. Also many who had the appearance of wealth and yet not a thimbleful to their names, but they were happy with just the look, the idea of their social mobility. It was a gaudy mixture of the haves and the want-tos.

Dotted amongst them were the cash kings. Men like them might take a notion and buy not one but four or five houses, pay a deposit in cash and then possibly go and buy cattle at the mart. He had seen it. But the big fish were rare to bite, and it was better to cast the net wide.

'Now I'll run through the process for those who have not yet seen the show houses – I know some have, but humour me on this, please, ladies and gentlemen. Rubin or myself will be conducting the tours and feel free to ask whatever questions you might have,' he continued.

'For those of you who are decided, the paperwork is here with me at the top table. We are only taking deposits today, folks, so please don't feel you have to break the bank on this. We have financial advice in the form of our local bank representatives to my right, and you can discuss your business with them in private regarding purchase options. I don't need to go more into that, I daresay we all know how this works!' And he let out a small laugh, at which some of the younger couples gave confused stares.

'Mr Kane has kindly agreed to make himself available should you have any further questions. Please make your way to his table, and don't forget there is some literature beside me here should you need reminding of just how good Birchview Estate really is.'

It had been quick and clean. Rubin smiled at him as he straightened his tweed blazer.

Some would be ready to buy immediately. The crowd began to rise and mingle, and with that the bankers sprang to action. Mr Cullen drained the last of his coffee in a breath and took out a gold pen from his inside jacket pocket. How many farms had that pen bought and sold? It was all there and there for the taking.

Austin and Sean, filled with a sudden energy, relayed customers from Kane to the bankers and on towards the paperwork at the front desk. The forms were basic: ten per cent deposit, initial here, sign there; it was formulaic.

Rubin organised the tour groups. Like some Florentine guide he raised his arm and called for, '*Attenzion, attenzion*. To me, ladies and gentlemen, to me for the tour.'

Nobby accompanied them on the first tour to ensure that everything was in order. As they walked the empty tarmac road to the show house a nervous chatter filled the air. Middle-aged women dressed in their Sunday best began to cackle. Rubin led by the arm an elderly pensioner who delighted in telling him how fine a young man he was, and wasn't this a lovely place.

'Is that your father who was speaking?' Nobby heard her ask.

'It was,' Rubin said and smiled.

'Aren't you a grand fella. And do you like the work? I expect you do.'

'It has its moments, mam,' he answered respectfully.

'I thought I might retire out here,' she confided as they walked further into the cul-de-sac. 'My niece thinks it would be a good idea. She's about your age,' she added.

'Right,' said Rubin.

He was for it now, Nobby thought as he watched the scene unfold. If he didn't unhitch the old bat it would be a half-hour of nieces and recent family history. She hadn't a notion to buy, this was a social occasion, and yet they could not leave an old woman on a half-finished road in a half-finished estate. Could they?

Nobby interjected and took the woman by the arm; he indicated to Rubin to continue with the group and that they would catch up. She greeted him and they talked in the safety of times past.

The reds and yellows of the show house were warm and inviting; a gas fire burned in the sitting room with the blue flame of imitation. In the kitchen the smell of baking bread filled the air; he'd need to spray that scent for the next tour, he reminded himself.

Rubin led the group upstairs and began to explain the details of the house. 'Now, the Oak View is my favourite. Beautiful landing and carpets, and as you can see the space upstairs is just bright, there's a real sense of air here.'

The ladies nodded their heads, the men knocked on walls and opened and closed doors forcefully.

Nobby seated the old woman by the fire and, excusing himself, followed after the group.

'The master bedroom is just a beauty, look at this view,' Rubin said as he indicated the treeline in the distance. 'There's Londoners who'd kill for such a picture.'

'It beats the old tenement in Hackney all right,' a man laughed.

'You're right there,' Nobby said and smiled at the man.

Returning downstairs, they checked on the woman, who was by now lost amidst a sea of throws and cushions.

'Are you all right, dear?' Rubin enquired of her.

'I'm just fine,' she said and gave a limp dismissive wave.

'Gas?' a man interrupted, the word thrown at Rubin.

'Sorry?'

'Is it gas or oil? The house, I mean.'

'Oh, it's gas, sir.'

'Hmm, gas is expensive, have you factored that in?'

'The Russians have, I'm sure,' Rubin laughed.

'What?' the man returned, his eyes now furrowed deep as warrens.

'We have,' Nobby interjected and frowned at his son.

They demonstrated the shower and flushed the toilet; the crowd watched like a group of tourists as the water whirled around the brim and disappeared.

'Great to see good pressure,' he heard someone comment.

'If you don't have pressure, you're fecked,' another added.

The conversation continued another five minutes before Rubin could escape the confines of his Portuguese-tiled prison.

They walked back to the kitchen and Nobby opened the doors to the patio. The weather had been with them today, he thought. How often might one really open those same doors? The night of a binge or a long-promised barbecue. Or maybe to smoke if cigarettes were banned in the house.

'Well now, this is the place, folks. I think you'll agree it's a lovely number,' Rubin said in summation.

'A great weekend pad,' Nobby added with a wink to a middle-aged couple.

'Or a great first house.' Rubin smiled at a young couple.

They all nodded and agreed that yes it was lovely. They gathered on the footpath outside and made to return to the tent. Nobby looked for the elderly woman but she was not to be seen. He returned inside to find the old bat still in her position on the couch, half-asleep. He had to rouse her.

'Sorry, but it's time to go, mam. We're about to head back,' he said.

'Oh, sorry, dear,' she said and placed her hand on his arm.

He helped her up and they walked out the door. She remarked how lovely the place was and then began to fumble with her purse. 'Is it cash or cheque?' she enquired and produced a wad of notes. 'Only I was going to ask your son, but I can see you're the man to talk to.'

'Oh . . .' Nobby took a step back. 'I see, well, cheque would be better, would be safer for you,' he said as evenly as he could.

'I see, I wasn't sure. Well, I'll take two, one for me and one for my niece. She'd make a lovely match for that son of yours,' she said.

He was at a loss for words and smiled in earnest. She returned that smile with a cunning grin as if to say, *You had thought less of me.* He shook his head and handed her back to Rubin. Closing the front door, he paused a moment to watch the group file up the unfinished cul-de-sac.

At two, refreshments were served and the crowd began to loosen up. Women pecked at food and men bellowed low into wine glasses. There was a grotesqueness about it all, like pigs gorging themselves at the trough. One could not help but stare. A strange new emotion had entered Ireland these last few years, Nobby thought, and it began to play out in the room as the drink washed through the crowd.

'Well, I'm a property manager and Mary works with the prison service,' one man explained to him.

'Build them and lock them up!' Mary snorted in a piggish sort of way.

'We have three properties already, this one is an investment, maybe one of the kids could live here in the future, you never can tell.'

'Never can tell.' She snorted again.

'It's a wonderful place,' Nobby repeated patiently and excused himself on account of paperwork.

'We drove the Beamer down today,' he heard another young man bawl.

'It's the only way to go. Audis are only shite,' his comrade replied.

'But a Land Rover won't see you wrong,' a stranger added.

'True. Hang on a tick, man, the office is calling.'

The more the drink flowed, the worse it became. A greed, a hunger-driven pride, and humility nowhere in sight. Nobby took a seat by the bar and exhaled; the day was nearly over. He instructed Rubin to gather up the paperwork.

He watched as John Kane walked the room and talked with the couples, his presence like that of an attentive maître d'.

'How may I help you?' he heard him say.

'Well, we are looking at a house,' they said.

And Kane regaled them with his story; he talked as if it were wine, a nice sauvignon blanc, house number 25, only two hundred and fifty thousand euro, it goes well with beef or lamb, and here's a mint for afterwards. And they nodded their heads as he talked and began to produce purchase papers.

Poor children, Nobby thought. They had come up at the wrong time, right in the middle of this boom, too old to live at home, not old enough to know better. It was a life sentence, this contract. He watched as Kane passed the cheap Bic pen to them. They hesitated, the man looking at his pretty young wife; she smiled encouragingly and it was done.

Nobby shook his head and drained his glass of wine. It would be a long drive back to Westport.

22
Lefoyle

1830

The slate roof of the courtyard houses shone black after the midday rain. Puddles of cloud and sky. Wild orchids had taken root by a ditch. How odd that beauty appeared in such unlikely places, he thought. Always so diplomatic in its favours.

Fixing himself he walked from the house to the stables. Past the front hall with those great stag antlers. The muzzle flash of excitement long gone. The carriage would be waiting.

Murphy stood by the stable door, the horses ready. Lefoyle thought of his conversation with Harmon months before. He had dwelled on the information, analysed the facts. White had indeed taken the Roscommon seat and more. Lefoyle had made the brave face then and proclaimed that the battle would go on. Had made it still when Harmon had acted queerly at the news of his appointment to the Privy Council. And yet?

And yet it was a fight grown harder, not by intimidation; no, he could deal with that. Right and title could not be so easily maimed as the cattle these nationalists now attacked. But age had begun to tell. All the trips showed now: a face grown thinner, or perhaps it was the colour of his skin that was looser? No, his colour was good, he reminded himself. Or does the eye of the beholder see what it wants to see? A colour blindness to mortality? Perhaps it was a good ailment to have.

Murphy clicked his tongue and the carriage moved forwards with a slow shunt. The sweet trundle of the wheels over stone filled the cabin, the metronome of hooves keeping time.

It was dark inside; indeed, the day had grown darker, he thought, save for those sunlight-yellow leaves glimpsed from his window. He looked out at the green fields and spied a cock pheasant at an oak's base; with a flutter of its wings it flew overhead as they passed by.

He rested his head against the sideboard and followed the green verge of the roadside. He could see the silhouette of the trees and houses against the horizon. At times a solitary animal looked up at them from bedded fields and then, its curiosity satisfied, returned to eating.

There would be a movement against him tonight, this he felt. But who? Harmon? No, an intelligent man but he lacked the hunger for leadership. Perhaps Stanley with his cumbersome wealth, or Foster? All would be known this evening. The party was indeed suffering. Exiled in opposition, and Melbourne having cities named after him. Perhaps the wilderness would make Pitt and the Tories hungry, like Ovid.

Outside he could hear the muffled sounds of Murphy talking to the horses. In tones not words did they understand and answer him. He rarely used the whip, they had come to know him so well.

They crossed the first bridge to town, by the flowing Camlin. In the river some wild ducks bobbed in the current.

They paused at the church to allow another carriage to pass. He would come to pray after the meeting; the parson would be glad to see him, dear Reverend Jenkins who knew the topography of the soul so well. Hadn't all these battles been for that?

They moved up through the town towards the market square, by the old gaol and the hanging elm, past the courthouse and the bank. Murphy nodded to men he knew and greeted them loftily. Lefoyle would give him a few coins to have a drink while he waited.

The meeting was to take place in the private rooms of the Market Hotel. Its owner, a Mr Edwards, had offered it as neutral ground where men would not be disturbed. The hotel was old, its carpeted floors worn, though luxuriantly so. A series of humorous lithographic riding scenes chased across the restaurant walls.

Lefoyle would eat before the meeting, and perhaps take a small drink for courage. A brandy or sherry might be in order, he thought. He took a seat in view of the front door; if Stanley or Foster were indeed to move against him, his would be the first face they saw upon entering. His eating might be perceived as weakness, a man who could not see his end. But it could also be a sign of confidence, that he was so relaxed as to be hungry, so sure in his position.

He took a small confit of duck accompanied by a moody red. The brown flesh had flaked in textured layers. He looked at the clock. The men would be entering soon.

Stanley was the first. He smiled at Lefoyle as he came in. And made gestures to join him. His broad grin approached the table. 'Henry, how are you?' he said with an outstretched hand.

Lefoyle made a show of pretending to rise out of his seat to greet him.

Stanley motioned to the waiter and ordered a brandy. 'To warm myself,' he explained.

He moved in tics and nervousness. His business in Canada

had brought him rewards, and yet despite his wealth he seemed so eager to please other men. 'So we'll be meeting upstairs?' he enquired.

Lefoyle nodded and continued eating. It was not Stanley, but with his nervousness it was hard to tell if some contempt lay behind that broad grin. They discussed local news and various concerns. It was the perfect mimicry of polite conversation.

Foster and Harmon entered together. Explaining they had ridden together and apologising for their lateness. Foster took a whiskey immediately.

'Well, we should get on with this meeting,' he said after he had returned the empty glass to the table.

'Yes, you're probably right, no point in dragging it out to all hours,' said Harmon.

They gestured to the waiter, who promptly returned with Edwards.

'Well, if it isn't the finest men in Longford,' said Edwards, his tone full of bravado. His neatly trimmed beard and balding head gave him the look of an old he-goat. 'I have a lovely room ready and set up. If you'll follow me.'

They walked from the restaurant through to the hallway. Edwards spoke quietly to a servant girl, who ran briskly upstairs.

'Now, gentlemen, this way, please,' he said, and with a wave of his hand led them upstairs, drawing their attention to his numerous art purchases along the way.

'And I'm particularly fond of this one,' he said, stopping to point out a dreary landscape.

The party looked at the picture. Stanley made a small coo and nodded his head as if he knew.

After a moment of waiting, Edwards nodded to himself and now moved the group upstairs to the meeting room. The dark oak doors were open and a fire lit. The maid they had seen earlier left by a side passage, a cloth and some polish in her hands.

'There are some drinks there in the cabinet, please feel free to help yourselves. I've a lovely brandy my son sent from the continent in that bottle there. Compliments of some fellow officer.'

Lefoyle smiled a dry smile. Edwards played the diplomatic barman so well. He'd even managed to slip in a comment about his son, to ensure all present knew where his loyalties lay.

'Now, gentlemen, can I be of any other help?' he said, showing his palms and looking from face to face.

'We're fine,' Lefoyle answered simply.

And Edwards, knowing his place, left.

Lamplight and the fire gave the room a warmth. Stanley poured himself another brandy, turned and waved the bottle at the other men, who declined the offer.

'Henry, congratulations are in order,' said Stanley, raising his glass.

'How so?'

'It is so rare to see you in Longford town these days – a toast for homecomings.'

Lefoyle smiled and nodded politely.

They gathered around the broad table and settled themselves. Foster produced some papers and his ink.

'Now, it is to be noted to thank all parties for coming to this informal meeting,' said Foster, fixing his glasses in that habitual nervous tic of efficiency. 'I apologise that we did not meet in the club rooms but I thought this better than having to go through the motions of secretaries and note-taking.'

'Quite fine,' said Lefoyle.

Stanley played with his glass tumbler, turning the fine crystal in his hands. Harmon alone looked calm and smiled at him reassuringly.

'We are all aware how busy you are these days, Henry. Your appointment to the Privy Council has left you with little time,' said Harmon.

Lefoyle nodded in courtesy.

'But,' Harmon went on, 'Longford is a changed place.'

'You speak in reference to the Whites?' Lefoyle remarked.

'Just so,' said Foster, looking up quickly. 'Hugh White has taken the Roscommon seat for O'Connell this many months, and now his brother looks set to stand against us here in Longford.'

'I'm aware of this,' Lefoyle said calmly.

Harmon resumed speaking but was interrupted by Stanley.

'It is good you are aware, Henry, but what is to be done?'

'It seems to me, gentlemen, that we have not known a peaceful year in the last six with O'Connell and his men, but the seat has always been safe here.'

'Safe, aye, but for how long?' said Stanley in his inebriated, blunt fashion.

'What Stanley means to say, Henry, is that under you, the Longford seat has always been Tory. But the worry now is these new voters, and O'Connell has got the population behind him,' said Harmon.

'He's got the priests, you mean,' said Lefoyle.

'Those too,' said Foster.

'These are troubling times,' said Harmon calmly once again.

'I have never known different,' replied Lefoyle. 'None regrets the loss of the Philip's seat more than I,' he said. 'He was more a farmer than a politician but a likeable fellow nonetheless.'

The men laughed. He could hear the fire crackle as the room returned to silence. He sat back in his seat. Of course he had known all this, of White and O'Connell and the priests rallying the labourers and small farmers. Wasn't it a fight he had been leading these last many years? A fight for the very soul of Longford. All those letters and talks and debates on belonging.

It was Harmon who spoke next. 'Henry, you talk with lords and leaders of men regularly; we do not. I can only speak for local people and address my issues. These reform acts have brought change, new voters, new lines and allegiances to the county. And it is necessary that we use these new voters. To alienate them now will harm us. It is my fear that Longford will be a battleground if we do not embrace change.' Harmon paused.

So this was how it was to come. It had been Harmon. A negotiation to be punctuated with some harmless betrayal.

'Am I to be Melos to these O'Connellites? Is that what you are saying, Harmon?'

'I do not go so far as that, though the maiming of cattle may escalate. Who here can say they may not turn to burning houses next?'

'So better to placate the junta now and join with them, is that what you are saying, Harmon?'

'Henry, I . . . I am . . . just concerned at how best placed we are to get these votes.'

'We, is it, Harmon, or you? Or indeed you, Mr Stanley, or you, Mr Foster,' Lefoyle said, turning now to the others.

'I would . . . never,' said Stanley, pulling at his coat sleeves. An ignominious look upon his shrew-like face.

'Return to your beloved bottle, Stanley. I can see you are but an accessory in all this,' said Lefoyle. 'We must defend our position, not barter it away to meet their terms. Perpetual charity leads only to one's destitution, gentlemen.'

'So you would have us continue as we are, Henry?' enquired Foster.

'By God, yes. I will not have good Protestant men intimidated by the mob.'

'Then we shall truly fail,' said Harmon gravely.

'Tell me, Harmon, how long have you sought to take my seat? Or rather give it to O'Connell's repealers?'

The party looked from one to the other. Beads of sweat sat on Harmon's brow. He wiped them hastily with a worn silk handkerchief. 'I seek to give the seat to no man,' he said.

'Then what, pray tell, is your intention?'

'It is self-preservation, Henry.' And the words lingered in the air. 'I had thought, thought vainly,' Harmon continued, 'that you might have been persuaded to see reason today, to join with us, to lead us even, to do what is right. If Ireland is to change, then it is better we be part of it.'

'Men speak nobly of virtues, of rights and wrongs, when they themselves are not threatened,' said Lefoyle. 'But, Harmon, your criticism I see is biography. Do you think that when the Papists' demands are met they will be content to allow you to be preserved? In your house, on your lands?'

'The times dictate moderation,' replied Harmon. 'Is it not better to still control the seat? Whatever the banner?'

'So you would have me step aside?' Lefoyle said, the fire now growing in his belly.

'If you do not support our changes, then yes. It is not the end, it is the beginning. The county, the country is changing.'

It was odd now to look at Harmon, he thought. Once they were great friends, but he had taken on a perfect loathing. His hair, his clothes, his movements. He was seeing him now through new eyes, as one sees a former lover, imperfections worn. There was no friend, there was no brother to be gained in the marriage of the children. There was stark truth. What, he wondered, became of gods when no one believed?

He drew a deep breath. 'Harmon, you call for moderation, but you sign your own warrant. Emancipation, franchise, and now our own church to be pulled down around our heads and Rome rule where there was Orange. There will be no moderation: there will be extinction, our ten thousand usurped by their hundred. A break of nations.'

He breathed out now and wiped spittle from his lips. 'And then, Harmon, then you will be walled in with a view to infinity of your own failure. Priests to your left and right. Remember that Athens, too, once all was said and done, did fall,' he added.

'So there is to be no talking to you, Henry? Is that it?' said Harmon.

'If the talk is of appeasement, then yes, you are correct.'

'If only your passion had clarity, Henry.'

'So you will support White?' said Lefoyle, looking around the party as some wounded animal. 'Is that it? Hmm?'

'We support ourselves. It is only right to know one's mind rightly.'

'Oh, be thyself, Harmon, be thyself. But know we are the beneficiaries of all those who have gone before us and you trounce them in the muck with this.'

Friendship the rare commodity, he thought. Wait long enough and even the most loyal dog turns against its master.

'Tell me the truth. Is it White or you, Harmon, who will run against me?'

Before the men could speak, however, the oak doors burst open and a red-faced Edwards stood before them. His breath heavy, he bent over, offering up a hand to beg a moment's pardon.

'Gentlemen . . . I am sorry . . .' he rasped, '. . . but the King is dead,' he said with practised solemnity. 'I thought it only right to inform you. We have just this moment heard the news, poor George.'

A servant girl ran past behind Edwards, shouting of the monarch's death. He chased after the excited help and shook her to her senses. The party watched as a slap and then a hug were administered. The maid was sent downstairs.

Harmon walked to the drinks cabinet and poured each of the party a glass of Edwards's brandy.

'God save the King,' he said, raising his tumbler and looking at Lefoyle all the while.

23
McQuaid

It was boxes and boxes that arrived that day on the backs of those lorries. Tied down with straps like wild animals, and the cranes to pick over them.

The men ran chains through the precast apartment walls. Raised up, they were then bolted and screwed into place with the noisy twist of ratchets and brutish spanner groans. Consaws nicked at reinforcing bars, the sparks flying out in fantails. The walls bore the white stains and air bubbles of their concrete moulding on some sections, while others were smooth to the touch. Suddenly floors and stairs began to materialise. Even the toilets came ready-made.

'Very little for us to do with these apartments,' Willy joked to McQuaid.

'Oh, Lego sets,' he replied.

The work was methodical, constant, moving. There was little time for craft or taste with this precast, he thought. It was follow orders and get the job done. Reflection was only a puddle on a rainy day. Perhaps that was why so much was said at lunch break and so little.

'Will anyone local buy these? Do you think?' Willy now enquired, looking to him.

'It's hard to say, they're not our culture really. Country people like having a bit of earth beneath their feet.'

'True enough,' Willy replied.

The men had taken pleasure in seeing it rise. For that week the focus of the site turned towards these inert slabs. The work was different and perhaps it was a welcome break, a new challenge.

John and Pat joked as their grinders greedily chewed the concrete for wiring and covered them both in talc-like powder.

'Bad luck to them claws of yers,' one called to the other, beseeching him to hold the water in place.

'Was it the monks of Buckfast Abbey that have you shaking so much?' John cried now over the roaring of the grinder.

'I might have been praying to them last night,' answered Pat as he put down the grinder and slapped the dust from his comrade's shoulder.

'Children,' Willy said, looking at the two of them.

'We were like that,' McQuaid said in a moment of honesty.

'That's a long time ago,' Willy said and returned to work.

And it was, McQuaid agreed to himself, things were different now. He set to work on the cables and wiring for the apartments. He unrolled reel after reel, from lighting to sockets. He marked the various lengths with coloured tape and snipped them where appropriate.

Paddy Reilly appeared in the stairwell, watching the scene, a soft smile upon his face. 'Well, isn't this a fine sight!' he announced. 'He has youse working.'

'We have to get the finger out some days,' replied John with a mistimed laugh.

'Indeedin' you do, lad, even the dead rise once.'

Reilly shook hands with McQuaid and stood, arms folded, watching the men work. 'Flying up, isn't it?' he said after a time.

'Oh, yeah, it's more or less alphabetical.'

They walked the length of the first floor, inspecting the work, McQuaid pointing out areas that might be awkward, Reilly agreeing or offering his own problems.

'Will we take tae?' said Reilly after notes had been compared.

McQuaid made to call Willy to join them, but Reilly asked for their own company. They walked into one of the many empty apartments and threw their feet over the window cavity.

Reilly produced a flask of tea and some biscuits from his lunch bag. They looked out over the view of the entire site, the cranes, the golf course, the manor house, the lawns, the houses. It was a vast unruly place.

'How is everything going with work?' Reilly enquired.

'Oh, good, busy,' said McQuaid.

'But not busy enough, not yet?' said Reilly.

'Oh that, no, not busy enough,' said McQuaid. 'It's still just this place.'

'I see. And the girl, how are things with her?'

'Well, I got the plans drawn up and then there was, a sort of a, I don't know what it was rightly . . .'

'A row?' said Reilly.

'Yes, a row,' McQuaid admitted.

Reilly paused, sipped his tea and turned towards him. 'It just so happens I've had a look around for you about your little situation since we talked.'

'Oh,' said McQuaid in surprise.

'And there's a job going in Ballymahon, another housing estate. And I happened to put in a word with the boys for you.'

'Ah, right, well, I appreciate that, Paddy.'

'No, you're not getting my meaning. They've closed the tenders, you're doing the sparky work on it, you've got the job on my good word. I mean, you have to price it and not rob them either,' said Reilly with a small laugh.

'Well, of course . . . I'd be happy . . . Jesus, Paddy, that's great news!'

'The only thing I'll say, Ger, this is a lot of work to have on your plate at one time, the manor here, and now this job. I know you want it, but are you able to do it all at once? Only, it would be an awful thing to start and find you're not able to finish. It's a lot of stress and no one would think less of you if you said no.'

McQuaid was silent a moment. If he took this job he might be able to think of his own dreams, his own house. He could have it all *now*, instead of in four or five years, or God knows when. It would be an end to all the worry and rows. There would be more work, yes, that he knew, but this would bring him so close to having everything, how could he refuse?

And Sinead, Sinead would come round when the blocks and windows appeared. Wouldn't it be a fine thing to look out from that old-style country house on a wintry morning and see the snow on Cairn Hill? To have those few prize-winning cattle in the front field and a nice Land Rover for the weekend. And later still a child, a family. It was not all a fantasy. Every reality starts, must start as a dream, he told himself. Life could move steadily into place with this job.

'I'll take it,' he said and shook Reilly's hand, a smile on both their faces. And he wished in that moment to give the man a hug for all this meant.

'There's more to homes than bricks and mortar when women are involved,' Reilly said sagely, as if knowing his thoughts.

'I know, I know,' McQuaid agreed.

'Cement can come off timber very quickly, is all I'm saying,' Reilly said, returning his gaze to the horizon.

'I know,' McQuaid repeated.

'Good. Well then, it's yours to take.' Reilly gestured with his mug out the empty window and with a quick flick of his wrist his tea bag went straining into the air, a paint splash of brown landing on the ground below. He cleared his nose and made to stand up.

'Any account of our man Lefoyle?' asked McQuaid, wanting to delay their parting and enjoy Reilly's company a while longer.

'Oh, same place we left him the other day,' said Reilly, sitting back down.

'Demesne walls and Orange men, wasn't it?' asked McQuaid.

'And Orange women, too,' said Reilly.

'Oh yes, Maggie Bond,' said McQuaid, remembering.

'The bitch with the soft face,' sang Reilly. 'Making out to be feeding the poor Irish when times were bad, but no mistake she was in the Lefoyle camp, an auld bitch!' and a piece of spit emerged from his mouth.

'Just so, they were a different breed, all right,' said McQuaid.

'Back then the Anglo gentry had it all, and yet many didn't even want to work to keep it. Lefoyle was a different sort, political and conniving, and yet you see what a ball it is now.' Reilly waved his hand at the desolate estate.

'It looks bad all right, but she'll come good,' McQuaid said.

'I suppose she will,' said Reilly. 'But is it needed?' he questioned softly.

'Needed or not, it's here same as ourselves,' McQuaid replied.

They walked back through the concrete corridors; sparks flew in different directions as men moved through doorways, lengths of piping in hand. The work though monotonous was freeing, he thought. Outsiders would never understand that; to these men there was more shame to a wasted day than wasted money.

Reilly bade the men farewell and returned to his work. He gave a polite nod to McQuaid and disappeared.

'What was that all about?' said Willy as they laboured to mount the safety rails.

'More work,' said McQuaid and smiled.

'Oh, good enough so,' said Willy and left the subject at that.

By the close of the day, the apartment block was rigged with temporary lights, the squat bulbs giving an orange glow to the evening. When seen from a distance they looked like Chinese lanterns. With all those lights, indeed it could be China. The site seemed fuller now, it had felt real growth this week, in this their Ballinalee-cum-Beijing.

Driving home, he stopped by the hill on their land where Kennedy had dug the test holes. He walked the noisy grass to the top. It had good drainage, and if he put in a word with Reilly he might tap into the water mains under cover of night and there would be no rates to pay.

I'm standing on the hill where our house will be, he typed on his phone and attached a picture of the view.

His heart suddenly beat very fast. He and Sinead hadn't spoken since the fight; he'd got up early that morning and left her house before she had woken up, before they'd had to face one another. There'd been a few meaningless texts since but nothing had been resolved, he still the bogger man not capable of understanding her weighty load of education.

Perhaps, he thought now, it was better not to send the text, to instead call her and apologise – even though he had done nothing wrong, he reminded himself – and get things back on an even keel. Perhaps he should wait and drive her here from the train station when she was next home.

But then what if she does not like it? his mind began. He quietened those thoughts and decided a text was best. He would send her the picture and she would see that it was all real, and that this new job was going to make everything happen. There would be no more waiting.

And what if she doesn't respond? She would respond, he assured himself, maybe not straight away but that would not be a concern.

He took another picture of the site to show the real beauty of the place.

Well then, you might want to think about the fact that if she agrees you're locked in, locked in for the train trip to babytown. You want that, though, don't you? The thoughts rallied against him now, making him doubt his actions.

I do, I do, he affirmed. I want this house, this dream, and I'll work to achieve it, he thought and clicked the send button.

He stood now in the long grass, returning to his surroundings; a lone frog slowly made its way up the hill and moved over his boot. He could kick it away, but then again what harm was it doing. The frog might meet a nice frog woman and they could live in one of the test holes, rear a little clan of tadpoles and be happy. At least there would be one family on that bloody hill.

24
McQuaid

Four men was not enough. Four men was not enough to start this new job, he thought as the van moved down the motorway to Ballymahon.

The dashboard was covered with wrappers and dockets, dirty mugs and out-of-date yoghurt. He seemed to live in that van now, moving most hours of most days back and forth between the sites. From the manor through to the villages. Joe Duffy was on the radio talking about the misery.

He stopped and bought a coffee from the Esso station, and quickly poured two sugars and a glob of milk into the black mix. Four was not enough. He would have to take on new labour. Perhaps Willy might lead them in Ballymahon. It was forty houses and the work would be easier than the manor. Willy could take the back out of it. He sipped the coffee and paused. He could get some Polish men cheaper, but would Willy work with foreigners?

Taking his phone in his hand, he called Crossan's the electrical supplier and complained that the orders were still not at the new job. 'Tell your man to pull his finger out,' he said to the receptionist.

The radio was still on as he drove further but he did not hear it, it was white noise to a busy mind. He had set out at twelve from the manor to get a new consaw from the plant hire, but it was three now and he had not yet returned. The Ballymahon developer had called him to discuss the price, which on account of Reilly's advice he had lowered.

He passed through Clondra and on towards the new estate. Houses and houses surrounded every village now, encircling them so deep they were in danger of becoming towns. It would all be one big town soon, he thought. The city in the country. Every block was different and yet the same, just like these houses, just like these towns in every corner of the country. Perhaps the council should just build a footpath through the nation and link it all up.

The drive was long and he had time to think. He ruminated on the pace of change, on how the local had become the world. Intel, Dell, IBM, Apple, KPMG, Morgan Stanley: they were all part of the New Ireland. From the docklands of Dublin to the walls of Limerick, the last great plantation had occurred; the Americans. Everyone working and no one to think where it would all end. Every Tom, Dick and Polski happy as Larry. But did Larry do as much driving as he did now?

He passed rushes and small fields, drove over drumlins and then saw the grandeur of old oak trees in the mighty presence of the large farms and neat stone walls of South Longford, where the landlords had held out as long as they could.

He could see the men on the scaffolding as he approached Ballymahon. They had made good progress in the day. The blocks had arrived, bound in white tape.

Soon they would be ready for them.

'Ger, hello!' Lech the Polish foreman greeted him.

'You've made great progress,' McQuaid said, gesturing towards the houses.

'Yes, soon it will all be ready for you. You will be ready, yes?' said Lech in his strained English.

'We will be ready. My orders should be arriving to you today. But I'm wondering if you might be able to help me?'

'I try.'

'I'm looking for a few extra men,' McQuaid explained.

'I know people,' Lech said calmly.

'And are they Irish?' McQuaid said carefully.

'Some Irish, some Polish, but they good sparkies.'

McQuaid smiled and shook his hand and asked him to text about the new men. Willy would have to take a hold of this place and bring it to life. He would explain the new workers, and if they did not work they could be removed. He would give Willy that freedom, there were men enough to replace any dead wood.

'They are not very pretty houses, Lech,' McQuaid confided as they walked the grounds.

'No, they breakfast roll houses, ugly but sell.' Lech laughed.

McQuaid's phone vibrated. *Need that consaw boss. Dec.*

He excused himself, explaining that he needed to go but that things were in order and to tell the developer they would be ready come Monday.

He started the van again and with haste drove back towards the manor. The radio squealed about contraction in the US, and wasn't he squeezed enough himself, he laughed. He moved over country lanes and endless yellow road markings. He gave a finger salute to a cement lorry parked at the roadside and spied a lazy crow watching the scene from an old fencing post.

The stone walls of the manor loomed large on the horizon as he neared the entrance to the estate. Oh, how the place had grown, the houses nearly finished, the apartment blocks growing each day, and the manor waiting for its rebirth. For its walls to be stripped away and it to become a hotel. The crown of the county.

The manor in its stone solidity had come out of the ground, it was part of the earth; its huge mass seemed to grow upwards, melded with the grass and ivy. Its connection to the place was real. But these new structures, what were they, only dropped there, and sitting atop it all; tiles from China, timber from Norway, walls from factory floors. They were so temporary.

He waved at Peter the security guard and continued up the driveway. He would be glad to be away from the van and his thoughts for a time.

Isolation does strange things, Ger, his mind sang. He dismissed the negativity and took the consaw from the back.

Four men was not enough.

25
Begley

Begley rounded the corner of the main street of Granard past the barracks and the bakery. The trailer rattled behind him with the squeak and mutter of stainless steel and cattle. The evening was already dark as he pulled into the mart. Trailers and lorries reversed to the loading bay and floodlights illuminated the rows and rows of parked vehicles.

The tinkers had set up their stalls in the yard, tools laid out on mats and blankets, consaws, drills, generators, every bit of it stolen, of course, the serial numbers mysteriously missing or worn away. A decent man would not buy those tools, but there were not many of those left.

Brady the planter had laurels for sale by the dozen. 'Perfect time of year to plant,' he remarked to a passer-by, 'the sap is up.'

'So is the price,' came the reply.

Begley reversed the trailer, looking out the window by times to check his vision.

'Let 'er back, c'mon, c'mon, whoa,' an attendant wailed as the tail-lights flashed red against the metal loading gates.

Begley unscrewed the door handles and lowered the spring-loaded gate. The animals came bounding out into the confusion of the space and were ushered towards the crush.

He had three animals to sell. The first two as fine as any others, and the last not nearly worth the effort: her mother had died in birth and he'd reared her on the bucket. Suck, suck, suck, it had gone as he had laboured with the formula and false tit three times a day until he had moved her on to crunch and hay. She still had the belly of a sucked calf, all bloated and bulbous like some African baby. He shook his head; whatever price he got he would take, she would not return home tonight.

Still and all, it passed the time, he mused. It wasn't as if life was so busy any more.

He walked inside and hushed the heifers on with shoos and prods. One of the cattlemen passed him his numbers while another daubed the sticky horse glue on the animals' backs and slapped their lot numbers on them: 117, 118, 119.

He was lucky this time, he was in the middle of the sale; early lots were never strong, as he had learned to his own detriment.

They'd never see their fields again, these same heifers. There was a tinge of emotion as he saw them led away, but the money would be a welcome replacement.

'John, how's things?' he called to a neighbour. 'Have they started yet?'

'A few minutes, prices are good,' replied the neighbour, not stopping.

Begley walked through the shed, climbing over the guards and turnstiles, dodging men and animals alike. Up ahead a bullock slipped on the wet concrete and fell with a mighty crack.

They stood around the ring with its plain blocked walls and adverts for agricultural supplies. The area was busy with the quick slip of bids and shifts of hairy men. Looking around the gallery, he spied familiar faces and dealers. So many of the men were now in construction, with a smell of cement as opposed to cow dung about their person. There were boots and measuring tapes where wellies had been. The builders bought because that was what their fathers had done, he reasoned. And in this New Ireland, cattle were still part of the dream. Táin Bó Cúailnge was not ended, it had but changed its form. Build the business, then the big house, control the area and land around you, and then the pedigree stock, and tribalism was complete anew.

The auctioneer looked down on it all over the grey rust and sawdust. He used a piece of rubber piping as a gavel and commanded the men's attention.

'What are they making with their weight?' Begley asked a stranger.

'Oh, three hundred easy,' came the reply.

They hushed as the bids came in.

Four fifty, four fifty, four fifty, four fifty, for fiffy, for fiffy, fooooooor sixty, four sixie, for sixie, for sixie, for sixie, sixie, sixie, sixie, and on it rang, an opera of lowing and coughs and winks and wagging fingers. Soap-strange jobbers in dirty long coats picked over the cheaper animals, waiting for the lowest bid and desperation to set in before they attacked.

Begley walked to the auctioneer's podium as his animals came up. He stood behind the seller's window, a small slit in the concrete, and watched as his first heifer made it into the ring.

The bids were fast and quick, up and up she went, fine animal that she was, he thought, and as the frenzy quietened, the auctioneer turned to him. 'Are you happy?'

'I am.'

'Oooon the market,' the auctioneer called to the crowd, and with those words her fate was sealed.

Whale Mouth Cullen bought the bucket calf at a low price but Begley did not mind, she was better gone. He, the Mouth, might make use of her somehow.

When all was finished he excused himself, allowed the next man into the confessional and walked to the office to collect his pay slip from the cooper. He was happy with the prices.

'It's warm,' he said.

'It's shocking close,' said the cooper as he handed him the docket.

'It's that all right,' Begley agreed and thanked him for the business.

Done now, he felt a hunger enter him and decided he had earned a fry in the canteen. The aproned girl greeted him and said it had been too long since his last visit; she enquired after his wife Mary and took his order.

She hummed the words to a Willie Nelson number as she poured him a pot of tea.

Mama don't let your babies grow up to be cowboys
Don't let 'em pick guitars and drive limo trucks
Make them be doctors and lawyers and such.

He took a seat alone and waited for his food. He looked around the sparse room with its glittering of cheap aluminium kettles and cutlery. A fat jobber forced a large fry into his sturdy jaws and thanked the girl for the extra bread and then proceeded to dribble the yolk of an egg upon his chin.

Did many of these poor divils know of love, he wondered as he sipped on his tea. Not many, not by the looks of their unwashed faces. A cow was a poor replacement on long wintry nights.

'You were selling, I see,' called Patch Riordan, the blueshirt, from the opposite table. A gossip and news bag, he was shunned in most places, he who was as subtle as a heart attack.

'I was,' Begley replied calmly.

'Oh, I knew that,' said Patch snidely. 'That Diana of a heifer is another man's problem now,' he added with a curling laugh.

'She is,' said Begley, not wanting to talk. 'If you're not out you'll do no deals,' he said in what he hoped was an end to the discussion.

'Shor, you'll buy all around you with all the money you have,' replied Patch in bully wit, to which his companions laughed.

'Land commission property makes a great pedestal, Riordan, it suits you,' said Begley.

'Your shower are in power now, we'll see how good they do,' came the reply.

'I don't need the other side of the political house to tell me how we're doing. Work for any man that wants it, that's how we're doing.'

Riordan could not argue the point and so returned to eating.

Begley finished his fry, pushed the plate to one side and took a newspaper from a nearby table. He wished for some peace and quiet now as he read the headline. *BEAR STEARNS' SHOCK CLOSURE.*

How would this affect the few shares he and Mary had, he wondered. America didn't seem to be doing too well. The late news would be able to tell him more. They might have to go and talk to the bank manager in Mullingar. They could make a day of it, he supposed, finances and then a bowl of soup. It could go anyway; they had enough to keep them now: the savings, the farm cheques in the post, it was enough for now. The trip would fill the day, fill the time indeed, and wasn't that what he was at nowadays, filling time.

He was alone but he wasn't lonely, he told himself. A man just gets used to a life of hard work and early starts, it's difficult to break a pattern. And he envied McQuaid his youth and willingness to work. Ger had it all before him. He was a good lad, he thought and smiled.

A fog had rolled into the shed as he walked back through the holding pens to the jeep. Sweet Jack emerged from the mist, driving the animals to their various destinations, his face and hands covered in dirt, his mouth a canvas of missing teeth. He all smiles and nods, the poor simple lad, and Begley gave him a cigarette as he passed him, at which Jack thanked him profusely and smiled his big vacant grin.

Sweet Jack, he had them all figured out. He was just as happy, happier than they, in his ignorance. He owned nothing except the clothes on his back, and the mart provided him with meals for his help.

And here he was, old Begley, slaving away at these cows, mowing meadows, birthing calves, losing calves, fighting over five measly euro for a bad heifer. The cows seemed to have the better end of the deal, he thought. A human to pick up your shit when you're in the shed and gather hay for you in the summer come rain or shine. No, Jack had it figured out.

Begley decided to take the air before going home and walked up the town towards the pub. He might have one pint to settle himself before he went and presented the slip to Mary for her approval. She might comment on the price of the good Limousin and say she expected more, but secretly she would be happy and she'd put the slip in the good china vase above the television until the cheque came in the post.

But when he neared the door of Val Donoghue's pub he found himself walking on by and up towards the motte and churches. He slowly trudged up the steep ground, past the Protestant and

Catholic churches where Ruske and Reilly were divided by the road and always would be.

He walked up the small lane to the motte, where the broken statue of Saint Patrick sat looking out over the town. He passed the grotto of the Virgin Mary, where little Anne and her baby had died, alone.

He could look out and see the town and the barracks and the bakery and the fields, the graves and the factories. To his left, Kiernan milling, and to his right the mart and *buachalán*'s growing in the distance. Empty beer cans littered the statue's base and Saint Patrick's broken hands gave a ruined feel to the place. He looked out on the town and the quiet shame of it all.

He was alone but he wasn't lonely, he told himself. And it must be true, it must be.

26
McQuaid

He sat at the kitchen table making out the wages for the week. The list had grown to include Lech's new men: Matt, Majus, Colm and Andrew. Willy had put them to work three weeks ago and their progress had been astounding. They had run with those wires through the houses, and the Polish were, he had to admit, as skilled as any Irish man; the language of electricity overcame all barriers. Willy had taken control of the job, and as stressful as things had become, he was a pillar during this time. Begley would be happy to see them now with so much work, so much more than they had ever done with him.

His mother fixed the dinner and put a plate of bacon and cabbage in front of him. 'Now Ger, you eat that, you're getting thin of yourself,' she clucked as she dished out the steamed potatoes.

'Yeah, yeah,' he said dismissively.

He pushed the accounts book to one side and opened the plans for Ballymahon. If they could manage to get the first fixing done in two weeks he might move the men back to the manor during that downtime and push on with the apartment block. His days now seemed to be spent on schedules and time sheets. He sighed heavily, at which his mother clucked again. If they could get through these few weeks, things might get back to the old way.

His dinner was cold when he finally began to eat, the bacon soft and stringy. He peeled the potatoes and poured himself a glass of milk. Just these next few weeks, he told himself.

His mother sat down, her jobs done for the day, and turned on the television.

'Can't you turn that *off*?' he snapped. 'I need a few minutes to think.'

'I'm just trying to get the news, son.'

Fuck that same news, he thought. He had stopped listening to it, it seemed to occupy everyone these days: America, the UK, it was only ever bad.

Frustrated, he pushed the tepid food around the plate but found he no longer had an appetite. He drank the milk and poured himself a coffee.

He walked outside and rolled a cigarette. Exhaling, he blew the smoke into the air. Perhaps he might reward himself and look over the house plans. He had grown so covetous of them lately, they had become dog-eared and stained from his constant opening and closing of them in the van, in the bedroom, on the building site. A few more weeks, a few more weeks of this stress and the block work could start.

He walked inside, took out the blueprint and rolled it flat across the kitchen table.

'That will be a fine place,' his mother commented, looking over his shoulder.

'Don't praise it too much, it's not started yet,' he barked.

'Is that my room?' she asked, nosing herself closer to the table.

'Yes, Mam, that's your room downstairs, like I explained,' and he pointed out the spacious room. It had an ensuite, and when the time came they would place a shower assist for her there. She would not, would never go to a nursing home, he told himself.

'Ah, the granny flat,' she laughed.

'Well, you're no flower.'

'No,' she said and paused in hurt. 'Well, your father would be proud. To think of one of our own with a big house like that. We started in the mobile home.'

'I know, the mobile home and no electricity, and you built up the farm when you both came back from England with only a teapot and the clothes on your back.'

'You know the story well,' she sang, missing his sarcasm. 'Is Sinead happy with it? I'm sure she is, I'm sure she can't wait to get moved in. I met her father the other day, proud as punch he was. I'll have a little Gerard in no time,' she added dreamily.

Sinead, he thought, she who hadn't talked to him at all, who refused to come home. Oh, she was the madam. And he the country fool who refused even to think to call her.

'She is very happy,' he lied.

'What did she say exactly? What room was her favourite?' his mother questioned further.

'She . . . she didn't say. The whole thing, I suppose.'

'Ah, but won't it be grand.'

'Yes, it will be grand. Now, can you give me a moment, Mammy, I need to figure out a few things.'

She held up her hands in appeasement and excused herself; she would fill the hot water bottles and go to bed soon, she wanted an early night before the school day.

He traced the lines of the blueprints with his finger, savouring each twist and turn, each right angle, the nooks, the crannies.

The planning permission had gone through and Reilly had connected the water as he said he would. McQuaid had been praised on the street and in the pub after the notice had gone into the paper.

He'd get Limerick Mick, the block layer, to build it. McQuaid would do as much as he could himself to keep costs down. Willy had offered to help too. His face had been so full of happiness the day he'd told him.

'So that's what Ballymahon is,' he had exclaimed.

'Well, partly,' McQuaid had admitted, fearing Willy's resentment.

'Well, fuck it, we'll make a go of her so,' Willy said and clapped him on the back. 'Didn't I tell you God would provide?'

'You did,' McQuaid agreed.

'But you'll be buying the pints tonight, lad,' Willy said.

'I will, I will,' McQuaid said and was glad that Willy was not jealous.

They had packed up the tools for the day and driven to the village for a celebratory drink. Willy was gleeful in the knowledge that all this work was leading somewhere.

'Some day I'll build me own and you can return the favour,' he said.

McQuaid promised he would and bought the first round. Maguire, one of the regulars, sent them a glass of whiskey and wished them health. It was a nice evening. And Willy was so happy, as happy as if it were his own place.

'These Polish lads you're getting me,' he said, breaking the mirth.

'Yeah?'

'Are they any good? Will they be fit for the work?'

'Ah, they're interchangeable. If they're no good, the road is the place for them,' McQuaid said.

'Grand so. I'll take care of things, don't worry, Ger.'

He had ordered another pint, shown Willy the plans on the way home and slept soundly that night. He hadn't rested so well in a long time.

Removing the paperweights now, he rolled up the plans. It was coming together, albeit slowly.

His mother walked back into the kitchen, her nightclothes already on her. 'Will you lock up?' she asked.

'Yes, yes,' he said, breaking from his thoughts.

'Ger, you'd tell me, you'd talk to me if anything was wrong, wouldn't you?' she began hesitantly.

'What? Nothing is wrong.'

'I know, I know, but if something was the matter, you'd talk to me?'

'Yes,' he eventually agreed.

'Only, it's . . . it's just the two of us now,' she said.

'I know, Mam. Go to bed, or there'll be no granny flat.'

'All right, son,' she said quietly, as if trying to find other words that would not come.

He put the plans by the front door.

'I love you, you know,' she said, and with that walked down the hallway and to bed, a heavy look about her shoulders.

There was nothing to talk about, he told himself, just a bit of pressure and he needed his space, that was all. He needed his own space.

You'll have to see her, you know, you can't dodge around that much longer, his thoughts sang. *I bloody know, I know, I know everything.*

He put his phone in the charger and decided he might go to bed early too. The night had wasted away now.

27
Lefoyle

1835

There could be no solace in fabric that night; silk, cotton, eiderdown. The bedsheets could not drown out the storm outside his window.

They had spoken of bad weather coming but nothing like this, nothing. Lefoyle dressed himself and made his way downstairs. Branches rattled furiously against the windows as he hurried to light an oil lamp.

The moon was the full of itself, its light draped against the trees of the estate, over the cedars and the elm, the oak and the ash. They were a riot of boisterous movement.

Rain began to fall in heavy drops that soaked in an instant. He watched from the streaming window, what else could be done? At least there was the security of the house.

Crash!

He turned to see a maid wild-eyed by the doorway, a chair on the ground in front of her.

'What's to be done, sir?' she asked frantically.

'Make sure all the windows and doors are secure, Marie,' he said. 'And get Murphy to check the stables and yards, I want no animal out in that weather,' he added, thinking of his prize hunter.

She curtsied and made her way to the servants' quarters to instruct the staff.

Had he ever seen a night, a storm, like this before? Not in years, not since childhood when they had been out in the fields picking wild mushrooms and a downpour had come worse than this one. Hen of the woods, puffballs, chanterelles, bolletes, Destroying Angel. He still savoured their names but the memory of their taste was long gone.

Caught in the rain picking mushrooms, he thought. Caught in the rain because there was no other food that day, save for what they, the children, might find themselves.

A man can only be the defendant of his own life, his own experience. And what had been *his* case? The dispute of poverty and how to escape it.

The precedent of education and a patron had taken him away from that bankrupt drunken father. *Stare decisis* of a promise never to be poor again. With work would come success; with law, order.

That poor youth had passed, as would this storm.

A flash of lightning scattered over Lefoyle's face as he stared out the window, and then came the unmistakable crack of thunder. The maid returned and waited a moment, watching.

'Sorry, sir, but I've checked all the doors and windows and everything is secure.'

'What's that?' he said, waking from his daze.

'Everything is shut, sir.'

'Very good. And Murphy?'

'Murphy is out checking the animals now, sir.'

Lefoyle nodded his head. 'Very well, go back to bed, Marie.'

She turned and left the room. He might as well go back to bed himself, he thought; what sleep could be salvaged from this night might as well be his. He walked the lower floor of the house, inspecting the front doors. Through the day room window he thought he glimpsed the figure of Murphy in the moonlight, stooped low like some lonesome scarecrow.

Back in bed he gathered the blankets around himself and felt their warmth and security, the pattern of a disturbed night worn in their folds.

It was past ten the next morning when he woke with a gasp. He dressed quickly. The rain and wind had ended, water covered the grounds and the trees looked like dishevelled lovers, leaves and branches askew.

After breakfast he waited for Murphy and his carriage to appear. The minutes began to pass: five, six, seven . . . ten minutes late. Dammit, didn't the man know he had to be at the bank this morning, had he not told the lout to be ready?

He rang for Marie, and as he waited his anger grew.

'Marie, where is Murphy!' he snapped as the maid appeared. 'Did I not tell him to have the carriage ready for me this morning?'

'You did, sir, but . . .' and she hesitated.

'But what, girl? Can't you see I'm already late?'

'But, well, sir, Murphy didn't come to breakfast this morning, sir.'

'Sick, is he? A fine lot of good that is.'

'No, sir, he's not in bed either, we thought perhaps you had sent him on a job, on account of the storm, and the horses are missing too, so young Sean in the yard tells me.'

'Missing? Did he come in last night, Marie? From the storm?'

'Well, I went to bed, sir, as you told me,' she replied.

'Did you hear him come in?' he questioned, a hint of worry in his voice.

'No, sir – I mean, it was very loud because of the wind, sir, so perhaps maybe he did or . . .'

'So what you are telling me is you don't know?'

'No . . . I don't,' she answered, her eyes on the ground in shame.

Lefoyle ran his hand across his forehead. 'Tell the men to search the yard, the grounds; surely someone has seen him.'

The bank would have to wait. He put on his heavy coat and made his way outside. The storm had indeed been terrific. Worse than he had thought. The air was fresh and moist, and the soft garden stone squeezed under his boots in a mucky talc as he walked. He must inspect the damage.

Branches and leaves roamed the grounds, scattered in disarray; a gutter torn from the wall dripped lazily with the last of the storm water. The roof of the storehouse had been ripped open, its slate sheets dotted here and there. By the driveway the remains of the pine tree crop stood in ruins. The ceremony of planting and thinning was but a thing of the past now. A failure of investment.

Lefoyle walked quietly; occasionally in the distance he saw one of the staff pottering around. And where was Murphy, he wondered. He had been too kind to him on those trips to town and beyond, and this was his thanks. A disappearing act, with God knew how much stock.

A white dust covered the grass and rosebushes of the western gardens; as he looked closer he realised it was crystals of sea salt. How far had this storm blown? How much havoc had it caused? Dead fish lay on the grass of the riverbank, plucked out by the net of the wind.

And what of his prized cedars of Lebanon, he thought now.

He prayed they had not been hurt. Those rare beauties brought from so far, far away. He quickened his pace across the lawns and began to fret their fate. It was his whole thought, of all those years, all that time and patience. He knew before he saw the disembowelled bodies that they had indeed been destroyed, their roots torn from the ground, the dark wet earth still clinging to them.

The sight was a blow; their beauty, so fragile, was gone.

Word slowly began to filter into the manor that the damage was equal all over the country: houses destroyed, stock lost, rivers burst, towns on fire, lives blown asunder by this kraken of wind and rain.

The staff worked to clear the debris, and he alongside them. This day there was no master or labourer, no serf and lord, just men united in their efforts. The maids brought out tea and sandwiches and he invited the men to lunch with him there on the grounds in the open air, on the belly of a fallen oak. The talk was a polite quietness, but on the subject of the storm there was much comment.

'Shocking, sir, wasn't it?'

'It was bad, Kennedy . . . bad,' Lefoyle replied, bringing his cup to his mouth.

'The divil's work, sir. Do you suppose it was a punishment, sir?' another man asked.

'How do you mean, Peter?'

'Well, for O'Connell upsetting the order of things, for the country folk trying to get one over on their betters, sir.'

'I do not see how the two could be linked. Haven't we suffered as much as any here in Birchview, and O'Connell is no friend of mine,' said Lefoyle with a laugh.

'Never be minding Peter, sir, full of auld notions he is,' said Kennedy.

Lefoyle took his pipe out of his waistcoat pocket and prepared his tobacco; he would relax a moment longer with the men and then get back to work. Superstition indeed, he laughed to himself.

By the oak planting a small figure appeared on the horizon. It was moving at speed towards them.

'Who is that?' questioned Kennedy as he brought his hand to shade his eyes.

'It's very small . . . It's young Sean, I think, sir,' answered Peter, turning to Lefoyle.

'What on earth is he doing?'

The men walked cautiously towards the moving shape. Young Sean reached them moments later, his face red. The men huddled around him and talked briefly. Lefoyle strained to hear.

'What's that? What's he got to say?' he shouted now at the men.

'Sir, Sean has some bad news, sir,' said Peter.

'Well, let the lad tell me himself.'

The boy walked forward slowly, eyes on the ground. 'It's Murphy, sir, I found him,' he began.

'Well, some news at last. Drunk, is he? I daresay he took to the whiskey last night,' said Lefoyle and laughed.

'No, sir, he's not drunk, sir,' said Sean and his voice broke.

Lefoyle straightened up immediately, the gravity of the situation clear. 'Take me there, Sean. You men go back to work,' he said.

The two of them did not speak as they walked across the lawn to the oak forest. At a clearing Sean pointed to a wildflower patch; he did not move any closer and remained thus in an immobile state.

A thin vein of sunlight shone upon the scene. There were no visible marks, just a softness of the lips, a fade in colour. Lefoyle had seen a man pulled from the Camlin River once and it had been that same look. The small trampled flowers came away from him, a yellow streak of pollen dashed across his face, a purple twist of wildflowers on his hands.

Lefoyle looked at him and thought of all those carriage rides, and had he ever once called the man by his first name?

Richard.

In his hand lay a horse's collar. The leather was black with wet.

And what of the mare and the champion hunter? Where were they? They had searched the grounds, called for them, but to no avail. Perhaps they too had been lost, the good horses no more. He cursed himself for last night's order.

He bent down and closed Murphy's eyelids, paused a moment and stood up.

He walked quietly towards the house, shaken by the day's events. The *caoin* of the women would soon fill the grounds. The body would be brought down to the servants' quarters, washed and dressed. He would do the right thing by Murphy and give his people some money.

As he went in the front door the shrieking neigh of a horse was heard and suddenly the hunter emerged from the woods and burst out through the thicket, his flank torn and cut, all blood and briars. The men ran after him, and as the news of Murphy's death spread, the grounds were a pandemonium of wails and neighs and sobs and cries. He closed the heavy front door and found he could not tell the sounds apart.

The loss of Murphy was a blow, but there was another loss, he thought, that others might not understand. Murphy would be mourned, he would be buried in the local church, he would be missed. But what of the cedars of Lebanon, who had they to grieve for them? Who would mourn their loss? Never would he know them again. It would be a private grief.

And what of good news? Was there any to be had?

No firewood had yet been stolen, he noted in his diary. He poured himself a brandy and resumed writing. And with all the felled trees the view of the local mountain had improved that same Cairn Hill.

He closed his diary and sat for a moment. He would let the day's events wash over him, as a river, as rain, as an end in itself.

28
McQuaid

The van moved smoothly into fifth gear and with a flash of his indicator he overtook the old woman in her Nissan Micra. He drove on towards the M50, the radio blaring out some mindless pop.

The attendant on the toll road had a thick Dublin accent. 'That'll be four eighty, love.'

He gave her a twenty crisp and fresh from the ATM at the filling station in Rathowen. The gate lifted and he sped off, past lorries and cars, by roadworks and the Sisk contractors, by the Spa Hotel and the Dead Man's Inn.

He could see the walls of Phoenix Park now and the cranes on the skyline, there like a thousand candles in the night, over Ballymun, Drumcondra, Glasnevin, Tallaght, Finglas, over the whole bloody city.

He'd called Sinead that day, finally mustering the bravery to do it. They agreed to meet up for a meal and a chat. They hadn't seen each other in weeks, not since the fight, and an oddness had come between them. He'd spent longer than usual on his appearance, tried on different shirts, a blazer, a jumper, but nothing seemed to fit. He'd put gel in his hair but could not get it right, could not get it to sit, and that calf's lick at the back had stayed defiantly erect.

'Fuck,' he'd said, looking at himself in the mirror. He didn't look right. He took some Dax from the old tin that had belonged to his father and flattened his hair, or rather beat it down. He returned the pomade to the shelf beside *his* toothbrush; it was so peculiar that his mother had never thrown out his father's things, not after all these years. Still a presence in the house, like he might come back one day to wash himself, comb his hair and call out for someone to leave him to the pub as he had an awful thirst for a pint.

McQuaid and Sinead had decided to meet at the Passage restaurant; it was once their favourite place, they'd had many happy times there, and yet it had been so long. Andy the manager would be behind the bar, all smiles and a drink on the house for them.

'Well, we haven't seen you in an age,' came the call as he walked in the front door.

'Been busy,' McQuaid explained. 'How is trade?'

'Business is good, a nice flow of punters these days, we're going late on the weekends too,' replied Andy.

McQuaid nodded distractedly.

The barman poured two whiskeys, one for himself and one for McQuaid. He swallowed it whole and it burned his throat. He was, he realised, nervous, nervous about seeing her, as he had not been for a long time and he was not sure whether to text straight away or wait until the next day.

He'd started the house. Would he tell her that, he wondered. Started the dream house. Maybe she already knew; Longford was a small place, the word would have already gone out across the parish. From her father to Whale Mouth, the grocer Kings, the Farrells; she would know, he was sure.

'Young McQuaid is building a mansion of a place up on that hill,' they would shout to one another.

'The bollox!'

Sinead arrived in the black Alphaville dress he had bought her on her last birthday. Red lipstick and black mascara. She was beautiful.

Andy turned his eyes towards the doorway and smiled. 'Sinead. What'll you have?'

'A vodka, please,' he heard her say quietly.

'Hey,' she said and looked at him.

He gave her a peck on the cheek and he thought she trembled at his touch. She too was afraid, he thought, and her shy smile spoke it loud. He savoured her perfume as if it were the first time. A rose blossom like he had never smelled before.

'We'll take a seat,' he explained to Andy, who nodded.

'The girl will be down with the menus in a few minutes.'

'How are things?' McQuaid began cautiously.

'Oh, good, busy with college, and you?'

'Yeah, work is . . . intense at the moment.'

She played with her drink and he looked fixedly at the wall behind her, at the customer going into the toilets, at the barman cleaning glasses; where was the fucking waitress, he thought.

'Where's that waitress got to?'

'Oh, I don't know,' she replied and searched across her shoulder.

They had the stuffed zucchini flowers and a bowl of olives to accompany their drinks. She sucked on the olive pits as she always did, devouring the last of the flesh.

'And college is good?' he asked.

'Yeah, you asked me that already, it's fine, just a few essays left.'

He wiped his forehead. He was sweating now as only she could make him; he rubbed the back of his neck with his handkerchief, his shirt was wringing wet. He stood up and excused himself. 'Just need the toilet,' he said, overexplaining.

In the bathroom he washed his face, dried himself with paper towels and looked in the mirror. 'Take a hold of yourself, man,' he said aloud in the privacy of the room. 'It's Sinead, it's only Sinead.'

And what, what must she be thinking out there on her own? He would go out, have dinner and talk to her. 'Just talk to her, Ger,' he said, looking at himself in the mirror.

He wiped a new layer of sweat from his forehead, washed his hands again and breathed deeply. He dampened his hair a little then fixed his suit and walked back outside.

'The main course arrived,' she explained. 'I waited for you . . .'

He thanked her and took his seat again. He shovelled the food into him, he did not care who saw him eat like this in public. He ate as he did when he was on the building site, as he had before he'd learned to eat like a well-bred city boy.

Tread softly, Ger. There's dreams at stake. His mind now ran. He paused a moment, took another sip of his whiskey to settle himself.

He was shaking now, he saw the tremor in his hand, small and slow as if he had been breaking concrete all day. Tread softly, he repeated to himself. It was easy for a big house man to eulogise on dreams and love and twilight when you had all day to do it.

Had he spoken in the last five minutes, he thought now, or had they been sitting in silence for longer? Jesus, he would want to say something.

You'll need to speak, Ger. Ar, Ger, you'll need to speak.

'How is the fish?'

'It's lovely,' she said in monotone, and yet her eyes told of anything other than fish.

'Can we get another drink?' she asked politely.

'Yeah, God yeah,' he said and relaxed slightly. 'Another whiskey and a vodka please,' he said to the waitress, pointing at the empty glasses.

There was such melancholy to them both, eyes not looking at each other, food pushed around plates, eaten only for show. When he knew full well her stomach was as sick as his.

He was afraid to speak, to really speak, as this was all the love they had ever known and, young as they were, they did not know those rules of love. That one must work, must talk even when it is hard. And what if this same love ended, he wondered. What then? It did not bear thinking about.

The drinks arrived and they smiled and gulped them down quickly.

'Will we . . . will we have dessert?' he asked tentatively.

'We might as well,' said Sinead with a small smile.

Andy came down with the dessert menu. He gave McQuaid a nudge as he explained the options. Go easy, man, he seemed to say, it's fifteen-love, it's your serve and you're in the last set, make it count.

'We'll have the cheese board, and could you pick a dessert wine to go with that?' asked McQuaid.

'No problem,' said Andy and he made his way to the kitchen. Andy, who had seen it all before, McQuaid mused; meetings and love, and endings too.

The restaurant was quiet this night, the candles flickered with the subtle hiss of wax and twine. The waitress cleaned away the plates and wiped the table.

Had he held Sinead's hand once tonight, he thought. Had he rubbed her thigh under the table as he had so often done before? The rub, the pet that said, look at us, like adults having a fancy meal and no worry about expense. No, was the answer, but it had not been out of spite.

The cheese was provedore fresh, strong blues, creamy whites, and sun-dried raisins with the seeds still in them. The dessert wine was sticky and rolled across the palate as Andy had said it would.

McQuaid signed the bill with his earnest scrawl, still the handwriting of a schoolboy, despite all the fanciness. Andy shook hands with him on the way out; he had never done that before, he thought, not in all their visits.

He and Sinead walked by the Liffey in silence, down the quays towards the port and the red and white chimneys of Dublin Bay, by the theatres and the docklands, by the old weighing bridge for the canal. The river was high and flowed its dirty current out into the Irish Sea. Sinead shivered and he took off his jacket and put it around her. She thanked him and draped it over her naked shoulders.

He walked with his hands behind his back, fists clasped tightly, like a man in deep thought, like a poet searching for the word and the word was 'the' or 'love' or 'no', but words were hard to come by tonight.

The Guinness factory had let out its belch and the city smelled like barley and wheat, he knew the smell so well from the summer he'd spent at his City and Guilds training, walking by it every evening.

The number 19 bus was stopped across the road to let the last of the late-night passengers off; oh, how nice it would be to make for Sandymount or Blackrock, go out on the DART to the beach he liked, or to Malahide where that ghost was supposed to appear at midnight.

At eleven they caught a taxi to Sinead's sharehouse; he could see the streetlights roll by, and the white road markings zigzag their way to the suburbs.

'Well, this is us,' said Sinead to the taxi driver, touching him on the shoulder and pointing out the small terrace house, the weeds still in the gutter, the bins not taken out.

McQuaid opened the garden gate and walked her to the door. He wished now to embrace her, to take her inside and hold her in his arms in the double bed. Not to make love, just to hold her, and to know that it would be okay.

And yet no words came, he was no poet, no man of quips or sonnets.

'Well, I better go,' he said.

'You could come in for a cup of tea,' she offered. 'If you wanted, that is.'

'Ah, no . . . no. I've an early start. I have this new job . . .' and he trailed off, rubbing the back of his neck in awkwardness.

'Oh right, I understand,' she said and slipped the key into the door as she had done so many times before, so many times they had rolled in that door with only thoughts of heavy breaths and passion and tongues and movement.

He walked away from the house, ran almost.

'Jesus,' he sighed.

Jesus, his mind rang.

He walked further still and calmed his breathing; he would take a drink, it didn't matter the pub, he would settle himself. He walked in the door and ordered a pint, and then another and then another still. A repeat of *The Late Late Show* played on television.

'What's the secret to your success?' the host enquired of his guest.

'Hard work, exercise and my wife,' the guest replied.

'Turn that fucker off, will you,' he said to the barman.

He took a double whiskey and a can for the road and stumbled out of the pub. He rolled down the sleeves of his shirt and found he was without his jacket. She had it still. He had an excuse, he told himself, he could go back and ask for the jacket and talk to her. No, she would be asleep now; she needed her sleep for class. He'd not bother her, he'd not interrupt her.

He walked back towards the city to where the van was parked; he passed a young couple walking home, hands held tightly. He sipped his can and spat on the ground. Fuck them, fuck the lot of these Dubs.

He'd sleep in the van, that same dirty van she had been so disgusted with. He opened the red sliding door and clambered in. There amongst the drills and wires and dirt he lay, arms crossed. His teeth chattered and he pulled the safety vests over his body to warm himself.

He vomited on his new grinder, and as the tears of the bile and sick fell down his face he was not sure if they were all from drink. The van stank now and he huddled himself down.

She just streets away and yet so far, and he sighed, closed his eyes and prayed for ease. Lord that the porter might make him sleep, he thought, and blacked out soon after.

29
McQuaid

She hadn't texted for days. That wasn't entirely true, he reminded himself, but her texts had been of no consequence. *Busy in class!* or *Hey, I'm out sorry!* And that bastard of an exclamation mark on everything. What did that mean, McQuaid wondered. Never an answer on the phone any more. Never the hint of remorse.

'Aul bitch,' he muttered under his breath as he unpacked the tools from the van.

Scrupulous meanness. His thoughts now ran. What?

Language of economy, Ger Ger. She only cares about the good times. You brought her for dinner and paid and she didn't even invite you in.

He tried to push away these thoughts. She *had* invited him in, she had and he was the one to refuse. It was all too awkward, he thought, and yet he ruminated further: she was a bitch, she the one who felt he was some country fool, some dreamer. And now his mother was asking questions, looking for answers he did not have. The only solid thing in his life was work and that house.

There seemed to be no end to the estate work at Birchview. They were still stuck in this maze of an apartment block and he surrounded by a shower of bolloxy Bills with no bit of a rush under them. It was the same every day; a life lived between copper rolls and the jaws of pliers, his balls in the snips.

He'd started the house without her. Limerick Mick had arrived and begun the work and yet she still had not come. Perhaps tonight he would send her a picture. Ballymahon had moved with speed and Willy so good as he was had come to Birchview on his downtime to help with the last push. Once the apartments were done he could relax. Once Ballymahon's first fixing was done *they* could relax and see life on the old terms. She'd come around, he told himself; he would send the picture and she would see the progress and it would all come together.

What was it, only a tiff. It all equalled itself out, everything happened for a reason. Or so his mother had always said.

Or maybe, maybe, that was just something widows told themselves to keep going, he thought. The dead cannot sustain the living and so the living take comfort in mantras. He shrugged his shoulders and set to work.

As he carried the drill into the building his thoughts rattled still. Of course she, his mother, was not talking to him either. They barely spoke now, he so busy with work and she with exams before the school break. Home life was notes on the fridge, the microwave, the oven. He still brought her to mass, still had the Sunday lunch with her, but it had all become a sort of ceremony. In his mind he had already moved out, already moved into the new house, and perhaps she knew this and resented him for it.

He could see the men through the opening working on the upper level, placing the last of the heavy gauge wires. Willy calmly instructed them to fix their drills on various points, his safety vest billowing in the growing wind. He had Willy at least.

Pat and Declan sat talking about last night's match, cigarettes in their hands.

'I'm telling you Rooney won't last the season,' he heard Pat say.

'Would you fuck off, he's in prime health,' Declan said.

'He won't make it,' Pat laughed and relaxed with the last of the smoke.

McQuaid put the drill on the floor and walked into the middle of the room. 'What the fuck are you at?' he asked sternly.

'Having a fag break, boss,' said Pat innocently, holding up his lighter in illustration.

'You can have your fucking fag at fucking break time. Didn't I say we're to get this job done today?' said McQuaid, his eyebrows raised.

'But Willy said, we thought . . .' Declan stammered.

'There was your first mistake: thinking. Fucking thinking when you should be working. It's not a philosophy class.'

'No,' said Pat, his eyes on the ground. They dropped their cigarettes and closed their boots to them. The pair stood and returned to work.

He turned and walked out of the room. He thought he heard Declan mutter an insult as he left. But he no longer cared; he was not their friend, he was their employer. It was he who signed those cheques.

He was angry, he knew, and yet what could he do about it? The house, Sinead, his mother, the old job dragging on too long, the new one not fast enough. The best thing would be for the men to stay out of his way today, to do their work and keep their heads down.

Willy, hearing the encounter, took him aside and explained that he had given the boys a break. 'They're working at this since seven this morning. The lads were tired and I didn't want any mistakes made.'

'I'll decide when the breaks are, Willy. The estate is my responsibility.'

'The floor will be done today, Ger. The men needed a break,' Willy said and offered him a smile.

Willy told the boys they could finish their fags and that he wanted the floor cleaned and ready by four. 'He's just under the gun,' he heard Willy say. 'Give it a few days.'

A white noise of labour soon filled the air. McQuaid set the heavy-duty drill against the shuttered wall. The masonry bit pushed and pulled and tore at the concrete until eventually the light of day shone through. He bored again and again, threaded the wire as he went and moved with purpose through the rooms. He continued with force for more than an hour and found the squeal of the metal an escape from his thoughts.

As he set the drill against the wall for what must have been the twentieth time, the bit shore and broke. He had gone too hard and not let the metal cool.

'For fuck's sake!' he spat and kicked out at the wall, hurting his foot.

He wiped the sweat from his forehead and paused. In the absence of machine noise, he could hear two voices calling out to each other.

'Do tribunals ever end?' said the first lazily.

'No, not when we're paying for them,' said the second firmly.

'There's no end to our money,' returned the first and they both laughed.

Had he not told them, had he not told them to stop with all this talk and do their work? He stomped down the hallway and found Willy in one apartment and John in the next, the pair talking through the shuttered wall as they fed an awkward cable through.

'Is that the right cable?' McQuaid asked.

'It is,' said Willy with a bemused look.

'And you're marking as you go?'

'We are.'

Trying to find fault where there was none, he turned to John. 'Have you them batteries charging?' he shouted through the wall.

'What batteries? Ah . . . no,' John shouted back.

'The batteries should always be charging when a man is using the drill. Have you not heard me this last hour, I'm near out and now I'll have to wait for the fucking thing to charge.'

'I didn't know,' said John, who now walked into the room, covered in dust and dirt. 'It's just you have the batteries in the van. I thought you had one in for yourself.'

'Jesus, but it's a dear-bought bit of shamrock, this country of ours. Aren't you the labourer, it's your job to have that done.'

'Easy now,' said Willy, moving towards the men. 'John will do it now, won't you, John?'

'I will, I will surely,' said John with a slight break in his voice.

'You should know better, Willy, and him working with you. A let-down, a fucking let-down this place is today,' said McQuaid. Fucking louts, fucking lazy pricks, and all the money he spent on these men, and what did he get in return? Not a charged battery, that's for sure.

There would be no lunch break today, he decided; they would work through like real men and get the floor finished. He replaced the bit and set to work again. His phone did not ring, and no calls or questions came to him. Each hole emerged and he filled it now with anger and frustration.

At five he wiped the sweat from his brow and took a break. The sun had moved low and darkness looked set. He rolled himself a cigarette and found he had calmed. He was covered from head to toe in dust, the drill hot and the holes finally complete, they looked like parallel pinpricks in the flank of some huge leathery grey beast. Today was nearly done.

God but you're a scutter face, his mind said as he dangled his feet over the open landing. Fuck those same thoughts, and he hocked a yellowed phlegm towards the ground.

Fuck the lads, is it? Yes, fuck them, he thought, and drained yet more of the cigarette.

Fuck the lads? And them the same men who'd lie down in traffic for you, Ger, what were you rearing on them for? He had so much on his plate, perhaps he should not be so harsh on them.

You were hissing at them like a monkey. It was true; he would apologise to the men and take them for a pint. He got up and walked back down the hallway. His anger was not at the men, it was at her. He'd buy them a round and explain that Big Jack was on his arse about the deadlines.

He smiled now at John's confusion over the battery. He began to pack up his tools and breathe a little easier. As he detached the bit a sudden commotion filled the air. Declan began to shout and bodies began to appear from across the floors, following the sounds. Drills and saws lowered to a purr and then stopped altogether as the shouts continued.

'Oh God, oh God,' came the cry.

McQuaid gritted his teeth. What was it now? He pursued the shouts, running through the block, moving as quickly as he could but not quick enough, and the shouts came again.

'Oh God, oh God, oh God.'

He found Declan stood in the middle of the room, hands to his head, pulling at his hair. His eyes a mix of tears and concrete dust.

'What is it?' he asked. But Declan did not, could not reply and began to rock back and forth.

McQuaid pushed him out of the way and walked towards the window opening. Far below on the ground lay a body and blood splattered on the blue granite.

'John!' he shouted and men poured into the room. 'Go and see who that is, quickly now,' and he moved towards Declan and grasped his shoulders.

*

There on the blue stone earth he lay. He could see only blackness and the occasional flash of oozy red. His ears rang, his body stiff, there was no pain though. People do not live in decades or history, they live in moments.

'One, two, three, four,' came the muffled words.

'One, two, three, four.'

'One, two, three, four.'

'One, two, three, four.'

There was another sound, but he could not put a word to it; he listened intently as it grew louder, but still he had no words, there was no word for it. The noise of a cow pulling grass maybe, stalk by stalk and the tear of the green from the earth. That must be it, he thought.

Everything changes into something else, he mused, and then all went dark.

*

'Oh God, oh God,' Declan cried.

McQuaid took him by the shoulders and told him to calm down and explain what had happened.

'Willy was on the scaffold and –' Declan stopped short, unable to finish.

'And?' asked McQuaid, shaking him now.

'And a plank came away and he missed his footing or . . . I'm not sure,' and he returned to his shaking.

McQuaid walked towards the window opening again. John and Pat had torn open Willy's clothes to check for the source of the blood; the rip of his boilersuit had filled the air. Another man knelt beside the body checking the pulse, counting the beat rhythmically.

'One, two, three, four . . .' he chimed.

'Call the ambulance,' shouted McQuaid.

Yellow vests soon flooded the grounds and the men looked on helplessly.

He would be taken to Mullingar hospital, he had been lucky, the ambulance driver said, a few feet higher and it would be death.

'Who's in charge here?' he enquired.

'I am,' said McQuaid, brushing through the crowd.

'Do you want to come in the ambulance with William?'

'No,' he snapped. 'I have work to do.'

The driver looked at him a moment, frowned and helped Declan into the back seat.

'That floor isn't finished, John. Don't stand around gawking. We're not leaving until it's done,' said McQuaid.

A queer silence came over the assembled group, and the men parted and let him through. No one said a word. His face hard and set, he walked back up to the apartment and began to drill. The noise echoed out in the emptiness of the site. Willy was gone, he told himself, his pillar had fallen. And as the tears rolled down his face he drilled harder still.

What would become of the work now, he thought, and hated himself for that same reflection. He should have gone in the ambulance, but the moment was done and the choice had been made.

30
McQuaid

He was on twenty a day now; light, suck, quench, repeat. The empty packets and silver foil had begun to mount up in the door panel and on the dashboard. Peggy in the local shop had begun to reach for them every time he entered. Tea was no longer strong enough, it would be coffee, black and sugarless. When he took a drink there was no ease, only a bitter aftertaste, and so he drank all the more, but there was no relief in those empty glasses.

Willy was fucked, as John had put it. Out of action for weeks and Ballymahon had gone backwards, if such a thing were possible; the Irish men had begun to boss the Polish around, and as much as he drove back and forth between the two jobs there was nothing to be done. Not one man to rely on, only baby steps and hand-holding with Declan and the others. It was a blow, Willy's loss, and only now in his absence did he see how much work the man had done, how many squabbles he had managed.

The apartments were nearly finished, and the second phase would start. He would be glad to be rid of those same apartments;

no man looked on them in wonder or awe now, only the wink and nod of that was where the accident had happened.

He drove to Mullingar hospital to see him and brought grapes and a bottle of soft drink. He asked the receptionist for directions and an elevator ride later he found himself standing in a ward, Willy asleep in the bed. He did not wake him, for what would be the point?

'How are you feeling?' it would go.

'Grand,' Willy would reply and sit up ever so slightly in the bed.

'You'll be up and about in no time,' McQuaid would say.

'I will surely.'

But he wouldn't, he would not be up nor back to work for weeks or months and McQuaid would have to pay his wages all the same, despite the absence.

No, he would not wake him, he affirmed. He left the grapes on the bedside locker and told the nurse on duty to inform Willy of his visit when he woke.

He walked back to the car park and lit a fag; beside him a patient puffed on his King Size Players, all the while holding on to his mobile drip. What irony it was, all those people fighting to keep the wretch alive and he still smoking.

He drove back to Longford, passing Lough Owel on the way; he looked out and saw the water lap against the train line and wished he might break a while by the water's edge. He sped up and drove on towards Ballymahon.

He had texted Sinead about the accident and she had expressed concern, saying she would visit Willy soon. It was over between them now, and yet it wasn't. If he could somehow get through this time without Willy, things might come back around. God might well provide.

And yet even on thinking it, something in his stomach spoke

otherwise. Was it the voice of his body trying to speak? The voice that was only used to hard work, its only comments 'I'm tired' or 'I'm hungry', but now it seemed to speak new words he could not understand.

It would be a welcome break if someone might come in and take control of it all for him. Set the brain in one area and the *corp* in another.

Limerick Mick had completed the first floor of block work on his house. He had, in the beginning, arrived every day to see the progress. But after Sinead had not replied to yet another picture, he had stopped. He was building a dream she might never set foot in. It was a blotch upon the canvas.

As he approached Edgeworthstown he could see the chimneys of the pet food factory belching smoke and the seagulls swarming the grounds. The factory was full of Eastern Europeans now, no Irish man would pack lumps of meat any more. No, they'd all be doctors and lawyers and such. A chip van was a step down for a girl with an arts degree from Athlone or Sligo. They were all professors and professionals now.

The change had come in the mind of the nation almost overnight. They were top dog. And yet what was it all for? Were they any happier? It wasn't shebeens any more, no, but none of the fuckers had time to speak to you either, to say good morning and mean it. Only get every last bit out of you with parking meters on country roads, mobile bills, internet bills, and roaming charges when you crossed the border on the same bloody island. He sighed and took the roundabout exit for Ballymahon and the estate.

A security guard greeted him at the site and waved him in. Forty houses to be wired and finished in what had once been some man's prideful meadow field. What tragedies and rows that ground might have known, he thought. Perhaps it had been sold by a son who no longer wanted to farm, or left to a niece in Dublin who did not know how to. Regardless, it was blocks and stone now.

Declan greeted him as he walked into number 4 Goldsmith Drive. 'How was Willy?' he enquired.

'No loss, up and about,' McQuaid lied, not looking at him. 'How are we doing here?' he added.

'Good,' said Declan, leaning against the wall, ready for a chat. 'Majus and Andrew are at each other's throats but they're getting the work done.'

'Good. I've those lengths in the van for you and I'll leave you the kango for later,' McQuaid said and turned quickly on his heel.

He opened the back door of the van, left the materials on the ground and shouted to Declan that he would be back before the evening. 'I'm on the phone if you need me,' he said as he climbed into the driver's seat.

Declan nodded from the doorway; there was nothing more to add. Declan had not been the same since the accident, but that was not for him to say. They could not talk about their feelings, that was not their way.

The road was quieter on the return journey to Birchview. He turned on the radio and listened to the news.

'*The US closures will not, will not affect the banking system*,' the thick Offaly accent assured the host.

'*But we've had two factory closures this week*,' the journalist interrupted.

'*I think you're confusing relocation and international finance*,' the man returned. '*Our market is fine, the banks have posted their biggest profits to date*,' he went on, talking over the interviewer.

'*So it was simply a black Monday?*' quizzed the journalist.

'*Simply*,' the man responded.

McQuaid changed the station, it was enough to hear the

news once in the day. He turned the dial to the local radio; he might get the day's deaths before he reached the estate. A young neighbour had been killed joyriding the night before and it would be a big funeral.

The manor loomed in front of him as he rounded the last corner. Bad weather had surrounded the estate for weeks now, hampering their progress. How this place had been made into something it did not want to be.

They were on the last rooms of the apartment block; they would be finished by the end of the week. It was a small grace, but one less thing on the list.

Big Jack waved to him from the office hut and beckoned him inside. 'There's the man I was looking for,' he began and invited McQuaid to take a seat. 'The manor house you'll be starting next week?'

'Should be,' McQuaid replied.

'Deadlines, Ger, deadlines. Can you give me the firm that you'll be there Monday? Paddy and his men moved in today. It's a total mess.' Jack sighed, leaning back in his chair.

'Monday it is,' McQuaid agreed.

Jack rested his hands upon his large stomach and smiled at the news.

'Was Kane in today?' McQuaid questioned, now leaning in closer.

'No, no sign of John today,' said Jack earnestly. 'I barely see him myself.'

'Just,' said McQuaid.

'Just,' said Jack.

Kane had not been seen on site since the auction. He would have to appear soon, McQuaid thought. Men would need money soon. Grumbles and rumours had started to spread. And McQuaid himself needed to pay Limerick for his own house and buy more materials for Ballymahon. He had more at stake than Paddy and the others, who could weather the wait with their own wealth, and so much now depended on these next few weeks and this next cheque. Begley had said Kane was rotten with money; well, if that was the case he would be happy to smell the stink.

'Well, you know your business with the manor, I dare say,' said Jack, breaking the silence.

'I do,' McQuaid said, and taking this as his cue to leave, walked out the door.

'Oh,' called Jack as he stepped outside. 'That stuff with Willy, it was a bad business. How is he?'

'He'll live.'

'Grand, we'll say no more about it so,' said Jack and returned to his paperwork.

McQuaid walked towards the manor house, past the laurels and the willows, by the front lawn and the golf course. He could hear the drills working inside as he approached the main door.

Paddy Reilly sat on the floor of the ballroom surrounded by copper piping, schematics and tools, his legs splayed out in front of him, toes upturned, like a child in a playpen.

'You're in,' said McQuaid.

'I am, though I'd rather be out,' said Reilly from the floor.

'Ah, but doesn't the big house look well under you,' said McQuaid.

'It'd suit me better if it wasn't as fucked as it is, bad luck and all,' said Reilly. 'You're to start Monday, I hear?'

'So they say.'

'How is your house going?' Reilly asked.

'They're blocking it now,' said McQuaid as he lit what must have been his twentieth cigarette of the day. He threw the empty box on the floor and walked towards the bay window.

From here he could see the entirety of Birchview and all its ripped glory.

'They're going to build a few lakes,' he said, pointing with his cigarette towards the golf course.

'I heard that,' said Reilly indifferently.

'Some change,' said McQuaid, and he let the smoke seep from his nostrils.

'There's always change.'

He looked at his watch; it was nearly five. He'd call Declan and see how things were progressing at Goldsmith Drive. John could finish here.

He would go for a pint this evening as he had fallen into the fashion of doing each night. Always alone since the accident, he needed and wanted it that way.

31
McQuaid

The weekend brought no rest, only the realisation that Monday was a day closer. Sunday and mass seemed paltry, seemed pale beside all he had to do. He was filled with a nervous energy, sleep was only a chore that had to be done, had to be trudged through before work could begin again.

Monday came as it always did and he looked at his work clothes laid out on the bed like some wedding suit and oh how he was married to them, to the work, to the job, to the New Ireland, he supposed.

When he got to the manor house, Paddy Reilly and his sons were already inside. John and Pat waited by the front door as he had told them to do.

'Gut her, boys, gut her,' said McQuaid.

They took to the task with relish, with the satisfaction that only comes from destruction. Wires and conduit and switches torn apart, torn asunder. The mouldy wallpaper folded like cobwebs and fell to the floor in waves, layer upon layer as the years revealed themselves, until only the rotten wood and rafters remained. How long it had been, they remarked, since those rafters had seen sunlight, not since the sawmill.

She was coming, McQuaid told himself. He was calm in the rip and tear; it would be harder to wire, to begin again those new veins of lights and sockets, to put a new nervous system in a dead thing.

The floors wore the stains of a thousand dressers and beds. There were scrapes in the ballroom where heels had perhaps fallen drunkenly on some happy night, hollows in the bathroom where men had stood and shaved. An old floor could tell a story as much as a wall, as much as a painting, if only one knew the language of the squeak and echo of houses, where the groans and drips called back to previous owners and better days.

It had been beautiful once and it would be again. But never the same.

They cleared the last of the wallpaper from one room and a raft of insect bodies fell to the floor, the shell-like remnants of some spider's web where bodies had been hung, dangled, smashed and eventually turned to greasy mould.

At lunch they sat amongst the piles of debris and bird shit and ate in near silence. There was no tea and yet he found he had no taste for liquids, nor his sandwiches; eating had become as sleeping, only done because he had to, because it would seem odd not to.

They'd think you queer if you went to the site at two in the morning as you had wanted to do last night, Gerard. He knew that truth; however, it did not stop the want to work, the want to start alone in the night and have peace away from everyone. To not be bothered by calls or questions as he ripped at a wall or wired a light.

Working in the middle of the night, the poor lad has lost it, that's what they'll say, Ger Ger. I know, he told himself. And yet fuck them, fuck what they'd say. It would make no difference to Big Jack when he was there, so long as deadlines were met.

McQuaid threw the half-eaten sandwich to the ground and returned to work.

Paddy Reilly came and went through the building with lengths of copper piping; there was a caw and rattle of drills and kangos as Reilly broke through floors and walls. The house was alive with the sound of labour. In a few days it would look skeletal.

He wondered was the picture to be found still. There in the bedroom where Sinead and he had made love that Halloween night, and it the only witness to their happiness. He would look for it another day and see if he might find more details in its weathered face; perhaps he, Lefoyle, would have handled these problems better.

By the stairwell an old stove sat all green and fresh. It would be good money in scrap, John had remarked, but perhaps it would be left as an ornament, a place to keep brochures or indeed flowers from the gardens, the chrysanthemums and orchids, roses, daisies and birds of paradise. They would certainly brighten the place.

The cheap waste wire mounted in bundles as they cleared each room, metres and metres of it snaked its way to the skip. They pulled and pulled and yet still there was more.

When he'd finished the hallway he took a seat by the stained-glass window and rolled himself a cigarette.

'Oh, but you're in deep thought,' came a voice from a doorway.

He looked up and saw Reilly standing before him.

'Could I get one off you?' he asked, looking at the cigarette. McQuaid handed him the box and Reilly took a seat as he rolled himself a smoke.

'How's it going with yourselves?' he said distractedly as he prepared the tobacco.

'Not too bad,' McQuaid answered. 'Not too bad. And where are you in all this?' he said, looking now at Reilly.

'Oh, the kitchen today, a fucking maze, ripping with the hope of an end and a straight edge.'

'She's damp all right. Did it ever know water before?'

'Only the cunt of a bathroom, and a bad job it was too. God, but they must have been living in filth here.'

'Filth and grandeur,' McQuaid laughed.

'Something like that,' said Reilly. He handed back the smoke box and lit his cigarette. 'You'll never find till I'm at your house,' he said in glee as he blew out a smoke ring.

'No, not far away. Fox the roofer is coming to take a look at her this week,' McQuaid said.

'A right man,' affirmed Reilly.

They smoked a moment in silence. The occasional shout or clang of a machine echoed through the building; outside they could hear a van turning on the gravel driveway, and further still the beep of a digger in reverse on the golf course. The silence was warming, it was comfort. He and Reilly had come to such ease with each other now, to a place beyond bullshit, beyond idle talk.

He smiled at him and Reilly returned it with a big toothy grin and they puffed away like schoolboys.

'How are youse holding up after that accident?' Reilly asked in a moment of candour.

'Ah, Willy is on the mend. He'll be out of the hospital in a few days,' McQuaid replied.

'But how are *you* holding up?' said Reilly, turning to him now.

McQuaid paused a moment. Reilly was the first to ask of him how he was faring in all this.

'I'm okay, I suppose,' he answered truthfully.

'I thought so. We'll go for a pint one of the evenings and have a chat,' said Reilly paternally.

'I'd like that.'

'Good,' said Reilly and nodded in approval.

They ended their break thus as the bay window shone bright and lit the room with the dead glow of winter. Reilly excused himself and returned to work.

John and Pat finished the last room and they brought the rubbish to the skip. McQuaid swept the floors and breathed a sigh of relief as the gutting came to a close for the day.

He was tired as he sat into the van for the drive home, so tired and yet could not find rest. The house plans stuck out from beneath the passenger seat but he did not wish to see them.

You'll have to call Sinead. You miss her, Ger Ger. But it was hard to dredge courage from a well that was all but dry. And the words, oh the words, he could not find them, never could. Lord but he had the feelings.

'Jesus, I've an awful amount of love to give you,' he had once remarked to her. It was these feelings that seemed to propel him forward like a hurricane, it was like this for all the men on the site indeed and their feelings. They were the real romantics, on tractors and diggers and lorries. There was more passion to a 'fuck' or 'gawd' or 'bollox' than any latte and talk of kabbalah by those cunts in Dublin or Galway. They might be the cultured people but weren't we the culture, he mused. No one wrote songs about Irish studies lecturers but they wrote plays about the ordinary working man because, because for all they said that was unsaid, their actions spoke a thousand words, stanzas of brick and wire and loneliness, and dreams, dreams of betterment. A drunken bollox crying in the middle of the night for the village he had left, not because he missed it but because he loved the place so much it was a part of him. And his forced departure for want of work was worse than any death.

He wouldn't want a child of his to have to chase wires for the rest of his life. He would want him to go to college and get a handy number in the civil service, finish at four in the afternoon, walk the dog and sleep in on weekends.

A son, what would he look like now, he thought. Would he have Sinead's eyes? That imaginary boy who had once been so vivid had begun to fade; he no longer looked like anyone, only the ghost of a wish. Everything starts as a dream, he thought, but when a dream dies, where does it go?

He coughed dryly and thought he felt a tear, but it was only the fags, he told himself, it was only the fags.

32
Lefoyle

1838

They had been marching past the front gate all morning, since before dawn. Banners and placards held high in a joyous blood chorus. *Ireland for the Irish* and *Repeal and Separation*, they read. Lefoyle watched them on his walk, stopped, stared, but their shouts only grew louder at the sight of him. Him the *enemy*.

And what were they marching to? Why, to him of course, that brigand, that dervish O'Connell, the rotund peasant king. The priests had marshalled the crowds for his arrival. It had been weeks in the making, Bishop Murray presiding over it all and the great wound that was Harmon James to speak before the monster meeting.

They had not spoken since that night in the Market Hotel when the act of *Et tu* had occurred. How long had that been; it numbered in years now, he thought.

The loss of a friend was a strange thing; death brought only a physical barrier, but betrayal in all its malicious forms carried much more, a wounding to the soul. For indeed it had been a wounding that night when his friends had turned against him, against law and order. That night a death had occurred. And long ago as it had been, as much as he had aged and his hair had faded to grey, he seemed unable to find peace.

He turned his face and walked back to the house. The grounds had returned to much of their former glory. The new tract of land in the south of the county had proved a worthy investment. Its rents had helped do much around Birchview. He stopped a moment to fix his belt and in the silence watched as a kestrel chased a small bird across the sky. From the stables to the servants' quarters their dance of fluid death moved. He held his breath as the small bird disappeared and he thought it all done, only to see it emerge once again defiantly and zip and dart its way back to flight. The kestrel dived once more and stung its talons into the other bird's back but not seeing its descent was so quick, both now crashed to the ground and were lost to his view. He walked towards the stables to find the victor but there was no sign of either. Perhaps their quarrel was far from over.

A shout came again from the road. The staff did not look at him directly today, and the servant girls did what they could to keep him happy and his mind away from the massing crowds.

More than one hundred thousand were to gather, he had heard said, indeed some of the workmen had asked for the day off; it was better to let them go than have them festering in the yards, brewing trouble. He had heard of the fears of Ballymahon, their petition for a garrison to be assembled; he would not be burned out of his home by the very men he clothed and fed. No, it was better to let them go, tire themselves out and return the next day ready to work. O'Connell would not pay them a wage, and freedom and scenery did not make for a full stomach.

Lady Bond was to visit, good sweet Maggie, she who had the measure of men. He would have the drawing room made ready and they might enjoy a light supper. The weather this May had been good, so perhaps they could dine outside under the willow. It would provide a distraction from the crowds at least.

By times he heard shouts and cries: 'England's cause is Ireland's curse' and 'The green is coming.' But mostly they just walked by silently, afraid to speak, afraid to show their true feelings in case it might be reported back.

They had come from as far as Meath, the reports had said. He would not set foot in Longford town this day. Would not even grace the same street as that man, he who would uproot all that had been done. It would be Murphy and Reilly and Connor in place of the old names of Rutledge and Foster, and yes, Lefoyle too. But little would change: there would always be a ruling order, always a poor. A real revolution was not fought with swords or muskets, a real revolution was what happened after the dust had settled and bureaucracy must work again. No, little would change, only a new elite of former butchers and publicans and priests.

Lady Bond's carriage arrived at three o'clock. He met her at the front door. 'My dear, how was your journey?' he asked, clasping her hands.

'Long, Henry, long and exhausting, crowds as far back as Ballinalee,' she replied.

'Droves?'

'Droves,' she said, shaking her head in emphasis. 'Haydn himself wouldn't gather so many.'

'And more's the pity, his notes would be lost on that lot,' laughed Lefoyle. He took her by the arm and led her inside.

Tea was served and the maid welcomed her ladyship with great courtesy.

'Thank you,' she replied and took a gentle sip from her cup, her long fingers delicately holding the handle.

'Mam,' murmured the maid and left the room.

'So, how are things in Mostrim?' enquired Lefoyle.

'It goes as it ever did, Henry, slowly, though this monster meeting business is a great worry. They don't drink any more, they march, they eulogise, they gather.'

'Temperance is ninety-eight reborn quietly,' said Lefoyle solemnly.

'Has he arrived yet?' she asked.

'No, not until this evening, I'm told.'

'That he may never come,' she returned and drained her cup.

Lefoyle reached for the teapot, looking at her questioningly, to which she waved her hand in decline.

'I think perhaps we might go for a walk, you can show me your grounds,' said Maggie.

'It is mostly the same.'

'Well then, I would love to see your flowers and you can tell me your news.'

They sauntered through the yard and grounds. It had turned into a fine day, no clouds, no sign of rain, and the grass was soft and fresh underfoot.

'I find great pleasure in walking, Henry. It grows the older I get. Lord knows we do it every day, to the parlour, to the bedroom, but the act of a social walk is all the greater. To walk for pleasure alone, for no other reason. Do you follow?'

'I do indeed. I myself walk the grounds each day for exercise.'

'Ah, but there you have it, a purpose already. No, Henry, the social walk is one which has no aim, no exercise in mind, to walk to simply enjoy, and one can take in nature all the more.'

'I take it in all the same.'

'I'm sure you do.'

They walked by the monkey puzzle, by the beech trees, by the willows that curled around the river. A lone hare watched from the front lawn until they came too close and then it broke, darting back to its warren.

The cadence of their speech was interrupted at times by shouts from the roadside. The crowds were still marching by.

'Things are good in Dublin?' she asked.

'They are at a stalemate. Every day we lose and we gain, it is a stock exchange this politics.'

'Have you dreamed lately, Henry?'

'Of Rose?' he asked.

'Yes, Rose,' she said.

'From time to time I think of her in my dreams. We are almost as long separated by the eternal as we were together.'

'They say that if one doesn't dream of the dead at their passing it means they are at peace.'

'Then she must be at peace,' said Lefoyle, who often missed his wife's presence on wintry nights. 'And you, Maggie, do you dream?'

'I do, but it is a haunting in a way, to wake up to a world of difference: left has become right, black white, mirrors show what is on the interior. It is a recurring fantasy, but I pay it no mind, for I find my hair still grows on my head and not my teeth when I wake.' She laughed.

Still the shouts came from the road, they grew louder as the day wore on. Temperance might have lost its appeal, he thought. One could not expect so large a gathering and no drink to be taken. It would end in rows as it always did.

'They will have mass for him, of course,' said Maggie after a time.

'Of course,' he agreed.

'As if it were Solomon himself,' she said and they both laughed.

Crossing the front lawn towards the house, Lefoyle suggested they take a light supper inside. The noise of the crowds outside would interfere too greatly with any attempt to dine under the willow. Two chickens had been killed that morning, and there would be a salad of fresh lettuce and some tomatoes from his greenhouse.

'How sweet these tomatoes are,' she complimented him as they began to dine.

He watched her poise as she nibbled on the various portions of her supper. Fine woman that she was, she had been brought up not to chew in the company of men. She put down her knife and fork, patted her lips with a napkin, and smiled in satisfaction at him.

'Shall we repair to the drawing room, you'll take a sherry or perhaps something stronger?' he enquired, rising from the table.

'A sherry will do nicely, Henry.' She smiled and followed him.

He poured two glasses from the decanter, the liquid rolling into the crystal with twists and turns like a small whirlpool. The shouts from the road grew louder now, sustained for minutes on end.

'Ghastly noise that, will it ever stop?'

'Here's to it stopping,' he said and raised his glass in a toast.

'It will be goodnight to Mostrim if ever they should be in charge. I know it is best to endure patiently whatever God has in store and yet we shall be stranded and alone if all fails,' said Maggie quietly, speaking as if to herself. She had not yet tasted her drink, he noticed, her eyes set on the floor, melancholy descending on her.

Still the shouts came from the road.

'Good Lord, but that's a horrid noise,' said Lady Bond again, more defiantly now.

'Your drink, Maggie,' he indicated. 'And perhaps you would give us a song?' he added, gesturing towards the piano. 'It's hardly used any more, I was never the player, that was Rose . . .' He stopped short, thinking of all the happy moments around that same piano, waltzes and foxtrots and singsongs too. He still had it tuned every year on her anniversary.

'Oh, I couldn't really,' she replied in false modesty.

'Well, it is either listen to the rabble or to ourselves. And your voice is much the sweeter. What was it they used to call you in your youth, the Mostrim cuckoo?' he said and raised his eyebrows in exaggerated good humour.

'The Mostrim *lark*, as you know full well. I never stole another's nest.'

'Ah, but you might have tried.'

'Trying and doing are quite different, you fiend.'

'Then play and let us hear the lark for old times' sake, play until *that* ceases,' he said.

'Very well, on the old terms I shall play,' and she moved towards the piano, ran her fingers across the keys, gaining the memory of the movements, of the touch, the feel of notes.

'Something cheerful, I think,' she said, looking up at Lefoyle, who stood by the mantelpiece.

'*Did you ever see a morn*
So dull and lack and grey
The snipe, the hen, the duck
Lay forlorn beneath the bay

But I don't mind, I pay no heed
For I'll be at the races in Kildare.
The races in Kildare, Oh
How they'll stop and stare at the races in Kildare,
The races in Kildare, oh how they'll stop and stare
At the races in Kildare!'

Her voice sang brightly and her fingers played a foxtrot to the words. She finished with much gusto and a flourish, at which they both laughed.

'Ah, the cuckoo returns!' said Lefoyle and clapped the mantel in mirth. 'As sweet as birdsong.'

Still the shouts came, through the glass, the curtains, over the mantel and the oil paintings.

'Perhaps another, a ballad?'

'One of Moore's perhaps?' she suggested after thinking for a time.

'Ah, but we have heard his rebel tones invoked too often of late,' he replied. 'No, I have a work, but I shall hardly remember it all,' he confessed.

He downed his drink, cleared his throat and stood as he had done as a schoolboy giving oratory, or as he might do in the courtroom in closing a case.

'*Even now*
If I see in my soul the citron-breasted fair one
Still gold-tinted, her face like our night stars,
Drawing unto her; her body beaten about with flame,
Wounded by the flaring spear of love,
My first of all by reason of her fresh years,
Then is my heart buried alive in snow.

Even now
If my girl with lotus eyes came to me again
Weary with the dear weight of young love,
Again I would give her to these starved twins of arms
And from her mouth drink down the heavy wine,
As a reeling pirate bee in fluttered ease
Steals up the honey from the nenuphar.

Even now
If I saw her lying all wide eyes
And with collyrium the indent of her cheek
Lengthened to the bright ear and her pale side
So suffering the fever of my distance,
Then would my love for her be ropes of flowers, and night
A black-haired lover on the breasts of day.

Even now
My eyes that hurry to see no more are painting, painting
Faces of my lost girl. O golden rings
That tap against cheeks of small magnolia leaves,
O whitest so soft parchment where
My poor divorced lips have written excellent
Stanzas of kisses, and will write no more.

Even now
Death sends me the flickering of powdery lids
Over wild eyes and the pity of her slim body
All broken up with the weariness of joy;
The little red flowers of her breasts to be my comfort
Moving above scarves, and for my sorrow
Wet crimson lips that once I marked as mine.

Even now
They chatter her weakness through the two bazaars
Who was so strong to love me. And small men
That buy and sell for silver being slaves
Crinkle the fat about their eyes; and yet
No Prince of the Cities of the Sea has taken her,
Leading to his grim bed. Little lonely one,
You cling to me as a garment clings; my girl.'

'I am at a loss to remember the rest, Maggie,' he said, shaking his head, and he could see the tears in her eyes, and his own moistened as they were.

'It does not matter,' she said softly after a moment of silence. 'That is an old piece. How marvellous.'

'From Sanskrit,' said Henry calmly.

'Old,' said Maggie simply.

'Old,' returned Lefoyle.

The shouts came again from the road.

'Quick, Maggie, play another; we shall drown out that which seeks to topple us,' said Lefoyle and laughed. He would take another drink and outlast these shouts. Tomorrow would come and they would have silence again.

33
McQuaid

They started a fire that evening with the remaining wallpaper and scrap from the manor. John giddily poured the petrol and watched as the flame swam up into the air, higher and higher, and then relaxed into a gentle warming glow.

'This shit is curling up like tissue paper,' said John as he held out his hands to warm them and laughed.

'Time wears anything down,' said Pat as he poured mugs of tea from his flask.

'True. Willy would've enjoyed this,' replied John.

The gutting work was finished and they would begin the wiring tomorrow. McQuaid looked over the blueprints: the openings, the partitions, the gauges and switches. The hardest part was yet to come, but they might as well enjoy this moment of immolation.

'Will you have a cup of tea?' they enquired, looking at McQuaid.

'No, I'm fine,' he said with a wave of his hand.

They all looked at him differently now, talked differently too, there was more concern and yet less concern in their voices.

Offering tea was in reality the subtle ask of 'Are you all right?' Nothing ever to be said outright.

A black smoke began to pour from the flames as plastic bottles and wrapping melted.

'Isn't this nice,' came a soft voice from behind them.

They turned around to see the slim figure of Rhian, the interior designer.

'Having a barbie, boys?' she asked, walking closer.

'Just burning a bit of rubbish,' said Pat awkwardly.

McQuaid invited her to sit and pushed an upturned bucket towards her.

'I'd rather like to keep this dress,' smiled Rhian, running her fingers over the black lace.

'Suit yourself,' he replied.

After hovering for a moment, she gingerly lowered herself to the bucket.

'Would Mr Saint Laurent approve of you coming onto a building site in such finery?'

'I should think he'd admire the guts it took to wear it,' she retorted and smiled curiously at him. 'Cig?' she offered.

He rolled up the blueprints and placed them on the ground. Turned to her and took the cigarette. 'You're here for the manor, I suppose?' he asked lazily.

'Yes, we did a small installation for the auction but now it's the real thing. The Irish country house rises again.'

'At least we didn't burn this one.'

He watched her a moment as the flames played across her face, highlighting her lipstick, her mascara, her freshly washed hair. And revealed something different in her from the last time they had met, her eyes more inviting perhaps.

'I haven't been upstairs and I wondered if you might be able to show me around,' she continued.

'Jack said I would, I suppose.'

'He did.'

He coughed, reluctantly dusted his knees, and stood up. 'I can take you now if you like,' he said.

She consented, excused herself to the other men, and the two of them walked towards the manor. He led her through the house, explaining what they were doing and how long was left on each area. He pointed out the ceilings and explained that the moulding was damaged in parts but there were efforts underway to salvage the ornate swirls and baroque twist of ivy and oak. She nodded her head in approval and paused at the smoke-stained marble fireplaces, touching them reverently.

They strolled the house for pleasure now it seemed, as she in turn explained her plans and gave him insights into the unnoticed beauty of the doric and ionic columns in the ballroom and great hall.

They ascended a flight of stairs towards the bedrooms. Through the rubble and debris and cobwebs they moved, and again she ran her hands along the walls and rails, stopping to evoke a colour or mood. At the final landing, Rhian tripped on a broken board but he caught her in his arms before she could fall.

His breath was heavy in the quick movement. They locked eyes for a brief moment but he returned her to herself forthwith.

'There's a magic to this place,' she said, marvelling at the endless corridors and rooms, her red lips slightly agape.

She diverged from their path and walked into a circular room. 'What's this place?'

He explained that it was the nursery and that as they had cleared the wallpaper a scene of clouds and trees had been exposed on the wall before the plaster crumbled and fell.

'Yellow,' she said, closing her eyes. 'This room needs yellow.'

'It needs plaster first,' he laughed briefly.

'Well, that too,' she conceded.

They moved further through the children's bedrooms. It was a sort of exploring, he thought, for there were still places he had not yet seen in the cavernous building.

They entered the master bedroom, empty now, the remnants of a headboard fixed to the wall all that was left. The painting of Lefoyle was indeed gone, for McQuaid had cleared this very room himself.

'This is where he slept, isn't it?' asked Rhian.

'Who, Lefoyle? I think so,' McQuaid answered.

In its sheer bareness, there was a sadness to the place, all dull and grey, like a thing that had never been loved, only lived in. So much of the house was decrepit, dying and decaying. The sadness was not Lefoyle's, nor his descendants', but an absence of something McQuaid could not pinpoint.

'This room needs a lot of light,' Rhian said slowly.

'We can have spots on the ceiling, or add a chandelier,' he suggested.

Rhian walked to the window and opened the wooden shutters. Outside he could see the fields and trees, and the cars as they passed by on the road.

Breathing in the window's light, Rhian turned to him, an odd smirk on her face. 'What did you think of me when we first met?' she asked.

'Think of you?' he stumbled.

'Yes.'

'I thought nothing, it was work, I had to show you around . . . I . . .' and he trailed off into an awkward silence.

'That was work, yes, but what did you think of *me*?'

'I, I thought you dressed nice,' he said with a subtle gesture towards her clothes.

'Yes,' she encouraged.

'And, well, I thought, I thought you were a bit mad, if you really ask me, with all the colours and the rooms,' he laughed and then cursed himself for having said so much. 'I mean . . .' He found he was nervous and sweating. It would be a welcome feeling if one woman did not make him nervous these days.

'It was funny, though.' She laughed.

McQuaid relaxed and scratched the back of his head; a smirk had grown across his own face he could not suppress. 'It was,' he said and they both smiled.

Moving so the light of the window played on her face once more, she continued. 'Do you think I'm nice?'

'You're . . .' he began, knowing his cheeks must surely be a bright red.

This is a moral ambush, Ger. It's not, he told himself, and stuttered as he tried to find the words. *You're here in the manor house with a woman, a woman, Ger, not a girl like Sinead.*

He breathed out in nervousness and tried to dismiss the thoughts from his mind. He tried to find the words to talk to her honestly, and a clarity of passion began to descend, and his darker thoughts were quieter now, easing themselves away into the distance.

Tell her if you want.

'You're, you're beautiful,' he said and found the words were not so hard to say, and so he repeated them. 'The beautiful Rhian.' The syllables did not carry with them the guilt of Sinead and he found he could say them again and again. And he thought not of her now but of all the weeks and months of the absence of her affection.

Rhian smiled and fixed her hair; she walked towards him purposefully, her eyes unblinking, and kissed him. Her lips so soft to the touch and he wondered when he had last been kissed like this. She kissed him again and how sweet the rhyme of her skin was.

It was his turn now and he kissed her with the force of pent-up desire, of lonely nights and bedtimes and the solitude of all those hours alone in the van each day. He sucked upon her lips and savoured them. He graced her unfamiliar tongue and breathed in her smell. And found in the nucleus of this house the remnants of his passion.

The sounds of the machinery and men below receded and there was only their heavy breath and the movement of hands over fabric.

He blushed and laughed. He took a step back and yet she came closer and he did not refuse, she would give herself to him here in this old house if he wanted.

'I . . .' he began.

'You have someone,' she said.

'I, well, sort of . . .' he said and the emotion of passion turned to water in his eyes. He was not crying, he told himself, and yet he knew she could see his vulnerability clearly. And he went to tell her of Sinead but she silenced him with a wave.

'But it is at an ending?' she asked calmly, to which he nodded in assent.

'I want to be here for you,' she said and he felt her willingness to be his pillar.

'You do?' he said and found her wiping the tears from his cheeks.

For they were tears, and with each of her kisses waves of loss came upon him, washed over him; Willy and Sinead and the work and the worry of money came forth, only to fall away in her arms.

But Sinead, he thought now, this wasn't right. He had a duty to her, he told himself. He would have left if he were not so shocked. The only woman on the building site and here he was kissing her and to do more if he wished, and wished he did. The denial now seemed only more an invitation to his loins, the guilt was an ecstasy in this moment. And the regret, the regret would come, but let it be later, her lips seemed to say.

She undid her dress and let it fall to the floor silkily. She stood before him now in her nakedness. Her smell filled him and he moved towards her, embracing her, their tongues a swirl of lovers, his clasp of her nectarine bottom, so soft and white. They lay on the floor and he entered her, and how different she felt, how different to Sinead, and yet the sensation, that sensation which drove men to do anything, filled him with a vividness and sensuality.

They made love wildly there in the room where he had taken Sinead so long ago, and yet all was different, utterly different. They lay on the ground in their skin amongst the wattle walls and flaking plaster, they lay there until such time as their surroundings took shape again, and he looked upon her love-smeared makeup and smiled.

'I . . .' he began but found no words.

'It's okay,' she said and began to get dressed.

They gathered their belongings and returned to their clothes.

'Here is my number,' she said and handed him her card. 'Red is the colour for this room, rose-blossom red,' she added, and smiled as she backed out the door.

He fixed himself, tied his boots and wrapped his toolbelt around him. He felt alive, and yet, and yet nothing, he mused. He would enjoy this moment over all the clamorous ones of recent weeks. He looked at her card and placed it in his shirt pocket.

The day was nearly over, he would go for a pint, and for the first time in so long he felt he might enjoy it. This evening at least his worries could stay amongst the blackened ruins of Birchview Manor.

34
McQuaid

'Willy is coming out of the hospital.'

'What?'

'Willy is coming out today,' Declan repeated to him over the phone.

'Are you serious?' McQuaid held the mobile closer to his ear. He took a step outside and listened closely.

'He called me this morning to say so,' said Declan.

'Jesus, but that's great news,' McQuaid said.

And it was, it was the best news he had heard in days, weeks even. Ballymahon was at a near standstill, the Polish had flatly refused to work with Declan, and try as he might, he was not able to manage the task. If Willy came back they might listen, they might reconvene on the old terms. They might get the fixing finished and at last some long-overdue money might roll into that drained account.

'I can't believe that. He didn't call me,' McQuaid said.

'Ah well, he probably thought the one call would do,' replied Declan.

'True enough,' McQuaid said absentmindedly. And wondered why the one had not been to him. 'I'll come over to Ballymahon today, and we'll see if we can't get a handle on these lads.'

'That would be great,' said Declan.

McQuaid hung up the phone and breathed out forcefully.

The clangs and rattles of the manor echoed around him, as John and Pat moved with wires and drill through the rooms. He had spent the better part of the day inside the old partition walls, chasing, boring, ripping, with the hope of bringing light to the floor by evening.

The pressures of work had steadily built, the wages and invoices for materials had mounted, and yet Rhian had made him forget those worries. They had met the last few evenings, made love on the site or in her car, always in secret places as secret lovers do. There was a thrill to the affair which both shared. He was, however, still with and not with Sinead. They had spoken on the phone, texted occasionally, but they had not brought themselves to meet, not yet at least.

He turned to walk inside and the manor seemed not so gloomy, not so forlorn; perhaps it had been the news of Willy or the texts from Rhian that had flown throughout the day. She had sent him a passionate picture in the afternoon: her body exposed in a sunlit room, pink and raw. The words underneath had read: *Come fuck me.*

He found too he could look upon the plans for his house again and had taken to visiting the site once more. Fox the roofer had all but finished and the wiring could begin soon after. He had begun himself, in ways, to create a new dream, a dream of Rhian and the house. It was no longer Sinead who looked out upon Cairn Hill with him but she. After all, she had said she was there for him, there for him in everything he did. So why not this, he thought. Why not the house and the land and the car?

He had tried hard not to see Rhian, for he knew it was wrong. Why could he not talk with Sinead, she supported him, still he knew this, she was his rock, and yet he would have a new rock now, a new foundation. Sinead was lost to him.

And if he were lost to himself, he mused, at least he might be lost inside Rhian. And there was a comfort in that. Wasn't there?

You might want to get back to yourself there, Ger. He would, he was. He wiped the sweat from his brow and took up his drill again. The deadlines had to be met. He would finish the drawing room and run the different gauge wires through its walls and rafters.

He sang to himself as he picked up the grey cables.

'*Twist the knife*
Because you hate your life
My life you want to spoil
I'm never going to let
Your negative vibes and comments
Get through to my psyche and cripple me
I'm never going to let
Your negative vibes and comments
Get through to my psyche and cripple me
I never will forget
The suffering that my people went through
In my country and overseas.'

'You're looking happy with yourself,' said Paddy Reilly from the door opening, he had been listening to him sing.

'Ah, I'm okay, can't a man have a sing, it's a decent day,' McQuaid replied.

'He can,' said Reilly.

'A decent day,' McQuaid repeated, affirming himself.

'How is the work with the designer going?' asked Reilly slowly.

'Oh, I showed her around, not much to it, paints and lights.'

'I see,' said Reilly, examining the dry rot in the door frame. 'You have to finish one job before you start another.'

'What?'

'Moving from the big room to the nursery today, aren't you?' said Reilly in explanation.

'Oh right, oh yeah, they're all linked, it shouldn't be too big of a job,' said McQuaid, no longer sure what they were talking about.

Reilly was quiet and refused a cigarette, saying he was trying to cut down.

'I better get back to work,' said McQuaid awkwardly.

'You better so,' said Reilly solemnly.

'Will we take that pint this evening?' McQuaid enquired.

'Tomorrow,' said Reilly and walked back to the boiler room.

McQuaid returned to work. What had Reilly been saying? It was more than talk of work, he felt. Ah, the bollox, what did he know? Finish one thing before you start another. Didn't he know that. He returned to his song and work. He would finish this room and then go to Ballymahon to see Declan.

He packed up the tools and told John he would be in the pub this evening if they wanted to join. The men declined, saying they were tired and needed the rest.

By four he was on the long journey to Ballymahon; he would drop more materials and see if they might put manners on the new men. Now that Willy was out, things could be different.

As he approached the site, a large traffic light stood in his path. The council had broken open the road to repair a burst water main and the vehicles would have to wait. He cursed to himself at the slowdown and slapped the steering wheel in frustration.

'What's going on? What's the hold-up?' he shouted to one of the council workers after what must have been fifteen minutes of waiting.

The man informed him that the digger was burst and they would just have to wait.

'Fucking burst, fucking burst, can't you see there are people who need to get where they're going?'

'Nothing I can do about it,' the man replied and promptly walked back towards his colleagues, leaving McQuaid stuck behind two cars.

The man had not even the decency to take his anger, he thought, only a wash of indifference. He cursed again and decided he would get out of the van to stretch his legs. Reilly's comments had festered in him and he now felt a wave of anger rise. He just wanted to get to Ballymahon, talk to Declan and find out when Willy would be back at work. Why were things always so hard? In a moment of rage he kicked out at his van and dented the sliding door with his heavy work boots.

'Are you all right?' a lorry driver asked from the vehicle behind him.

'Arra, fuck off, will you,' McQuaid said.

'Fuck you and the horse you came in on,' the driver replied and rolled up his window.

McQuaid felt the frustration grow inside himself. He tried to sing again and think of Rhian.

'I'm never going to let
Your negative vibes and comments
Get through to my psyche . . .'

But the words did not help now. Suddenly cars began to honk. He tried to mime the words over the vehicle engines.

'Will you get in your fucking van, we're moving,' the lorry driver shouted.

'Fuck you,' McQuaid spat and waited now a few moments. If the council was going to make him wait, he would make them wait.

The road worker returned down the line in search of the hold-up and source of commotion.

'What's going on here, the digger is working again there,' he explained, looking at McQuaid singing on the side of the road. 'We're moving,' he said, softly touching him on the shoulder.

'All right, all right, I'm going, I'm going,' McQuaid snapped and sulkily sat back into the van.

Red, yellow, green.

You might want to watch yourself there. Time to keep the head down, son. A throb grew in his stomach as it had done these last few weeks. He ignored it, telling himself it would pass. He would get to the site, sort things out with Declan and have a pint.

Eventually the vehicles made their slow procession past the roadworks. After some twenty minutes he approached Ballymahon and found Declan explaining to Majus the need for the junction boxes to be labelled.

'Is everything good here?' he said as he walked into the building.

'Fine, we're fine,' said Declan.

'We not fine, boss, I cannot work with Declan, he knows nothing,' Majus said.

'What's the problem?'

'He tells me to do house number four but I do not want to work with Andrew and he is there.'

'And what's the problem with Andrew then, eh?'

'Andrew not neat, his work is messy, I can't work with man like that,' Majus said.

McQuaid sighed and rolled himself a cigarette. 'Fucken nuisances, that's what you all are.'

'What?' Majus asked, straining to understand his words.

'Nothing, nothing.' It would be easier to be rid of them all, and yet he could not find men at such short notice. No, it was better to lead from the front.

'Majus, I tell you what, you work with me in the manor and John will come work here. Is that all right for everyone?'

The men agreed.

'And don't let me hear of any fighting at the manor or it's the fucking road for all of you,' he continued.

'No fights,' said Majus, offering his hands in peace.

McQuaid dismissed the men and inspected the work. It was sloppy, that could not be denied. He scratched his head and tried to think how the work might be remedied. Perhaps this move would bring peace to the job. He was, he could admit, not giving it his full attention. And with that had come mistakes, and perhaps word might spread of the sloppiness.

He called Declan over and they spoke in confidence.

'Is it any better here?'

'I don't know,' said Declan, and he could see the strain growing on the young man's face.

'Well, what about Willy, so he's coming out of hospital?'

'He is, thank God,' said Declan and smiled.

'Well, that is a relief,' McQuaid agreed. 'So did he say when he'll be back at work?'

'At work?'

'Yeah, at work, to take the reins back here.'

'But . . .' stammered Declan.

'But what? This is clearly too much for you,' McQuaid said.

'It is, but, but . . .'

'But what, Dec?'

'But Willy isn't coming back to work. He just got out of the hospital, he has to do physio for three months, I thought you knew that.'

'You mean he's not coming back?' said McQuaid in confusion now.

'Yeah, I mean I was ringing to tell you the good news that he was out, but he's barely able to move his leg, he won't be at work for a long time,' said Declan.

'Oh . . . right.'

'I thought you knew that.'

'Oh, I did, I did,' McQuaid lied and cursed himself for having been so stupid as to think Willy might return to him. 'So, three months, is it?'

'About that, he says.'

'Right,' he said and spat on the ground.

You thought it was all green lights from here on, Ger me auld son. We're still in that traffic jam, aren't we, he returned. *Ah, sort of. But she'll come green in time.*

He told Majus to meet him at the manor tomorrow and left shortly after.

35
Neary

'What's a recession?' said Neary again for what must have been the fifth time that evening.

'Well, it's, it's when something recedes, isn't it,' said Limerick from the far end of the counter as he sipped his pint.

'Yeah, but what does it mean?' returned Neary.

'Ah, shor fuck sake, man, weren't you here in the eighties? It's that sort of thing, the banks aren't in order,' said Limerick.

'Hmm,' said Neary, wiping his moustache. 'But how, how will it affect us?'

'Well, it won't affect you,' said the Patch Riordan as he swished his half one in the glass.

'No, I suppose not,' said Neary with thoughts on his social. 'But these stocks falling, the run on the banks, that's not right like,' he said as an afterthought.

'No, it's not right,' said Limerick. 'Not like a banker to run,' he added with mirth.

'But a run on the banks, what does that mean like?' said Neary.

'Ah, Jaysus, Neary, you're in here more than us, and the telly on all the time. Paul, Paul,' called Limerick to the barman. 'Is this man in here most days?'

'He is,' said Paul in his thick drawl.

'And does he watch the telly when he's in?'

'He does.'

'The news?'

'When it's on,' said Paul as he poured another round for the men; they never asked for another round but he knew them well now, knew their drinks, a Guinness for Limerick, a half one for Patch and Heineken for Neary.

'Well, that's enough said, isn't it,' said Limerick. 'Ann and Brian and the rest of the RTÉ crowd will have you well filled in.'

'They do,' said Neary. 'But,' he began, scratching his chin again. 'But like that's only half the truth, I mean where did it come from? One minute the place is going like the clappers and suddenly we have to worry, some are saying we're fucked like, but then I hear the crowd in the Dáil and you'd think it was only a flat tyre we had.'

'Someone hand Neary a pump, he's going to fix it.'

'Well now, I didn't say that, but by God I could. Fix her right up I could.'

The men goaded Neary, waiting to hear his bar stool epitaph on the state of the nation. For it was in a right state, it was all they talked of any more, banks and finance and economists. These men that politics had never bothered in the last ten years, who did not have to think about it, that was another's concern, and suddenly they had to have an opinion, one that went beyond the old party lines. It was no longer blueshirts and Fianna Fáilers, it was real thoughts and opinions.

'Well, a banking system is a system, like,' began Neary.

The men nodded silently.

'Well, a system has gears and cogs and that. So if you have a breakdown you look for the problem and you fix it, a new chain like, a bit of an oil and you're away.'

'But it's more than that, Neary,' said the Patch.

'This system, like . . . it's like mass,' Neary said with an emphasis of the hand, and paused.

Paul smiled from behind the bar and raised his eyes to Limerick.

'Mass and money are a bit the same.' Neary reached into his pocket to pay for his pint. 'This note, it's like holy communion like, you have to believe that it has value, it's only bread until the priest consecrates it, and this is only paper until you believe in it.'

'You believe it's God, is it?' said the Patch snidely.

'Shut up there, Riordan, we haven't seen you at mass in a long time,' said Limerick. 'Go on, Neary,' he said softly.

'Well, like the mass and the money like. The paper, you have to believe the paper has a value, and Paul there has to believe it has a value, and the bank has to believe it has a value. Even though it's only *paper* like.'

He was silent for a moment, scratched his chin and sighed. 'I mean a banking system is an act of faith, isn't it?' he asked, looking around the pub. 'And, well, it's only bread until the priest says the words and you believe it's the flesh. So did they stop believing? Is that it?' he asked and then shook his head.

'Happy are those who have not seen and yet believe,' said Paul solemnly.

'I always thought Jesus must have been horrid fat to give up the flesh each Sunday and still have more for next week,' said Limerick.

'Gluttony,' cooed the Patch.

Neary scratched his head. He had watched the news every day these last few weeks, but it was still confusing. The banks weren't good but they said they were. The boom was over but everyone was still driving around in their Land Rovers, houses were still being built, there was still lots of money.

It had passed him by in a way, this boom; he had sold a few sites, who hadn't. But he hadn't lost the run of himself, he still lived in the old cottage that had belonged to his mother, still kept the ten cows and got the social on a Friday. He was consubstantial with the old ways, he thought.

'This guarantee,' he said. 'Is it to guarantee there'll be money in the ATMs? Or to guarantee that the money will still be worth something?'

'Bit of both, I suppose,' said Limerick.

'I mean, would we ever wake up and we wouldn't have money?'

'Didn't we do fine without it for a long time?' said Paul.

'But the money, the boom money, where did that come from?'

'Computers and that,' said Limerick. 'All them Intels.'

'And Europe,' added the Patch.

'We earned it, didn't we?' said Paul.

'Neary didn't,' said the Patch.

Neary scratched his head again. It was a problem he had been thinking of, in the fields, on his bicycle ride to the pub, at mass. Where had it come from? And where was it going now? Like a flight of the earls, they might wake up to nothing.

'Neary, I'll tell you now, you needn't worry yourself about that, them bucks in Dublin will sort it out, we've never been as well off, work and a house for everyone, and no one has to leave any more. You only go away for a holiday these days.'

'I suppose so,' said Neary. 'Do you see any signs of a slow-down?' he asked Limerick.

'I'm as busy as I was last year.'

'So there's no sign of a slowdown?'

'Well, I think in Dublin they're slowing up a bit, no harm mind, they're rotten with houses up there.'

'What would happen if it did slow up? If it went arseways?'

'We'd get by. America is doing all right and two of their banks closed.'

'Will ours close?'

'No, isn't this what all the talk is about, to stop them closing, they'll guarantee the money so that whole show keeps going,' said Limerick with confidence.

'Bertie and his crowd,' said the Patch.

'It was them that brought the boom,' said Limerick.

'They took enough out of it,' returned Patch with a rat-like smile.

'I didn't see your boys complain when they got the raise.'

'Would the foreigners have something to do with it?' said Neary.

'Who?'

'The Polish, the blacks like.'

'Aren't the Poles like us? They're here working same as we always did.'

'But the money is going home back to Poland.'

'Same as when we were in England,' replied Limerick, who would not go against the Polish; many of his men were from the east, they were rough but they were workers.

'Do the blacks work?' asked Neary.

'They go to mass. I do see them at the cathedral, ones with big transport box arses.'

'They're dressed well enough, shor, they must be working.'

'Still and all, this bust . . .' said Neary as he finished the last of his pint. The suds rolled down the glass.

'Happy are those who have not seen and yet believe,' repeated Paul and smiled.

'Men, I'll be seeing ya,' said Neary. He would cycle home in the dusk; a cow was near calving, she might drop tonight under the pale fluorescent light of the byre.

The banking system wouldn't stop nature, he told himself, but it would still be a defeat to lose the calf; he'd sit out in the shed tonight as he did on those nights.

'An awful haveral of a man,' said Paul to the remaining few.

'A bollox,' said the Patch.

'Give us another one, Paul,' said Limerick and silence resumed in the bar.

36
McQuaid

Rhian had arrived at the site unannounced and told him to get his things. She had bought a dozen fresh Galway oysters, a bottle of wine and some sourdough.

'I thought we might have an impromptu picnic,' she explained as he sat into her small sporty car.

'A picnic in this weather?'

'I provide the food, you provide the venue,' she laughed and touched him.

McQuaid thought for a moment; perhaps he might show her his house. Fox the roofer had texted him that morning to let him know that the Valencia-blue Bangor slates were in position.

'I have the place,' he said and directed her down the road.

'Where are we going?' she asked after a time.

'It's a surprise,' he said, and indicated she take the next left.

She smiled and ran her hand over his thigh playfully, sensually. 'Okay, but I don't want this wine to get warm.'

He promised it wouldn't and they made the final turn and drove up the gravelled hill towards his house. There had been times when he had stopped going to see it, but since Rhian's arrival it had become a pleasure once again.

The plans had come to life, the old-style country house with the bay windows and spiral staircase. The slates gleamed in the misty rain, and the view, the view was everything he had hoped for: Cairn Hill in the distance, sunbeams playing upon its woolly tree-topped crest, and to the right the Camlin River lazily flowing towards the town and later the Shannon.

She parked the car and he explained that this was his house.

'But my, it's beautiful,' she said, as was her fashion.

'It is, isn't it. Only one like it in the country, Kennedy the engineer drew it up for me.'

'It's wonderful,' she said.

They walked towards the back of the house, wine and oysters in hand, and found Fox the roofer packing away the last of his tools.

'Ger, I didn't expect to see you today,' Fox said in surprise.

'I got finished early. It's a great job,' McQuaid said and gestured to the roof.

'She came out nice in the end, aye,' said Fox, happy in the praise. 'And you must be Sinead?' He extended his hand towards Rhian. 'I've heard lots about you from the lads, and you're as good-looking as they said. You're a lucky git, Ger.' Fox laughed.

McQuaid was awkwardly silent for a moment. 'No, this is Rhian,' he said hesitantly.

'Pleased to meet you,' she now chimed and shook Fox's hand again.

'Oh right, God, sorry now about that, I just saw the wine and I thought . . .' Fox backtracked, his face turning red.

'No, it's fine. Rhian is my girl, you must have heard wrong about Sinead.'

'Oh right,' said Fox uncomfortably. 'I'm only a fool of a

roofer, what would I know?' he added, looking at Rhian. He packed his remaining tools and left shortly after.

They walked into the house and McQuaid took her through the rooms, pointing out the kitchen, the living room, the laundry.

'This is where my mother will sleep,' he explained as they walked into the granny flat.

'Oh, your mother?' Rhian said.

'Yes, not for a while but when she gets a bit older. There's just the two of us.'

'Oh, I see,' Rhian said.

They climbed a temporary metal staircase and he showed her the upper floor, the master bedroom, the ensuites, the views. He explained how the blueprint was so special, how the house was what he had always wanted.

'It's lovely,' Rhian agreed, but she did not touch the walls or whisper colours to herself as he had hoped she might.

'I thought, I thought you could decorate it,' he said.

'Of course, that wouldn't be a problem.'

'For the two of us,' he added coyly.

'Okay,' she said and then insisted they eat the oysters and drink the wine before everything got stale.

They sucked on the fleshy jelly and ate chunks of the sourdough. Having no glasses they drank straight from the wine bottle and giggled as the acidic taste rolled down their throats. He made a sort of bed from the coats and rolls of insulation and they rested upon it. When the oysters were finished he kissed her and tore at her lips violently.

She hesitated a moment and then pulled back.

'Is everything okay?' McQuaid asked as he pulled at her skirt.

'I can't today,' she explained. 'I have a work meeting after this.'

'Oh . . . I thought we might have a bit of fun,' he said.

'I'd love to, I just don't have time . . . sorry,' she said.

He released her from his arms and nodded. Said that of course it was fine. He was disappointed in a sense, he had hoped she would be in awe of the place and they would make love there in the house, christen every room as he and Sinead had spoken of.

'I just thought . . .' he ventured. 'Ah, it's nothing.'

'Are you sure?' she asked as she gathered the empty oyster shells.

'Well, I thought you might like the house more.'

'I do, I think it's very sweet,' she said.

'Just sweet?'

'It really suits you. It just, well, honestly it wouldn't be to my taste,' she said calmly.

'Well, maybe we can change something,' he began.

'When I come to do the work for you, I'll bring some ideas,' she said.

He nodded. She was being funny because Fox had called her Sinead, he reasoned. That must be it. That was all it would be.

'The oysters were great, weren't they,' she said, changing the subject.

'They were,' he agreed and took another mouthful of the wine.

She thanked him for showing her the house, and apologised that she couldn't stay longer, it was a flying visit, but they would meet again another evening and go for a meal and have a full night of romance. They were overdue a fuck.

He helped her pack away the remaining bits and pieces. They sat back into the car and she returned to the estate, dropping him at the manor house.

'I'll call you when I'm free again,' she stated.

'A longer stay, I hope,' he said earnestly.

She nodded and kissed him from across the gearstick.

He inspected the men's work in the manor. The ballroom was all but finished. A few more days and they would heft and shove the large wires upstairs and a new shape might take place.

That Rhian is herself. She was busy, that was all, you can't be fucking every day of the week.

I suppose, but Sinead would have liked it better, she might not have brought oysters but she'd have loved the place. She would, he thought, and tried to dismiss the negativity from his mind.

She's out for herself is all I'm saying. Not at all, Rhian was his new woman, she hadn't baulked when he'd told Fox that. No, she was his all right, she was just, she was just her own woman.

If you say so. I do, he thought and decided to take up the drill for a half-hour to escape himself.

He set to boring the drawing room rafters and worked a sweat onto himself. The setting sun's blazing rays cast a light upon the room as he worked, clicking across the rafters as the minutes went by, allowing the shadow to reclaim the bat-clustered haunt for another night. There were few other sounds from the mighty building except his bit and bore. He threaded the wires through and found solace in the labour.

He had seen the house at least and it had not hurt him as it had before. He had seen it and shown it to Rhian and she had agreed that she would decorate it for them; she would come to love the place as he did and they could share a tea and look out the windows and wake to the filtered light of the morning sun through the blinds and curtains.

He had done nothing wrong in showing her, nothing at all. That poor fool in Leitrim had missed out on such a place.

*

At seven he struck the ballroom off his mental list. He had enjoyed the solitary busyness. He found his mind had changed in recent weeks, since the departure of Willy, into a place of numbers and lists and to-dos.

He emerged from his diving bell of labour, wiped his face and gathered his tools.

A drink was on the menu, and though he drank most evenings now, his mind never cursed him the next day, rather it was just a dull throb, and though the throb had followed him for weeks, it had not interfered with work.

As he entered, Paul the barman greeted him and moved towards the taps.

'You're nearly a homeowner,' said Paul as he lifted the Guinness onto the counter.

'For all the trouble it's worth.'

'Not at all, isn't it a lovely time, did your woman see it yet?'

'No,' McQuaid answered and quickly sipped from his glass.

'I remember our Madge was at the house every evening when we were building. Mind you, we lived in the caravan on the site then, she had little choice,' said Paul and laughed at his own wit.

'She'll come and all though,' said Reilly loudly, emerging from behind a pillar.

'Ah begod, I didn't think I'd see you here,' said McQuaid.

'Well, even a camel needs a well,' said Reilly and invited him to sit.

The two discussed the work and weather. Paul interjected occasionally with a remark and the three enjoyed the merriment.

'Are you keeping up with the news?' said Paul as he fixed another round.

'Who's dead?' McQuaid asked.

'Oh, no one dead – well, the Nipper is on the way out but he's done that a few times. No, the news in Dublin.'

'Dublin, a shower of cunts,' he replied and hunched over his drink.

'Doesn't look great though,' said Paul. 'But I'm sure it'll pass.'

'Course it will,' McQuaid replied.

The drinks mounted as the evening went on; there'd be no dinner, only a dried-out husk. He had broken with his mother of late and abandoned their evening meal together. Reilly's spirits began to lift too and he told joke after joke.

'Did you ever hear the one about the Yank who came on holidays?'

'No.'

'Well, a Yank came visiting.'

'Looking for his roots, I suppose,' said Paul.

'Aye, something like that. Anyway, he goes into a pub, small pub, something like here. Has a few drinks, buys the barman a drink, buys the locals a drink. Having a grand time. A grand time.'

They nodded in mirth.

'Nature calls anyway, break the seal and all. Goes to the bathroom.'

'I know this one,' said Paul with a smile.

'Shut up, you.'

'So he goes to the toilet, does his business, shite and all that, ready for a few more.'

'As you do be.'

'Exactly. Well, he walks back out, walks straight over to the barman who's serving people, and he says in that Yank way, "Gee whiz, this is a great bar, and you're great guys, but man I just got one problem – those toilets."

'"Oh, the toilets," says the barman. "No toilet roll, is it?" he says. And the Yank says, "No, it's just that there's no locks on the doors."

'So the barman squares up to him real proper like. "God,

son," he says. "We've been here a long time and no one tried to steal a shite yet. I don't know how they do it in America!"' and Reilly laughed.

'An old one,' said Paul.

'An old one,' agreed Reilly.

'Ah, they're awful gullible them Yanks,' said McQuaid as he clapped the counter in happiness.

'Compass trouble,' said Paul and removed himself to serve an elderly couple.

'Compass trouble is right,' McQuaid repeated.

'Are you having a bit of that?' said Reilly, suddenly turning to him.

'What?'

'With Sinead, is it compass trouble?' asked Reilly quietly.

'Ah now, Pat,' said McQuaid, laughing it aside.

'Or is it prick trouble, that's a nuisance when it comes,' Reilly continued.

McQuaid stood up, saying he was going to have a smoke. Prick trouble, he repeated to himself. Reilly was drunk, he wasn't a bit wiser than the rest of them, just another labourer with a fondness for beer. Prick trouble; wasn't he seeing better now than he had in weeks, the clarity of passion had opened his eyes. There was no prick trouble.

He lit a cigarette and inhaled the crisp evening air. He found he was drunk himself, the pints and chat had been quick, had gone to his head.

The front door opened and Reilly walked outside and took a smoke from him.

'Well, we're here,' said McQuaid.

'We are,' Reilly said and put his hand upon McQuaid's shoulder for support. He stumbled slightly and laughed. 'I'm not used to drinking so much any more.'

'You'll be fine,' McQuaid said and let him continue with his hand. 'You never finished that story,' he said.

'What?' said Reilly and hiccupped dryly.

'Lefoyle, you never told me how it ended.'

'Oh, that; in disaster – don't they all end that way?'

'Ah, but how did he end up, Lefoyle like?' McQuaid persisted with the zeal of inebriation.

'That prick, the same as ourselves: alone. Alone and in madness.'

He wished to ask Reilly in truth now why he had been so reluctant to tell that story, all through the year. Why did he hate the man so much? Hadn't Lefoyle's demise in a way brought them all this work, headache as it might be?

'Did I ever tell you my own people were tenants of his?' said Reilly after a time.

'No.'

'Well, there you go, we suffered under the bastard.'

'And?'

'And nothing, he was our lord and master, and a cunt what's more, and that's it.'

'That's it?'

'That's it.'

'That's not much of a story, if you don't mind me saying,' said McQuaid with a chortle.

'Well, I said it wasn't worth telling,' answered Reilly.

'Fucking wish you hadn't. I thought you were going to say you were related to him or something.'

'Not a drop of blood,' said Reilly and spat on the ground.

'But there must be more?'

'There is. But it's best to let the dead bury the dead. I do not want to bring up those stories. The ghosts are better left where they are,' said Reilly and blessed himself. He took his hand from McQuaid's shoulder and walked back inside quietly.

Suddenly his phone vibrated. It was Rhian, he told himself even before he had taken out the mobile, she had been odd about the house but she'd thought better of it. She wanted a roll around and that suited him. But when he blearily looked at the screen the words were not hers but Sinead's.

Can we meet up? Let's talk ☺

So she was home, after all this time. He coughed, hiccupped, and reflected that it had been so long since the days of smiley faces and big Xs and Os.

His mind was a chatter of voices and yet no clarity seemed to emerge. Maybe it was better to leave the ghosts where they were, to exorcise himself of them totally.

He went inside, ordered another drink and downed it. He would confide in Paddy Reilly and seek his advice; he who was as close to a father as he had would not steer him wrong.

Rhian and the business with Sinead came out, poured out of him, to which Reilly nodded and listened quietly.

'I knew, I knew,' Reilly repeated mournfully.

'How?'

'I knew something was wrong, and you're going to tell Sinead now, is it?'

'Well, I have to, I suppose,' McQuaid responded honestly.

'Go easy, lad, you have to end it right, you have to finish one job before you start another.'

'I suppose, but Rhian is great, she wants to support me, she loves the house, she's my woman, I said as much to Fox today when he met her.'

'Fox met her?'

McQuaid nodded.

'And you are sure Rhian is with you on this?'

'I am.'

'Well then, you have to.'

'Right,' said McQuaid, and he stood up.

'What, you're going to do it now?'

'Might as well.'

'Jesus, you're a braver man than me,' hiccupped Reilly.

'Well, you just told me,' McQuaid said and downed a short of whiskey. 'It's shovel or shite.'

The words seemed to echo in him as he walked to the door. He did not look back. He heard Reilly say something to Paul but he did not listen.

He stumbled towards the van and drove to her house. Just lay it out straight and get out, he told himself. He'd be free then and no more worries, no more complaints. He and Rhian could be in peace and the dream could resume on the old terms. It would be an end and a start.

The lights were off in the house, all the souls were in bed for the night as he walked towards her bedroom window. He knocked on the glass and when no reply came he climbed in.

'Sinead, Sinead,' he called.

'Hmmm,' she stirred from her sleep.

'Ger,' she cried. 'What are you doing here, they're all asleep. How did you get in?' she said, sitting up in the bed very suddenly. She was wearing his blue knit jumper.

He walked towards her and sat on the bed. He looked at the ground, at the bedside table, at anything but her sweet blue eyes.

'I don't love you any more, it's over,' he said and found the words had drummed out of him.

'What?' she said and rubbed her eyes.

'It's over, I'm not in love with you any more,' he said again, slower now, and fixed his attention on the carpet pattern.

'What do you mean?' she stammered.

'I mean I met someone else.'

'Who?'

'It doesn't matter, I love her.'

'Who?' she repeated; a queer panic had entered her voice.

'Her name is Rhian, she's a designer on the site.'

'What?' and she began to cry, the tears rolling down her still-waking face.

He looked at her now, finding the drink had induced a new confidence. 'I love her, the way she kisses me. You and me, we've been growing apart for months, Sinead, it's over.'

'Oh my God. I think I'm going to be sick,' she said and the tears were coming faster now. 'But what's wrong?'

'Nothing is wrong. Rhian is just the fit for me, she loves me, she visits me at work, she thinks the house is wonderful and she's going to live in it with me, she's my woman now. Besides, it's only love, you'll get over it,' he added and looked her in the eye.

'What? Oh my God, I'm going to be sick,' she repeated and hunched over in the bed, clinging her sides, wrapping herself in her blankets as if to escape this nightmare.

He sat motionless and turned his eyes towards the floor once more.

'But you could have talked to me.'

'I tried but . . .' and he stopped short, he no longer had an answer. 'I'm sorry but you'll get over it, it's just, it's just not working out, it's too hard,' he said and slowly stood up. 'It's better with her. She wants to support me, she believes in me.'

'I believe in you,' Sinead cried.

'Not like her.'

'Don't go, can't we fix it? What did I do wrong?'

'Nothing. Nothing,' he repeated, softer still, and stumbled towards the window. 'I'm going to go, have a good sleep,' he said and smiled drunkenly, piggishly it seemed, as he climbed out the window.

It was done and he was free. He could hear the sobs from her room, and a light switched on in the hallway.

He walked towards the van. It was done. It was done.

37
Kane

His phone rang constantly; dring . . . ring . . . dring . . . ring went the polyphonic tone as it had done these last few weeks. And who would be calling? Why, Big Jack or the contractors or the investors or indeed the bank. The bank that called every day.

He didn't go out, he didn't answer the phone, he didn't sleep well. He no longer did much of anything. And yet for all the money and jobs he'd created, none of those calls were to ask after him, his wellbeing. Only take, take, take.

Kane moved from the sitting room to the kitchen. He had done this lap many times today, moving through the house, looking, searching for some quietness and solitude. He carried an old calculator in his hand and paused by increments, adding the same sums again and again. There was no way of getting away from the figures: the repayments to the bank were late.

Five million, and he checked the sums yet again.

Sean and Austin knew something of the truth, he thought. He'd told them he was waiting for cheques to be cleared from the deposits on the first houses. And they had coughed and spluttered and insisted that they needed to know that everything was fine.

He paused by the kitchen sink, checked the calculator again, took a pen in his hand and wrote the number down. Five million and all its loitering zeros, and yet not so long ago it was small money. Five million: hadn't he been well able to pay that, and had done last year and the year before.

'Five million,' he sighed, speaking what must have been his first words in an hour or more.

That was a lot of pigs, a lot of long nights in marts and lorries and offices. He'd come so far from those few small acres to all this. To achieve such success in one lifetime, he'd employed men he had gone to school with, cousins, friends. Wasn't he the rising tide that had lifted the boats of these men? But that would all be forgotten once the truth came out, as the bank would make sure it did. They'd cut the socks from underneath him.

Failure to make a payment and his name would be in the papers, and the letters and litany of hate would begin. But he still had Birchview, still had part of the deeds, they could not take that from him, could not take what was rightfully his.

He cast his mind back to that school lesson of long ago, when so much had been clear to him.

'How does one make money?' the master had asked.

'A job,' had come the reply.

'But there are other ways, boys,' the master returned slyly. '*Verecundus* Kane, can you enlighten us?'

'Please, sir, my father says . . . my father says there are three ways for a man to make money.'

'Three, Mr Kane, and what might they be?'

'Well, sir, my father says, says you can buy it, you can inherit it, or you can steal it.'

'*Gratias tibi ago*, Mr Kane,' said the master with a smile. 'You boys might do well to remember John in years to come.'

He had smiled at the praise that day and the master had asked him to stay behind to talk. He wanted him to go on to secondary, to sit the junior and maybe think of finishing and college. He could go to St Pat's or Maynooth, he had promise, or so the master said. But that dream would never eventuate, his father needed him at home on the farm, needed the wage coming in when he was old enough to begin an apprenticeship.

Books were for better people, he was told.

He thought now of that day at school when big Connie McGahern, who'd stayed back several times over, had taken money from the poor box to buy sweets. And the parish priest had come to tell them all that hell had plenty of room for a thief. But Connie would not confess; despite his size and age, he was a coward. And so he, John, who needed education no longer, owned up to the crime and took the bare-arsed beating from the sally rod in front of all the other boys, and even though he'd cried when he walked home that evening, he had the respect of those same boys. He knew then he had made the choice to be upstanding, to be a leader.

There were no books in his house, only brochures and newspapers and dockets. He had often dreamed of that other life; perhaps if he'd had support, he might have ended up a priest or a teacher, or even . . . even maybe a doctor. He'd earned more now than any doctor but in polite company his money was never the same, it still had the smell of the farm and the pigs; no matter how high he might go, or how many men he might employ, he'd never be an Austin or a Sean. And even though he too attended the theatre, had met the Taoiseach, had a box at Croke Park, he'd never be one of them.

'Five million,' he sighed yet again. He was well short of that.

And he'd heard the quiet word that other men were short too, like a snail run out of ink, the shimmer of slime seemed to be slowing down, the money was not so easily come by any more. The rest of the country didn't know yet, but it was a growing feeling, a whisper in the snug. Blight must move like this, he thought; quiet and slow, and both left a smell of rot, for that was what was coming, rot and damp.

He crumpled the notepaper, put the calculator away and moved himself abruptly.

A decision. He had to make a decision, that much was clear. Confess to the bank and take the sally again and all that went with it: the bitter resentment, the false talk, the begrudgery. Oh, how they would revel in tearing him down.

Or, and he thought carefully now, he could choose to not pay the contractors and use that money to make up part of the payment. It would hold the bank at bay, it would buy him time at least, the market could have, no, it *would* have picked up by then, he told himself.

'Fuck,' he said and felt a pang of emotion engulf him.

There was, of course, no one to talk to, no wife or companion, hadn't he put all that aside to achieve, to build this life, and yet now he had no one to share it with, no one to turn to. Austin and Sean would not understand, they might even baulk at the idea and ask for their investments back. A snide solicitor's letter might be their only response.

No, the choice was clearer now, the men would have to wait. He was not shafting them, he was only delaying their cheques. Yes, that was it, he mused, and repeated the mantra to combat those strange feelings in his stomach.

Hadn't he given them all so much already; what was a few months? There would be another development and he would take them all on again. Even those who had let him down.

He was the rising tide, he would take care of those same men. They wouldn't have an arse in their trousers if he had not taken the plunge, the risk. Birchview would still be rotting away silently under some decrepit half-bred-out Anglo. No, he was right in his actions; the men could take the hit for now.

He breathed out slowly, boiled the kettle and prepared himself a cup of tea.

He would call the bank manager, explain that he was waiting on certain investments to come through but that he would pay part of the instalment this week. He would hold back the waves that were starting to lick at his heels.

He drank from the hot cup and savoured the taste. It was the first morsel to pass his lips all day. The tension began to leave his shoulders and arms as he sipped on the liquid, but then the pang of hurt returned suddenly to his stomach, moving up his torso.

The men, his mind now rallied, they were not fools, they might see his truth for what it was: a lie. That the cheques might never come in the post, that his delays were the first sign of total failure. And then they might stop working for him altogether.

Kane felt a dry retch in his stomach and nearly spat out the tea.

'No,' he said out loud.

No, he would not collapse, it would be only a few months, only a few months until the market picked up, and then all would be well. He could pay the men, in cash if they wanted; the apartments would go under the hammer and he'd have more than enough to satisfy all.

He poured out the rest of his tea and walked back into the living room. He absentmindedly picked up the colour chart Rhian had left him. He had to choose the main colours for the manor house. It would be a pleasant task and a welcome distraction. He sat at the table, put on his reading glasses and flicked through the booklet.

Goosewing grey, juniper green, Van Dyke brown. Thoughts of those swatches had seemed so far away when they had broken through that first ditch and built the temporary road into the estate, and now he was so close to the end.

Goosewing grey, that had a lovely sound, like flight, like the birds that wintered on the Camlin River each year on their way to Russia or France or wherever they were going. It would be nice to be that free. He settled on a green for the hallway and various blues and creams for the ballroom.

He looked up at the wall clock; the day had moved slowly. He resisted going back to the office, where all those problems seemed to reside. Catriona, his secretary, could handle the callers; he needed this time. Perhaps he might go for a walk, or a drink. He needed to get out of the house, to get out of Longford, if only for a short while.

He walked to the front door and took his overcoat from the cloakroom. He had the best house on the Battery Road, where the old gentry had once lived. He had the Merc and the Land Rover, he had the land and the turf and still took his holidays in Donegal each year. And yet what good was all that to him now?

He had not been to the site in days, nor to the piggery. He rubbed his eyes and walked outside. He would drive to the farm and take a look at the stock. He did not need to do it for he had a man for that, he had a man for everything now, and yet the land had been calling to him. Calling him back to those same fields where it had all begun, where he had played in the meadows, watched the pheasants dart through the rushes, seen the fox that dusty evening and each had looked at the other with a respect that called out across the divide of species.

He drove towards the farm and told himself that he would

stand under that lone blackthorn and a new idea might emerge, a new dream to fix this nightmare. When he returned he would come to a firm decision and phone Catriona. And yet as he passed the roundabout turn his mind seemed to say it had been done already, and maybe it was right. But the walk, the walk would do him good.

38
McQuaid

The cheque had not arrived, it was late, late by weeks. Kane the bastard was holed up in his house or office and was never to be seen. And the work, could the work continue without the money? He did not know.

Big Jack said it was coming, it was coming. But when, McQuaid wondered. When is a long time, with many twists and turns. He was busier now it seemed than ever before: Ballymahon, Birchview, his house, wages for the men, for Willy. It was all going ahead and yet in the pit of his stomach a feeling grew that said it's not, not in the very slightest.

He could still pay the men's wages, there was still enough for that, but for how long? He had called into Kane's office but the receptionist, that *snottery* bitch that she was, had said he was in a meeting.

'Well, I'll wait until he is finished.'

'He's in a meeting out of the office,' she explained.

'Well, I'll wait until he comes back.'

'That may be some time. Why don't you leave a message and I'll get him to call you.'

'I've left messages all week and got no reply,' he returned sternly.

'Mr Kane is a busy man. I'm sure he will get to you in time.'

'Oh, he'll get to me. He's bloody got to me already. I'll wait,' he said gruffly and took a seat in the foyer.

Old magazines littered the coffee table; he flicked the pages, looked at the photos. And jigged his leg impatiently. The receptionist went for lunch at two and remembered herself at the sight of him.

'Oh, you're still here. I'm afraid I'm going out to lunch. I'll have to lock up,' she said and rattled the keys in her hand.

'Isn't there someone else here?'

'No, not today, you can wait outside for the hour.'

'Fuck waiting outside,' he had said and walked out the door.

Fuck waiting and fuck Kane and his receptionist, he told himself. Fuck them all. There was no option but to keep working and hope the man would show up soon. The word had begun to spread. Neither Reilly nor Limerick had been paid, but the painters had received some cash, so perhaps there was hope. Perhaps time was the answer.

The manor house had proved difficult but the majority of the work was finished. Majus had settled into his new role and it was as if they had always worked together. They would begin the second fitting soon after the plasterers had tidied up. It would be switches and lights, nothing too strenuous, and maybe then he would make Kane wait, make him sweat as he was now doing.

But at that thought the feeling grew in his stomach again and the pressure in his head intensified, like some screw into old timber, deeper and deeper it went and then knotted with a torque twist.

He drove to Ballymahon and worked the day through; the wire squeaked and rattled as it slowly came off the reel, grey and stiff. The zip of the cable ties zagged through the air as he bundled the cords together. Bundled and zipped, bundled and zipped.

The houses seemed lost in the greyness of the day, their cement and plaster a poor imitation of the skyline. And when he paused he could hear a mixer trundle in the distance.

He would see Rhian in the manor this evening. He had tried hard to keep his space from her this last while, not to crowd her. It had been wrong when Sinead and he were still together, but now, now the way was clear. That night had never been on their emotional calendar, that disaster, that breakup was best not thought of.

Rhian and he had much to discuss: the future, the house. He had his new foundation and a better, more solid dream could take place.

At five he left Ballymahon, telling Declan that he needed to get supplies. They were to meet in the ballroom. As he gripped the steering wheel he imagined the event again and again in his head: he would tell her about Sinead, and she would be a bit skittish, but eventually they would embrace and he would take her to the master bedroom as they had done the first time and make love. Afterwards they would plan out their future, and maybe go for a drink or something to eat.

McQuaid smiled to himself as he lit another cigarette and quickly passed through the towns and villages. A dog darted by on a country lane, not bothering to look up at the van.

A red glow shone out through the ballroom windows and illuminated the carved marble fireplaces. He heard his boots clop through the empty house, the sound reverberating off the freshly plastered walls and stucco moulding.

In the distance the golf course men still worked turning up the soil; how long it took to make a lawn, he remarked to himself and laughed.

Rhian's heeled boots tittered through the front doorway and he heard her rhythmic walk slow then pause and begin again. She was admiring the work, he decided; the sound of her footsteps drew closer and then stopped. He turned and found her leaning by the eastern ballroom window, her long dress of black and red trailing to the floor.

'Hello,' he said and shyly embraced her.

She kissed him politely and he felt her lipstick stain his cheeks. 'I haven't seen you in a while,' she said.

'Well, I needed a bit of time,' he replied.

'Oh?'

'Well, I know you were busy,' he countered.

'I was but I wouldn't have minded some fun either,' she said and smirked.

'Well, the thing was,' he said and found himself nervous. 'The thing is, I broke up with Sinead,' he said quickly.

'You did?'

'Yeah, so you and I can be together now, properly be together,' he said and found a renewed confidence in his words. 'I mean, I know you were a bit awkward the other day when I brought you to my house, because I suppose Fox thought you were Sinead, and then the house was all a bit much, and then you didn't sleep with me because you didn't want to be going behind Sinead's back any more. But it's all fine now, it's all okay,' he said and smiled and reached out towards her.

Rhian was quiet a moment and took a step back from the window. 'I never –' she started.

'I know you're a bit overcome with it all, but it's just us now, it's all fine,' he cut her off.

'I never . . .' she tried again and cast his words aside, 'asked you to break up with her. I never asked you to do that.'

'I know you didn't, but I knew when I brought you to my house that day, that's why you didn't sleep with me.'

'I didn't fuck you that day because I was busy, Gerard. I came to see you and surprise you with oysters because I had some time to kill.'

'That's fine, what I'm saying is, though, it's us, it's us now.'

'What are you talking about?' she asked and her words seemed to linger in the room. 'I never asked you to break up with her, because I don't want to be with you.'

'But it's fine now, Sinead is in the past. You're the future.'

'Gerard, you're not listening to me.' Rhian's voice grew stern. 'There is no us. There never was. This, all this,' she gestured around the ballroom, 'this is all we are, just a fling in the middle of a dull building site in the middle of rural Ireland. Just a bit of fun and sex in the middle of this dump.'

'But our meetings?' he said.

'They were just that – meetings, meetings and sex and laughter.'

'But you said, I thought you said you were here for me.'

'Yes, I did say that,' she admitted and cast her eyes towards the ground.

'And we're here now, and I know this is just a row but we'll get over it,' he rallied.

'There's nothing to get over. I did say I was here for you, but I only said it because I thought you needed to hear it, there was so much energy in the room that day, and you looked so lost. I said it because you needed me to.'

'But I love you.'

'How could you love me, we've only met a handful of times.'

'I thought . . .' and he found himself stepping backwards, the gap between them growing. This was not what was supposed to happen, and his stomach lurched. His thoughts grew heavy but he struck out once again. 'You said you would design the house for *us*, my house.'

'As a job, Gerard, as a job.'

'But you didn't say anything when I introduced you as my girl to that roofer.'

'I don't love you. There is no combination of words or complex wiring panel to this. I'm not some circuit breaker you can switch on or take apart. I'm not in love with you. There was never more to this; that house isn't mine, that dream isn't mine, and try as you might you can't put me into it.'

'But . . .' he stammered.

'I'm sorry for being so harsh but I had to be straight with you,' she said and reached her hand towards his face.

'But I broke up with Sinead for you.'

'That was your choice.'

'But I showed you my dream house, *our* dream house.'

'It's just a building, Gerard. It's the same as any other. I really am sorry, you're a really sweet fella and it was lovely the time we had, but it was only a fun thing, I was just, *we* were just having fun.'

'No. No,' he repeated. 'No, this can't happen. You said you were going to support me. After everything I've been through with work, with accidents, with Sinead, you can't go, I won't let you.'

Rhian grew angry now and slapped his outstretched hand away from her. 'You never told me any of these things. You invented this relationship, but it was never anything more than fun. I said I would support you but we said a lot of things that day. It's over.'

'Oh my God,' he said and found that the tears were indeed

rolling down his cheeks. He backed away from her and turned his eyes towards the window. 'Oh my God,' he said again, and the words that echoed through the ballroom seemed to stir his mind to life. That conscience that had been so quiet all this time.

You have that nicely fucked up, Ger Ger. Oh Jesus, he thought, and felt himself drift away from Rhian and further into himself.

You are some man, Ger Ger. You had two women and now you have none. But I can fix things, I can fix this, he thought, and tried hard to hold strong against the negative thoughts.

Fix it? Fix it? This isn't a faulty wire, man, this is your life. What have you been playing at? I was busy, he thought, work was busy, and then . . . I don't know.

He walked towards the fireplace and cursed out in the open; he rapped his fist upon the cold marble and felt its hardness; he gripped it, clung to it now as he felt a weight come over him, weighing his very back and legs to the ground.

You don't know. You don't know, Ger. Shall I tell you? Yes, he thought, and then no, and clung to the fireplace tighter as the weight grew and he felt his knees bend.

You're only after breaking poor Sinead's heart because you couldn't talk to her. All you had to do was tell her you were under pressure, instead you were chasing that aul jumped-up bitch. She's made a right bollox of you with all her talk of energy and light and mirrors. Well, here's the mirror now and you may take a good long look, Ger. You're fucked.

'I'm not. I can fix this,' he said and he was not sure if he spoke the words aloud.

You can't fix this. I can, he thought, pushed with his weight and strength and years of work to lift himself up, up and away from the fireplace, wiping the tears from his eyes. He started to sing.

'I'm never going to let
Your negative vibes and comments
Get through to my psyche and cripple me
I'm never going to let . . .'

No amount of verse will save you now, Ger. You're fucked. Can't you see it, that fucked look in your eye, on your brow, in the lines and greying hairs on your head. Jesus you are some bollox.

'*Your negative vibes and comments, Get through to my psyche and cripple me . . .*' he tried once again but the words petered out and he sobbed once more.

'I'm fucked,' he said and looked up to see that Rhian had already left, no goodbyes, no perfume, no kisses.

'What happened?' he mouthed and saw a tear fall on his clay-stained work boots.

Ah, nothing much, Ger, only you lost the plot. I didn't, I haven't, he countered.

It's fine, Ger, you lost it a long time ago. Don't worry about it now.

He moved out of the ballroom now in search of Rhian; if only he could find her they might talk, might start as friends and build something real. He went through the house but took a wrong turn and found himself in the kitchens; he retraced his steps and found he was in the drawing room. He was lost now in this cavern of a place.

'Rhian, Rhian!' he shouted but there was no answer. He took his phone from his pocket and called her number but she did not pick up.

I can fix this ☺ he texted.

There's nothing to fix. You've been broke this long while, Ger, that day when Willy fell, that evening when the council digger broke down. There's no cheque, no Willy, and no Sinead.

He cried now at the thought of Sinead and what he had done. I love her, he thought, I never stopped loving her.

Climbing in a window pissed, is that love? Breaking in a window and she asleep in your own jumper. Is that love, Ger? I was lost, he thought, and wished this blackness would leave his head, would leave if only for a moment so he might think clearly and reason and see that he just needed to call Sinead.

It's time to forget about the house now, Ger. It was not too late, he could talk to her, he had not been free of the stress, the jobs, the worry. It had been too much. And he had listened to Paddy Reilly that night, Paddy Reilly had suggested he end it with her, he had not even wanted to.

He searched now for Sinead's number on his phone. He would call her and explain everything.

So you have it, Ger Ger. And he paused now and found he had no answer to the blackness of himself.

'No,' he said and wiped the tears from his eyes.

You haven't been thinking, Ger . . . Gerard, your head has been miles away. Too busy with this bloody place, going to work at two in the morning, driving back and forth each day, every day between here and Ballymahon to build this dream fucking house. You haven't been thinking in a long, long time.

A sudden silence filled the room and the full reality of mouth and brain and numbed feeling descended upon him. The tears cleared from his eyes. How long he had been in this quiet state of shock he did not know, and his mind laughing all the while, laughing still, only now he fought against it and regained his composure. And yet still the words rang, drilled into his skull.

You bollox. You bollox. You bollox.

39
Crawford

The rental BMW was clean and smooth. He always requested this model, he might as well have some small comfort during this horrible task. The M4 had been busy today. Lorries, trucks, four-wheel drives and cars speeding back and forth, up and down the dual carriageway.

He looked at the printout of the email and the Google Map directions to the different locations. He had four more today in the midlands region: Leitrim, Cavan, Westmeath and Longford.

'They never shoot the messenger,' he had joked in the office that morning.

'But you better have a thick skin, Crawford,' replied his supervisor as the door closed behind him.

A thick skin, he thought now. He'd surely developed that in the last few weeks. Insults of every sort, threats of violence, the front wheels of the car slashed that day in Kerry and he stranded waiting for the AA for two hours, nodding politely at the German tourists on their bicycles.

He stopped at a filling station for coffee and a chocolate bar. He asked the attendant for two plastic bags and some rubber bands. He poured the packet sugar into his paper cup and stirred. It was weak but it would have to do. He could have a decent coffee when he got home. The new Nespresso machine made a great latte. That would be his evening's treat after all this bedlam.

He looked for the road signs to Longford; he passed Glennons sawmill and took the Leo Casey roundabout to Birchview Estate. It seemed like a fairly big development. But Longford? Who'd want to live here? No one now, he reminded himself. No one at all.

He could see the large stone wall in the distance and the trucks and vans coming in and out through the gateway. A security guard sat in a cabin at the roadside.

'Hello, I'm here from the bank,' Crawford explained and read the guard's name badge, '. . . Peter.'

'Oh yes, have you on the list, sir,' said Peter, and he limped slowly towards the gate and lifted the security arm. 'Everything okay?' he enquired.

'Yes, just fine,' Crawford coolly replied and brought the tinted car window to a close once more. They had no idea, he told himself, no idea at all, but it was the same every place he visited. The news had not filtered down, not yet.

The gravel crunched under the car tyres. He slowly turned off the ignition and checked his hair in the rear-view mirror. He walked to the boot and retrieved the plastic bags to methodically place over his expensive leather shoes, then fixed the rubber bands around his ankles. The plastic rustled as he walked towards the site office, papers in hand.

'Hello, Jack, is it?' He knocked confidently, then walked in the cabin door.

'Yes,' said the large man from behind his desk. A yellow safety vest and blue hard hat hung from the door handle.

'I'm here from the bank,' Crawford said and thrust the papers into the man's hand.

Jack's expression changed from warm to a grimace as he read the opening paragraphs of the legal documents.

'Failure to pay remittance,' Crawford explained.

'But surely there's some mistake?' asked Jack, looking up from the papers.

'No, there's no mistake. John Kane has been informed, he's been aware of the situation for the last few weeks,' Crawford said calmly.

'It's the first I've heard,' said Jack, grasping, clutching for an understanding. 'I'll call him,' he said, fumbling for his phone.

'Call if you like, but I've spoken with him already, it's happening today.'

'But . . .' said Jack, letting the phone hang limp in his hand. 'I'll call him,' he reaffirmed.

Crawford walked outside and left the foreman to his conversation.

'Well, it's me . . . There's a fella here from the bank,' he heard Jack say. A long pause followed. 'Yeah, he's handed me some papers . . . What?'

The man's footsteps rattled in the cabin, he was pacing the floor, they all paced at this stage.

'But for Jesus' sake, John, what about the men? And me? The place is nearly . . .' and he stopped. 'Right,' he said and hung up the phone.

It was a different man who opened the door. His face was drawn and pale with the news of a world that had come crashing to a halt.

'He knows, said he spoke with you.'

'Yes. Well, we better get on with this,' Crawford said.

Jack slowly lifted his safety vest and placed it on his large frame. 'Jesus,' he sighed.

'Do you want to tell them or shall I?'

It was a dry throat that choked: 'I think you should.'

They walked through the site to the houses and the apartments, to the golf course and the hotel. Crawford stepped carefully to avoid the puddles and muck; freckles of dirt splashed onto the bags over his feet.

They stopped at the first housing estate on Boolavogue Place where a group of men worked on the gutters of a house.

'I'm sorry but this site is closed,' Crawford called to a young man up a ladder.

'What?' replied the man.

'It's closed. I'm here from the bank, this job is finished,' Crawford patiently explained. 'Please stop what you're doing and pack up your tools, there's to be no more work done here.'

On and on the conversation went. Jack quietly walked off and returned with groups of men: bricklayers, electricians, plumbers, carpenters, painters.

Word quickly spread throughout the site, and a new energy filled this place of work. Panic was the word, he always thought. A panic of the unknown.

Again and again he repeated the words: 'Please stop what you're doing, this job is finished.'

'But for fuck's sake, we're right in the middle of work here,' men protested.

'That is not my concern. I'm here under directions from the bank. It's my job to ensure all work stops immediately.'

'And what about our money?' said another man.

'That's not my area. You have to talk with the developer Mr Kane and Jack here.'

'Jesus, Jack, what the fuck is going on?' they began to shout. 'What's all this about?'

'It's finished,' Jack murmured.

'What?'

'It's finished, it's finished, it's fucking finished, he's gone bust,' shouted Jack. The emotion in both his words and face was plain. 'He's gone bust,' he repeated.

'Look, I'm sorry about all this, I'm just here to do my job,' Crawford told the distressed group. 'If you're concerned about your money you'll have to talk to Mr Kane, but today you have to leave, the site is closed.'

The plastic bags scrunched and rattled over the muck and dirt. Jack was sullen and shrunken.

'It's a shame, it's a lovely place,' Crawford said as they paused and he admired the view.

'It would have been,' returned Jack. 'It was getting there, it was nearly there.'

'Can you get one of the men to tack up these notices?' Crawford said, handing Jack the laminated foreclosure signs. 'They need to be on all the site entrances and exits. And you'll need to give me the keys, and whatever copies the men have can be dropped to your office. Is that okay?'

'Yes,' said Jack. 'They're in my office, I'll give them to you on the way out.'

'We can't have any of the men coming back vandalising the place. It has to be secure.'

'They won't do that, they're good lads,' said Jack.

'It happens, Jack. It happens. The best of men can go a bit off with this sort of news.'

By lunchtime the vans and trucks began to move off. There had been no big protest, no scathing remarks. They had quietly followed his orders. The whole site had capitulated to his will.

This suited man with plastic bags on his feet, armed with no more than legal documents and a ballpoint pen.

There was no victory in his efforts, he did not like to see the defeated look upon their faces, the open contempt with which they viewed him. He had friends, cousins, in the construction industry; he had heard their cries and laments. But it was not his job to be their comforter.

By three o'clock all the men had left the site. Jack had retreated to his office and produced a small naggin of whiskey from some nook or cranny.

'Jack, I'll need those keys.'

'Oh right,' Jack said and handed him the bundles.

'You can lock up if you like,' Crawford offered and returned him the keys.

'I'd like that.' Jack gave a weak smile. 'I thought,' he stood up slowly, 'I thought we might survive, I thought with the sales that we might make it through. I knew things were bad around the place, but I . . . I . . .' and he could not find any more words.

'I'm sorry,' said Crawford.

'So am I.'

Crawford closed the office door and walked back through the site. Boots and safety vests littered the grounds. Bales of unopened blocks, cranes stranded in mid-reach. A temporary traffic light blinked on and off. It was always the same, the deserted look about the grounds, as if all the occupants had suddenly vanished. As though it were a war zone and everyone had been evacuated. Only the wind now moved through the buildings, and the silence, the silence filled the grounds. Like the grave.

He had worn holes in the plastic bags, he would have to get a pair of wellingtons for himself. Get a pair for the next job. He sat back into the rental car. Took out his pen and scratched out the word Longford. The day was not over yet, there would be another site and another before the Nespresso machine and the nine o'clock news on his new widescreen television.

They never shoot the messenger, he told himself, but his skin, his skin was not so thick for the news he brought.

40
Lefoyle

1847

'What did I say? Those gates are to be kept shut. Shut,' he repeated and wiped his sullen brow.

Lefoyle dismissed the maid, who nodded and left the study. Too many called to the gates now, too many, charity had to end, it had to. It was not his doing, this, this rot.

He picked up the newspaper; endless reports of inevitable disaster. Disaster, he thought, it is already upon us. From Mexico a potato blight to kill all Europe.

He had survived O'Connell, survived and prospered; repeal was dead, had died indeed with big Dan. Harmon's treachery a brief pain that could be ignored, but now a new death loomed. These pointless roads, inland lighthouses, railways to God knows where. Public works in aid of food and the work, the work that led nowhere, and nowhere was the destination of this place. They reap corn and sow corpses.

But they must work for their keep, he mused now, food and money could not be handed out ceaselessly, they would grow dependent on the charity of others. They must work.

Lefoyle walked towards the window. It was a calm day, bright in fact, odd that this day was like any other; the birds sang, the trees still stood, rain fell where it was needed, and yet disaster gripped the nation. Death, endless death. Bodies ravaged with hunger, lines of marching mouths. Famine.

It seemed that these last few years had been one disaster after another. The very soul of Longford ripped from its being by spiritual agitators, connivers and now disease. All would change and change utterly. And was not he already a man and was that not tragedy enough?

He left the manor seldom now, left only when he had to for a court sitting or a council meeting. Indeed few moved about by choice. Maggie had boarded herself up in Mostrim, she had taken pity on many and paid visits to the workhouses and infirmaries. She looked upon them as children; she, spinster that she was, could afford to feel pity. She gave them hope, she had said when last they met. But hope was an expensive commodity.

It had already been two years and still the rot spread. He had seen firsthand the sickly death upon their faces, the tenants no longer able to pay their rent. He had been tolerant at first, next year would be better, they had said, but the years were no better, rather a downward spiral, each day worse than the last. He could not continue to be tolerant. It would be eviction. It was the logical thing to do, too many mouths on land that would be better merged into larger fields. Animals where people had been. And Harmon, bankrupt from his generosity, would see this wisdom before too long, before he too had nothing but the clothes on his back. Perhaps the modest proposal was more feasible now.

Apples, cup, black and lumpers. The names flowed around his brain like the flies around their small white flowers. Little hope of any of them now. Living on lumpers and growing into lumps on that lazy vegetable. Only relief committees and soup kitchens. They had taken to drinking cattle's blood again as in antiquity. Vampirism, like some tribal Africans. They should have been out planting and tilling new fields, sowing new crops; how the land had grown neglected.

And they the poor gentry to pay for it all, expected to pay for it all. Moral landlordism, they called it; well, did tenants not belong to a place, should they not show allegiance to their betters? Instead of sacking storerooms, stealing, shooting. Law and Order, that great companion, was a broken thing now. All was changed.

He cast his mind back to the courtroom and the trial not two weeks ago of John Murtagh, that Young Irelander, that criminal. Oh, temperance and peace were forgotten things, all right. Famine and rebellion all that seemed to exist now. They had shot Stephenson the overseer for a few shillings. Shot the poor man. Molly Maguires, Ribbon men, White boys.

It had been hot in the courtroom that day, and his wig and gown had itched as the prisoner was brought forward.

'John Murtagh, you stand accused of sedition and plotting to incite rebellion,' Lefoyle had said. 'You are an educated man and will not be brought before the scaffold; martyrdom is what you seek so as to incite more young men to take your place. Well, it is transportation that is your reality. Fifteen years in Van Diemen's Land shall be your scaffold and may it teach you humility. What have you to say in your defence?'

Murtagh walked towards the bar and scratched his wrists. A cut on his forehead had congealed and shone dark red. 'On the subject of rebellion I have much to say. I have heard much talk of obligation today. Obligation to the crown, to England, to the moral tyrants who call themselves the gentry. Honour belongs to all men, cottiers and gentlemen alike, it is not a monopoly of one.'

'We are not here for a lesson in morality, Mr Murtagh,' Lefoyle had interrupted.

'I am here to be heard. Is not a man entitled to speak his piece before deportation?'

'In that it may be brief, yes.'

'It will.'

'Then proceed.'

Murtagh coughed then and raised his voice louder still. 'I have watched as the people of this country have given up their land for soup, soup from outsiders who parade as insiders. Evictions that have served only to clear land for animals now that trade has resumed on the old terms with England. They sell grain still while mouths wag for crumbs.'

'We are aware of the situation the country is in, Mr Murtagh, you are amongst the literate now,' said Lefoyle slowly, and a quiet mirth filled the room.

'Then more is the shame in this room. For I have seen more piety in the dunkle and mud hut of a cottier than in any big house. Your evictions in Newtown did not go unnoticed, Baron Lefoyle. The outsider by virtue of his birth may call himself Irish and lay claim to confiscated lands but he will never own them truly. I am to be sent to Australia to be amongst the forgotten people, the people you wish to forget. The mind may relegate us to the past, to that nether region, but what do a forgotten people do? They remember. A scaffold of hurts will breathe new life into us and those that remain here.'

'Your crimes dictate death but we the court have pleaded leniency in your favour that you may serve use to the building of that new country. You are a lucky man,' Lefoyle told him.

'Leniency is the virtue of the tyrant who fears to meet his maker and finds he is alone. For that is what will happen. You will be alone, this class will fall. Should you offer us freedom now, it would be a spent word. Gifts too long withheld lose all value. Your tenants do not have an obligation to you, this is not England or Russia, we are not your property. Hibernia is our master and she calls strong men daily to fight.'

'Then let it call, you will be too far away to hear,' Lefoyle shouted and brought down his gavel in furious energy.

Murtagh was led out of the court to shouts and calls of freedom and rebellion. His zeal had filled the room and brought resentments to bear. He, Lefoyle, was no absentee; was it not men like him who had fought to keep the peace, to bring order? Was it not men like him, he reasoned now, who had lobbied for the cheap maize to be imported? What would come after him, he feared to think.

'Sir.'

'Sir,' came the voice again, more urgently now.

'Yes.'

'Sir, an emergency, sir, we've caught a trespasser in the storeroom stealing food,' said Marie the maid.

'Is there to be no end? An example is what we need,' said Lefoyle, still angry from the thoughts of Murtagh.

He stormed out of the room and towards the store. He could hear shouts down below. When he opened the door a dirty emaciated figure stood before its captors.

'Let me go!' screamed the boy in his still-unbroken voice.

'So this is the rat,' said Lefoyle, looking at the boy.

'I'm no rat.'

'You will speak when spoken to,' said Marie sternly and clipped the boy's ear.

'What's your name? Hmm?' Lefoyle enquired.

The child was silent.

'What's your name, or are you deaf?' said Marie.

'Reilly . . . James Reilly,' stammered the boy.

'And what was he stealing, Marie?'

'Flour, eggs and some of the pheasants.'

'Greed knows no bounds,' said Lefoyle. 'You may not know it, boy, but I am a judge and can try you where you stand.'

'I don't care, let me go.' The boy kicked out at Lefoyle, hitting him on the shin.

A sudden darkness took over his mind and he seized the child, hitting him about the head and arms and chest. 'How dare you, how dare you!' he shouted.

Each blow fell harder and harder, he repeated the words as the blows, until a foam appeared on his lips. He beat him now from a place beyond anger, he beat him out of sorrow for the loss of Rose, for the treachery of Harmon. He beat him for the changes that seemed to come every day, for the world that was changing around him and which he did not wish to change. He beat him for O'Connell and his monster meetings, for Murphy and the cedars of Lebanon. He beat him for Jane his first love, for his own cowardice which had lost him a chance at happiness with her, he beat him for her letters that he still kept in his chest. He beat him for this famine and disease. He beat him for this stench of rot that filled the air and the bodies that lined the ditches. He beat him for Murtagh and his true words, that yes he was alone, and had always been, and it terrified him.

He cried now as the boy was crying, tears on both their faces, the stain of anger and regret and pain.

'Sir!' shouted Marie and pulled him off the boy.

Lefoyle swung for Marie, who backed into the corner, knocking a bag of flour to the ground. The powder filled the air, forming a thick cloud, blinding him.

'Aarrrgh,' he shouted and swung now at the flour dust hanging in the air. He was old but he could still fight. He would not surrender.

'Sir, *please*,' begged Marie. 'Please. Please,' she repeated again and again through her own tears of horror. And the mantra flowed through the room as the dust settled, settled over the eggs and the pheasants, over the rabbits and the bacon. Over the bags and the grain and the small lifeless form crumpled on the floor. 'Please, please, please, please,' babbled Marie, hunched down with hands over her face.

The figure did not move. Lefoyle pushed him with his foot and there was no response. Marie crawled to the boy and turned up his face, checking for signs of life. Blood flowed from his head and drops now fell on the floured floor and caked.

And he, Baron Henry Lefoyle, stood erect and looked at his own hands stained and raw, red and white, like the flag of home. Like the bodies of the rebels hung at St Johnstown and buried in the lime. Everything changes into something else.

Marie rocked back and forth, cradling the child in her arms.

'Can one see the future in those stars?' he said queerly and walked silently out the door.

He walked through the hallway and up the stairs towards the front door and outside. He had not taken his daily walk by the wall, his mind kept telling him, it was time for his walk. He would walk the wall, walk the wall so as to improve the mood. Walk the wall. A healthy mind needs a healthy body. Walk the wall.

The boy had struck first, he told himself, they had struck first. And as the screams of Marie filled the house he closed the door and felt the grass beneath his feet. He would walk the wall.

He was inside and the junta could stay out there with their mobs to the left and right. Change would not, would never change him.

41
McQuaid

He got into the van to drive to the manor but he found himself still driving, past the manor, and on past the town, on the motorway, by Carrick-on-Shannon and on to Sligo and the road to Strandhill.

It was all fucked, he kept repeating to himself. The job was finished. Closed in a day and he not even there, only come to the locked gates. And now no Sinead. No Sinead and no work. How had it all come suddenly to a halt? Ballymahon was limping along, it seemed it too would close, it was only a matter of time. The world was closing in around him.

For sale signs littered the motorways and towns. How they seemed to mock him. Didn't they know? Didn't they know that it was all falling apart? Falling into utter shite.

We were supposed to be the lucky generation, he thought. The big things would not break us, because there would be no big things, there would only be college and cars and the house and the job.

He held back the threatening tears. Oh, what had happened to him? How lost had he become.

McQuaid lit yet another cigarette and drove faster. Strandhill was calling him. Calling him as it had done when he had last been there, with Sinead, and they had walked the beach and the mountain.

The car had been steamy with possibility on their first trip together. And Strandhill might as well have been New York for how exciting it all was.

Shopping on the main street of the town they'd come across a local artist selling landscape paintings: Benbulben Mountain, the bloody forelands of Donegal, the beach in the early morning.

'God, wouldn't that picture of the mountain be lovely to wake up to,' Sinead had said.

'Yeah, yeah, I suppose it would,' he'd replied. 'And that one of the whin bushes, Jaysus, we could put that in the hallway,' he had said after a time, pointing to another picture.

'In the hallway? What hallway would that be?' she had asked in an excited tone.

'Well, the hallway of our house,' he answered, looking at her and squeezing her hand.

They smiled happily at each other and he handed money to the artist, who wrapped the canvases in brown paper and tied them with string. They had looked like parcels from the movies, he remembered now.

'Will we go for a walk by the beach?'

'Let's have dinner first,' she said.

'Ha, thinking with your belly. Well, fair enough, don't want you getting grumpy,' he had replied.

They walked to a nearby restaurant and had the seafood chowder for starters and shared a tasting plate of cured meats. McQuaid was generous that day and ordered whatever she wanted. The wine, of which there was plenty, reduced the room to just them, sitting across from one another, eyes locked, all smiles and giggles. Forks floated back and forth in the frivolity of food shared with a lover. It wasn't the food that was sexual, it was the people.

When the bill came he would not let her see it. After dinner they walked along the shoreline and down to the beach. The lights of the town in the growing darkness took on a special quality. They had talked and talked, his arm around her waist as they traversed the sand. Occasionally he would rub her neck or squeeze her hand, and when the emotion grew too much they would stop and embrace.

It had all been so easy, so carefree.

Eventually growing tired, they had sat on the sand and listened to the wash of the waves in the background. They had just sat there in silence, her arm rested on his shoulder. And it had been lovely, he remembered.

'What will we do next?' she enquired after a time.

'We'll finish the walk and go to the B&B, and tomorrow . . .' he paused.

'Yes, tomorrow?'

'Tomorrow is a new day,' he said a little nervously. 'Oh God, Sinead,' he said, turning to her excitedly. 'I can't wait until tomorrow, or the day after that. You're the thing I think about first thing in the morning, not work, not Mam, not even bloody going back to sleep. I'm . . . I'm bursting here for you,' he said bashfully.

'Oh darling,' she said and placed her hands on his face. His eyes were huge and black.

'It's just, I do imagine us,' he began afresh.

'You do?'

'I do,' he said, his gaze catching hers. 'I imagine a house, our house, a mix of the two of us. Open fires and . . .'

'Yes,' she had said and he remembered her breathy excitement then.

'And children running around, a boy like me, we'd call him Fionn or maybe Mick after my father, and a girl.'

'We'd call her Deirdre,' she said.

'Yes, Deirdre and Mick and maybe more, too. I'd be a hard enough father on them, they'd have to work hard at school and the boys would help me with the business when the time came.'

'And be good-looking, of course,' she added.

'Oh, of course, well, look at the two of us!' he had said with a big smile and laugh and kissed her with his trembling lips. 'And we'd have a farm, my father's farm. Would you work it with me?'

'If you showed me how.'

'Oh Sinead, there's nothing we couldn't do. But it's just . . .' and he hesitated. 'Will I be a success, Sinead?' he continued with that wave of insecurity that seemed to overcome him by times.

'You already are.'

'But will I be rich?' he had pressed further.

'You've got plenty of money already,' she answered calmly.

'But not enough, not enough to have my dream, not yet.'

'That will all come, you just have to be patient,' she had said and touched his face.

'I just worry,' he had said. Now he remembered how much she had loved him, her concern had been so genuine, so earnest and tangible. 'I'm good at making money, and Begley is going to hand me on the business any day now. I mean, I could build a place soon enough.'

'You could,' she had said and put her hands over his face once again. 'But you don't need to worry about that tonight,' she added and kissed him tenderly. She leaned in to his ear and whispered about going to bed. Or had he suggested it? He was not sure now.

On the way home he had stopped the van and made her promise, promise to always be his.

'Always,' she had agreed. 'Always, I'll love you always.'

And she had smiled and they knew it was the truth that they would be together for life. This was the woman he wanted, he had thrown his chips down on her number. And then that job, that job had started and he had got so lost in it, the stress of it, wearing on him, and that bitch Rhian had arrived and ruined everything. Ruined his dream, why could he not have walked away? He had fought it so hard, and yet he had made the mistake, he cursed himself for it. Cursed himself every moment of the day. What had happened to him? Who had he become, in the pub with Willy or Paddy Reilly when he should have been with Sinead? At work late when he should have been with Sinead. With her, when he should have been with Sinead.

Of course now he could see he didn't really love Rhian at all. He had only just met the girl. What had made him cling to her? Cling to her as some life raft in the storm that had grown up all around him. And that drowning feeling consumed him again. But hadn't he felt like he was drowning all these months? Drowning in a sea of wires and bills and concern.

He just needed someone to talk to, someone to understand.

The dream was dead. But wasn't it dead for the whole bloody country? Every last scrap of land packaged and sold for development. All of them buying and selling from one another.

What was it all for, he questioned now. What the hell was it all for? All that work. Wasn't the place bankrupt now? A wounded people, a maimed people, who had spent so long looking at the past that they could not see the future that was coming, coming straight bloody at them.

'You fucking bollox, you fucking bollox, you fucking bollox,' he repeated again and again.

The words he knew were babbling, he was babbling to himself here in the van on the way to Strandhill for what bloody reason he did not know. To be close to her, close to the notion of the happier times they had lived. Had enjoyed.

You fucked it all up, Ger Ger. You destroyed your whole life. You were supposed to be getting married to her. You fucking idiot. Why couldn't you stop and think? Why couldn't you stop? Too lost in that bloody work and pub to see what was coming. A fucking disaster. A moral failure.

He was crying now and he wiped the snot and tears on his sleeve. Oh God, what had he done? He had texted Sinead but her anger only brought anger in him. He just did not understand how in the space of a few weeks he had gone from loving her to breaking up with her. It did not make sense. And now he was alone, alone for the first time in his life, and it terrified him. The house had become a folly, a folly to how lost he had become. It was a ghost, a haunting of what could have been. And the work. Fuck the work, he would gladly throw it all away to undo the error he had made. But he could not undo it, he could not. And it hurt him so.

In the distance he could see Benbulben and the sea. He was close now and he might get some ease from Knocknarea, climb it and look out over the Atlantic, past the waves and the swarf, out over the lighthouse and the small airstrip to happier times. To times they had spent together.

'You fucking bollox, you fucking bollox!' he shouted. And blasted his fist against his skull. How could he have been so stupid? Again and again he thumped his skull.

Ah, Ger Ger, why could you not have listened when I talked? I was scared, I just got so caught up, I don't know. I don't know, he whimpered and hit his skull once again, in an effort to quiet these dark waves.

You're nicely fucked now. Driving to Strandhill like a madman, but then of course you are mad, on top of this mountain howling to the wind. I can fix things, he seemed to say, and was not sure if he spoke the words there to the wind.

You cannot fix this, Ger, it's beyond us now, it was only work, there would be other jobs, other work. You made it God and now look what it has brought you.

'It's brought me nothing,' he cried and sat on a clump of rushes as the sheep nearby bleated and ran at the sight of him.

You are a gobshite, it brought you nothing, only loss. And you broke that poor girl's heart. You never stopped, never stopped to think what you were doing. No, he had not thought, not once. He had been unable to see what stress he had brought upon himself, and that Faustian bargain of Ballymahon had been his undoing. Paddy Reilly had betrayed him.

Everything had been fine, better than fine, and then it had all started to fall away, fall apart, the whole bloody thing.

Like a house of cards, Gerard. You took on too much in search of that view of Cairn Hill, for that car and those cows and the footsteps of tiny children. That manor won't save you. The work won't free you.

He hit his skull again and stood up. His hands shook and trembled in the wind and rain of the mountain as he lit yet another fag. And the tears stung his eyes. Stung them worse than any childhood fall and mammy had put a plaster on that cut knee. There was no mammy now to fix things. This was real life and it was shovel or shite.

He walked the stony lane to the top of the mountain, past the ruined cottages and the boggy rush-infested ground. They said Queen Meabh was buried on that mountain, Sinead had once told him. Amongst the fossilised coral and granite stones. In the cairn on the hill that looked out over the town.

He walked faster and faster, walked so his legs hurt and there was relief in the pain, anything to take him away from his mind.

The mountain top was deserted; a goat grazed lazily on the heather and grass, a blackbird cawed, but there was no other soul there, no release. But maybe it was better he be alone. He did not know what he might say to a stranger now, spill his heart to him or her, tell of his tragedy, his loss, his utter failure. *Uaigneas gan ciuneas.*

He sat on top of the cairn and, head held between his hands, he wept.

'Sinead,' he muttered.

'Sinead, come back to me,' he cried out loudly.

It was the cry of the desperate, he knew, and she would not want a desperate man, a drowning man with no love or support to give. He had to pull himself together. Make himself a better man. It could not all be lost. It couldn't. He prayed furious prayers, as if prayers might work in this the dark night of his soul.

He took out an old invoice from Crossan's electrical supplies. On the back he wrote his desperate note to her.

Come back to me, Sinead. Mo ghra.

He stood up and let the wind whip it out of his hand, a wish, a plea to the universe, to God, to the Celtic gods that might still hold sway in remote places such as this.

'Come back,' he said.

He turned and walked back down the mountain. He did not look back, would not look back, afraid the wish might be broken. It was to the wind and fate and the universe now.

He walked down through the town towards the beach. This

place too had not escaped the boom. Houses dotted the coastline, neat rows of scaffolding stretching out to the horizon.

He went to the beach, past the bathhouse and the surf school. The sand changed colour from grey to white under his feet as he walked. He could hear the tourists speaking in different accents: German, French, Japanese. All the different accents, yet all he wanted was to hear her accent, her voice.

By the lifebuoy sign he stopped and read the gritty words. A stolen lifebuoy – a stolen life. And wasn't his life stolen, stolen and he drowning and no water needed. Drowned in stress and work and loss.

You bollox, you bollox, you bollox, his mind ran, and he sank again into all those memories.

A passer-by stopped to watch him, to watch this fine man reduced by a lifebuoy sign. They shrugged their shoulders, turned their face from him and moved along quickly and silently.

42
McQuaid

Ballymahon had closed, as he knew it would. He had woken up one morning and felt that the day was better left to itself. An artificial night seemed a kinder ease. To stay in bed and cry and weep and look for her face under the covers. He no longer showered or put on the work boots, it was a pointless effort, for what was it all for? There was no work, no Sinead, no light. His thoughts had trapped him unto himself.

The cheque had not come, would never come, and the bills and legal letters mounted.

'Another one for you, son,' his mother said.

'Leave it at the door,' he weakly called out.

There was no ease, only a tiredness, a tiredness of the body and mind. A body that had been too long ignored and pushed aside and a mind that had finally given up. It was pointless, he told himself, and the dark thoughts had grown stronger and harsher in the last few weeks.

You're useless, Ger. His mind would laugh, laugh at him there in the privacy of his room, on his way to the kitchen, in the toilet. Kane and he were not so different now, both men trapped in their houses. Kane by choice and he by life.

His mother knocked on the door, his work clothes, that wedding suit, lay folded on the foot of the bed, but he had refused to get up, refused to get dressed.

'Son, maybe we should go see the doctor,' she tried.

'I'm fine,' he lied and turned his face back into the pillow.

'Gerard, you haven't been out of bed, you don't eat, and you're just puffing away on them bloody fags and drinking cups of cold coffee. I'll not go through what we did with your father. It's time we saw the doctor.'

She helped him out of bed, placed his work clothes to one side and brought him a clean pair of jeans and a shirt.

The clinic was full of splutters and wheezes, as the sick and the dying sat side by side, waiting to see the man. His mother placed her hand softly on his knee and smiled at him. It had been so long since she had treated him this way, as a child.

'The doctor will see you and it will all be fine. God will provide,' she said and held a sad look from her eye.

'He will,' he lied and turned his eyes towards the ground.

The doctor examined, listened, made him cough and jump and wheeze. When he did ask what was his ailment, McQuaid said it was trouble sleeping and that he needed rest.

'Well, exercise is very important when you are suffering with fatigue,' the doctor replied. 'I'll give you a few sleeping pills, to get the pattern back, but only on the condition that you join the gym and start running every day.'

'I will,' McQuaid said and in that moment believed his words.

He met his mother in front of the surgery.

'Now a bit of a break is all you need, Gerard, and the gym will do you good,' she said as they purchased a new jogging suit and runners from the shopping centre. 'I've been meaning to speak with Sinead's father,' she said on the drive home. 'So I might go visit them later today.'

He did not answer her, nor did he care.

He laid the new tracksuit on his bed when he was at home, looked at it, all clean and crisp, the smell of new runners filling his nostrils. It was a nice smell, like summer holidays, he told himself.

When he did go to the gym he ran for five minutes, felt an utter tit, gave up and went outside to smoke a cigarette.

Fuck it, he told himself. Like some health nazi to be in there every day. Wasn't he fit already? Didn't he lift and heft enough tools and wires and cables to make him the match of any man, on any site? He did not need to exercise.

The clothes stayed in the bag thereafter.

He had taken to walking by himself, to lonely places, or places he and Sinead had once been. He would sit and dwell. Smoke cigarette after cigarette. When the phone rang it was never her, only Providers or Crossan's or Plant Hire looking for bills to be paid. It had all got so much, the whole bloody lot. He could not pay the bills for he had no money. He could not earn money because there was no work. And he could not get out of the house now because it all seemed so hard. It had been a sore blow to his remaining pride to tell the men on Friday that they needn't come in Monday. He had solemnly given them their last pay cheques and shaken their hands. It was yet another parting.

'Will you be all right?' Declan had asked, he had been the only one to.

'Oh shor, I'll be fine, I'll give you a bell when we get a bit more work,' McQuaid said.

Declan nodded; that had not been the intention of his question but McQuaid was too proud to ask for help, too proud to admit defeat. It was a brave face from a man who had no bravery left.

He went to the pub some evenings when he had enough energy, but the drink had only a bitter taste now. To listen to Paul and Neary and Limerick lament it all.

'It's all gone arseways,' they would say.

But did he not know that already. He did not need to hear it spoken aloud. But there was no other conversation, only the bust and the banks, and the government about to fall in on itself. He refused to see Paddy Reilly any more, though Reilly had called and texted; he refused to see that man who had lost him Sinead.

The outward was the inward, he thought. He had become a twin to the whole bloody country. He remembered something from Shakespeare from school, how the weather reflected the mood. Well, the rain surely spoke pages. Rain, wasn't it always fucking raining, and if it wasn't raining it was grey.

And the waves of anger would come again. Why had it all suddenly come to a halt? Wasn't he a good man? Why did it happen? How could he go from having it all, the business, the girl he was going to marry, the dream house, to having nothing? Barely able to put diesel in the van. God would provide, and had he not had faith?

He was in a spiral now, darker and darker, and his mind's dark thoughts growing stronger and stronger and then the odd thoughts had come. Repeats of times with Sinead, those happy, happy times, over and over again. And why he'd not thought of all those happy moments when Rhian had been chasing him, kissing him, he did not know. He had become so distant to the men, he could see, distant to the mother, distant to himself.

He laughed when one day he found he had been staring at the floor for an hour. Just staring at it, like some bloody lunatic. Jesus, if they only knew, it would be straight to St Loman's into the day ward with the other defectives. Like his grand-uncle

Sean, a nurse to wipe his arse the rest of his life. Well, that wouldn't happen to him.

'Fuck it,' he said.

'Fuck it,' he cried.

Fuck it.

And with each fuck the anger grew. What was it all for? This country, what do you do with your country once you have it? he asked himself. You fucking make a mess of it. Wasn't it better you left it to the Brits, hand it back to them even? The place wasn't even a hundred years old and they had all made a right *state* of it.

Fuck it, he repeated. Fuck Pearse and his bloodlust, fuck Connolly, fuck Emmet and his speech from the dock, fuck Parnell, fuck Dev the long string all priestly and queer. Fuck Wolfe Tone and the shinners and the bloody marching to Bodenstown. Fuck Collins and the bitch Julia Roberts playing a Longford woman with a northern accent. Fuck the Unionists and the Twelfth and Bobby Sands. Fuck Dr No and Maggie. Fuck Haughey who got away with all. Fuck Cowen the big fish-lipped yoke and Bertie with his smiling from the press. Fuck Fianna Fáil. Fuck Fine Gael, fuck the civil war politics that still held sway in every fucking village and town in the country. Fuck partition.

Fuck Yeats and Gregory and the Celtic twilight, fuck Raglan Road, fuck O'Casey and Friel, fuck the Playboy and the poor aul gombeen men. Fuck dancing at the crossroads, fuck the comely maidens, fuck the cottier and the landlords. Fuck Lefoyle who built the whole bloody manor and all the shite it had cost him. Fuck Behan and the anthem. Fuck the hostage and the céilí music. Fuck the Chieftains, fuck MacGowan and dirty old town. Fuck Luke and the foggy dew. Fuck Damien Dempsey and Sinead. Fuck Dana. Fuck Joe Dolan and the statue the tinkers stole.

Fuck the Normans and their rabbits, fuck the Vikings and Dublin, fuck the Celts who couldn't keep the show together. Fuck Strongbow. Fuck the Brits for fucking us. Fuck the land commission and the new Irish. Fuck the developers. Fuck Kane for fucking him over.

Fuck Joyce that blind auld bollox, portrait of a gobshite. Fuck McGahern and lonely Leitrim. Fuck the priests and the abuse. Fuck RTÉ and the Late Late. Fuck Bono. And Geldof when he was at it. Fuck Paddy and his ghosts of Birchview, he who was haunted and did not even know it.

Fuck the bull and the field. Fuck Christy Brown the cripple and Day-Lewis too. Fuck Father Ted and Glenore. Fuck Setanta and Ferdia, Diarmuid and Grainne. Fuck the cattle and the potatoes. The Kerr's pinks and the golden wonders, fucking steamed and boiled and mashed.

Fuck the Kerry babies, fuck Irish the language we all pretended we could speak. Fuck O'Leary and the grave, fuck the Fenian dead. Fuck Kathleen Ni Houlihan, she who never got the ride, fuck the GPO, history didn't start there. Fuck Peg and everyone sick of her laments, fuck the round towers and the dolmens and Newgrange with its sunbox. Fuck the bog bodies and the bogside. Fuck Ned Kelly. Fuck Eoin O'Duffy and the blueshirts. Fuck the blacksmith of Ballinalee. Fuck the Catholics, fuck the Protestants. Fuck the chains that took us to Australia. Fuck the Famine and the Irish Americans. Fuck emigration. Fuck the Polish who'd arrived like an older version of ourselves. Fuck the new cars, and the houses built everywhere. Fuck the planning officers. Fuck Noel Browne and the mothers. Fuck O'Connell and the Children of Lir.

Fuck Paul McGrath and Jack Charlton, fuck O'Driscoll and the Blackrock boys. Fuck the GAA and headquarters. Fuck Bloody Sunday.

Fuck Van Morrison. 'Fuck it,' he shouted.

Fuck the schools for teaching us all this shite and to praise our country. Fuck nationalism, what had it achieved? All the great touchstones of this supposed state and we had forgotten every bit of it. Every last morsel we had packaged and sold. Having a Coke doesn't make you a Yank but drinking a pint of Guinness makes you one of us. Never was a product more tied to a place. Fuck the last little bit of culture we had left and lost in this boom.

The dream was dead, he told himself, but wasn't it dead long ago. The blueprints of his dream house were nothing more than an index of his failure, an elegy to all that was gone. And at the thought it saddened him so. What had it all been for? Nothing, he admitted now. No glorious dead were going to bring him back Sinead or put work in front of him. No hunger strikers were going to sort out the bills with Crossan's or Providers or pay the wages for the men.

We were so busy sacrificing ourselves, he told himself, so busy being the maimed people, that we couldn't see we were maiming ourselves.

Happiness is only singular and each case speaks only for itself, nothing more. He got up out of the bed, put his work boots on and made his way to his van.

43
McQuaid

It was 25 June and he had returned to the manor. There had been time since he last visited. Had it been weeks or months, he was no longer sure. Days had bled into each other. The feel of a Monday was lost to that of a Sunday.

He climbed the locked gate and walked amongst the place he had known so well.

It was still very much a site. Discarded bales of blocks, wire coils abandoned, safety vests hung out rusted with rain. He could hear a church bell call a hallow chime, call out over the emptiness.

The cranes had come to a standstill. A tricolour wrapped round itself blew as best it could. It blew for nothing now and to no one.

He walked the grounds where they had worked. Some houses were near while others lay like half-built slums. In many the plasterboard sat still stacked on its pallets, the chalk wearing through in tufts.

A retired garda now patrolled the gates in place of Peter. He grazed his cattle on the front lawn. That lawn which should have never felt the insult of those lumbering beasts.

He walked through the oak forests towards the manor house and could hear the wild neighing of the tinkers' horses playing in the undergrowth. Their calls echoed through the grounds, this way and that, and in the distance by the manor house, scene of his great moral failure, stood a majestic white stallion. He stood as if waiting all this while for him and him alone. Weeds had begun to grow from the great house's gutters again. He looked in the windows, looked in the hope of seeing something of that old life, to maybe see himself working. To speak with himself and say slow down, it's not the be-all, lad. It's not, but would he have listened?

He had been so full of pride that he would never have admitted how lost he was, how the water was up around his lugs, pulling him down. Never to ask, my soul, my soul, where are you?

He had pleaded with Sinead, pleaded and called and cried, she had become an obsession. If he could only have her back things would be okay. The good times would come again. Work would appear, he could finish their house and they could pick up where they had left off. They could begin again.

But she would not take him back. He had broken her heart, that poor sweet girl, and she had broken his. If only they could both understand what had gone wrong. But even he did not know what had gone wrong. What had caused everything to fall apart.

His mind moved now clearly, clear as water. It was in a space of purpose that he had not felt in so long. And the thoughts, the thoughts were not of construction, or bills, or Sinead and his mother. Not Kane, or Big Jack. Not Paddy Reilly whom he had come to forgive. Not Lefoyle or Rhian, nor Declan, nor poor Willy who would, he was told, never walk properly again. Not any of them.

He had heard men talk about going to Australia to work in

the mines. Ride out on the western railway and don the work shorts, drink a tinnie and do the hard yakka. They were making as much, more than they had ever made at home. But he would not, would never abandon home. Longford had made him, and broken him, but he would not leave it; if he could not find peace here he would not find it in the depths of some godforsaken hole in the Pilbara.

He sent her one last text.

Please Sinead, take me back, please. Always, always I'll love you.

How many of these pleading messages had he sent, too many, he had sickened her of him. He had pushed and pushed and though he knew it was wrong he could not control himself. If he could only have pulled back a bit and calmed down and talked to her, told her the truth, she might have understood, but the truth now seemed too late. It was all too late.

The bills had gone unpaid; he was bankrupt, as bankrupt as Kane, his dream house would never be finished now. It was as big a relic now as the manor. They would take it from him, the bank, some plastic-bagged fucker would walk in and take the whole lot, like Birchview, like Ballymahon, like Colmcille, like Drumlish, like Granard, like every town and village in the county and country. Filled with emptiness. It had been too much for a young lad to take on, maybe Begley had given him too much too soon. Or was it Paddy Reilly and Ballymahon? He was not sure.

Was it all a dream and he to wake in fright, he asked himself now. No, it was life and its living. He looked out over the site past the trees to Cairn Hill. That half-mountain that had defined his whole life. It was their skyscraper, their guideline to height and the power of nature. It did not move, it never asked anything of the people of Longford, but it was there and would be there long after he.

As he moved closer now to the front door of the manor house, the stallion nodded its large head in defiance and suddenly galloped away, neighing out to his harem. McQuaid pushed and beat a side door, forcing his way into the building. The sunlight shone through the rooms as he had never seen before. Nature saves its best cards to the end, he thought. Shows her power and beauty, but he was beyond beauty now. Beyond sunlight and scents, flowers and otters playing in the Camlin.

He walked up the creaking stairs to the bedroom where he and Sinead had made love, where he and Rhian had fucked, to that room of ghosts and memories. Where Lefoyle had slept, where he himself had committed his greatest error and where it had all gone wrong.

Half-peeled wallpaper drifted on the floors, empty paint cans sat in one corner. Some chairs and used grinder discs. He found the burnt-out cask of a picture frame amongst some rubbish. It was surely Lefoyle, and he smiled to himself.

He stood now silently. He breathed deeply, he was calm, he told himself, calmer than any day he could remember. His hands did not shake or tremble. His mind was clear, his decision real.

He opened the window slightly and let the cool air fill his nostrils. To breathe, one, two, three, fill the lungs, fill them with cleanliness, he needed no more cigarettes.

And the brain began, but softer now, softer and calmer than in months, a whisper, a gentle conversation, like that between two lovers in each other's arms.

Do you remember those security towers the first time we went to the North on holidays? I do, he replied.

And how were they? . . . Empty.

That's right, empty, Gerard, the first ceasefire and the mam and dad wanted you to see the North, to see the other side of this little country. Going across that line and all the talk and you only little, what were you? Ten, ten years of age, but you knew. You knew. And do you remember the feeling? I do.

Ah . . . that empty feeling, it'll all be like that now, towers all over the country, empty towers and houses littering the place, until it gets so much you can't breathe, because the history, boy, the history is suffocating us. And these same fucking houses all wire and steel will be just memories of all the work and pain and labour. Monuments to a time when they were important.

There'll be no passport needed to get across this border so, it's the green light now, he replied.

He waited but the brain did not speak again. Would not speak again. But of course hadn't it been this way all these months, he speaking only to himself lost in his own head.

And he smiled that soft smile one does when reality comes all too late, at the end. For what else is there to do.

His phone vibrated in his pocket, a text from Sinead. Probably an insult, or maybe, maybe, she had forgiven him, had understood more than he thought she did and would take him back. Maybe the mother had said something to her family. He sighed now. Let it wait, he said to himself. Let it wait. I'll deal with that tomorrow.

The open ceiling exposed the oak rafters, thick and strong. They had borne the weight of this house for two hundred years, they could bear a little more this day.

The grey cable was stiff, two juts of copper stabbed out its end. The wire was tight, he looped it again and again, tying a knot as he had done so many times before; for a socket, for a switch, for light, and wasn't that what he was searching for now.

He stood up on the cheap stool and placed the cable around his neck. The deed was fast, the *cathair* fell and with it Ireland.

Acknowledgements

Thank you to David Malouf for his wonderful advice and friendship, my mother and father for everything, and my brother, sisters and family. Matthew Tevlin, a dear man in whose company this story was born, Father Sean Casey, Julie Koh, Duncan Graham, Paddy Doherty, Liam Heslin, Ronan McDonald, Nashen Moodley, Mark and Steven, Harry Sanna, Robert Barton, Fergus Grady, Belinda Aucott, Jimmi James, Andrew Emerson. Paul Meredith, Elliot James Shaw, Conor O'Shea, Yonta Taiwo, Oliver Watts, Ollie and Diane, Brody, my uncles Mickey and John Connell. Rod Morrison for seeing my potential. Rose Forster. Donal Ryan. Daniel Saez, Charles Clapshaw. To Vivian Huynh, my editors and publishers, the people of County Longford. To Angela for all the teaching and help, and the amazing Faryl Reisman and the Reisman/Small family.

Thank you also to Varuna writers retreat and Bundanon Trust, Damien Dempsey for the use of his song 'Negative vibes', Ed Bruce for 'Don't take your love to town' and Radiohead for the use of 'Just'.

MORE BESTSELLING TITLES FROM PICADOR

The Miniaturist

Jessie Burton

'There is nothing hidden that will not be revealed …'

On a cold winter's day in 1686, eighteen-year-old Nella Oortman knocks at the door of a grand house in the wealthiest quarter of Amsterdam. She has come from the country to begin a new life as the wife of illustrious merchant trader Johannes Brandt, but instead she is met by his sharp-tongued sister, Marin.

Only later does Johannes appear and present her with an extraordinary wedding gift: a cabinet-sized replica of their home. It is to be furnished by an elusive miniaturist, whose tiny creations mirror their real-life counterparts in unexpected ways …

Nella is at first mystified by the closed world of the Brandt household, but as she uncovers its secrets she realises the escalating dangers that await them all. Does the miniaturist hold their fate in her hands? And will she be the key to their salvation or the architect of their downfall?

Euphoria

Lily King

English anthropologist Andrew Bankson has been alone in the field for several years, studying the Kiona river tribe in the Territory of New Guinea. Haunted by the memory of his brothers' deaths and increasingly frustrated and isolated by his research, Bankson is on the verge of suicide when a chance encounter with colleagues, the controversial Nell Stone and her wry and mercurial Australian husband Fen, pulls him back from the brink. Nell and Fen have just fled the bloodthirsty Mumbanyo and, in spite of Nell's poor health, are hungry for a new discovery. When Bankson finds them a new tribe to divert them from leaving Papua New Guinea, the artistic, female-dominated Tam, he ignites an intellectual and romantic firestorm between the three of them that burns out of anyone's control.

Set between two World Wars and inspired by events in the life of revolutionary anthropologist Margaret Mead, *Euphoria* is an enthralling story of passion, possession, exploration, and sacrifice.

WINNER OF THE 2014 KIRKUS PRIZE FOR FICTION

Solace

Belinda McKeon

Mark Casey did not expect to fall in love. But from the minute he saw Joanne Lynch across the garden of a Dublin pub, it seemed that nothing else was possible. They soon start a relationship that is as chaotic and exciting as the city they share.

But Mark is guiltily drawn back to his family and the land they have farmed for generations, as he discovers the truth behind a feud that threatens to destroy this passionate love affair. Just as they appear to have brought the warring factions together, one single tragic moment undoes everything.

Solace is a beautiful, breathtaking story about the city and the country, the old and the new, the thrill of new love and the inescapable bond between parents and children.

Burial Rites

Hannah Kent

In northern Iceland, 1829, Agnes Magnúsdóttir is condemned to death for her part in the brutal murder of two men.

Agnes is sent to wait on the farm of District Officer Jón Jónsson and his family, who are horrified and avoid Agnes. Only Tóti, the young assistant reverend appointed as Agnes's spiritual guardian, is compelled to try to understand her. As the summer months fall away to winter, Agnes's story begins to emerge. And as the days to her execution draw closer, the question burns: did she or didn't she?

Based on a true story, *Burial Rites* is a deeply moving novel about freedom and the ways we will risk everything for love. In beautiful, cut-glass prose, Hannah Kent portrays Iceland's formidable landscape, and asks: how can one woman endure when her life depends upon the stories told by others?

WINNER OF THE INDIE AWARDS DEBUT FICTION OF THE YEAR 2014

WINNER OF THE VICTORIAN PREMIER'S LITERARY AWARD PEOPLE'S CHOICE AWARD 2014

WINNER OF THE FAW CHRISTINA STEAD AWARD 2014

WINNER OF THE ABA NIELSEN BOOKDATA BOOKSELLERS' CHOICE AWARD 2014

WINNER OF THE ABIA LITERARY FICTION BOOK OF THE YEAR 2014

WINNER OF THE SMH BEST YOUNG AUSTRALIAN NOVELIST 2014

WINNER OF THE BOOKTOPIA PEOPLE'S CHOICE AWARD 2014

SHORTLISTED FOR THE STELLA PRIZE 2014

SHORTLISTED FOR THE BAILEYS WOMEN'S PRIZE FOR FICTION 2014

SHORTLISTED FOR THE VICTORIAN PREMIER'S LITERARY AWARD FOR FICTION 2014

SHORTLISTED FOR THE ALS GOLD MEDAL 2014

SHORTLISTED FOR THE GUARDIAN FIRST BOOK AWARD 2013

SHORTLISTED FOR THE NIB WAVERLEY AWARD FOR LITERATURE 2013

Rachael's Gift

Alexandra Cameron

Rachael is a child prodigy, a talented artist whose maturity and eloquence is far beyond her fourteen years. She's also energetic, charming and beautiful, beguiling everyone around her. To her mother, Camille, she is perfect. But perfection requires work, as Camille knows all too well.

For Rachael has another extraordinary gift: a murky one that rears its head from time to time, threatening to unbalance all the family has been working towards. When Rachael accuses her art teacher of sexual misconduct, Camille and Rachael's father, Wolfe, are drawn into a complex web of secrets and lies that pits husband against wife and has the power to destroy all of their lives.

Set in the contrasting worlds of Australia and Paris, *Rachael's Gift* is a mystery story of the heart, about a mother's uncompromising love for her daughter, and a father's quest for the truth.

Game Day

Miriam Sved

'The ruckmen face off over the centre circle and for a moment everything is frozen possibility: players, umpire, the ball suspended overhead, the softly clouded sky. Everything except the fans, a circus beyond the stillness. Then the ball swings down and cracks it all open.'

The new draft pick, the tired has-been, the up-and-comer, the might-have-been. The talent scout, the coach on the edge, the beleaguered umpire, the concerned medic. The number-one fan, the lifetime members, the desperate gamblers. The footballers' mums, the WAGs, the groupies. The tags, the rivals, the sledging. The pressure.

Mick Reece and Jake Dooley, best mates since childhood, began their first professional season playing AFL with little notion of what they're getting into or the complexity of the beast that the game must feed.

In *Game Day*, Miriam Sved brings this beast into the light over the course of one season of Aussie Rules. Revelling in their battles, their victories and their relentless interdependence, *Game Day* asks whether what unites the true believers is stronger than what divides them, and if love of the game can transcend our flaws and imperfections to result in something beautiful.

Author photo: John Minihan